THE MYSTERIES OF GLASS

THE
MYSTERIES OF
GLASS

SUE GEE

review

First published in 2004
by HEADLINE BOOK PUBLISHING

A REVIEW hardback

10 9 8 7 6 5 4 3 2 1

Cataloguing in Publication Data is
available from the British Library

ISBN 0 7553 0309 1

Typeset in GaramondMT by
Letterpart Limited, Reigate, Surrey

Printed and bound in Great Britain by
Clays Ltd, St Ives plc

HEADLINE BOOK PUBLISHING
A division of Hodder Headline
338 Euston Road
LONDON NW1 3BH

www.reviewbooks.co.uk
www.hodderheadline.com

For Marek

Author's Note

The drama of this novel is played out in real places: in towns, villages and churches lying in a corner of Herefordshire border country which I find uniquely beautiful. The events of the story, set a century and a half ago, are entirely fictional, are based on no real person, living or dead, and draw on no real incident know to me. Any resemblances are entirely coincidental. One or two real people from the past do make brief appearances – the local historian Richard Parry, the clockmaker Thomas Skarratt. I have also used many old local names.

I thank Miss Vera Harrison, Secretary of the Kington History Society, for so readily and kindly lending me maps and documents of the period. Beryl Lewis was also kind enough to furnish me with some local material. In London, Dr W.M. Jacob generously responded to questions about the Victorian church. Any inaccuracies about location or period detail are mine alone.

Part One

1860

————————

1

---

ecember afternoon, the light fading, frost. As he pulled out his bags and slammed the carriage door, the engine's escaping steam rose like a wraith to the gathering cloud. He called up along the track to where the guard was leaning out of the window, his features barely distinguishable in the dusk.

'Thank you!'

'Good night, sir!'

Then, as the train began slowly to move again, the wraiths of steam became great billowing clouds, and he stood back on the whitened grass and watched it puff away over the crossing and along the wooded track to Kington. The whistle blew, the last of the carriages clanked on the rail and the marvellous clouds dissolved into the winter air. Now, from beyond the trees on the other side of the line, he could hear the river, and from somewhere in the dusky lane behind him the turning wheel of the mill.

The first stars hung in the sky. There was a crossing gate, a keeper's cottage. He crunched across the frosty grass, feeling the cold, in just a few yards, begin to bite as he let himself out to the lane. A lantern stood in the keeper's porch and above, at a lighted window, a little girl was leaning against the glass and watching him. He put down his bags and raised his hat, unable to discern, from the lamplight deep in the room behind her, more than the fall of hair, a pinafore. He felt her gaze; then she withdrew. After a moment the door of the cottage opened: he glimpsed the play of a fire on the hearth, a candle on a table. Then the crossing keeper came out, pulling the door to, and picked up his lantern.

'I'm to show you to the house, Mr Allen. She ain't far.'

'That's very kind.'

'I'll close the gates first, if you don't mind.'

'Of course not.' And he watched the man swing them to, over the dull gleam of the rails, and then walk back to him.

'Will I take that big bag, sir?'

'No, no, you just show the way.'

The lantern swung before them, shining on frozen ruts of earth, on bank and frosty hedgerow. Beyond its reach he could make out nothing but the dim outlines of the few buildings lying on either side of the lane: the mill house, a cowshed, a couple of cottages set back from the lane, each with a crack of light at the shutters. He heard, after a little while, the musical tinkle of a stream.

'It has not frozen over?'

They were rounding the bend, and he set down his bags for a moment to pull up his muffler. Just to speak a few words made him catch his breath.

'Even in snowfall he sometimes has a trickle.' The man stopped to wait for him: as the lantern was held high, Richard saw the still outlines of apple trees in a little orchard, and then the dark depths of the woods, climbing the hillside, silvered here and there by the gathering stars. He made out Orion, and the Plough. 'In the autumn he floods right across the lane. High as my boots, he's been.'

'Is that so? You've lived here a good few years?' He felt his breath condense within the muffler.

'Just four, since the line opened. You had a good journey?'

'Very good.'

They came round the bend and he saw all at once the rising moon. It came from behind the eastern hill and shone upon the long line of trees on the ridge and down across the long sloping field towards the stream bed.

'Here she be.'

The lantern swung out to the right. He saw by its beam and the pure clear light of the moon part of a great black barn set far up a track from a five-barred gate. Before it stood the cottage, set within a garden, bordered by a picket fence white with frost. It was right by the stream, and he could see now that its insistent music came from a little waterfall, tumbling through a gap in the field hedge.

'I'll see you up to the door, sir.'

The keeper was nodding at the wicket gate. His gate now. He lifted the stiffened latch, and they walked up the frozen path. He could smell wood smoke, saw the misty puff of blue against the inky sky. Downstairs the pale globe of an oil lamp shone at the window, and the key had been left in the lock. He had to take off his glove to turn it: it glistened in the lantern light and felt so cold he could hardly do so.

The keeper was stamping his feet.

'I'll say good night, then.'

He helped him lift in the bags, and then he was off, his lantern swinging away down the path, his footsteps scrunching. Richard called out his thanks as the man clicked the gate, then closed his front door on utter silence.

That night the cold was so intense he was almost afraid to sleep upstairs. He had been left a pot of soup on the range, a loaf and apples, the rector's letter of welcome. He turned up the oil lamp to read it, and ate by the banked-up fire in the snug. In his bedroom he heaped up coat and cape and travelling rug upon the quilt, kept alive the fire in the tiny grate, then shivered at the window, watching the moon rise higher and higher, over the pitch-black hills.

The bedroom boards were bare save for a little rug beside his bed, whereon he kneeled for the briefest prayer: gratitude for his safe arrival; the commending into infinite care of his father's soul, and the lives of his mother and sisters. When he pulled back the covers and blew out the candle, only the firelight showed him the room, and he lay watching its flicker over chest and washstand, the pegs on the door, the simple chair and wardrobe. Then, in the cold which crept back as the fire began to die, he tried to sleep.

But he found that the day's long journey and the motion of the railway carriage were still within him: he rocked and swayed from Ironbridge to Shrewsbury, from Shrewsbury to Ludlow to Leominster. Here he changed trains. They puffed away through the winter land-scape as the afternoon light began to fade, past Kingsland, Pembridge and Titley, Herefordshire Tudor villages of which he caught only glimpses. In Kingsland a butcher's boy swept out sawdust by a window hung with game; in Pembridge a man tramped home with a Christmas tree. The train ran through woods and tussocky fields, scattered with sheep and cattle; through frozen ploughland; past a sudden sight of the river Arrow, red with blood as the sun sank low. That had unsettled him. Then he alighted, here in Bullocks Mill.

Richard turned in the narrow bed, tugging the blankets round him. He began to drift towards sleep and was startled awake by the call of an owl, hunting through the woods. At once he felt the thrill of fear and awe he had felt as a child, envisioning then something huge, mysterious, implacable. Now, in a new house, held in winter's grip, he imagined as he used to do the sudden swoop upon trembling mouse or shrew, the dreadful soaring up, held limp and helpless. Childhood was long behind him, but as the call came and went through the heart of the woods he felt the same shiver of dread.

At last came the shriek, then silence.

At last he slept.

In the morning, the window was thick with frost. Downstairs there was ice on every pane and the shutters in the snug cloaked a passage of freezing air. The world was yet in darkness: for a moment he felt like a ghost, returned to an unlit empty house, with no one to hear his voice or have any sense of his presence here at all.

He lit the fire, closed the door, huddled over the snapping wood and leaping flames. After an hour the room was warm and the sky began to lighten. He breathed upon the melting ice until a misty circle formed on the glass, and through this he beheld the glittering garden as the sun broke through; beheld the lane winding up and away through the woods, the frosty fields and leafless trees all held in a miraculous stillness.

2

He was in border country in Bullocks Mill, some mile and a half from the market town of Kington; just outside its parish, and within the parish of St Michael and All Angels, Lyonshall, where he was to take up his duties: curate for a year to the Reverend Oliver Bowen. Later this morning he must walk up through the woods to meet him, as the letter awaiting him last night had bade him do, joining Mr Bowen and Susannah, his wife, for luncheon.

Save for a half-remembered childhood journey, Richard had never ventured into Wales, nor even travelled so far into Herefordshire, but he knew that where he lived now lay between two great topographical features. He had been told about them; he had looked them up on the map. The earthern ramparts of Offa's Dyke, which ran a hundred and twenty miles from the Severn to the Dee, here were to be found in stony heaps on the hills above the town, and in deep ditches by the paths along the river. And Hergest Ridge, which rose from beyond Kington's last few houses, stretched like the spine of a broad-backed sleeping animal, out towards Wales: from its grassy, bracken-bordered height, riders and walkers looked out across the dense forests of firs which clad the Radnor Hills. Wild ponies roamed on the top of the Ridge, and in summer skylarks sang.

Walking country. Rich woodland and fertile farmland, cut through by the Dyke and by the rushing Arrow, tributary of the greater Wye, which ran to the south. The Arrow's pools and depths, its flashing kingfishers, the motionless fishermen on the banks, its waterfalls and glinting shallows – all these were to wind in and out of the time he spent here, the plash of the turning wheel of the mill and the ceaseless rush of water always there, always with him, on every walk along the lane, in whatsoever frame of mind, and there were many; save when a train came whistling through the valley, and all sounds beyond it faded.

Now, in the dead of winter, the river ran slowly between its freezing banks and the wheel turned slowly too, ice gleaming on the blades.

The windowpane was running with melted frost. Through the watered glass he watched a pheasant slip through the picket fence and come stepping over the grass. His eye was bright, his plumage brilliant but for the clerical ring of white at the neck. Richard watched him cock his head this way and that, and bend to the ground for a husk or frozen grub; behind, his soft brown mate slipped through the fence to join him. Richard eased open the casement, and they ran. He flung out the crumbs from his breakfast and the birds flew up, whirring away to the woods. He closed the window quickly against the cold, gathered up his breakfast things and took them to the kitchen. When he returned, the pheasants were back again, and a little flock of songbirds, quarrelling over every speck.

He must bestir himself. He must unpack and acquaint himself with his new home before he set off, make some start at settling in; and he threw another log on the fire and warmed himself, then stood in the middle of the little room and looked about him, thinking where to place his few books and pictures.

There was a mantelpiece of good Welsh slate: here he might put the silhouette of his father, made on his ordination in 1826, at just the age he himself was now; and next to it the portrait photograph of all of them, taken just before his father's wholly unexpected, unimagined death. They were gathered in the studio before some ferny backdrop, the five of them holding still and grave until Emily could manage it no longer and began to giggle, and though they struggled to maintain their composure the shroud of black cloth cloaking the photographer's head began to twitch, and soon they were quite helpless. So that the photograph, when it came, showed them all at their happiest, only weeks before they discovered sorrow.

It was less than a year ago, and the melancholy which had settled upon him as he walked slowly behind his father's pall had never left him; was something he could not dispel, try as he might. His mother and his sisters wept; he felt his very blood slow down.

Now he must make a fresh start, in this lonely place.

And he left the small warmth of the fire, took brush and pan and climbed the narrow flight of stairs to his bedroom, where the chill once again enveloped him. He blew on his hands, pulled up the covers and smoothed the quilt, taking his coat and cape to the banister to hang downstairs in the hall. Then he bent to clear the grate, put the pailful of cinders and ash by the door and rinsed his hands in the pitcher and bowl on the washstand, where he had had to break ice on rising.

He could hear the pheasant croak outside, but he could not keep still in the cold to watch him any longer, and hurried to unfasten the straps on the big leather bag, which once had been his father's; to unfold and put away the perfectly ironed shirts and collars, the clerical white ties, the underclothes and handkerchiefs; to slip in the muslin bags of lavender which Emily had given him with a kiss.

'I've made one for every day of the week. I *wish* you weren't going.'

Tonight he would write to them all.

He hung up his two suits in the wardrobe, set brushes and box of cufflinks on the embroidered cloth, which Verity had found in a sale and thought just right for his chest of drawers. Then he opened the smaller bag and took out his Bible, inscribed by his father on his own ordination, and laid it by the candle at the bedside.

Last of all, he withdrew the chamber pot from beneath the bed, something he was quite unused to doing. He would, after a day or two, have a local woman in to do the work, Mr Bowen had told him in the letter. For now – well, Our Lord had had to do much worse. And he carried the pot carefully downstairs and set it behind the front door, to take down to the stream.

Up and down, up and down. He brought his coat and cape, and hung them in the hall, where the flagstones were dark with damp all round the blue and red rug. He collected the pailful of ash and carried it to the kitchen, where a mighty draught was blowing through the back door. Another thing to see to. He unpacked his pair of old skates and hung them on a hook, for who knew but that he might go skating here one day? He stood his fishing rod in the corner: something else to look forward to, with the river his companion, though in this cold it was hard to imagine that. And he took up the last of the wood and coal from the snug and laid a fresh fire for the night, knowing he would be glad of it. He brought down the little bag and set the pictures upon the Welsh slate with a kiss. Then he took out his handful of books.

The perfect place for a handful of books was above the desk in the corner. Here, no doubt, he would try to write his sermons. What weak things they still were. Above this desk a little window had been cut deep into the southern wall, offering a stout sill and the prospect of a good broad field, where a crow was sitting on the topmost branch of an ash tree covered in ivy. It towered over the hawthorn and hazel that grew alongside the stream bed, dividing the field from the long slope of the next, where the moon had risen last night to guide him. With the partial thawing of the frost in the weakened winter sun the air was damp and misty, and as Richard put up his hymnal and Book of Common Prayer in their slipcase, the volumes of Herbert and Donne, Donne's *Sermons*, he looked up at the crow and felt the rawness of the air up there, the pockets of wetness within those glossy wings, the haughtiness. He slipped on to the sill *The Imitation of Christ* and then, at a little distance, Hooper's *Birds of Field and Garden*, White's *Natural History of Selborne* and Newman's *Butterflies and Moths*.

He thought of the butterfly collection in his room at home, pinned out in the shallow case beneath the glass; of the careful way he had graded the colours, the Common Whites above the Clouded Yellow, the Grayling and Heath and Brimstone above the Tortoiseshell, then the long line of Red Admirals and the single prize, the Camberwell Beauty, caught on a summer afternoon in a pause in a game of croquet.

'Look! There!' His father tugged at his sleeve, pointing towards the open door of the summerhouse, where a bowl of Victoria plums stood in the sun, the butterfly gorging upon them. He was inside the house for the net in a flash.

Long-distant sunlit days: he was twelve, then. Twelve or thirteen, and home from school for the holidays, Emily and Verity and Mama all lined up to greet him as he came home with Father in the trap.

☆

12

In the hearth, the fire was sinking. He ran a hand over his books, then pulled on coat and gloves and went out to the back of the house with empty scuttle and basket.

Out here – ah, when the cold eased up, he could see himself out here, chopping wood before the black barn with the woodshed next to it. He saw another wicket gate, set between overgrown laurels at the side of the barn, and looked over it into a neglected field fenced off from the larger one beyond. Clumps of dead thistles stood limp amongst long grass fronded with frost; two little apple trees were in need of pruning. In spring he would come out here and see to all of it.

Now he slipped up the latch on the barn door and peered into the darkness. At once something scurried away and he stepped back quickly, then tried again, letting his eyes adjust to the dim light filtering through gaps in the boards. The space was huge, with room enough for a pony, even. And there was a low partition beyond which the trap might stand. He walked over the earth floor towards it, brushing away dangling strands of spider web, thickened with dust. Behind the partition stood a rough broad plank on a pair of old kegs: faintly, in the icy air, he could smell apples. Cider-making. He tapped each keg, but both were hollow. Still – he might try his hand at a little, and perhaps, in the orchard he had glimpsed across the low wall by the path, keep a hive or two.

He went out again, beating his arms across his chest, and carried his things to the woodshed, which, when he opened the door, smelled most wonderfully of resin. A bill hook and scythe hung on the back wall next to a good keen axe and saw; beyond the wood pile lay a glistening heap of coal.

He would not be without fuel and he would not be idle.

He filled basket and scuttle, then stood at the door looking back at the house, dull stone and timber beneath the slate. From the woods beyond he could hear the croaking pheasant, and then, all at once, the faint high mew of buzzard, and he looked up to see a pair wheeling far above, calling and calling as the morning mist rolled back over the fields and the hazy sun grew stronger.

All the birds of the air around him.

In some fashion he would not be without companions.

Within the hour, he was walking up the lane, wrapped up well and clapping gloved hands together. Just as well that the lane was frozen: as he picked his way over rut and hollow, the puddles glazed with ice, he wondered that anyone could walk here except in summer. Perhaps a pony and trap were indeed something else to think about.

Dearest Emily – What kind of pony should I look for? A chestnut with a star? A little skewbald?

At the turn in the lane he stopped, and looked back down at the house, his first proper sight of it in daylight at some distance. How well it was set within its garden, within the spread of the fields; how simple it was, but how well-proportioned, a room on either side of the door and three above. Quite roomy – roomy enough to entertain, perhaps, when it grew warmer. Who should be his first visitors?

He must call on his new neighbours once this day's duties were done. No doubt he would see some of them in church. And he thought of the crossing-keeper's little girl, pressed up against the lighted glass last night, looking down at him so gravely.

He could hear the tumbling fall of the stream, and the mew of the buzzard, circling still. And he heard something else – a footstep from somewhere in the quiet woods. He turned and listened: who might this be? There came the snap of a twig, then silence, and although he called out a tentative greeting not another footfall came, nor answering voice.

It must be a bird: as children they had been forever hopeful of finding some shy creature in the shrubbery, hearing a rustling there – something furry and soft, an orphaned mouse or rabbit to take indoors in a box and care for. Always, as they peered through box or laurel, a thrush or blackbird foraging in the undergrowth hopped quickly away.

He walked on, climbing the lane, the woods spread soundlessly around him.

It was over a mile to the Leominster road, which ran past the top of the woods, and by the time he approached it he was warm from exertion, though his feet were like blocks of ice. He had passed paths running this way and that through the trees, with here a resting farm cart, there a pile of logs. He had passed no dwelling, though from these signs he knew there must be at least a cottage or two some-where. Now he came to a lodge, no doubt the dwelling of a gamekeeper, for if he had not seen houses he had seen plenty of pheasants picking their way along the verge, whirring up at his approach. No doubt it had been a pheasant he had heard earlier, and no doubt there were partridge too, and a regular winter shoot. Perhaps he could join it.

Beyond the lodge was the sign for a farm, but it was set so far back up the drive he could not see the house. I could live here for a year and see no one, he thought; then reminded himself that he had duties to fulfil and a community to serve, and within no time at all would be greeting his new parishioners in church. And at Christmas too.

'*You can't go away before Christmas – you simply can't …*'

'*Hush! A vacancy has come and I am to take it. I am directed by the Bishop of Hereford, Emily, think of that! Now come, don't cry. Father would not wish to see his dear girl crying …*'

But he had had to fight down tears when he left, and turn away so they would not see them, and all through the journey his heart had been like lead. With his father's death a little of him had gone too, he knew it, and he did not expect to feel things again as he used to do, try though he might this morning to cheer himself with the thought of country pleasures.

A carriage was rumbling along the road ahead. He quickened his pace to see it go by, and stepped out from the lane just in time to see the coachman flick the whip and the horses steam. They were making for Kington, down to the right, but he turned off to the left, and walked down the hill towards his destination, glancing at his watch and filled, all at once, with apprehension. He was still so young, so recently ordained. It was one thing to serve alongside his father in a parish he had known from boyhood: how would he measure up to this, his first appointment?

But you are not the incumbent, he reminded himself, hurrying down the hill. You are only the raw young curate, and must be guided by what you find here. Seek humility; forget yourself in service.

The Church of St Michael and All Angels was set high up on a walled bank rising from the road, and the track which led up to it was steep. It was quite a way for parishioners to come out here, a good half-mile up the hill from the village of Lyonshall, and then this climb. But come here they did: Richard's letter of appointment had described a good strong attendance both for the services and for the village school, which, like the vicarage, lay within the churchyard.

'You will find, however,' the Bishop of Hereford had written, 'that the fabric of the church, its roof and interior, are in urgent requirement of repairs and restoration. I believe that the vicarage, too, is in need of some attention.'

Richard stood at the foot of the track, looking up. Even from here he could see that the roof of the church had a great number of missing tiles and that the battlements of the tower had gaps like a mouthful of broken teeth. There was a rusting weathervane but no clock, and he fumbled beneath his greatcoat for his pocket watch. A good quarter-hour before noon: he hesitated. So anxious had he been to arrive on time that now he was early. What should he do? If he went up to look round and were seen from the vicarage windows, he might be thought to be lacking in circumspection: he should wait to be shown round this afternoon, not go prowling around on his own.

Yet he could not stand about here in the cold and, besides, he found himself wanting to get a sense of it all without an introduction, to have his first impressions and knowledge of it all alone. Perhaps, shifting from one foot to another, he felt that he would not in any case be quite alone: that the church's empty interior and the cold sweep of the hillside churchyard might be filled not only with the presence of God but with his father's spirit, come to watch over him on this momentous day.

And was it wrong to want to cherish these last few minutes of freedom?

Quickly, he climbed the long track between hedge and churchyard wall. A rook cawed in an elm; Richard pulled up his gloves, stamping his frozen feet as he reached the lich-gate. It was glassy with ice, and the latch, like that on his own wicket gate last night, was stiff to the touch. Inside, beyond the church, he saw pressed up against the north-west wall the low dark house that must be the vicarage. Ivy clung round porch and windows; he could see no one watching for him there, and walked up the long flagged path towards the south door of the church, the cold slicing into him, chapping his lips. He pulled up his muffler again and looked about him: at the elms, and the three or four yews, at the gravestones shimmering with frost. Winter's stillness – but there must be many times when the wind came keen and terrible up here. He stood with his back to the crumbling tower and looked out across the road below to the unbroken fields and distant hills beyond, with nothing but the hedgerows and, on the road, a timber-framed house and a villa set behind gloomy laurels, to stop wind and weather come howling over the land.

And there in the south-east corner of the churchyard was the little schoolhouse. All shut up now for the Christmas holidays, the shutters barred and a great padlock on the door, but in term-time it must be a lively place. No doubt he would often be coming here to tell the children their Bible stories. Yet where did they run and play? Was there perhaps a yard at the back? He walked down a few paces, saw no enclosure and realised that the churchyard itself was the playground – it was here that the children must race about in their games of hare and hounds and hide-and-seek: in and out amongst tombs and gravestones.

For a moment this gave him real pause. He thought of the crossing-keeper's child, glimpsed looking down at him last evening in the winter dusk: she must attend this parish school, and learn her letters and struggle, perhaps, with her sums, as Emily used to, though Verity was so quick. Was it right for a little girl like her to skip over the dead or stumble on the headstone of some other child – for he saw, as you always saw, how small were some of those dotted here and there, like lambs in a field. Then he reproached himself: children were children, and innocent – they did not think of these things. And as he turned and walked back to the church he tried in the cold to imagine summer, sunlight playing over the grass beneath the trees, and laughing faces peeping out behind old mossy stones. After all, if God were with them, why should they not play where their fathers lay at rest?

He was approaching the gabled south porch of the church and, even before he reached it, could see how the timbers were rotting and eaten with worm. He walked inside, and his footsteps echoed. Then he slowly turned the handle of the great oak door.

And as he swung it open he had one of the first great experiences of his adult life, for it seemed for an ethereal moment that an icy choir sung in the sudden disturbance of air, as pure and cold as glass, and as fragile, for at once the high clear sound was gone, and he stepped in, shivering, and quickly kneeled in a pew chosen quite at random, on a worn hassock embroidered long ago with lilies on the purple ground of Advent, and let his prayer of awe fly upwards, like sparks, into cold heaven.

When he lifted his head he was dazed. He took in the dreadful cold, the smell of damp and its stains on every wall, the rafters ravaged by worm and beetle. Then he got stiffly to his feet, knowing he must by now be late, and made his way outside again, and round to the vicarage.

So very dark and closed in did it look, with its low, broken-tiled roof and massive growth of ivy, and so deep did it lie within the shadow of the tower, that he wondered as he walked up the path how endurable it was to live here. But smoke was rising from the chimneys and he saw the flicker of firelight in the rooms on either side of the front door and guessed at parlour and study. A dish of water was set outside, next to the boot scraper. So there must be a dog or a cat, something homely. This steadied him a little.

Dearest Emily, Today a thing indescribably beautiful took place in the church where I am to assume my duties. Would he – could he – try to describe that ethereal music? *And today (in such cold!) I meet at last the Reverend Oliver Bowen, and his wife, Susannah. The vicarage has a rather gloomy and forbidding aspect, but inside—*

The door swung wide, and a round-face maid was there.

'Mr Allen?'

'Indeed.' He smiled, wiping his feet. 'You are most prompt.'

'You're expected, sir. They are waiting to receive you.'

'I fear I am late.'

He stepped across the threshold; he handed his hat and coat; he entered a low dark hall. A hat stand was on his left, and a towering grandfather clock stood in the corner by the parlour door, its mahogany casing just beneath a beam. On a little table a great stuffed hawk glared from beneath a dome of glass; on a whatnot stood a potted fern beneath a candle sconce and an engraving on a mildewed mount. He made out the picture's subject at once: Christ raising Lazarus from the dead. It was a scene familiar since childhood – the outstretched hand, the look of gratitude in hollowed eyes. As a child he had wondered at the miracle, but that had been with the pages of a whole volume of biblical scenes. Hung alone in this gloomy hall it felt an ambiguous welcome.

'Mr Allen.' There was a cough. He turned as the door to the parlour opened. 'Welcome. I am delighted to meet you.'

'And I to meet you, sir, at last.'

What had he been expecting? Oliver Bowen was tall, as his father had been. His handshake was almost as firm, his voice a little hoarser. There was perhaps a difference of no more than a few years between them. But this man had white in his hair and shadows beneath his eyes, and where his father had had such an easy, loose-limbed stride, Bowen moved rather stiffly to stand aside at the parlour door. Impossible to know if reserve or discomfort caused this.

'Come in by the fire.'

'Thank you, sir.'

Richard entered the room. He saw the cold winter light at the casement overlooking the churchyard; the faded carpet, and horsehair ottoman; the round table with a pile of *Blackwood's Magazine*; the oil lamp. He took in the plainness and darkness of it all, the leaping flames of the fire almost the only colour in the room, for the cat asleep on the fireside chair was the most solid black, and the young woman standing by the mantelpiece had hair and skin as pale as milk, and her gown was as pale as a dove.

And for ever afterwards, remembering her swift smile as she came towards him, remembering everything about that day, it seemed that an absence at the heart of important things was what so strangely marked it: a footfall in a wood, though no one made it; an unseen choir, half heard for an incandescent moment; the exquisite absence of colour – as if there were simply no need of it, was that what he felt? As if pale silken hair and dove-grey gown were everything – in the appearance of the woman who now put her hand in his.

3

L uncheon in the vicarage. Save for the terms at school and his theological college, Richard had sat at a vicarage dining table every day of his life, as the family accompanied his father in the move from living to living. They unpacked the trunks of clothes and books and china in the houses of his childhood: the gaunt grey house in the hills outside Buxton, in whose church he had been christened, and, his mother told him, made not a murmur at the sudden shock of water – unlike Verity, two years later, who had screamed until she was purple. Then came the villa in the Potteries, where his mother began her modest collection of Coalport and he, hurling sticks into a chestnut tree one autumn, brought down a spiky case upon his upturned face so hard it split his lip wide open. That he did remember – the blood pouring through his fingers as he clamped them to his mouth and ran indoors; his mother's gasp, his father coming out of the study, murmuring boys will be boys, swiftly pressing his own handkerchief against the painfully swelling lip.

Later, they had moved to Shropshire, to the rectory in Ironbridge, where Emily was born. From there he was sent to school, and something of his childhood ended; but in the long holidays something of his growing-up began: an elder brother, an only son, sitting at the right hand of his father at the table, sitting at the head of the pew, watching his father climb the steps to the pulpit, and bow his head.

'Let the words of my mouth and the meditation of my heart be always acceptable in Thy sight, o Lord, my Strength and my Redeemer.'

He thought on a Sunday just before his confirmation: one day perhaps I shall climb such steps and say that prayer. At the confirmation service, kneeling with all the others before the altar rail, he closed his eyes, heard the rustle of robes, felt the stern press of the hand upon his head; he opened his own hands to receive for the very first time the pellet of bread that was the Host, the sharp metallic sip from the chalice that was the Blood, and he knew. No doubt, no speculation.

'Take, eat, this is my Body, which is given for you: Do this in remembrance of me …this is my Blood … which is shed for you and for many … Do this, as oft as ye shall drink it, in remembrance of me …'

He swallowed, his mouth dry: he drank, and his heart was pounding. Light poured in through the crimson and blue of the altar window. This was his life.

'You will take some cold mutton?'

He had been taking cold mutton at the vicarage dining table since he was old enough to come out of the nursery and assume his place there. Roast on Sundays, after the communion fast; cold on Monday or Tuesday; into a pie on Wednesday, with the very last scraps for the vicarage cat – they had always kept one – and the bones straight into the pot for broth on Thursday. The joint did vary, of course – spring lamb; a rare side of beef; poultry; and now and then pigeon pie or rabbit, if he and his father had gone tramping out with their gun.

'There! Quick!'

The first time he fired he was blown straight backwards, landing whole yards away, while the rabbit went tearing over the tussocky field and his father fired, then came running towards him.

'Are you hurt?'

'No, no …' Richard scrambled, dazed, to his feet. 'Did you get him?'

'I think not.' His father patted his shoulder. 'You're bruised?'

'A little.'

That first time they went home empty-handed. But once he had learned to brace himself for the kick, they'd bag one or two, bring them home to the back door still warm, hanging them up in the pantry to drip on to paper, nose down, ears back, long limbs outstretched.

Emily always wept.

'Look at his poor little face – I shan't eat a morsel!'

'Yes, you will.' He put his arm around her. 'It was very quick, Em. He knew nothing about it.'

'Do rabbits go to Heaven?'

'Don't be so foolish. Of course not.'

But their father, taking his boots off, greeting Verity with a kiss, said that Emily was asking a very big question, and was not to be dismissed. 'If there is a corner in Heaven for rabbits, you may be sure that this one will take his place among them.'

He went to his study. Emily dried her tears. They all went out to the garden, their father's eye upon them, as he looked up from his desk.

He had been beside them always. Now he was gone.

Now, on a bitter winter day, with the fire in this dark little dining room burning brightly, Richard sat watching a man of his father's generation sharpen the bone-handled carving knife upon the steel. The room was at the back of the house, looking out on the churchyard wall. In the fields beyond it, sheep were grazing beneath a leaden sky.

'We were so sorry to hear of the loss of your father.' Oliver Bowen made the first cut.

'Thank you, sir.'

'A very fine man, from all accounts. The Bishop spoke of him most warmly.'

'Thank you,' said Richard again. He could hear himself struggling to speak steadily: it was surprisingly hard to do so.

'You must miss him greatly.' Across the table, Susannah Bowen was regarding him.

He nodded. 'My mother and my sisters – it is hard for them.'

'And for yourself – I am sure the breaking of the great bond between father and son must leave you quite bereft—' She broke off, and he knew she was sensing how difficult indeed it was. 'Forgive me,' she said quietly.

'Please. You are most kind to enquire.' But he could not meet her eyes, and for a moment the silence in the room was like a pall.

Then he was passed his dish of cold meat, a log broke apart in the blazing grate, and the door opened. The comfortable maid was bringing in dishes of fragrant roast swede, and roast potato.

'Thank you, Millie.' Susannah Bowen lifted the first lid.

How good it smelled. This too was the fare of his dear home life, and as they began to eat, each hot mouthful filled Richard both with comfort and the kind of sudden lurching homesickness he had not known since those hideous first weeks of school.

'You're not crying, are you, Allen? Only weaklings cry.'

How he had hated it all, at first: the noise, the bells, the cold, the shoving – always someone to push him, to pinch or poke him, to threaten the sting of the cane. By the end, as his father had promised, there were things he loved: the scent of cut grass in long afternoons in the deep of the cricket field, where, in truth, it was butterflies, dancing over willowherb and cow parsley which had taken his attention quite as much as the game itself. *'Dearest Father, Today I have seen a Purple Emperor!'* He had liked the polished floor of the chapel and the great, roof-raising hymns; he had learned to like Latin, though he never shone, and Greek, though he always struggled, and history, in which he had done rather well. He had loved his friends, still wrote to Symes and Moore, had brought their letters of condolence with him: 'My dear Allen, What a truly dreadful blow …'; 'My dear Allen, May I extend my very deepest sympathy …' By the end of his last term he had, indeed, entirely forgotten the misery of his first.

Yet now, eating a familiar lunch with strangers, kind as they were, he felt himself once more a lonely, homesick boy; and where in boyhood he had felt his parents' love as strong as the arms of God around him, now there was a most terrible black absence. His father was in Heaven, and he must rejoice; his father was watching over him, over all of them, and would do so always. But here, at a meal prepared to welcome him, where his new life must begin, he sensed that boyhood had never left him, and that those feelings of abandonment and loss could quite unman him now.

He put down his knife and fork, and reached for his glass.

Susannah Bowen said gently across the table: 'This is your first visit to Herefordshire, Mr Allen?'

'It is.' He swallowed, and forced a smile. 'Although, of course, I have come only from the next county.'

'You had a good journey, I hope?'

'Very good, thank you. I much enjoy travelling by train.'

'Sometimes the train is as bumpy as the horse-drawn carriage.'

'But so much faster – though it still took some hours to get here.

And you, Mrs Bowen? Have you travelled much?'

She shook her head, and he saw the place where her knot of pale hair was held with a marcasite clip. For the first time he saw, too, some little tension about her eyes, as if she had slept badly.

'I have travelled very little, I fear,' she told him. 'Indeed, I found my first steam train quite alarming.'

'And where was that? What journey were you making?'

'Oh, it was just a little trip to see my aunts in Worcester, but it felt as if we were being borne away to a distant country.' She took the plate her husband passed her. 'Now I am a little more at ease with it all. And as the wife of a clergyman I expect to move about.'

'Indeed. As we did.'

And as he began to eat again, he thought all at once what an orderly progress his family had made across England, moving through adjoining counties – Derbyshire, Staffordshire, Shropshire, as if they were following a line of hills, or the path of a mighty river. Now he was over the border again.

Well. Perhaps God had always intended him to come here.

'My dear,' said Oliver Bowen to his young wife, as the meal was concluded, and she rose from her chair and rang the bell.

'I shall be sewing in the parlour,' she said. 'I shall leave you both now – I'm sure you have much to discuss.'

Richard rose to thank her. Then Millie came in to clear the table, and Susannah Bowen, with a rustle of her dove-grey gown, retired.

'We shall take ourselves into my study, I think,' said Bowen. He rose, and as he did so gave a cough again, and at once put his hand to the middle of his back.

'Sir?'

'It's nothing.' He took a breath, walked slowly to the door. 'Come.'

A fitful sun struggled through the ivy overhanging the study window, and Richard, looking around him, took in by its light the volumes of Gibbon, Macaulay and Carlyle in the bookcase; and of Lindley's *Botany*: everything his father, too, had kept on his own study shelves. He saw the place for the *Quarterly Review* and *Blackwood's Magazine*: familiar spines he had known since boyhood, as much a part of the texture of his life as the candle sconce above the bookcase, or the drawing of his father and Uncle Henry, made when they were boys.

And there was something else which spoke of home, for another engraving hung on the wall: *Christ in the House of His Parents*. His father had seen Millais's painting itself on a rare trip to London and a visit to the Royal Academy. He had said it was filled with a light which evoked both Palestine and eternity.

Bowen was looking about him. 'I had thought Millie was to bring in a tray – excuse me one moment.'

'Sir.'

He went out, and Richard went closer to the bookcase. Bowen was up to date. Here was the July–October volume of the *Quarterly Review*, which he had not seen, for with his father's death many economies had had to be made, and such subscriptions cancelled. But so familiar did he feel with them that almost without thinking, as if he were at home with his family, talking and browsing, he pulled this last one out, and ran his finger down the contents page.

'The Missing Link, or Bible Women in the Homes of the London Poor'; 'Ragged Homes and How to Mend Them' by Mrs Bagley; '*On the Origin of Species by Means of Natural Selection* by Charles Darwin: A review of Bishop Wilberforce of Oxford'.

Richard's finger stopped, then he turned the pages. His father had spoken of Darwin, and of Alfred Wallace, who had prepared the ground for extraordinary new theories. Keen naturalist that his father was, he took a lively interest in all God's creatures, but Darwin had startled him, as he seemed to startle many. And Bishop Wilberforce, it appeared, was taking him to task.

'With Mr Darwin's "argument" we may say at the outset we shall have much and grave fault to find …' Richard skimmed the pages. 'The words graven on the everlasting rocks are the words of God, and they are graven by His hand … Mr Darwin writes as a Christian, and we doubt not that he is one. We do not for a moment believe him to be one of those who retain in some corner of their hearts a secret unbelief which they dare not vent; and we therefore pray him to consider well the grounds on which we brand his speculations with the charge of such a tendency …'

There was a cough; there was a chink of glasses. Richard looked up to see Oliver Bowen returning with a tray, and glancing at him quizzically.

'I see you have found something of interest.'

Richard flushed, and snapped the volume to. 'Sir. Pray forgive me – something caught my eye.'

'And what was that?' The tray was set down on the desk.

'A review of Mr Darwin, sir, by the Bishop of Oxford. My father read of his work with some curiosity.'

'Did he now? I imagine he found Mr Darwin's ideas as abhorrent as I do. I was very glad to see Bishop Wilberforce quite thoroughly undermine him.' Bowen gestured to the fireside, coughed again. 'I trust I am not to find I have taken on a curate who finds this heresy in any way attractive. Take a seat.'

'Sir.' Richard slipped the book back into the bookcase, flushing still as though he were back at school. Clearly, it was of no interest to Bowen what he might think, and since, in truth, he did not know himself, then let this moment pass; please, let him not offend on his very first day here …

'Let us talk of other things,' said Bowen, unstopping the decanter. 'There is work to be done, Mr Allen. Will you join me in a little port wine?'

'A little. Thank you, sir.'

'Across the border, the temperance movement is very strong. Here—' Bowen poured a little glass and held it up to the light – 'here, we have today a special occasion.' He gave a dry little laugh. 'I hope I did not speak too harshly. It is a serious matter, is it not, to question the very nature of Creation? But you are welcome, Mr Allen. Please—' he gestured to the chair on the left of the fire – 'please, sit down. Your very good health.'

'And yours, sir.'

And they sat, as the grandfather clock in the hall struck a sonorous half-hour. Richard's chair was a worn horsehair, one of whose castors was missing, so that he found himself tilted towards the blaze of the fire, and tilted back again, whenever he shifted in his seat. He took his glass, and tried to settle.

The hesitant sun lit the china dogs on the mantelpiece, the brass of oil lamp and fender, a set of little brass scales on the rector's desk, placed beneath the window. Richard sipped his port wine and felt stronger. The sun went in again. He regarded his host in the shadows, settling in to the high wing chair across the hearth, coughing, and pausing, then reaching for papers from the table. Oliver Bowen was not quite in good health, but here he sat, sipping his wine, glancing through papers, while Richard's own dear father, who had strode like a young man across the fields and swung so easily into the saddle, now lay beneath a yew.

Bowen pushed up his pince-nez and regarded him: had he felt too intense a gaze? Richard's eyes dropped to the place on the damask-covered chair where the solid black cat must have been scratching. He found himself imagining Susannah's quick reproof, the way her hand might shoo the creature away, and smooth the torn loose threads.

'So. Our duties.' There was another little smile: Bowen passed a sheet of foolscap. Richard ran his eyes over the service times. There followed the notes of a funeral to be held within the week, of a baptism two days later. A winter child – he should have liked to think that one of his first acts here might be to baptise such a one, born so close to Christ's Nativity, but the flowing initials O.B. were set against both services.

He went on reading: the dates of the Parish Council meetings in the first quarter of the New Year; the dates of the inter-parish meetings, chaired by the vicar of Kington; the start-of-term date for the parish school in the churchyard, which he must attend. There were three boys to be prepared for confirmation. Then came a list of the names of the sick who must be visited; an appointment with a church warden; an introduction this very day to the verger, Philip Prosser; the name of the Kington builder who must urgently patch the roof. And here were his own initials beside the last sermon in Advent, less than a fortnight away. He was to preach here for the first time in the very week before Christmas. At the thought of it, his mouth went dry. He drained the glass of wine, and cleared his throat.

'There is plenty to do, it seems.'

'Indeed. And although on winter days such as this you may feel you have come to the quietest place on earth, there is a great deal going on here. Kington is a lively little town, and of course the coming of the railway has brought changes; it is putting us in touch with the wider world.' Bowen bent to the scuttle. 'Bringing us good Welsh coal, for example.' He cast a shovelful upon the flames. 'The old ways persist, of course. We still see the drovers, as well as the railway cattle trucks. Old women still walk over the hills on market day.'

'And when is that?'

'Every Wednesday. I shall accompany you there next week.'

'That is very kind, sir.'

'And your domestic arrangements?' Bowen leaned back in his chair. 'I fear you would prefer to be housed closer to the church, to be somewhere rather less spartan, with a good servant living in. Is this so?'

'In truth, it was bitterly cold last night, sir. But this morning – I felt myself begin to settle.' Richard thought of his books on the deep stone windowsill; of the desk set before them, with the prospect of the field, and the glossy crow shaking water from his wings at the top of the ash tree. He would live alone for the first time in his life: perhaps, within such solitude, he might grow closer to God. And perhaps, in so doing, he might become a man.

'The cottage fell vacant,' Oliver Bowen was saying, 'and since it lies so exactly between two parishes, it seemed an opportunity too good to ignore. But you must tell me if you find it too remote or too cold to bear. My last curate, Mr Davies, enjoyed comfortable quarters within the village here until his marriage and first incumbency took him away. I am sure we could arrange something similar for you. In the meantime, as I said in my letter, the woman Martha Price will come in each morning from Rushock Bank. You will see her cottage when you walk up to the Presteigne road: it lies just on the other side.'

'Very good. Thank you, sir. I shall expect her.'

'And now—' Bowen tidied his papers again – 'now I must take you across to the church. No doubt you are anxious to see it.'

'Indeed, sir.' He felt himself colour, and looked away. Slight though it was, his response was a deception. Perhaps he really should have waited to be conducted round, for he was such a poor dissembler: how could he feign an entirely fresh interest in something he had already seen? Yet he had, in truth, only gained an impression of dilapidation. And had he not been alone, would he have been vouchsafed that extraordinary moment? The intimation of a miracle – was that what it had been?

Bowen was getting up slowly from his chair. 'And then I will take you down to the village and show you around a little. And then—' he gave a little smile – 'then your first day's duties are done. You will be able to walk home while it is still light.'

Susannah bade them farewell in the hall, as the grandfather clock chimed two.

'It has been a pleasure to meet you, Mr Allen. We do hope you will be happy here.'

Once more, he took her outstretched hand. He bowed.

'I am sure I shall be. You are most kind.'

'And your first sermon? When is that to be?'

'On the fourth Sunday in Advent.'

Millie approached; he turned to receive his outdoor clothes.

'We shall greatly look forward to hearing you. Shall we not, Oliver?'

'Indeed.' Bowen was pulling on his own heavy coat. Away from the fires the hall was cold and draughty. He took his hat, brushed his wife's cheek with a kiss. 'Go back to the fireside, my dear. I shall be home by teatime.'

'Very good. Millie? May we confer for a moment?'

And the two women returned to the parlour's warmth, as Richard and Oliver Bowen went out into the churchyard. Rooks on the path flew up; the sun was gone.

'We shan't linger long,' said Bowen, as they walked past leaning headstones. 'I fear that the building is in great disrepair, as no doubt you have been told.'

'I have, sir.'

'You have only to look at the roof.' They stopped, and looked at it. 'See those great holes? The rain has been driving in for years.' He shook his head. 'To raise sufficient funds for restoration is a tremendous task. I fear I have not begun to do what is needed. Still—' they came to the south porch and he led the way in – 'you are young, you have energy. We shall look to you. And now—' He swung open the door.

Richard held his breath, but though the chill from the interior met them at once, the mysterious music of that choir of air was not audible now, and he followed Bowen inside.

'We shall pray for a moment.'

They took off their hats; they kneeled side by side in a creaking pew. Outside, the rooks cawed in the elms; Richard, as he tried to pray, was aware of this, kneeling in silence beside a man he hardly knew, trying to concentrate. *Father*, he said in his heart, and could say no more.

Beside him, Bowen sighed, then rose stiffly.

'Amen,' murmured Richard, and followed him into the aisle.

'So.' They walked down the nave, their footsteps echoing. 'How does it strike you?'

Richard looked about him. A stain like a map of India lay upon crumbling plaster on the north aisle wall, beside a marble tablet to the Hooper family. For a moment he was transported to the schoolroom and the globe, reciting the names of those magical, half-imagined places – Poona, Mysore, Kashmir, Calcutta. India! The sikh, the sepoy, the gilded dome and marble minaret. The elephant, the slinking tiger, the Ganges and the jewelled prince. As a boy, fired up by stories and engravings, by letters home from Uncle Henry, making such a success of things in the East India Company, he had thought to sail there himself, perhaps to serve in a mission. Then, three years ago, came news of the Mutiny, and his mother's shocked white face. Then came the death of his father. He knew he would never travel now so far from his mother and sisters.

So, here he was, in quiet border country, and here was Oliver Bowen, coughing and pointing upwards.

'See there? And there? I fear that if one single rafter were removed then the whole would fall in upon us.' He stopped, and turned towards the west window, and the curtained recess beneath. 'We do have a fine ring of bells, and loyal ringers. And there is a stove, which our good verger lights early on Sundays.' He swung his arms across his chest. 'What cold, what cold!'

He coughed again; for a moment he could not speak. Then they walked on down towards the altar, noting the pew with the broken back, the pew with its door half off the hinges, the places in the cracked flags where the damp dark earth came through; the place where the bucketing rain had soaked a once-fine hanging, now removed. Panes were missing in the plain glass windows, the holes stuffed with rags and paper.

'And yet,' said Bowen, as they reached the transept, 'there are churches in far worse a state than this. I fear there are parishes where a less-than-dutiful incumbent has absented himself for months at a time, and something approaching ruin has been the result. I believe that in Cefnllys the bells rust, the furnishings rot and the pews are quite in pieces. Naturally, attendance is very poor.'

'Where did you say that was, sir?'

They had come to the chancel. 'Cefnllys, some miles across the border. You must learn to accustom yourself to the Welsh names – I shall lend you a dictionary. Of course, it is the Chapel which has the greater hold there, and I do not hear of those congregations allowing neglect of their good plain furnishings.'

Richard listened. How much he had to learn.

He looked around him at dark oak choir stalls, and the modest organ at which he longed to sit for a moment and try his hand at a little piece of Bach or Handel. 'In what condition is the organ, sir?' he asked, and Bowen said it was a poor wheezing creature, but served well enough, as it must.

'I should so love to—'

'In time, in time. You see we have one fine window.'

'Indeed.' And he gazed up at the stained-glass panels above the altar, where a ship broke up upon rocks in a mighty storm. 'A good naval officer from Lyonshall,' said Bowen. On the left panel, Christ walked upon the waters. 'Now, let me show you behind the scenes.'

He led the way to a small oak door to the left of the altar. Richard followed, and as Bowen unlocked it and they entered the vestry, he was at once at home. Here was the cupboard of mildewed sheets of music; here were the Books of Common Prayer with missing pages, the hymnals in need of rebinding. Here were the vestments on a row of pegs: the cassocks, the surplices of choir and clergy, the long embroidered stoles. In Advent, purple was everywhere. He stepped aside as Bowen took out the keys to a box on the floor, and barked his shin on a broken-backed chair.

'Here is the plate.' Bowen raised the lid of the oaken box and unwrapped from black cloth the chalice, a little tarnished; the mahogany collection plate. 'It is another sign of the times that we dare not leave this box unlocked, nor the vestry door.'

Richard rubbed his shin. He drank in the smell of old books, the sight of holy objects. He smelled polish and dust and stone and worn cotton; he smelled winter in a country church with every breath he took.

'We must go.' Bowen was relocking the box, straightening up again. As he did so, Richard saw him wince. He coughed again, and his face, when he ceased, was tight with pain. Then he gave a quick little smile and gestured towards the door. 'After you.'

They walked down the aisle beneath the marble tablets. The light from the altar window lit here and there in blue and green and silver the carved end of a pew, the rim of the font, the flags. Bowen indicated the pairs of glass mantels screwed into the walls. 'Since Kington has had gas we are able to hold evening services in winter, but in such cold we have only a very small congregation. I tend to hold evensong only until the end of November. We begin again in Lent.'

'I'm sure that's very wise, sir.'

They had come to the end of the aisle. At the top of the nave Bowen pulled aside the curtain, indicating the long loops of the bell pulls, hung on their hooks, and the rounds chalked up on a blackboard on the wall.

Richard made out Grandsire Doubles, and smiled. 'I shall like to hear them,' he said.

'They make a fine sound, though at home we can hardly hear ourselves speak.'

He let the curtain fall, and they turned and looked back, down the nave. Beyond the rood screen the dull gold cross gleamed on ghostly linen as the light began to fade.

'So,' said Oliver Bowen. 'This is your church. I pray you will serve it well.'

Outside, a wind was getting up, and the trees were soughing.

'We must call on Philip Prosser,' said Bowen, as they walked down to the lich-gate. 'Our verger, a true churchman. He is just across the road, the house behind the laurels. He will be affronted if I do not introduce you at the first opportunity. His wife is rather a poor weak thing: visitors cheer her, I think, though you will find her shy.'

The Prosser villa, whose roof Richard had glimpsed in his solitary moments on the churchyard slope, was screened from the highway by a long path lined with a towering laurel hedge. It darkened the downstairs windows; leaves blew about in the porch. Here was another house which, recalling the good plain rectory in Ironbridge, fronting on to the street, and passers-by, he thought might be a difficult place to live. But the maid who answered the door seemed cheerful enough, and the Prossers were all smiles.

'Come in, come in out of the cold.' The verger was small and sharp-eyed; he shook Richard's hand firmly. 'Delighted to make your acquaintance, Mr Allen. May I present my wife? To be sure, Tilda,' he added, as Mrs Prosser rose from her fireside chair, 'you need not look so anxious with the arrival of a visitor! We have heard all about our new curate, have we not?'

'Indeed we have,' said Tilda Prosser with a little laugh. 'Do excuse me, Mr Allen. It is just my way.'

The room had a fern or aspidistra in every corner; chenille draped every table. The company took their seats and began a little small talk – the weather, Richard's journey, the length of Mr Prosser's service. The maid came in and asked if she should light the lamps, so dull had the afternoon become.

'Oh, do,' said Mrs Prosser, but her husband checked her.

'No need for it yet, I think. How we run through oil in this house. We will call when we are ready, Josie.'

'Very good, sir.' And Josie made a bob, and left the room.

Tilda Prosser picked up her work.

'I wonder that you think of sewing when you have just complained about the light,' said her husband. 'Have you no more to say to our guest?'

'Of course, of course. I hope I did not complain. Do tell us, Mr Allen, how are you finding it here?'

'Indeed, I have only just arrived,' Richard began kindly, and Tilda flushed as her husband cleared his throat.

'I fear I have never been a great conversationalist,' she said, looking down at her lap. 'It is my husband who is so good with everyone.'

'Nonsense,' said Prosser, and patted her cheek as he got up to throw on more coal. She gave him a loving little look, but though

Richard and Oliver Bowen stayed for another twenty minutes, and touched only on the most undemanding topics – the approach of Christmas, the giving of alms, of how the organist, Thomas Hatton, was a true musician who brought out the very best in the choir – Tilda barely spoke again, though she bid them farewell most warmly and hoped Mr Allen would call again.

'Indeed I shall,' said Richard, pressing her hand in the cold tiled hall, and she blushed.

'There are children?' he asked Bowen, as they made their way back down the path.

'A son,' said Bowen. 'A clerk. He lives in Hereford.'

They came out on to the highway, and Richard felt the subject close as firmly as a shutter on a winter night. How foolish of me, he thought, as they walked down the hill. Surely they would have talked about their son had they wished to. And he thought: there are no children in the vicarage. I must wait to be told about that.

'Prosser is a good enough man,' said Bowen, raising his collar against the wind. 'A little limited, perhaps, but dutiful and reliable. Now, then, the village.'

They turned off into a byroad, and walked on, passing an inn. In the cold of the late afternoon, Lyonshall was almost deserted, but for a little coming and going at the single shop; through the dark glass of the window, a woman behind the counter could be seen wrapping cheese. Two women in widow's weeds were gossiping; a child took a toddler's hand as they came out down the step with their mother.

The little girl looked familiar. Richard studied her, then remembered. This was the crossing-keeper's daughter, whom he had seen gaze down at him from her lamplit gable when he arrived last night. He pointed her out to Bowen, who nodded.

'Yes indeed – your neighbours. A good strong little family. Birley saw you up the lane, I trust.'

'He did. I should like to greet them now, if I may?'

'But of course – you must meet everyone.'

Mother and children were stepping on to the unmade road, the mother lifting her skirts.

'Mrs Birley?'

Richard walked quickly up to her: she turned and dipped a curtsy as he raised his cleric's hat. Then Bowen was beside them, making introductions.

'My new curate, Mrs Birley, Mr Allen. Your neighbour!'

'Yes, sir. My husband has told me it all.' Her little boy was shrinking into her skirts, his thumb in his mouth; the girl regarded them. 'Alice, bid Mr Allen good afternoon.'

'Good afternoon, sir,' said Alice.

She was wearing a patched little coat and knitted gloves. From beneath her winter bonnet she looked gravely up for a moment at the two dark-coated men before her, then lowered her gaze. Something about her put Richard at once in mind of Emily, whose shyness with strangers concealed her spirit. This child, he felt instinctively, had even at her young age – seven? eight? – a strong sense of how to be true to herself. Which made her, indeed, like both the dear girls at home, and he told her, standing there in the street in the cold: 'I have two sisters at home in Shropshire, Alice. They are rather older than you, but you bring them to my mind a little.'

She nodded, but did not answer him, and her mother, burdened with her basket and the clinging hands of the little boy, said Alice was unused to new company, and please to excuse her shyness.

'I hope you will ask if there is anything you need, sir,' she added. 'We are just a step away, and very willing.'

'That's most kind. I hope you too will feel able to ask anything of me. I am the curate of the parish now: it is my privilege to serve you.'

'Thank you, sir.' She dropped a little bob to Oliver Bowen. 'I trust you and Mrs Bowen is keeping well, sir.'

'We are, we are. Well, now …' He was rubbing his hands. Richard noticed that the little Birley boy was gloveless, and his hands quite red and raw with cold and sucking. 'We must not detain you. I will hope to see you all in church on Sunday.'

'We shall try, sir.' And Mrs Birley blushed and drew the children to her, shifting her basket on her arm, and crossed the muddy street, setting off up the slope towards the highway from where they could hear the brisk clip-clop of a carriage pair travelling down into Kington.

'So,' said Bowen, as Richard watched them, 'a turn round the village, I think. Then you will have your bearings.'

And they walked on up the street. Quiet though it was, Richard was aware of eyes upon him: from the woman coming out of the shop, from faces at the windows of the cottages, still unlit. They glanced quickly out, and then withdrew. He was a curiosity – and he was curious himself now, some of the day's earlier hesitancy diminishing. He had a position. He had been made welcome. He had neighbours in whom, humble as they were, he felt some interest quicken. He liked that child. Susannah Bowen had made a deep impression: that pale but lovely face, that gentle manner, the hint of strain, or tiredness. Had she been ill? Did the long winter in that house oppress her?

'You are quite lost in thought,' said her husband, as they made their way back up the hill.

4

On Sunday, he rose while it was still dark, stumbling in the fragile candlelight to the frozen pitcher of water, breaking the ice and gasping at the violence of the cold.

He splashed his face; he was awake. He must pray.

'Our Father, which art in heaven, Hallowed be thy Name ...' He kneeled, shivering, at the bedside; he struggled to let the great words sink into him, to calm him. 'Thy Kingdom come. Thy will be done ...' He was trembling with nerves, his stomach rising and falling like butter in a churn. How was he to conduct himself this morning, how persuade his new parishioners that he was worthy to serve them; to offer the Sacrament; to pray that the peace of God might fill their hearts?

Once again, as he drew a long breath in the darkness, he reminded himself that such thoughts were vanity; that he was merely another young curate; that he must think not of himself but of his people, and, with them, of their Father in Heaven, in whose embrace they all were held as equals.

'Lord, grant me strength to serve Thee.'

He pulled off his nightshirt and dressed in the clothes laid out last night. His undergarments smelled of wood smoke: Martha Price had already taken and returned a basket of washing, dried before her fire. Shivering still, he had never felt more glad of the woollen undershirt and socks his mother had begun to knit as soon as he heard of his appointment.

'Whatever else you may need, you will need warm socks,' she had said, as she returned from the Ironbridge drapers with six grey balls of wool.

He tugged them on, took down his father's cassock from the hook upon the door. The clerical tailor in Shrewsbury had needed to make some alterations: to turn up the hem, for Richard had not quite reached his father's height; to turn in the cuffs, which were worn. His mother and the girls had wept when the tailor's boy delivered the altered cassock. Trying it on, in the privacy of his bedroom, Richard had found himself weeping too.

Now, as he drew the dear garment down over his head and fastened the black cloth-covered buttons, he felt as though his father's spirit were settling upon him. And in the hour before dawn, when people died – he knew that people slipped away in this shrouded time, and the deep small hours before it – he stood with his head bowed, asking for a little of his father's goodness and kindness to enter his own soul now.

He put on his white tie. He stepped to the window. The night had been clear and the last pure stars still pricked the sky. A glimmer of frost on the field showed the faint bulk, here and there, of sheep at rest. The silence was complete, and he wondered again at its utter depth and fullness, as if the whole world were contained within it. Then, as he listened, he heard the faint sound of the stream beyond the garden gate.

The stars had faded. Morning had come. He had prayed; he had tried to eat. In hat and coat and muffler he walked up the track through the woods. The sheep were moving now, over the great hill field that climbed alongside, heavy and quiet with lamb, heads bent to the frosty grass.

Dearest Mama, my dearest sisters – Today I am to take part in my first service. I shall write to you all about it. I am privileged to read the first lesson: as a way, says the Reverend Mr Bowen, of introducing myself to our parishioners. After the service I am to take luncheon at the vicarage again, to meet members of the parish council. I am filled with apprehension, vain though it may be: about the reading, the luncheon – about, quite simply, everything.

The text for today, of course, is Isaiah 44, verses 1–21. They are verses I love, for they are full of the natural world, and of homely, ordinary things, are they not? Willows and grass and water. Smiths and carpenters. I shall like to think of you all, listening in church to the same words, at the same time as I am reading them here. Dear home! How I think of you all ...

☆

He came on to the highway, saw the whitened expanse of fields on the other side. A clerical jackdaw was perched upon the gatepost: it cocked its head; he raised his hat. By the time he had walked the mile downhill and come to the entrance to the steep church path, he was steady and calm.

God was with him. A task was to be done.

'Dearly beloved brethren, the Scripture moveth us in sundry places to acknowledge and confess our manifold sins and wickedness; and that we should not dissemble nor cloke them before the face of Almighty God our heavenly Father; but confess them with an humble, lowly, penitent, and obedient heart; to the end that we might obtain forgiveness of the same, by his infinite goodness and mercy …'

The hoarse voice of the Reverend Oliver Bowen met the rustle of skirt and crinoline, the cough, the shuffled foot, the whispered hush to a child: in short, the congregation. They made perhaps sixty souls. From his seat behind the rood screen, Richard guessed at farmers, millers and agricultural labourers; tradesmen, shopkeepers, clerks – such men and their wives and children made up the greater part, filling the centre and rear pews. There, on the right, were the Birleys: she with Alice standing straight and still beside her; he in his Sunday suit quite a different man from the crossing-keeper in rough, smut-spattered jacket, who had swung a lantern before them on the night of his arrival. What a fine face he had. The little boy was not to be seen, though perhaps it was he who must be hushed a moment ago. Richard imagined him sunk now beneath the shelf in the pew for books and Bibles, fiddling with a thread of wool in a hassock.

Filling the front pews were the gentry, the men who might be landowners, lawyers, auditors and magistrates – subscribers to the new railway, perhaps.

Such secular thoughts.

This was his first sight of them all, his new parishioners: specula-tion perhaps was natural, as his first service began. Still, he checked himself as the invocation drew to its close, glancing once, and then quickly away, at the very front pew, where a grey silk bonnet showed a skein of milk-pale hair.

SUE GEE

'Wherefore I pray and beseech you, as many as are here present, to accompany me with a pure heart, and humble voice, unto the throne of the heavenly grace, saying after me ...'

There came the descent to the knee, like the fall of a wave upon the shore.

'Almighty and most merciful Father; We have erred, and strayed from thy ways like lost sheep ...'

Richard sank to his own knees, joining in the murmur of a country congregation in confession, as he had done every Sunday throughout his life. And to what now, on this freezing Advent morning, should he confess as his new life began?

'We have followed too much the devices and desires of our own hearts ...'

Beyond the rood screen, beyond the flagstoned transept, threescore Herefordshire voices rose and fell. In the very front pew, a grey silk bonnet was bent over clasped gloved hands. Richard's eyes were closed, his own head bent, his voice at one with the congregation; but he felt this image sink within him now like the impress of a thumb upon hot wax.

'Spare thou them, O God, which confess their faults. Restore thou them that are penitent ...'

He murmured the Amen. He kneeled upon the square of carpet upon the cold stone floor, as Oliver Bowen stood alone and pronounced the Absolution.

A door was slowly opening, into a room which he had never entered.

'Here beginneth Isaiah, Chapter 44, verses 1–21.' He cleared his throat, feeling their eyes upon him.

'Yet now hear, O Jacob my servant ... Fear not ... For I will pour water upon him that is thirsty, and floods upon the dry ground ...'

His trembling hands rested upon the pages of the open Bible. It lay upon the great carved outstretched wings of the church eagle, whose fierce proud face beheld the congregation. How, as a child, he had been in awe of this bird, standing beneath the polished wood, gazing up at the cruel curve of the beak, the glaring eye! Now, what comfort it gave him to lean his hands upon its solid oak. The pages of the Bible were pinpricked here and there with rust marks, leafed with gold. He read on, his voice a little steadier.

'The carpenter stretcheth out his rule; he marketh it out with a line; he fitteth it with planes, and he marketh it out with the compass, and maketh it after the figure of a man, according to the beauty of a man …'

The words described the making of a graven image of God: something terrible, and forbidden; and yet how full was the language, almost despite itself, with the love of making things, of something made well and straight and true, sprung from the holy beauty of the world.

'He heweth him down cedars, and taketh the cypress and the oak, which he straighteneth for himself among the trees of the forest; he planteth an ash, and the rain doth nourish it …'

And now he was at one with the words he was reading, all nerves forgotten. He felt the attention of the whole church upon him, he felt an Old Testament prophet's words sound clear as water in the cold, pouring through time, taking the congregation and him back to the ancient land of Palestine; out across England, to where his mother and sisters sat in the family pew in St Mary's, Ironbridge, listening, thinking of him, and of his father; taking him back to his childhood, when he had sat beside them and heard countless lessons. They had sunk into him for ever.

He bowed his head. 'Here endeth the First Lesson.'

And he lifted the long purple bookmark of Advent, and let it fall in the place in the New Testament where the Second Lesson must begin: at the marriage in Cana of Galilee, St John, Chapter 2. Here had Christ performed the miracle of turning water into wine.

Then Richard slowly returned to the chancel, and walked through the rood screen, and took his place.

The organ sounded. There was a great getting to the feet, the rustle of hymnals.

'Hymn number forty-nine,' announced Bowen, and sixty voices rose, with Richard's voice among them:

> 'O come, O come, Emmanuel,
> And ransom captive Israel ...'

A mighty piece of work, this Advent hymn, these words, this tune: he had always loved it. And he let his voice ring out in the cold: 'Rejoice! Rejoice!'

'The grace of our Lord Jesus Christ, and the love of God, and the fellowship of the Holy Ghost, be with us all, evermore. Amen.'

The service was over. For a few moments longer, the church was hushed. Then the organ began to sound once more, and the congregation to rise from its knees, as the rector and his new curate came down from their seats. Behind them the choristers gathered up their music and processed into the vestry. Before its door closed there was a perceptible buzz of voices, a burst of laughter, quickly hushed. As they walked down the aisle in the clouded morning light, Richard felt himself immeasurably self-conscious beneath the gaze of so many. They came to the southern transept; the verger swung wide the south door and a rush of cold air came in.

Outside was a flurry of icy rain, which turned all at once to hail, and the horses at the carriages waiting beyond the lich-gate tossed their heads, stung upon flank or fetlock. The hail bounced off path and gravestone, speckled the grass with white, and as Richard waited in the freezing porch to greet his new parishioners he watched it whirling everywhere. A handful blew suddenly in, and went rolling across the flags beneath the bench.

'Quite a little storm,' said Bowen, on the other side of the porch. His surplice blew about his ankles. 'You read well,' he added, rubbing his hands.

'Thank you, sir. They are fine verses.'

The organist was playing a piece of recessional music, a Bach Invention. In the cold and newness of it all, Richard found it especially melodious and sweet, threading in and out of the murmur of voices, the closing of hymnal and prayerbook, the violent spattering of hail. Then the first family was coming out into the porch, and Bowen was clearing his throat.

'Mr Southwood, Mrs Southwood, good morning. May I present our new curate, Mr Allen?'

A bony hand, a bow; a dip of a bonnet and a light gloved clasp. Richard murmured their names, he answered their kind enquiries, was told that their daughter, Charlotte, had a chill and had not attended church today and told that Will, their son, would soon be down from Oxford. Behind them the press of people grew; before them the hail blew away; beyond the lich-gate a coachman jumped down and unfastened a carriage door. The Southwoods moved on, with an invitation to Richard to come and dine one day. Richard shook hands with Mr Arthur Bodenham, the Kington solicitor, with Dr Probyn, with Mr Richard Parry, auditor; with Thomas Skarratt the clockmaker.

'You will admire the illuminated clock which hangs above Skarratt's premises,' said Parry, fastening his top coat button. Richard was sure that he would.

He turned to Mr Edward Turner and Miss Effie Bounds, delighted to learn of their recent betrothal. He promised to call on Mrs Thomas, Mrs Meadham, the Misses Jenkinson, and on Miss Dorothy Wilkinson and her aunt, who must take the Blessed Sacrament at home since her sudden fall in the autumn. He was sorry to learn about this, and sorrier still to hear of the great loss suffered by Alfred Arndell, whose young wife was buried not a twelvemonth since, out there in the churchyard, there, down the slope to the left, hard by the wall. Richard promised to visit this sad place, and to visit Arndell too, should he so wish it.

'I shouldn't mind,' said Arndell, moving slowly out among the rest.

As the greetings and introductions went on, Richard tucked a card into his sleeve; was invited to call at half a dozen houses; was taken aside and had the details of an unusual medical condition confided to him. He was drawn back into the throng with an enquiry about his strength as a walker, for the walking in the Radnorshire Hills was the finest of any border county, and he was fit for this?

He laughed, said he was sure it was so, and he was his father's son

45

and hoped he could keep up with any man. He heard himself relaxed and at ease, as if he had been making such parish small talk always. He felt a light touch on his arm, and he knew it was her, and the voices all around him faded.

'The whole world wishes to speak to you, Mr Allen.'

Beyond the gate a harness jangled. In a sudden bright glance of the sun the wind chased light and shadow through the bare trees and across the churchyard.

'I am touched to be made so welcome,' he said, and it was true, and then he had nothing to say.

She gave a little smile, and the face which had been so serious and intent during the service was lit like the quiet interior of a chapel by an opening window.

Sounds came in through the door of the porch: carriages were leaving, voices were calling farewell. Within the church the murmur of the organ died away.

'My dear,' said Oliver Bowen, stepping forward, 'how cold you look. How dreadfully cold we all are; we must go home for luncheon. Allen, you remember our good verger, Mr Prosser?'

'Indeed, I do,' said Richard, and he turned to shake his hand.

This luncheon in the vicarage was a very different affair from the one he had taken earlier in the week. Then, he had arrived alone, his mind a strange mixture of nerves and quietude and awe and grief. Now, walking across the churchyard in the company of Mr Prosser and his little wife, trying to concentrate upon the man's account of a robbery, his head was almost spinning with the impressions of the morning: the sea of the congregation, the service, the accumulation of introductions in the porch, the realisation of how much, in truth, was expected of him here.

And, in the midst of it all, was that still pure moment before her, when all else faded.

But this he must not think of, simply must not, and now he must absorb more information, and respond.

'Is that so?' he asked politely, at a pause, as a pony and trap clattered past the churchyard, down the hill. What was it that Prosser had been telling him?

'Aye, it is. 'Twas a theft such as would strike fear into the heart of any man, and all in broad daylight too. Since transportation all but ended we have had such lawlessness, and the lawless must remain amongst us now. I sometimes sit on the bench, Mr Allen, at the Presteigne Quarter Sessions, and I have experience. The County Gaol there is quite bursting, and the House of Correction alongside. The chaplain there has but a part-time post, but a visit at all from the Church is more than they deserve, the many of them, the vagabonds and thieves and harlots that they are.'

They came to the fork in the path. 'But at Christmas,' put in Tilda all at once, as Prosser drew breath, 'at Christmas, in this season of goodwill, my dear, then one might hope to harbour kinder feelings? There are poor girls within the House of Correction whom I am sure do not deserve such long confinement, but our charity.'

Prosser snorted. 'My wife is a good Christian soul, Mr Allen, and I thank the Lord for that, but I fear the truth is that charity is wasted on some of those that receive it.'

'Perhaps, as your good wife suggests, that is a little severe?' said Richard, seeing Tilda flush. 'Our Lord, after all, bid us open our hearts to the lowest sinner, did he not?' He found himself speaking with a muted passion. He knew this kind of man, he realised: his father had sometimes had to work with such parish councillors – self-important, narrow-minded, quick to pronounce. In response, his father's own spirit had been so generous, so truly Christian, a real example. And he now had a role to play here, had he not? He had a position, and must declare himself from the beginning. 'For as much as ye do it unto them, ye do it unto Me,' he said quietly, and knew he had found the text for a sermon. 'Is this not so?'

Prosser looked up at him. 'You are very young, Mr Allen, if I may say so. As one grows older, experience teaches certain things. Let us discuss this no further now.'

The silence that fell was as frosty as the grass between the graves. I am put in my place, thought Richard, before luncheon has even begun. He saw Tilda Prosser compress her lips: such a faded, sick little thing. How difficult marriage could be, it seemed, without the dear harmony which had lain between his parents, as closely woven as any quilt or cover.

They had come to the vicarage. There came all at once the rich and marvellous smell of Sunday roast. Richard was ravenously hungry.

'I am sure you are right, sir,' he said to Mr Prosser, speaking like the peacemaker his parents had taught him to be when Verity flared up. And he stood aside at the vicarage porch, letting the two go in before him, seeing faces at the window, hearing laughter.

Luncheon was for nine: three good men of the parish who formed the body of the council; their wives, active in charity work; Oliver and Susannah Bowen, and himself. Richard listened and listened and listened: in the firelit parlour, where they were all foregathered, and at the dining table, where he was placed between Mr and Mrs Arthur Bodenham, along from the Prossers and opposite the Neves.

Dearest Emily, If you could hear how they talk!

He heard from Mrs Bodenham, as the soup tureen came in, that a good Christmas turkey could be had in the market for four shillings, and that she had last week placed her order. She told him how the week before a horned black Cardiganshire bullock had all at once taken it into his head to turn off the High Street on market day and had lumbered away towards Mill Street, frightening everyone half to death until the Welsh drover and John Blakely had cornered and cowed him – if Mr Allen would forgive the little joke! – in the yard of the Burton Hotel.

He was told by Samuel Neve that some eight thousand black cattle came down the drovers roads each year and passed through Kington on their way to the Midland counties to be fattened up for the London market.

'Now we have the railway, no doubt we can expect fewer of such dramas,' said Neve, unfolding his napkin. 'The cattle truck will take them, and a good thing too.'

Roast mutton came in. Richard heard that it was by its sheep that Radnorshire chiefly lived, though the fluke had destroyed many flocks in the fifties, and ruined many a farmer in the hills.

'It is unfortunate that Southwood is unable to join us for luncheon,' said Oliver Bowen, sharpening the knife upon the steel. 'He serves us very well upon the council – indeed, he often chairs it. Still, you met him and his wife, Allen, and will do so again.'

Richard tried to recollect: he had met so many this morning. 'I believe I did, sir.'

'Such good people they are,' said Mrs Neve, 'and Mrs Southwood has been so kind to me in my indispositions.'

Richard knew at once what was wanted here: he made solicitous enquiries, and was told, as Liza Neve awaited her dish of mutton, that unfortunately her health was indeed rather poor, and that in particular she suffered most dreadfully from headcolds every winter, though in November, on Mrs Southwood's advice, she had for the first time purchased the new Beecham's pills – 'Worth a Guinea a Box is how they describe them,' she said with a little laugh – and recovered most remarkably. She told him, as Millie served the potatoes, about the medicinal waters at Llandrindod Wells. 'You must be sure to go there,' she said, passing the gravy boat, and he said he was certain that he would.

And if he cared for another fine expedition then he could, said Samuel Neve, take himself up the track from Bullocks Mill, which led to the Presteigne highway, and cross it to walk up Rushock Hill, where he would come to the three ancient yews just over the border, which they called the Three Shepherds, and from there could look out across three counties, a magnificent stretch of Offa's Dyke the one way and Radnor Forest the other.

Richard listened and nodded and smiled and said he would do all these things. He was told he had come to one of the loveliest places in England, the very heart of England, to be sure, and he said that he did not doubt it, and was very glad to have done so.

The sky had grown darker again. It began to rain as the carving dish was removed, and though no further hail arrived there was much talk of the weather, and how it was sure to freeze again tonight.

And how the poor of the parish, and the sick, suffered in this cold! Over pudding, Mrs Neve and Mrs Bodenham described some of their charitable activities. In addition to their frequent rounds of visits, taking broth and warm clothing where needed, Liza Neve, whose husband was a Poor Law Guardian, belonged to the Ladies Association in Aid of the Distribution of Bibles amongst the Jews, and sent parcels every month to Palestine. Florence Bodenham visited the girls of the Charity School in Hereford, to teach needlework and read improving books. How they had enjoyed *The Little Serving Maid*!

'And you, Mrs Prosser?' Richard asked, as she picked at crumbs of syrup pudding. 'Are you involved in such things?'

Tilda Prosser drew a breath, and he felt how hard it was for her to be called upon to speak in company. But she told him that she took an especial interest in the Servants Reward Society. 'It was founded in 1833,' she said. 'I think that is right. Philip? Is that so?'

'Is it important?' asked Prosser, and she quickly shook her head. 'Of course not, how foolish of me. Well, Mr Allen, it was founded for the encouragement of faithful domestic servants—'

'Of whom Millie is certainly one,' put in Liza Neve, as a tray arrived with glasses and decanter.

'We are indeed most fortunate in Millie,' said Susannah, overhearing this from her place at the end of the table. So far she had spoken little, presiding solicitously over the luncheon – passing a soup plate, uncovering a dish, handing down the silver gravy boat. 'My grand-mother's,' she told Richard, when he took a moment to remark upon its pretty shape, and she turned to listen attentively to Liza Neve's account of a nasty bout of influenza suffered by her aunt.

It seemed, indeed, to Richard, getting to his feet as Susannah rose now, to lead the ladies from the room, that in the midst of all this chatter she and he had perhaps been united by their silence; that neither had done much more throughout the meal than listen to their neighbours, and smile responsively, and make the right remark – and that this had left him, at least, with a quiet place within his mind to which he might withdraw himself entirely.

That night, he looked back on it all, lying beneath the covers in the candlelight, watching the fire sink low. Quietude lay all around him: within the house and out in the dark stretch of woods and fields. He could hear the stream; he could hear, now and then, the hunting owl, but its hollow cry troubled him less. He was growing accustomed to it. This was the countryside at night. He, in this candlelit room, had his place within it, as the mouse – he could hear him – had his place behind the wainscot.

'You are a soul kept safe in the hands of God,' his father had told him on his ordination, and he thought of this now, and of his father's own hand, resting upon the heads of each of his children in turn, blessing them every Sunday evening, before they went to bed. To follow him had never been in question: from the moment of confirmation, his vocation had run in his blood.

Now, his life in the Church had begun.

As the last logs glowed in the grate, Richard brought to mind the strong stern voice of Oliver Bowen, made hoarse with coughing, summoning his congregation to confess. He saw them all before him in the pews; lingered in memory, as his gaze had lingered then, on Susannah's grey silk bonnet and the glimpse of silken hair. He stopped himself now: this surely was not right. And he went through the lines of the lesson, where he had acquitted himself well enough, and heard the first deep notes of 'O come, O come, Emmanuel' sound as he made his way back to his seat. He heard the sweet conjunction of Bach and spattering hailstones as the service ended. Then the introductions in the freezing porch – and then the light touch of a hand upon his arm and his certainty at once whose hand it was. The churchyard was crowded with people, but he saw only her.

The candle beside him burned steady and pure. Richard turned over. Beside its steadfast flame, he felt himself search this way and that for a place without Susannah's face, or smile, or voice, and could not find it. He thought: something is happening to me. And then: I must not let it happen. I must not.

He pushed back the covers and kneeled in the cold to pray. The room smelled of tallow and burning wood and beeswax. Closing his eyes, he might be in the bedroom of his childhood, with his father's certainties and purpose woven into the very fabric of his life.

'Lord,' he whispered, into his folded hands, 'Lord, take me back.'

And then he prayed: that he would be given strength to serve as he had always meant to serve, that he would not let himself be led into any kind of distraction, that he would listen only to God's will.

He found he was shivering, murmured the Amen. In bed, he lay gazing once more at the candle. The heap of covers began to warm him; he began to feel calm again. And yet – his mind was still not quite fixed upon that pure pale light. He found himself thinking of the luncheon, of the quiet place in his mind to which, amidst the endless talk, he had retreated. And he let himself wonder, if only for

moments, if Susannah too had in silence listened not to the conversation of her neighbours but for his own voice, as he had listened for
hers, and in some imagined place had heard, as he did, the wind across
the grass, the nibbling of sheep on the turf outside a lonely chapel,
whose door and window swung open, letting the light pour in.

5

———

Midweek. Early morning: market day. Today he did not make the long climb through the woods, but turned left out of the garden gate, down towards the crossing and the mill, for the mile walk up to the Kington–Presteigne road. The cold from the river hung over the fields; there were icicles on the gabled porch of the crossing-keeper's cottage, and on the slow-turning wheel of the mill.

Ahead, the stonework of the bridge sparkled with frost. Richard stopped upon it and blew into cupped gloved hands, getting his bearings.

Fifty yards up on the western side came the rushing fall of water over a weir. He dropped a twig and crossed to the other side to see it come swirling through on the deep winter flow beneath the bridge, borne away between leafless wood and empty field. How full was the air with the sounds of water: the tumbling weir, the rhythmic splash of the wheel, the ripple over stone. He stood taking it in, accustoming his ear to this new music. Could he hear through it all the faint tinkling thread of his stream, the Arrow's little brother, racing down through the field and past his garden?

He could not, from this distance; but he heard all at once a bell, ringing from deep within the crossing cottage, and in a moment saw the door pulled open and Birley come out, all muffled up, to swing the five-barred gates across the lane. And in a few moments came the first train of the morning, puffing along the wooden track, and over the crossing, and Richard stood watching the cottage swallowed up in the swirling clouds of steam: like a fairy house, there one moment and then vanished. The train whistled piercingly into the still cold air, a bugle call in a magic kingdom; he saw the furnace of the engine blaze against whitened hedge and silver track; then it went pounding on, the carriage clanking behind it, and the steam cleared and the cottage was revealed once more, with its gabled window.

Might Alice Birley be there again? With the school shut up for the Christmas holidays, was she playing, or sewing, or minding the little boy? He looked, but saw only the soot-smutted glass. And he turned and walked on, hearing the scrape of the gates drawn back, the whistle of the train into the distance, and the flow of the river all around him.

The lane rose steeply now; on the great bend was a sign to Downfield Farm but its buildings were out of sight. Richard walked past, feeling his heart begin to quicken with the exertion of the climb, and then, on the straight again, strode between hedge and field, his breath in clouds before him.

He came out on to the main road as a cart clattered past towards the town. Ahead were the hills of Rushock Bank, where a plume of smoke from a farmhouse chimney rose to pale clouds, and a buzzard wheeled. He watched it for a moment, and then he turned after the cart.

At the entrance to the town, set back from the curve of Victoria Road within a cobbled yard, he passed Merediths Foundry, with a great sound of hammering from within, and the sudden magnificent sight of the furnace, through an open door. A fine bell hung in a bellcote on the roof, no doubt to ring the workers in and ring them out again at the long day's close. Close by stood a line of cottages, the sign Nail Row upon a garden wall. He could smell the pigs in the sties, and hear the clatter of dishes from inside – and how strange it felt, after his solitude in the cottage and lonely walk along the lane, to be amongst the press of people and activity once more.

Amongst those going in and out of the High Street shops, with their packages and parcels, he recognised here and there a face from Sunday's congregation, and was greeted with a nod or shy smile, a lifting of the hat. Almost every window had its bright bunch of holly, or scarlet-ribboned mistletoe: even amongst the bottles and pillboxes of Stanway's, the chemist and druggist, in whose interior Richard glimpsed Liza Neve, deep in conversation at the counter. What ailment troubled her now? He moved on rather quickly. He passed John Wilson, Wine and Spirit Merchant, stood looking in at the window of Francis Went, Printer and Bookseller. Here he might buy his ink and fresh quills, perhaps; here he might purchase a blank-paged notebook with marbled endpapers, such as was displayed in the window, and make it his journal – for surely he should keep a journal here, in this, the place of his first appointment. But first – provisions; the market. He walked on, past Hebb the Hatter, and George Bayrell, Butcher, the windows hung with poultry and game, a great dressed turkey upon the marble slab. Everywhere was packed.

The market hall, a low stone building, well set against the Tudor black and white of the town, stood behind the Talbot in Bridge Street. It was crowded with stalls, and though the cattle market lay some quarter-mile away, even from this distance Richard could hear the shouts, the lowing, the clang of pens, and with every breath drew in the smells of wool and hide, of straw and dung. They mingled with the acrid smell from the Sunset Gasworks and the unmistakable stench from the drains. He walked on up the High Street for a while, his muffler now drawn up against all this as much as the raw air. There was the clock outside Skarratts, which Mr Parry had spoken of after the service: it must indeed be a good sight when lit by gas at nightfall. And there was a great tin salmon, hung outside a fishing tackle shop with rod and line. Well. He stood at the window looking in at it all.

The fisherman's patient hours by a river were unthinkable in this raw December weather; the tackle shop spoke of summer afternoons, the rustle of trees, the peaceful play of light and shade upon the water, the murmured conversation in the long, long wait. He thought of those moments on the frosty bridge, an hour ago, and the icy waters that in spring would leap with wild trout and flicker with sticklebacks. He and his father had fished, as well as potted rabbits together; surely in the spring, he might take his old rod out, and fish again.

'Mr Allen! Good morning!'

Across the street, outside Webbs, Ironmongers and Drapers, a gentleman, tall, a little cadaverous, was raising his hat. An air of dry aristocratic melancholy hung about him. Richard recalled the pressing of a bony hand in the cold church porch, a kindly inclination of the head. There it was again. He raised his own clerical hat, pulled down his muffler and crossed the muddy street, stepping out of the way of a pony and trap making for the market at a trot.

'Southwood,' said the gentleman outside the drapers. 'James Southwood. We met in church on Sunday.'

'Indeed, sir. Good morning. I hope you are well.'

'Rather cold,' said Southwood. 'Like poor old Gauntlet here.'

Dearest Emily, I have met a dog called Gauntlet!

Richard looked down at grizzled head and mournful gaze. Even on his haunches the dog was tall, but beneath the rough grey coat how thin he was.

'Hello, old fellow.' He extended his gloved hand; Gauntlet gave a dutiful sniff. 'What a fine creature,' he said to Southwood.

'A wolfhound cross,' said his master, patting his head. 'With what exactly he is crossed, we do not enquire too closely, but in his youth he ran like a hare. Now he rather resembles his owner. We creak about together.'

Richard smiled. People stepped in and out of the drapers, an errand boy ran through the crowd, a winter sun glanced upon shop windows. He thought: I have met someone I like.

'And Mrs Southwood?' he enquired, as the shop bell rang. 'I hope she is keeping well.'

'She is within.' Southwood inclined his head towards the shop. 'Gauntlet and I are in attendance. Many purchases are required at Christmas, including new cushions, I believe.' He shifted on his cane. 'How are you finding it all? We were sorry to be unable to join the vicarage luncheon.'

'It was most enjoyable,' said Richard, 'and of course would have been all the more so had you both been there.'

'How kind. Well, there will be plenty of other opportunities, I have no doubt. And when are you preaching?'

'On the fourth Sunday in Advent – in a little over a week's time, indeed.' Surely it could not come so fast?

'We shall look forward to that. And then it is Christmas, of course. Will is just home at last: we feel like a family once more, though he will spend some time with his fiancée's family. And your cottage? It is tolerably comfortable? You are not too much alone?'

'I am growing accustomed to it, sir. And it is in a most picturesque location.'

'It is. We are quite often down there for the shoot. Well, I must not detain you. The market is rather splendid in the festive season. I trust you will enjoy it all.'

'I'm sure I shall, sir.' Richard bent to pat the grizzled head.

Another little sniff, then the gaze upwards at his master again. How good it was to have a dog at your side. Perhaps this was what he needed at the cottage: a dog to stretch out on the hearth while he wrote his sermons, to walk with him in the woods. There was something else to think about. And he turned and walked back towards the market hall, thinking.

Plenty of people were walking along Bridge Street, and here clopping past was an old carrier patched up on the side with planking, and perched on its plank of a seat were an old couple in clothes such as country people must have worn a generation or more ago. Perhaps, indeed, they had been taken out of their grandparents' chest. He wore a heavy old smock; she was in poke bonnet and cloak like a blanket, and she sat there knitting a long black stocking as her husband tugged on the reins.

'Whoa, there!' Their mud-caked grey drew up a few paces from the market.

'Minna Davies! How be thee this long time?' A stout woman behind a trestle laden with baskets of eggs was shouting through the crowded open doors.

'We be keeping, bach, we be keeping.' Minna Davies sat upon her planks, her needles flashing, as her husband jumped down and slipped the reins over a post.

'Not that he'm thinking of going far,' he said with a cackle, and the old grey stood meekly between the shafts and lifted a hoof in want of shoeing. Davies went round the back of the cart and let down the flap. Minna finished her row, and tucked away her knitting.

'Thee both be looking well.' Behind the trestle, the egg seller folded her arms across her great bosom.

'Her do pray every night as I'll be took before morning.' Davies, coming round to the front again, put out a sinewy arm, but his wife ignored it, and jumped nimbly down to the edge of the gutter. Between them, they swiftly unloaded a crate of swede and turnips, a crate of mangolds and another from which two scraggy turkeys poked out their heads, looking this way and that.

'How much will you want for that bird?' asked an old man leaning on a stick by the wall.

'That bird or that bird?' Davies held the crate before him.

'That bird.' The stick was pointing towards the smaller and scraggier, and the turkey shrank back, his beak opening and closing.

'Two shillings and sixpence.'

'And will you wring his neck for me?'

'I will.'

'And pluck him?'

'For threepence I will.'

'Twopence,' said the old fellow, fumbling in his purse.

The tired grey lifted his tail and a yellow stream ran swirling down the gutter. The turkey was swung out of the crate by his feet and had his neck wrung. Nobody took any notice.

'He'll do us,' said the old boy, leaning on his stick. In the crate set down upon the flags, the other bird stared about him, shifting from scaly foot to foot. There came, from here and there in the hall, the sudden cackle of a goose, the cluck of hens.

Richard observed all this. Used as he was to the gun, the rod and line, the pantry wherein rabbit or an occasional pheasant might hang until stiff and gamey, he had not liked to see that casual wring of the neck, and did not like the confinement of that other poor turkey now, nor the opening and closing of that thirsty beak. He moved between the stalls of winter vegetables, pots of jam and pickles, crocks of butter, muslin-wrapped cheeses, enormous plum cakes. There was a cloth-covered trestle of tin and wooden toys: little engines and carts and farmyard animals; peg dolls in scraps of cloak or knitted shawl. He saw Alice Birley standing before this trestle in a press of children, twisting a finger of her woollen gloves this way and that at the tip.

'Good morning, Miss Birley.' She turned and regarded him. He bowed. 'Or may I call you Alice?'

She said: 'I am always called Alice.'

'Of course you are. I fear I was teasing – you look so grown up.'

She looked back at the stall and he followed her gaze.

'Which of these dolls is the one you like?'

'I must not like any of them.' The finger of her glove was twisted tight.

'And why is that?'

But of course he knew, or could guess. There was little money for Christmas: she had been taught to expect little, never to ask. If she were good and helpful there might be something.

'Alice?' Mrs Birley was coming towards the stall, her basket on her arm, the little boy holding her hand. 'Do you mind Tommy,' she said to her daughter. 'Only for a moment or two.'

Richard lifted his hat: she saw him, smiled.

'Excuse me, Mr Allen, I had not seen you there.'

'Perhaps you did not expect to see a grown man at the toy stall.'

'Men young or grown will like toy trains, I think.'

Tommy's hands were straining up to the edge, where he could from his little height make out the entrancing outline of a red tin engine.

'See! See!'

'Hush, now,' said Mrs Birley, but she lifted him up, and he stretched out, squirming. 'You may look but you must not touch.' She shifted him to the other side. 'Now keep still, do! What a weight you are.'

'Shall I take him?' asked Richard, almost without thinking. 'May I?' He held out his arms.

'You won't want to be troubled with this great boy, sir. He's nothing but a nuisance, isn't that so, Tommy?'

'It is no trouble at all,' said Richard, and lifted him into the crook of his arm and stepped towards the stall once more. 'You have an unerring eye,' he told the wriggling Tommy. 'I should like that very engine myself.' He turned to Mrs Birley. 'If you have purchases to make, do leave the children with me. I shall be happy to watch over them for a little while.'

'Are you sure, sir?'

'Of course.' He ran a gloved finger down the little boy's flushed cheek. 'We shall make friends, shall we not?'

Alice was gazing up at them.

'Do you be very good,' said her mother, and as she shifted her basket to the other arm Richard could sense how great was her relief, all at once, at the prospect of a quarter-hour to herself. 'I shall be back in just a little while.' And she walked quickly away through the stalls, just as Tommy realised what was happening, and let out a wail.

'Mama! Mama!' He wrenched himself around; his face was scarlet and wet with tears. 'Mama!'

'Hush!' said Alice.

'Hush,' said Richard, and took him right up to the stall again, and pointed to the engine. 'Look at that magnificent piece of machinery,' he said. 'See where the steam comes out? Now tell me, if you will, how fast do you think it can run?'

The man behind the stall was laughing.

'I think it is you yourself who would like it at Christmas, sir.'

'Perhaps I should. What do you say?' he asked Tommy, wiping tears away. 'Might we share it? Would you permit that?'

Tommy stopped crying. The children around them chattered and pointed at this toy and that. Alice returned her gaze to the bundle of peg dolls in cape and bonnet.

'Which is the one you like?' Richard asked her again, and as she pointed her small gloved hand, with its intense little twist of worn wool on the forefinger, he felt as perhaps his father had felt when they were children: shot through with pangs of feeling, unable to afford very much, wanting to give them everything. Should he purchase Peg Doll – he knew that was what Verity and Emily would call this strange thin creature – and the little red engine, and give them at Christmas? Or was it too soon, was he too new here, whether as friend or neighbour or new curate, even to think of such an intrusion into family life? Might such gifts merely throw into relief what the parents could not give? He had, in any case, his own provisions to buy: bread, cheese, candles, bacon. And if he did not intend to give, was it not unkind to linger here, examining the merits of little blue or little scarlet cloak?

The noise within the pillared hall was growing with the Christmas crowd. A clock began to strike the hour. Tommy rested his head against Richard's shoulder and yawned.

'That one,' said Alice.

'Just the one I should choose,' said Richard, looking at painted black eyes beneath the hood. The bell rang out; a cold wind blew; he turned for a moment to see if it were about to hail again, and saw Susannah Bowen on her husband's arm, just outside the hall. Bowen himself was looking at the sky, and his face was drawn, but Susannah was looking directly at Richard, and the little boy in his arms. He knew at once that she had been watching him, for longer than a moment, and before he could collect himself to smile and raise his hat, he saw her blush and turn quickly to her husband.

And he turned back to the children: to Tommy, falling asleep on his shoulder; to Alice, whose small grave face was alight with longing, and felt his own colour rise, and between himself and Susannah the fall of an awkwardness, like a sudden shadow upon unclouded glass.

And this he could not put out of his mind.

It was early afternoon: he sat at his desk with his pen in his hand, looking out across the field. He had come home with his purchases from the busy town and felt the cold and silence of the cottage enclose him so profoundly that for a moment it was as if he was entering a cell. His spirits sank. Then he saw that the floors were swept, and the fire re-laid; he saw that the washing basket was gone, and a heap of clean linen lay on a chair. Martha Price, at least, had an eye upon the place, was keeping it as a house should be kept, and he was grateful.

He lit the fire, he put away his purchases. He toasted bread and cheese before the fire, threw on another log, sat at his desk, and prepared to write his sermon.

Then said Mary unto the angel, How shall this be, seeing I know not a man?

And the angel answered and said unto her, The Holy Ghost shall come upon thee, and the power of the Highest shall overshadow thee: therefore also that holy thing which shall be born of thee shall be called the Son of God.

This, from St Luke, was to be his text. As Advent drew to its close, and the great moment of the Nativity approached, he would focus every mind and heart on the power of innocence, and of humility. Only within the pure, unsullied life, the quiet soul, might the wing of an angel beat and come to rest; only here might the power of the Holy Spirit fill an entire soul, and thence the world.

He dipped his quill in the inkwell; he began to write. 'Then said Mary unto the Angel ...' He knew the words by heart, and he knew their provenance: St Luke, Chapter 1, verses 34 and 35.

He gazed out through the glass, thinking. Beyond this narrow window stretched the empty field, and between oak and hornbeam stood a distant gate to another. Above them, in the wintry heavens, the birds of the air rose and fell.

'*Let the words of my mouth and the meditation of my heart be always acceptable in Thy sight, O Lord, my Strength, and my Redeemer ...*'

His father's voice was quiet and strong within him, speaking the words he had heard all through his life. Now he stood in imagination in the pulpit of St Michael and All Angels; he looked down upon the congregation.

'Dearly beloved brethren, I who am so recently come amongst you am humbled by the occasion on which I have the great honour to preach to you for the first time.'

Below, in the front pew, he saw the pure clear eyes in that upturned face, with its frame of silken hair. How would she receive his words?

He put down his quill. Already, with such a thought and such distraction, he was proving himself unworthy even to mount the pulpit steps. And with a deep flush he realised that not since the first shivering moments of the morning, when he had kneeled at his bedside on rising, had he thought to pray. He had tried to settle to the first real task of his new life – for reading the lesson, after all, was not such a great thing – without the one act which should precede it.

And he had thought to preach upon humility?

He pushed back his chair; he kneeled at the desk.

'Lord, I am not fit ... I pray Thee to enter my unfit soul, to calm and prepare me as Thy most humble servant, that I may address this new congregation of souls in a state of grace ...'

Such fluency. Where did it come from, when in truth his mind was troubled?

The fire crackled. He buried his head in his hands. He prayed, kneeling on the worn red rug upon the cold stone floor, stumbling now over quite different words: 'Let this morning's shadow between us pass away. Let the light shine again. Let us be open with one another.'

He was shocked at this flood of longing. Yet this, he knew, was the day's true prayer.

'Lord, let she and I look purely upon one another, without any shade of awkwardness. Then I will rest, and will give myself to Thy service.'

Already, he was imposing conditions: grant me this, and I will give Thee my life. He knew that his words should be only: I give Thee my life. Do with it whatsoever Thou wilt. Without such surrender, how could he be fit to serve?

The fire crackled; the fire sank. His knees were aching with the pressure of the stone. At length he got to his feet.

The light of the winter afternoon was fading. Across the field from his desk he could see pigeons making for the trees beneath the clouded sky. He put on another couple of logs, and saw that the basket needed refilling for the night. He should do it now, before darkness fell.

He turned to go out to the hall for his coat; he glanced at the window on to the lane where no one came and no one went, on this cold December day. Yet something stirred, did it not?

Richard frowned. Was that a figure moving through the trees? A woodsman, at this hour? A worker from the mill, coming through the woods on his way up the hill to the highway? He strained his eyes. Perhaps it was Birley, out to gather kindling in the hour before the last train ran.

He looked out again, stepping closer to the window. Who was this man?

He glimpsed him again, and started, for the figure which moved like a ghost through the darkening trees wore a cloak, and her hood was up.

Richard opened the casement, and at once the woman vanished. He gazed through the dusk but could make out nothing. Had he dreamed her? He leaned out in the cold, and heard the faint snap of a twig. Then there was only the music of the stream, and the beating wings of birds.

6

'Let the words of my mouth and the meditation of my heart be always acceptable in Thy sight ...'

The words coursed through him, his father's voice shaping his own. 'Amen,' he said, and opened his eyes to see his hands tremble upon the pulpit's rim. Below, the mass of upturned faces swam before him, their blur partly the effect of his intense nervous state and partly due to the shimmer of heat from the stove at the back of the church, which had been lit at seven. Looking out across the congregation, he made out its fiery glow through blackened bars.

He cleared his throat; he felt the first page of his sermon shake within his fingers.

'My text for this morning is taken from the Gospel according to St Luke, our beloved physician apostle, the only one to tell us of the great moment of the Annunciation, when the young girl Mary is visited by an angel.

'Then Mary said unto the angel, How shall this be, seeing I know not a man?

'And the angel answered and said unto her, The Holy Ghost shall come upon thee, and the power of the Highest shall overshadow thee ...'

It was as it had been when he read the Lesson: the words had their own magnificence, and he was but a vessel for them, as Mary had been but a vessel for the great miracle that was to take place within her. He could hear his voice begin to steady, and grow stronger, as she bowed her head, and the angel departed from her. He could feel her dazed state, the hushed stillness in the shaded courtyard of her house in Nazareth, the heat of the narrow street outside; he could feel, in a country congregation, in the year of Our Lord 1860, a hush fall now.

Well – he was young, he was new to them: of course they gave him their attention. And with this glancing thought he knew humility – here it was, achieved without effort, through submission to the Word. He settled his feet more squarely upon the pulpit's piece of carpet, and began.

'I should like to talk to you this morning about this young woman, Mary. As the mysterious shining moment of Christ's Nativity draws near, I should like us to consider once again this miracle, and to think about how it was that the very Son of God, Our Lord, should be born to one so pure, so innocent; a young woman living a simple, humble life, away from the press of the world, obedient to whatever God might ask of her.

'Think of it! Think of Palestine in spring, the blue of the sea of Galilee, the warm winds blowing through the olive groves, the shutters opening on to the narrow streets of Nazareth, where Mary has lived all her young life, and now is betrothed to a carpenter.'

His gaze had been fixed upon the burning coals, whose shimmer of heat, it seemed to him now, was like the very veil of mystery through which the believer might apprehend the Spirit of God, moving across the face of the waters, as a new world began. Now he dared to look down upon his new flock, to let his eyes rest, just for a moment, upon an individual. The winter morning light was pale through plain glass windows, but here and there, where the glass was stained, a patch of crimson, gold or purple fell upon the door of a pew, the trim of a cloak, the rim of a hat or bonnet.

'And to this young woman, whose days consist, perhaps, in drawing water from the shady well, of fetching the new-ground corn and baking bread, of washing clothes and laying them to dry on the sunny hillside where the bells of sheep and goats come tinkling through the heat – to her is to be given the greatest Gift of all: to receive the Holy Spirit, and give birth to the Son of God.'

Country girl spoke to country congregation: he knew it, as he spoke on. Sheep on the hills, the golden corn, the swing of a bucket on its rope down the dark shaft to the gleam of water – all this was timeless, all this still lay deep in the life of the people here, no matter that the steam train rushed through their lives and bore them towards a new age. The rhythm of the country year went on, with its flock and herd and watermill, its new-mown hay and fresh-sawn timber.

'And though Christ's great life was lived amongst the hills and seas of a distant, ancient, burning land, He lives amongst us still, in the hills and valleys of this lovely place. He lives in the cold of winter, in the most humble shelter or stable on a little farm, where the snow blows in and the cattle stamp their feet, just as he was born in such a lowly place, and gave his first cries in a hay-filled manger. And he lives still in our own poor hearts, for ever, if we can only open ourselves to His grace and humbly offer ourselves and our lives in His service.' He paused. 'Thanks be to God.'

He bowed his head, he closed his eyes, he felt himself filled with an extraordinary stillness. Then he tapped together the pages of his sermon, and descended the pulpit steps, as the organ sounded and the people slowly rose to their feet, picking up their hymnals.

'Angels, from the realms of glory,
Wing your flight o'er all the earth...'

Outside, in the porch, he stood with Oliver Bowen awaiting the exit of the congregation. He waited, in the cold, for a word, a mention. None came. Bowen straightened his purple stole; he blew his nose and rubbed his hands. He glanced towards the wintry churchyard, where the cold wind stirred the yew. In the silence between them, Richard could hear the creak of the weather vane up on the tower, blowing north, blowing far away from here.

'Sir?'

'Mr Allen?'

'Forgive me – I do not wish to draw attention to myself, but would you be so kind as to tell me: did my poor sermon meet with your approval?'

Bowen cleared his throat. 'That you have an eloquence is not in doubt.'

He made it sound as though eloquence in the priesthood were the least desirable attribute on earth.

'Forgive me,' said Richard again, hearing the sweet notes of Charpentier's *Te Deum*, the rustle of skirt on stone, the murmur of conversation at the door. 'I have offended you in some way, I fear. Something is amiss. Please tell me, so I may correct it, sir.'

'It is a conversation for another time,' said Bowen, turning towards the first of his parishioners. 'But I fear I found something of popery within your words.'

'Popery ...' He was bewildered.

'Such elevation of the Virgin Mary,' said Bowen quietly. 'It does not become the Church of England. Least of all in such a place as this, perhaps, when we are so close to the Church in Wales.'

It was Christmas morning. The long whitened rim of the hills and the frosty clumps of fir within the woods glittered with a new intensity as the night rolled slowly away and the first faint light broke through.

Thus, for a blessed moment or two, was how it appeared to Richard, pulling back the shutters in his bedroom, standing in the darkness without lamp or candle, preparing himself for prayer. Here and there the stars shone faintly; beneath them the sheep moved slowly over the hillside, as they had done on the hills above Bethlehem, beneath that unearthly light. Would people, in another thousand years, still think of Bethlehem? Richard closed his eyes, felt himself as enfolded by sleep as a lamb in a shepherd's arms, opened them again and fixed his gaze upon a star that seemed to hold, even at daybreak, an especial brightness.

Was this the same star that had hung that night to guide king and shepherd towards a miracle? Was the earth such a tiny thing that the limitless expanse of heaven could unite that time and this? Might this light, shimmering in his gaze as he tried to hold it fast, shine still in another thousand years; and on what soul, what hill or city?

Such questions lay in the realm of science, of which he had so little. Gazing out over the starlit hills he remembered all at once his first conversation with Oliver Bowen – just that touch, that was all it had been, upon Mr Darwin's new ideas, upon the possibility that Creation might be more complex than a beloved Bible story; that nature, not

God's mystery, perhaps had shaped the world.

'I trust I have not taken on a curate who finds this heresy in any way attractive.'

Was that what Bowen had said? Something like that, and Richard did not like to think of it now. The first reproach, and now he had had another, so early in his ministry. Popery ... Was it justified? Did Bowen see in him something he could not see himself, some failure of faith or doctrine?

He stood at the open shutters, looking out over darkness, pin-pricked here and there by light. He bowed his head.

To wonder if the world, in time, would still consider Bethlehem, and believe in this most sacred moment – was this not close to doubt?

It was much too close.

And did doubt and heresy spring from the same source, like a polluted stream? Had he really, in his sermon, come so close to something outside his own Church, something which might offend his congregation?

He had been asking himself this all week; it seemed, indeed, that where he should be calm and still, filled with the anticipation of Christ's birth, he was churned up by a storm of questions: about the world, but also about himself.

And he thought again, as he tried once more to concentrate upon this holy hour, of the last person to come out to the porch on Sunday: she who occupied a pew so close to the front of the church, and therefore must leave at the very end. By the time she arrived, he was so filled with shame and distress at the reproach he had been given that it was all he could do to respond to those parishioners who came up to shake his hand.

'A fine sermon, Mr Allen.'

'Oh, I *much* enjoyed it! You made it so *alive!*'

They had seemed so genuine, so warm, but he felt from the other side of the open south door a chill which cut through him like a wind across a winter field. And then, as her husband's stern face was lit at last by a smile, Susannah Bowen was coming through the door, intent upon her neighbour.

'It is made so much worse by a sleepless night, of course,' said Liza Neve, 'and I can do nothing but toss and turn ...'

'Indeed, I am sorry to hear it.'

Susannah turned to her husband and murmured something. He nodded. Mrs Neve continued her lament, addressing it now to Bowen, who inclined his head. Inside the church, the organist, Thomas Hatton, was closing the stops. Prosser was fastening pew doors. Outside in the churchyard people were hurrying along the path in the cold. A carriage door slammed; a horse shook his head with a jangle of bridle and bit. Richard heard all these sounds with a heightened awareness, as he waited, in his discomfort, for her eyes to meet his once more.

They met. He saw within hers a new illumination. He thought, it is as I have prayed: we are at ease again. He smiled, and felt suddenly happy.

'Good morning, Mrs Bowen.'

'Good morning, Mr Allen. I must thank you for a most affecting sermon.'

Even as he opened his mouth he knew he was doing wrong, only compounding an offence. 'I fear that it did not please your husband.'

'Oh?' She frowned, and turned to him, as the litany of Liza Neve continued.

'... It is something which has tormented me since I was a child ...'

'My dear? Forgive me for interrupting, but how is it that Mr Allen's sermon has displeased you?'

Another frown, much darker. No more response than this. But when Susannah made to continue the exchange with Richard she was stopped all at once by her husband's hand on her arm as he stepped forward.

'My dear, this is not something which need trouble you. I shall join you at home directly.'

'Very good. Well, then ...' And she glanced once more at Richard but with the light quite gone. 'Good morning, Mr Allen.'

'Ma'am.' He bowed; she was gone, caught up at once in the churchyard by the unstoppable Liza Neve.

Richard and Oliver Bowen were left alone in the porch. They returned to the vestry in silence. The choir had gone, save for one or two of the trebles, who quickly made their retreat.

'Sir?'

Richard hung up his surplice and stole; he took down his coat. Everything in here smelled damp and cold and dead. At the far end of the church he could hear Prosser raking the coals.

'Sir?'

Oliver Bowen had taken off his own robes, was pulling on his boots. He winced as he bent to the task, then started to cough. The bubbling sound within this silence was horrible. Then he straightened up, and wiped his brow.

'Mr Allen. I have said we will discuss your sermon on another occasion. Already it seems that it has been discussed enough. I wish you a very good morning.'

And he took down his hat and left, his footsteps measured and loud in the empty nave.

Richard went home in a tumult.

Dearest Mama, I fear I have quite foolishly offended ...

He could not write it. He banked up his own small fire in the snug and sat before it, turning over question after question.

And now, on Christmas morning, days later, he was in tumult still.

He turned from the bedroom window, fastened so tightly against the cold, yet thickly patterned with the flowery frost. He crossed the bare boards, lit faintly by the breaking of the day, to the rug beside his bed, whereon he kneeled, and sought, on this holy morning, when the world was made anew, to fix his mind on God, on a still pure point of light.

Half-past seven. He had dressed, but had taken no breakfast, for this morning, for the first time since he had assumed his duties, he was to assist with and receive the Blessed Sacrament.

'Lord, make me worthy ...'

On the mantelpiece in the snug stood the Christmas cards from the family: dear, home-made cut-and-pasted things such as they had made when they were children, sent especially because of this, because he was far from home.

Dearest Richard, How we are all missing you! It is such joy to have your letters, but oh, that we had you here with us this Christmas! Still, I know that in your new parish you will be made welcome, and that when you serve Holy Communion we will be in your heart, as you, at the same moment, will be in ours. I pray for you every night and morning ...

His mother's hand was as strong and flowing as ever, but he saw in every dash her hesitation lest she pour out her sadness too much and burden him. Now, before banking up the fire, he kissed each card, each pasted berry and snow-trimmed sleigh, and cast a glance at the parcel which had come on the mail coach to the post office in Kington. He would open it this afternoon, on his return from Christmas luncheon in the vicarage – for to this he was still bidden.

'I have not yet been excommunicated,' he said aloud, and felt a little humour lighten the morning's intensity, as he pulled on his greatcoat, picked up two little packages, and closed the door.

As he stepped outside, he felt the icy air enter his throat with every breath. He pulled up his muffler. It was barely light and with the fading of moon and star the woods were dense, the conifers almost black.

Daybreak. Winter. Christmas. No bird, no bleating sheep, no whistling train – and yet, even in this near-silence, broken only by the tinkling of the stream, he thought: I am not alone here. Someone in these woods is watching me.

He stood; he watched and waited. There was nothing, only his sense of something.

But it was far too cold to linger. He walked fast, beating his hands, turning left down the lane, past shuttered cottages showing cracks of light, until he came to the crossing, and the crossing-keeper's house. And he stood and looked up at the gabled window, and thought: I am watching, too.

Was she awake? Every child in the Christian world was awake on Christmas morning. He made out the glow of a rushlight, deep within the room; he listened, and heard their voices.

And he stepped forward, and just inside the porch laid down the two small packages, each with a label: 'Master Thomas Birley, from Mr Allen', 'Miss Alice Birley, from Mr Allen'. Then he stepped out again, and walked rapidly back up the lane, his heart beating wildly, as if he had done wrong.

Eight o'clock. The church was hung with hoops of fir and holly; the air smelled of greenery and candlewax and hay, for the Nativity crib was filled with it. It stood in the eastern corner of the transept, and as

Richard walked down the aisle, the first to arrive, he made out in the dimness the faint shapes of plaster oxen, and the blue of Mary's robe. He compressed his lips, then would not think of it further: the sermon on the Virgin was behind him now, and though he was light-headed with fasting he was also cleansed: by his prayers at dawn, and the long cold walk through the woods.

Prosser had already lit the stove; he warmed himself before it. The smell of the coals, too, hung in the air. He walked on, his footsteps echoing, came to the vestry, pushed open the door.

He leaped.

He was not, after all, the first to arrive: Oliver Bowen was there already, standing by the small plain window, his hands held up to his face as if—

'Sir?'

Who had most startled whom?

Bowen's face was ashen.

'Forgive me,' said Richard. He seemed to be forever saying this. 'I had not meant to alarm you, sir. I thought no one was yet here.'

Bowen pressed his hands to his mouth. At length he said: 'I fear I am not quite well. A spasm of coughing has weakened me. It will pass. Will you be so good as to assist me?' He gestured at the communion plate lying wrapped at the bottom of the open trunk; he leaned against the cold stone wall.

'Of course.' Richard stepped forward. 'But may I fetch you some water, sir? Will you not sit down?'

There was the chair, with its unmended back. Bowen sank slowly on to it. The sky beyond the leaded glass had begun to lighten: Richard saw the sheen of sweat on the rector's brow. He looked about him. No glass, no carafe. He remembered a rainbutt in the church-yard, but no one could drink from that.

'It will pass,' said Bowen again, and leaned forward, his head in his hands. 'I pray you – make ready.'

Richard made ready. He took out worn folded linen, and silver chalice; he took out wine and wafers. He left Bowen sitting on the broken chair, and set everything out upon the altar. Then he returned, to find Bowen on his feet again. He was still pale, but his demeanour was recovered.

'It has passed.' He stretched out his hand. 'I thank you for your kindness.' He smiled faintly. 'May I wish you a very happy Christmas.'

'And you, sir. And you.'

They walked slowly back into the church. Prosser had returned, and was lighting candles. Outside, there came the sound of footsteps, and then a carriage, the horse clopping slowly up the slope in the early morning light. One by one, the communicants entered: the Bodenhams, the Southwoods, Susannah, widowed Alfred Arndell.

They took their places, as Richard and Oliver Bowen took theirs, on either side of the chancel. Snowy linen, silver chalice, plain gold cross – all had the sheen of candlelight.

Christmas began.

7

J ust after Christmas, it snowed. Richard had grown accustomed to the quiet of Bullocks Mill in early morning, to the hoot of the owl as he fell asleep, and the croak of the pheasant as he woke. He knew, he thought, the bleat of one particular sheep, throaty and low, and had described it in a letter home, knowing how they would laugh at him. He knew that once the first train had left Kington and come through Bullocks Mill, then the day fully began: the millworkers tramping down the lane soon after, and Birley swinging the gates across the line again, that cart and carrier might pass through. Sometimes he could hear the children, though he knew he would hear them much more when spring came, and they could play properly outside. He knew the slow footsteps of Martha Price, come to clean, or bring clean washing down from Rushock Bank.

This morning he could hear nothing, and as soon as he woke he saw the entire change in the light: so bright at the gap in the shutters, where he was used to a gradual breaking of the dark. And the quietness was complete: no wind in the trees, no birds. Something else was missing, too: he listened, and realised that even the stream was silent.

He got up, pulling on his woollen robe, and opened the shutters. At once, even though the panes were thickly frosted, the room was filled with light. The snow had fallen so thickly on the sill that at first he could not push the casement open, but then it gave way and snow fell upon snow, like a carol, into the garden beneath. And he looked out on to a landscape quite transformed.

The purity of it all, on field and tree and garden, was unblemished.

All he could see of the stream beyond the fence was an indentation between its narrow banks. He looked up the long white curve of the lane, which perhaps, with another fall, would be impassable; he searched the fields and the slope of the hill for sheep but saw not a movement, heard not a bleat, though he thought they would not be buried – the fall was but three or four inches at most. No doubt they would be huddled in some corner beneath the hedge; no doubt the farmer would somehow make his way to them with a bale.

He was shivering. Quickly he pulled the casement to, and when he kneeled at the bedside for morning prayers his teeth were chattering.

'Lord, as the snow has fallen in the silence of the night, keep Thy silent watch over us in the beauty and cold of the morning ...'

He rose; he dressed, slipping into his pocket a fresh white hand-kerchief with his initials stitched by Verity. There had been six in the Christmas parcel, with three pairs of socks, and a splendid cake: he thought that the mouse had discovered this, at night, on the pantry shelf. There had also been a notebook, from Emily, leather-bound, with a silken bookmark – 'for your observations'. Well: he had many. And he went downstairs to light the fire in the snug and stood before its small warmth, watching the frost on the pane begin to melt and the light from the snowy garden fill the room.

Snow without and a fire within. He must fetch fuel. And then this was a day to keep to the house, to read and write his letters home. He had, too, to write another sermon.

And on what should this be, when he knew, in his heart, that he was far from a state of grace?

The last log in the hearth caught. Through the melting frost on the pane he saw the perfect whiteness of the garden, glittering still brighter as the sun rose in slanting shafts through the trees. In the kitchen, he set a pan of milk upon the range. He pulled on coat and boots and unbolted the back door. All was silent still. Then he heard the scrape of a shovel, and knew that Birley must be clearing the ground by the gates.

Richard took pail and basket out to the woodshed, marking the yard with the day's first tracks. The sun was rising within a brilliant sky and, cold though he was, he stood for a moment surveying the entire beauty of his snow-filled corner of the world: the outlined plum and apple trees, the thick white hedge and slender wicket gates, the long stretch of path to the lane.

'Lord, Thou art everywhere,' he said aloud.

Even as he spoke it, he thought: But art Thou in my soul? Art Thou drawing away from me, Thy failing servant? Or is it I who am drawing away from Thee?

28 December 1860

I am resolved to keep a journal. The letters I write home must say so little, and my communion with God leaves me wanting. Sometimes I think I am merely repeating the familiar, well-loved phrases of a lifetime. At others I know that I am wrestling: I feel myself estranged from Him, and full of shame, for worldly thoughts crowd in upon me and I am not strong enough to resist and banish them. And what are these thoughts? Dare I commit them even to the pages of a private journal?

A log in the fire fell in pieces; he threw on another, then returned to his desk. Emily's notebook was perfect for the task. Had she known, when she wrapped it so carefully, that this was what he needed in his new solitude? He had considered buying just such a one from the Kington printers: lo, here it was, from his little sister, with a crimson silk ribbon to mark his page.

On Christmas morning, I assisted in giving the Blessed Sacrament. At my side, I felt a sick man struggle with the task; before me, at the altar rail, his wife opened her hands to receive the Wafer from me, and lifted her face to sip the chalice which he held. It was barely light. Southwood and his wife were there. Edward Turner kneeled next to his fiancée; poor young Arndell was facing his first Christmas without his wife. There were the Bodenhams, the Prossers – she so white and pinched; perhaps half a dozen more. But first I kneeled myself to receive Communion, and though I strove to feel the great holiness of the moment, as in the past I have felt it, now I heard the blessed words as in a daze.

'This is my Body … This is my Blood of the New Testament, which is shed for you and for many …'

Bowen's voice was almost a whisper; when he in his turn kneeled down to receive the Sacrament from me, I saw with what difficulty he sank to the step, how his open hands trembled, the one upon the other; I felt myself grasping the chalice as I held it for him, as if I, not he, might let it slip.

This has been my first experience of reciting, rather than living within the words of a service. No doubt it must happen in a long life within the Church; perhaps it happened to my father, though he never said so. But that it should happen so early in my ministry, and at such a moment – Christmas morning, Holy Communion, the first occasion of my assisting with the Sacrament. It shook and saddened me.

The service ended. We walked slowly up to the porch to receive the small congregation, which in a few hours would swell to become the great number which Christmas always draws in. I watched Oliver Bowen anxiously as we came out into the cold, and tried to concentrate on greeting each communicant as he or she deserved: James and Elizabeth Southwood, poor widowed Arndell ... And what, as we waited, and Bowen coughed in the cold, was now my greater anxiety and distraction? A sick man standing in an icy porch, or the lovely face of his young wife, for whom I stood waiting as for no one else, and for whom, I must now confess, I find I do hold such tender feelings?

Richard put down his quill, and buried his face in his hands. To think – to dare to think – of something so improper: more than that, so wicked – this was disturbing enough. To write of it now, to commit it to the page: it felt as if he were taking another step forward on a path he must not – must not – follow.

He looked up. The sun had gone, and the window above his desk showed the vast unbroken white of the field, the branches of the great oak and ash trees heavy with the weight of unfallen snow. The birds had begun their search for food: a pair of crows flapped slowly across the field and back; in the cloudy sky a buzzard mewed and circled, over and over again. He felt himself a speck, a small presence on the edge of the natural world, and yet filled with enormous feelings, of whose power he had had no knowledge or expectation.

What shall I do? he said aloud. What must I do?

There came a small tap at the front door. He felt it within him like a mighty knocking. With shaking fingers, he covered the pages.

When he went to answer the door, heaped-up snow fell in. Mrs Birley and the children stood before him, all muffled up. Behind them their footsteps made neat tracks from the gate; he saw that the scraps he had flung out after breakfast were all gone.

'We'm sorry to disturb you, sir. We was just wondering if you had everything you need.'

'It is I who should have walked down the lane to ask you that,' said Richard. How far away he had been all morning. He smiled down at the children, Tommy's raw little cheeks reddened still more by the cold, Alice's gaze so clear. 'Please – come in by the fire.'

'Thank you, sir. Only for a moment, if we don't trouble you.'

They stamped their feet on the hall flags. Small heaps of snow became dark pools. He ushered them in before the leaping fire and threw on another log. They stood looking about them, at the desk with its inkstand and papers, and the windowsill of books; at the table and rug and lamp. He saw Alice's gaze go to the family photograph on the mantelpiece, the potted studio ferns and laughing faces.

'Don't you be staring, Alice,' said her mother. 'What do you have to say to Mr Allen?'

'We've to thank you for the presents,' said Alice gravely. 'As you left in the porch on Christmas Day.'

He looked at Mrs Birley. 'You did not mind?'

'How should we mind, sir? You was very kind.'

'We knew it was you,' said Alice. 'Before I read the labels.'

'You can read well now?'

'Pretty well.'

'And are you enjoying your gifts?' He bent down to Tommy, who had in these new surroundings fallen quite silent. 'You like your new red engine, I hope? It was something of a struggle for me not to keep it for myself.'

Tommy stared at him, and his fingers went to his mouth.

'He's very shy, sir.'

'Of course he is.' Richard straightened up and looked at them all. How to understand the difference between stare and gaze? Perhaps it was only the difference in their years; perhaps Alice, at two, had also stared at people, but he sensed she had not done so, that her look had always been watchful and considered. 'I'm rather shy myself,' he said.

'That can't be true, sir.'

'Yet it is. This is my first appointment in the Church. You can't think how anxious I have been.'

'It don't show one bit. It feels as if you have always been a preacher.'

'Is that so? How kind of you to say so.'

Yet 'preacher' was not a word with which he could readily identify. It spoke of Methodism, of the open air, of a man who went walking between towns, pasting up notices to announce his arrival. A preacher set himself up upon bales at a summer fair, or leaned, shouting, from the window of an upper room – as John Wesley had done when he preached in Kington more than a hundred years ago. Bowen had told him this.

And he?

He, whether preacher, priest or curate, was already failing.

'We should have thanked you for your gifts in church on Christmas morning, sir, only there was such a press of people.'

'Indeed. But I was glad to see you all there.'

And so he had been. Looking out from his seat in the chancel at newly familiar faces singing 'O come, all ye faithful' with the choir, he had felt tears prick his eyes at the thought of his own small family, enduring the absence of husband, brother, son at Christmas. Seeing the Birleys somehow steadied him in his homesickness and new confusion. He glanced at his desk: the pages of his journal were safely covered, but he blushed to think of them and of how, with this dear good family come to call, he was already a deceiver.

'What presents did you have at Christmas, sir?'

'Alice! You don't ask such things.'

Alice flushed, and Richard said quickly, 'I don't mind you asking at all. My family sent a marvellous parcel, and in it there were—' he paused for effect, and saw Tommy's eyes widen – 'three pairs of socks and six new handkerchiefs, each with my initials.' He smiled at Tommy. 'You think that dull, and indeed it is not as exciting as I hope your red engine was. But for a man on his own such things are always useful. And also—' another pause – 'there was a splendid plum cake, which a naughty little mouse has come to share with me.'

Tommy looked at him with a new interest, but Mrs Birley was disconcerted.

'Oh, sir! I can fetch you a trap, if you will. Or Birley will come with the poker. They'm everywhere: once they get in the house there ain't no use in kindness. Even for a curate.' She gave a little smile and Richard saw in it the intelligence he had seen in her husband's face when it was clean of smuts and he had taken his place in the pew at the head of the family.

He smiled back. 'A foolish curate might be kind until the New Year, I think. Now then, what may I offer you? It seems a little early in the day for cake, but I feel sure that luncheon approaches.'

'It do. We must be getting back.' She tipped her little boy from her knee, and took his hand. But Tommy wriggled away, and pulled from the pocket of his winter jacket the little red engine, which he proceeded to run along the hearthstones, and all around the coal box.

'The seven forty-five from Kington,' said Richard, watching him. It was all he could do not to get down on his knees himself. Oh, to be a boy again!

He turned to Alice, standing by his side. 'And your doll? She pleases you?'

She reached into the pocket of her own patched coat, and withdrew the little figure. Cloaked in scarlet: that had been right, he felt, for Christmas.

'She sleeps in a box,' she said, 'and eats at table.'

'Very good. And her name?'

'Victoria,' said Alice.

'After Her Majesty?'

'Yes, sir.'

'It's a grand name for such a little person, but I do believe it suits her.'

He looked down at the scrap of hood and bright black eyes, and wanted all at once to sit by the fire with a child of his own on his lap, and talk nonsense until teatime.

At the door, Mrs Birley said, 'Are you sure you have everything you need, sir?'

He said he had.

'Fresh water?'

He looked at her.

'The well has not frozen?'

Of course the well had frozen. There was but a quarter-pail in the back porch. How had he been so foolish?

'I drew from the river this morning,' she said. 'We'll boil that up.'

'I shall do the same. I'll go down this afternoon, if Martha does not come. And, please, if you ever need anything, don't hesitate to call. If anyone, God forbid, were ever ill ...'

'Thank you, sir.'

She turned to the children, who were out in the garden now. Scarlet cloak and engine were joyous things against the snow.

As they ran down the path to the gate Richard scooped up a snowball and threw it to land at Tommy's feet, as accurately as if he were on the cricket field.

'Howzat?' he called, and watched them walk laughing down the lane like children from Emily's Christmas card. As he went back into the house he felt his spirits lifted. Inside, he slipped his journal into the middle drawer of the desk, and locked it.

8

New Year skating party! The morning after the Birleys' visit, Richard received an invitation, taken by surprise by the arrival of the letter carrier soon after the mid-morning train. He was writing his sermon, and looked up at the sound of whistling in the silent lane. Then came the click of the gate, and the man tramped up the snowy path.

'You are very good,' said Richard, pulling open the door. 'I had expected nothing until a thaw.'

'You would have had nothing in the old days, sir. Not afore the train. Afore the train, with another fall, 'twould have been impassable.' He was unfastening his bag; he handed over two letters.

One from home – and what was this? A good strong hand, a good thick seal with the impress of a sword.

'Will you come in for a moment?'

'No, thankee, sir. I'd best get on.'

'Do you walk right on through the woods?' Richard had yet to do more than walk up the lane to the Leominster highway and down to the church and village: there were lonelier houses than his along the paths through the trees, known so far only through the map, but they were part of the parish, and visiting must yet form a part of his duties.

'I do. Not that there's many that read and write up there – not much call for me. But I've something to take on now to Mansell Farm, if they've cleared the way.'

'And do you …?' Richard hesitated. Was it wise to confess that he had felt watched down here? That though now the snow-filled woods gave him no sense of another's presence, he had, he was sure, seen a cloaked woman walk through, and heard from time to time her footfall.

'Sir?'

'No, it's nothing.'

No doubt from the homesteads along the woodland paths people often came walking or gathering firewood, and why should they not? To say that he felt that a woman might be, for some reason, observing his own presence here sounded foolish, even risible.

'No matter,' he said, and bade the man good morning, and took his letters inside, to read at his desk. He broke open the seal impressed with a slender sword.

> Burgage Manor
> 29th December 1860
>
> My dear Allen,
> The lake is frozen solid, and we are having a little skating party on New Year's Day. This is something of an annual event – we generally begin at about eleven, and have a good fire burning at the lakeside for luncheon. We do hope you will be able to join us. Such snow! I trust you are keeping well, and have adequate fuel. I trust too that the track is not impassable.
> It was good to see you in church at Christmas, and I trust that you spent a very pleasant day in the vicarage, though I fear that poor Bowen has not been well. He and Mrs Bowen generally join our party, as do many of your new parishioners, upon whom you seem to be making something of an impression.
> With warmest good wishes for the season, and in anticipation of the pleasure of your company.
> James Southwood

What a kindly, courteous spirit flowed within these lines. Richard read them again. At New Year in Ironbridge, he and his father had each slipped out of the house in the starry darkness and returned on the stroke of midnight to hammer upon the door, bearing a lump of coal and a crust of bread, until Mama and the girls ran to open it and draw them in by the fireside once more. The bells ran out as the last stroke of midnight chimed the old year away; in came the new, and he and his father raised their glasses. And often, in January, they had all gone skating. What a joyful thing was a skating party indeed: the ring of blades on the ice, bright faces, a crackling fire with fat chops roasting. They had loved it as children, and now—

The snowy field beyond the window sparkled in the morning sun. He felt a great lifting of the heart.

Burgage Manor lay some half-mile beyond the turning down to the village, set back from the highway and approached by a drive through parkland. It was not a grand house, but it was substantial: grey stone with a terrace and balustrade, now prettily outlined with snow but where one might, in summer, stroll to look out over grazing deer or cattle, spill out from a dance, linger to breathe in the scent of a rambling rose. So Richard thought, walking up the cleared drive in wet boots, with his skates hung over his arm. As usual he was early; as usual he wondered if this were the mark of a good, sound man, or made him look puppyish and eager.

But he knew he was not the first to arrive, for the air was crystal clear and he could hear laughing voices ring out in the distance behind the house, and see, as he rounded the corner and came into the stableyard, two traps with their shafts laid down in the snow, and a carriage likewise. He saw a boy rubbing down the horses in a box and then, as he passed through the arch, had his first sight of the lake. It lay a good hundred yards across a field, and a long path made between shovelled-up heaps of snow led down to it. And as he approached and saw the bright blaze of the fire, and a young couple come gliding hand in hand over the ice, Richard realised that this was no formal, landscaped feature, wherein a fountain might tumble over fish or maiden, and a few skaters make their mark in winter, but a great rough country stretch of water, fringed now by frozen reeds, which in spring must be alive with wild duck – and offering, no doubt, good shooting in the autumn.

The expanse of it glittered in the sun. Rooks cawed hungrily from a distant stand of trees; the fire crackled and two or three figures ahead of him were talking in high spirits. Who were they? And who was on the ice? He made out Southwood, skating well, gliding to a halt now and then to greet a new arrival. He saw the dog Gauntlet on his haunches by the fire, Mrs Southwood in discussion there with the cook, a manservant moving about with a tray of steaming drinks. He did not recognise the people ahead of him, but he saw that the couple skating so fast and happily were Effie Bounds and her betrothed, whom he guessed had been skating together since they were children. He made out the lawyer Bodenham, helping his stout wife on to the edge, and watched their stately passage around the perimeter; he saw a half-dozen young people make a party of it, laughing and clinging to one another as they took their first steps. Then they set off one by one, graceful and sure as they gathered speed.

Oh, Em, how I wish you were here! How I wish you and Verity were one on either side of me, racing over the ice with all our cares forgotten – as if Father were still with us, and dear Mama laughing again—

For a moment he was so taken with this thought that he did not hear the footsteps coming along the path behind him, nor see, at the further side of the lake, a young woman bend to fasten her skates while her husband held her elbow. Then he recovered himself, and through the dazzling sun on the snow and the frozen lake, with its flying figures and sprays of fine ice glittering, he did see her.

He saw her smile up at her husband and let him help her down to the edge, where a space had been hacked down through the whitened reeds and rushes. He saw her step on to the ice and relinquish the helping hand, and he saw her begin to move, slowly at first, her gloved hands holding up her gown, and then with greater confidence, as her husband watched her, until she was skating far away from him, quite on her own, greeting and nodding to people but quite on her own, that pale hair almost silver in the brilliant winter sun, so that Richard had a sudden piercing sense of how she might look when she was old, and knew that he would love her then as he loved her now, for what must this feeling be if it were not love, as she came flying over the ice towards him, and on with a radiant smile, and all else faded.

'My dear Allen.' Southwood had come to a halt again, and was raising a hand in greeting. 'How good of you to come.'

'It was very good of you to ask me, sir. What a marvellous morning.'

'Is it not? Will you take some hot punch? Nothing alcoholic, I can assure you – Mrs Southwood concocts something with spices whose secrets I can only guess at, but we do find it assists one's prowess on the ice.'

And Southwood gestured at the tray of glasses held by the manservant who was now at Richard's side. He drank, and was wonderfully shot through with a piping-hot blend of cinnamon, cloves, lemon, honey and water – and surely a drop of brandy. What else could give this drink such a fiery heart? Or was it his own heightened emotional state, this sudden bolt of knowledge, which gave everything a sharp intensity? He could not look at the lake again.

'It's very good, sir.' He took another sip. 'You're quite sure—'

'Certain. Do say hello to this old fellow.'

And Richard bent to pat the grizzled head which had appeared beside him.

'Gauntlet's skating days are over,' said Southwood. 'He cut a fine figure once. Now, you must meet people. The Bowens are here already, as you see, though I doubt he will take to the ice. You know our young lovebirds, of course, and the Bodenhams. I don't think you've met my own dear children, though they are scarcely children now.' He turned as a woman came gliding up beside him. 'Charlotte, my dear, let me introduce our new curate, Mr Richard Allen.'

Charlotte Southwood wore crimson, and her dark eyes were clever and alive. She is Verity, thought Richard, bowing over her gloved hand. She has Verity's flashing wit and temper, she must struggle continually to keep herself in check. He knew this with complete certainty, just as he knew now that he was in love, with someone who was in truth quite mysterious to him.

'Mr Allen, I am delighted to make your acquaintance.'

'And I yours.' He released Charlotte Southwood's hand; he bowed again, and smiled. She turned to the tall young man who had appeared beside her.

'My brother Will.'

James Southwood to the life. What a fine-looking fellow Southwood must once have been.

'Delighted,' said Richard, shaking hands. 'How is that we have not met before? You cannot have only just come down?'

'Indeed not, Mr Allen. I spent Christmas with my fiancée's family. Do allow me to present Miss Debenham: she is talking to my mother.'

'And indeed I must greet your mother,' said Richard, following him over the snow towards the fire. 'She is supervising a feast.'

Clerical phrases. Clerical manners. Always the right remark for every social occasion. He was born to it, bred to it; to mingle easily amongst his parishioners was in his very bones, and how could he ever have thought that he would not quickly find a place here?

And how could he have imagined that his heart would stand still at the quick-silver sight of another man's wife; that she, shocking though it was, would in some way betoken everything he had ever wanted?

'Mrs Southwood. How good to see you again.'

'Mr Allen, how charming that you are here. You have met my dear children at last? Do let me present Miss Debenham.'

He bowed; he greeted; he stood by the fire, warming himself, observing the entry into its depths of trays of chops and sausages, great onions and potatoes, the smell of it all quite mouthwatering. Voices rang out from the lake in the bright cold air. He stood talking easily, never once lifting his gaze to where the skaters whirled, until Will Southwood said at last that this wouldn't do, they must take to the ice before luncheon. And Richard bent down to fasten on his skates, and offered his arm to Charlotte Southwood, as she was clearly waiting for him to do, and they all went galumphing across the thick snow towards the tall white clumps of reeds.

'You have skated much, Mr Allen?' asked Miss Southwood.

'I fear I am rather out of practice. I used to skate with my sisters when we were young. You put me a little in mind of one of them.'

'Oh? And which is that?'

'Verity, the elder. She is rather clever.'

'Then she must be quite unlike my sister,' said Will drily, and received a sharp reproach.

'You know I love to tease,' he said. 'Come, Charlie, don't take to your high horse.'

'I shall ignore you entirely. Pray continue, Mr Allen.'

And he continued. He did not say that Verity's temper was a legend, only described the two girls as well as he was able, Miss Southwood listening attentively as they stumbled over the tussocky ground.

THE MYSTERIES OF GLASS

They came to the edge of the ice. And once he had helped her to take her first steps, and found his own feet with far less confidence, now he must look up, and out through the skaters, their faces flushed in the cold, and seek out the only face which mattered.

And then? Then how should he dissemble?

'Good morning, Mr Allen.'

She was there, she had seen him assist Miss Southwood on to the ice, and in the moment in which he replied, as he might to anyone, 'Good morning,' she was gone again, gliding now, for surely she must be tired after such long exertion, until she had come to the place on the bank where her husband was standing in conversation with a group of good men of the parish – the lawyer Bodenham, and Neve, and Dr Probyn – and came to a halt before them.

'Miss Southwood, pray excuse me one moment ...'

He left her with her brother and Miss Debenham, and set out across the frozen lake – and how out of practice he was, and how far Susannah was from him. Surely she would not abandon the ice just as he had stepped out. Surely he might ask her to take his arm if her husband were not skating: that was quite innocent good manners, was it not?

The air was sharp in his throat as he gathered speed, and sprays of ice were everywhere, for there were truly quite a number of skaters now, and even in this great space it would not be difficult to go crashing into someone and cause an accident.

'Good morning, Mr Allen!'

'Good morning, good morning!'

He greeted Tom Skarratt, he greeted the Bampfields, he went on, faster and faster, and then, within a moment of his thinking of falls and accidents, there came from the middle of the lake a sudden, dreadful scream and he saw pretty Effie Bounds gazing down in horror.

'What is it? Whatever has happened?'

There were voices all around him, and then she screamed again, and everyone fell silent.

Edward Turner, thought Richard, slowing right down, as everyone was slowing. Someone has felled him – her childhood sweetheart. He has broken his head – he is dying ...

But when he looked again he saw no fallen body; saw, indeed, Edward Turner take his sweetheart in his arms, and then all colour drain from his face as he too looked down and saw what lay trapped beneath the ice.

'Stand back!'

Southwood's command rang out through the hush, and as they all slowly withdrew from the centre he came skating steadily towards it, with Gauntlet, at once alert to drama, danger, his master's need of him, limping painfully after. And nothing could more have heightened the strangeness and tension of the moment than the sight of his determination, the click of those old dry claws across the ice.

'Here,' Southwood said quietly, as he came to a halt. He reached out a hand; Gauntlet's head went into it; man and dog looked down. There came a low growl, and as the hackles rose visibly on Gauntlet's bony neck Richard felt his own skin prickle. What was it? What had they found?

Our Father, which art in heaven …

He could not tell if he spoke aloud. Then the dog gave a howl which tore the air apart and the rooks flew up from the trees beyond the lake, cawing wildly.

'Hush!' said Southwood, and tugged his dog away. 'Hush now!' And he raised his head and looked out across the ice to where his wife was standing by the fire, and slowly nodded, and her hands went up to her face. Beside her, the servant with his tray of drinks was absolutely still.

Then there were the sounds of Effie's weeping, the whimpers of the dog, the mad cawing of the rooks as they beat away across the snowy fields, until Southwood skated slowly to some distance, the dog at his heel. He made a gesture and drew all the company into a circle around him.

'My friends …' His voice shook a little; he began again. 'My dear good friends, I am so sorry that something so distressing should happen here. I must apologise to you all, and especially—' his eyes raked the throng, found Effie Bounds, sobbing still in the embrace of her young fiancé, who looked as white as she – 'especially I apologise to the dear young people who have so delighted us with the news of their engagement. What lies here—' He broke off, and gestured towards the dark place in the centre of the lake, where the ice was not as thickly formed, and where whatever had come drifting out here now lay visible beneath the surface.

'It grieves me to say,' Southwood continued, his hand tight upon Gauntlet's worn dark collar, 'that what lies here is, I am certain, the body of a young kitchen maid who left us without warning last November.' He hesitated. 'When young girls leave their employment so abruptly I fear there is often only one reason, though I shall not offend the ladies amongst us by describing that. Suffice it to say that she left us, and though my wife made enquiries we could find no news of her. In the autumn rains the lake becomes very deep indeed, and the tragic end she took for herself has been undiscovered until today. Again, I am so very sorry. I pray you will all come up to the house, for I fear that none of you will wish to linger here. Before we leave ...' His eyes scanned the silent throng once more, '... Mr Bowen? Where is Mr Bowen?'

'I am here,' said Oliver Bowen from his place amongst his friends on the snow-lined shore.

'Might we say a prayer for this poor girl before we leave her?'

There was a little pause. Then Southwood said quickly, 'How foolish of me – of course, you are not skating, you are not quite well—'

'I am well enough,' said Bowen. 'I can walk upon the ice if someone will assist me.'

'Sir.' Richard stepped forward. 'Will you permit me?'

'Good man,' said Southwood. 'Thank you, Allen.'

And Richard skated slowly over the ice, making a wide sweep away from its terrible dark centre, until he reached the further shore, where Bowen stood with his councillors and with his young wife, whose lovely face, Richard took in at a raking glance, was ashen. Perhaps he himself was pale: the party was become an assembly of shocked ghosts.

'Sir?' He put out a hand, and Bowen stepped slowly forward. Together they made their way across to where Southwood stood waiting. Bowen's footsteps were slow and cautious: as he leaned upon him Richard had once or twice to struggle to keep his own balance on the skates, and felt himself break into a sweat of nerves.

'Well done, sir, very well done.'

Bowen did not answer. For a horrible moment, Richard thought: I am taking a sick man out to a place of death, and his grip tightened. Then Southwood was moving carefully towards them, his hand still upon the restless Gauntlet's collar.

'Well done. Thank you. Bowen, you will lead us when you are ready?'

'I will.' And Bowen drew a breath and took off his broad-brimmed black hat, and held it before him.

The rooks had returned in slow pairs to the trees, and their caws came again across the field – a sound so associated with the English churchyard that the party might indeed all have been in church, as they bowed their heads and the pall of cold settled over them.

'Lord God, our Heavenly Father,' prayed Bowen, and not a sound came now, save for the intermittent call of the birds, and the crackle of the fire. 'Look down upon us, we beseech Thee, as we stand in this place of sin—'

Did Richard imagine it, or was there a sudden sharp intake of breath from James Southwood, standing on Bowen's other side, his old dog trembling beneath his hand?

'Grant that the troubled soul of this young girl may find rest and quietude, that her great wickedness might in Thy mercy be washed away, and that this place may hereafter be returned to innocence. And Father, as we stand before Thee now, hear us as we say together the words of our Lord Jesus Christ: Our Father, which art in heaven, Hallowed be thy Name ...'

Perhaps two score of sombre voices joined him, each mind, Richard guessed, filled with its own image of what lay gaping and drowned beneath the ice.

Then it was over.

In little knots and pairs they skated slowly to the lakeside, and gradually the silence broke into murmured conversations. A tragedy, a scandal, a wicked, wicked thing. Edward Turner wrapped his arms round Effie Bounds once more, and Southwood conducted Bowen back to the shore with a grave nod to Richard. Richard saw Will and Charlotte Southwood skim rapidly to their mother and embrace her, and found himself escorting Miss Debenham, Will's fiancée, over to join them.

'A dreadful occurrence,' he said. 'You must be very shaken.'

'I fear these things happen with servants,' said Miss Debenham.

'I …' For a moment he could not speak. Then he said carefully, 'Yes – I suppose they do.' And he left her with her new family, and looked about him.

Where was she? Were those her sentiments? Was he so young and raw that he thought it pitiful?

He saw the manservant who had been taking round hot punch now removing the trays of roasting lamb from the fire with enormous care, his face aflame. He saw Bodenham and his wife and the Neves and Richard Parry all walking slowly round the lake. Bowen and Southwood were with them, the dog loping stiffly over the snow. He saw Susannah – where had she been? – walking slowly across to join them, and hold her head as if she were listening attentively, though he knew from her bloodless face that this could not be so.

Might he join them? Of course he might join them – what hesitancy was this?

He knew what hesitancy it was.

But he took a breath, and skated across, and came hobbling out through the reeds with enormous clumsiness.

'May I accompany you?'

There was a murmur of assent, a general waiting while he bent to unfasten the skates and rub his ankles. Then they all set off again, and he took himself to Susannah's side, just in time to put out his arm as she stumbled.

'Please – let me help you.'

For a moment she leaned upon him, and he saw that her face was streaked with tears.

'I am so sorry,' he said quickly, as she struggled to hide this. 'You must be very distressed.'

Clerical phrases. Was he to go on saying them to everyone, for the rest of his life? And yet what else could he say now?

She murmured something he could not hear. The others were drawing ahead.

'What was that? I fear that I did not catch—'

'She was expecting a child.' The words were barely a whisper.

She looked down at her hands, and he had no phrase to answer her.

Then the others stopped and turned, and were waiting, and they walked in silence over the snow to join them.

9

He went walking. The thaw came at last and he went walking: away from the church and the village, down over the crossing and past the mill, up the long lane to the Kington–Presteigne highway, and on up to the Rushock hills. The track was rutted and deep. Ice shone on the puddles as he climbed and the temperature dropped; patches of snow still lay amongst the trees. He passed a farm, and a chained-up dog barked wildly and was cursed from within the house. Then a face appeared at the window. Richard raised his hat; there was a nod; he walked on, passing a barn whose door stood open, and saw cattle knee-deep in filthy straw, pushing their huge heads between the rails towards the hay trough. The wooden pens creaked; the great beasts stared at him as only cattle stared, their muzzles wet, their flanks caked. He climbed on for a long way, passing a building set so deep within the trees that at first, preoccupied, he did not notice it. But he heard something – what? – and stopped, and saw it: unfaced grey stone, shuttered windows, no doorway fronting on the track. It must be a storehouse for the farm below, and what he'd heard from within was a wintering animal – squirrel or rat or hedgehog – waking with the partial thaw, shifting about in its bedding. It was so quiet you could hear even this. Then a jay shrieked suddenly from deeper in the woods, and he started, looked for its flash of blue and saw it, and went on walking. And not until he had climbed another quarter-mile did he stop to rest, and turn to look down at how far he had come, and saw a thin blue line of wood smoke rising through the trees.

He frowned. He walked a little off the track, on to a carpeted bank of damp twigs and leaf mould, which, as he disturbed it, released its rich wet smell. When he could look down at the front of the building he saw that a door faced into the woods. It was tightly closed, and the windows were shuttered too, but for one, open a few inches to the light. From within he could hear, just, in the still winter morning, somebody moving about.

An old sick labourer from one of the farms, begging not to be sent to the workhouse, granted a primitive shelter until he died? Or was this a hermit's house, something he had only read about, picturing always somewhere far more remote than this, right up in the hills: an abandoned sheepfold or shepherd's hut wherein an old man might mutter and pray beneath the clouds.

Well, who knew who lived here? It was something to remark, and briefly think about, but he had much else on his mind, and he turned and walked back to the muddy track, rounding a bend and approaching open country.

Three ancient windblown yews stood on a summit, dwarfing wall and hedgerow. He looked out across the empty fields; he saw that the tops of the distant Radnor hills were still thick with snow, and walked on and on until he had come to a broad grassy place from where he could look out to the misty blue Malverns one way and the towering Black Mountains the other. Down in the valley the train was puffing through, steam streaming back through the hazy trees. Above him a buzzard soared, and save for the steady faint puff of the train its melancholy cry was almost the only sound in the world.

'Susannah,' he said aloud, and her name in this empty place entirely filled him. He said it again, and then he kneeled to pray.

'Lord, teach me; Lord show me – what must I do?'

When he rose to his feet he was stiff with the cold. Grass stained his knees, and he had no answer.

He was here for a year: he must fulfil his duties.

Already he had sinned. To look upon another man's wife – to covet her in his heart – this was a sin forbidden by the Commandments he had learned to recite as a little boy. The words were a part of him, ran in his bloodstream, as love ran now.

He had sought all his life to love God. Yet still—

'In my Father's house are many mansions' – Christ speaking to his

96

disciples after the Last Supper. Did human love lie in one of those mansions? Must there be only one kind of human love?

Richard walked on, as the buzzard wheeled in the heavens.

Lord ... as we stand in this place of sin— He heard the stern words of Oliver Bowen sound across the ice; he pictured the frozen drowned girl beneath. This was sin's punishment on earth, and beyond lay eternal torment.

She was expecting a child.

This, for Susannah, had been the most dreadful thing – because that poor girl had murdered her unborn baby, or because she herself was childless?

Lord, Lord—

How were love and tenderness a sin? How could a sudden rush of joy, a sense of the marvellous beauty of the world and of her perfect place within it – how could these feelings not lie close to God?

It began to rain: a sudden, sleeting fall, bouncing off bare rock and then soaking into the grass. Richard looked about for shelter, ran for the three mighty yews, and stood beneath them, already soaking, listening to the rain fall on and on through their branches and on to the hillside. The Three Shepherds: that was what they were, he recalled from his first week here, when everyone pouring out of the church and everyone at luncheon at the vicarage had been so eager to acquaint him with the place, to name hills and trees and breeds of sheep; to talk about themselves, their occupations and troubles, while he half listened and only afterwards realised that through it all he was seeking out her voice.

He had known even then; he had known the first moment they met.

Beneath the shelter of the Three Shepherds, guarding their flock on a hillside between three counties, two countries, he himself now stood on the border between love and fulfilment, purity and sin.

At last the rain stopped, and he shook out his hat and began the long walk back to the track, and down into the valley. Everything shone.

Lord, Heavenly Father—

What would his own father advise him to do? He asked himself this, squelching over the sodden grass, beginning the slow climb down again, and saw only a long, grave, loving look, then the invitation to prayer.

And lead us not into temptation—

All about him the trees dripped steadily.

He lifted his feet through the mud of the track and almost lost his boots. He sought out the bank, and the air was filled once again with the marvellous wet scent of leaf mould, earthy and strong. He came at last to the place high above the farm where stood the shuttered grey stone cottage, a hermit's house, with its hazy blue wood smoke rising through the trees – more thinly than ever now, after the rain – and then he saw her.

Not Susannah, though he had thought of nothing but her, and to see her now would have filled his heart with gladness.

Not Susannah, but a woman in a cloak, walking out from her lonely house to her rain-soaked winter garden in the woods.

He knew at once that this was the woman whom he had sensed watching him all this time. Now he stood on the bank above the track, watching her.

He saw a rough border of stones enclosing a square patch of ground, and a pail in a corner, set to catch snow or rain. That a woman might survive the cold and isolation of the snow up here was hard to imagine, yet here she was, in a cloak as coarse as sacking, stepping in rough wooden pattens over the wet ground, bending to pick up the pail with its few inches of fresh rainwater. And with her footsteps Richard became aware of movement in the branches of the trees, and of rooks and magpies gathering above her. She heard them too, and looked towards them.

Richard stood absolutely still. As she lifted her head, her hood fell back, and he saw her face: dark, weathered, intent, the face of a young woman unlike any he had ever seen – except, he thought now, watching her reach into the folds of her cloak and scatter crumbs and scraps about her, when as a boy he had walked with his father past a gypsy encampment which had appeared overnight in the fields where they went shooting.

But gypsies were always together. They arrived, and offered to a boy a brief enchantment, with their fires and cooking pots, their caravans and dogs and shaggy ponies. Then, overnight, they were gone. This woman had no clan or company, and the stones she had placed were an indication of settlement: she had lived here alone for a long time, and the woodland birds relied upon her. They were all around her now, and amongst the pigeons and corvids he saw a few songbirds which had survived the winter, no doubt because of her: blackbird and thrush and a bright thin robin. She was murmuring to them all. The smell of the woods after rain was heavenly, and the air was full of the sound of water – the dripping trees, rivulets of melting snow running into a brook. No doubt it ran down the hillside to join the Arrow, and though its source lay in a different place from his own garden stream, the sound of it was gladdening and familiar.

The birds ate and jostled; the young woman brushed the last crumb from her hands, and he expected her now to pick up her pail and return to the house. But a watery sun was filtering through the trees, and she pushed back her roughly knotted hair and then all at once turned up her face towards this new light, and stretched out her arms with upraised hands and stood quite motionless.

It was a gesture which both shocked and thrilled him. It felt pagan. It felt rapturously holy. Time and history fell away, his sermons were leaves in the wind. Here was something mortal touching something luminous, eternal. He thought, as he watched her, that perhaps she was closer to God than he had ever been.

The birds had finished feeding. They searched, they looked up, they saw her outstretched hands. And as he watched her a pigeon fluttered upwards, and landed on her hand, and rested there. Amidst all the turmoil of his thoughts, amidst the new-found knowledge of his love for Susannah, Richard felt now as if he had been granted a vision – as unexpected as the discovery of water by a diviner's rod.

Lord, Lord—

He folded his own gloved hands in prayer; he bowed his head.

When he looked up, she had gone, and the door of the house was closed. He took a step, and at once the birds flew up and away through the bare trees. In moments, the scene before him might never have taken place.

Part Two

10

It was the beginning of February. The last of the snow lay in
glistening patches on the Radnor Hills; the first clumps of
snowdrops lightened the churchyard.

Susannah sat sewing by the parlour fire. Morning sunshine filtered
through the ivy at the window; a heap of heavy blue school pinafores
lay on the footstool beside her. They were old and worn, and in want
of pockets or patches or turning up; they had been found by a
member of the Society for Promoting Christian Knowledge at the
back of a cupboard in her great-aunt's house in Pembridge, in the
turn-out after her death; they had been brought to a meeting in
January, for use in the churchyard school.

Susannah's needle flashed in the February sunshine; she pressed
down her thimble and winced. Beneath her grey gown she was
bleeding copiously into rags. This was something never directly
spoken of.

– I am not quite well today.

– You look pale. Stay in the warm and rest.

The rector's wife never rested. The rector's wife must be seen to be
active; must never, except in prayer, have a moment to herself.
Everyone and everything needed her: the decaying vicarage; her
husband's poorer parishioners, in their sickness, and need of warm
clothing, and schooling, and parish relief. Those who were more
prosperous made different claims upon her: meetings of the Bible
Society, the Benevolent Society, the Reading and Tract Societies, the
Society for the Relief of Jews in Palestine. There were pamphlets to
be written and read and distributed; there were letters and accounts;

there was the decoration of the dilapidated church – at Christmas, at Easter, for weddings and baptisms and for the Harvest Festival. There was the assisting at the school, hearing faltering readers, helping with sums on slates, the telling of the Bible stories, the listening to songs. As her mother used to say, yawning as she kissed them all good night: even without the blessing of children, the work of a clergyman's wife was never done.

Susannah had not the blessing of children. She was not quite well, but she had not earned that long period of rest that a lying-in gave a mother, away from the press of vicarage life in her vicarage bedroom, hearing the rooks in the churchyard elms and the cry of her newborn infant from the crib. When she climbed the stairs to bed, she was filled with a confusion of dread and longing. She received the dry press of lips upon her brow within the darkness; she endured the lifting of her nightgown, his entry into her, the sudden stickiness, the groan.

This was what must be done to have a child.

Yet there was no child.

Two years after their marriage, she had sought advice. Was it – was it because she found it all so distasteful? Were she able to give herself more freely, might an infant more readily be conceived? In her heart, she asked herself these questions. In Dr Probyn's Kington consulting room, she could not bring herself to ask them. Oliver was waiting in the ante-room, seated upon the ottoman, turning the pages of *The Times*. Even through the dark oak door she could hear him clearing his throat.

'Is it – it perhaps something in me?' she asked Dr Probyn, scarlet with embarrassment.

'I very much doubt it.' He leaned back in his chair behind the desk, pressed his fingers together and observed her. 'You are young, you are healthy and strong enough. Your good husband – he is rather older, is he not? Quite considerably older, I think.'

'Some twenty years,' said Susannah.

'As I thought. Well, there have been plenty of such marriages blessed by children. But perhaps – Mr Bowen is not always in perfect health. I know he finds the winters difficult. And though God has made us in such marvellous fashion, nature is a strange old thing.' He gave her a little smile, and she felt herself relax. 'Sometimes a weak chest, a weak heart, a little complication somewhere – any of this may affect a man's fitness to conceive.'

'My husband has a weak heart?' Now she was alarmed. 'You think there is something—'

'No, no, not at all, you must not think that. I am only speculating.' He tapped his compressed fingers against his lips, still watching her. Then: 'It is a love match?' he asked her kindly, and now her blush consumed her.

'His father—' she was stumbling over the words – 'Oliver's father and mine – they were very good friends. I have always known him. He was always fond of me ...' She dropped her gaze.

'I see.' There was a little pause. She swallowed a lump in her throat. Let her not weep, let her not spill it all out. How shameful that would be – to speak to another man, even kind Dr Probyn, in ways in which she could not speak to her own husband.

'My dear. My dear Mrs Bowen, please do not distress yourself. If this situation continues, then perhaps I may have to examine you. For now, put your mind at rest. Let nature take its course. In good time, I am sure you will both be blessed.'

She could not lift her eyes to his. She never went back.

Last year her husband developed a cough which would not leave him. Syrup and mixtures did not soothe it. He tossed and turned in their high iron bed.

– Oliver?

He pushed back the covers, felt for his slippers and gown, the cough a dreadful sound.

– Let me give you some water.

– Go back to sleep. I shall sit for a while.

She lay listening to the chink of glass and pitcher, the hideous cough, the steps along the landing, the dressing-room door pushed slowly open.

Now, on such nights, she lay alone thinking of the poor drowned girl beneath the lake at Burgage; of the quickening of the baby within her as she stepped through the reeds and gasped at the cold. She thought of her walking out, going deeper, deeper, the indifferent moon glinting on the inky water, the last candles blown out in the house in the distance, the last bolt shot and no one to miss her until dawn. He would not miss her. He did not care. She pushed out further, thinking: I must do this – I cannot do this – until with a sickening drop the bottom of the lake gave way to its real depth, and she thrashed, then sank unstoppably.

Save me, Father—

Who had died first, that desperate young woman or her baby? As the icy black water filled her mouth, her lungs, how long had her baby continued to swim in its own mysterious chamber?

Susannah lay in the darkness of her married bedroom, with its texts upon the walls and peeling paper, the cracks in the ceiling, and damp in the plaster, which no fire would cure, and asked herself what would become of the soul of Sarah Watkins, a suicide. Which was the greater sin? The conception out of wedlock? The taking of the life which God had given you? Or the taking of the life of your own poor baby?

When they dragged her out of the lake at the thaw a week ago – it was all over the *Kington Gazette*, everyone was talking about it – they tugged her to the shore and wrapped her, ravaged by fish and beetle, in a canvas shroud, and heaved her, streaming weed and water, into the back of a cart. Oliver had gone out to bury her in a suicide's grave – outside the churchyard, in a windswept field quite outside the village. If she had family, they did not stand there; the earth was shovelled over the cheapest coffin, Oliver asked the Lord for His forgiveness, and Sarah Watkins was left to lie in an unmarked grave, unmourned, with her unborn, unnamed infant.

Was it a boy or a girl?

Susannah, in her parlour, in the winter sun, bent over the heavy blue pinafore, so difficult to sew, and rocked.

It was noon. In his study across the hall her husband coughed at his desk. He had told her she must not dwell upon this death, this sin. When she woke from a terrible dream of that face beneath the ice he held her in his arms and prayed for her. She let him come into her. Then he began to cough; then he got up, said he was in a little pain, went creaking along the landing.

She lay in the darkness, seeing an unborn baby swimming in an underwater chamber, safe within her, waiting for her touch.

Lord, grant me this. Please – grant me this.

Then:

– I am not quite well today.

– Stay in the warm and rest.

Across the churchyard the school bell clanged, and the voices of the children sounded, as they ran out to play in the cold.

The fire was sinking. He rose from his desk, with its ivy-framed view of the graves, and bent to rekindle the flames with a shovel of coal. The pain gnawed at him from its lair beside his spine. He threw on the coal and the dust made him cough: the pain leaped, snarling, and sweat broke out everywhere – on his brow, beneath his arms, on the back of his neck, beneath the chafing white tie. He kneeled by the hearth and waited, breathing as carefully as he could, while his heart pounded; concentrating, concentrating – Lord, let me not cough, Lord, let me not cough. At last he was steady. The pain sank down, flared as he got to his feet, leaning on the arm, then the wing of the chair; he took the few steps to his desk. The pain settled down, waiting.

He pulled out his handkerchief and wiped his brow. From now on, in this new phase of illness, he must ring when the fire needed tending. While it lasted, he must conserve his energy, cosset and guard it. God was with him: he would come through. Already the pain was quite subsided – it was only exertion which roused it. For a little while he must keep to the house. The cold and the snow and the standing on the ice, the wind which cut across the suicide's burial ground, the deep winter chill of the church – all these had taken their toll. He would cherish the health which still remained in him, and with the coming of spring greater health would return, just as the snowdrops had sprung up once more, in tender white and green amongst the graves.

He leaned on his hands, his elbows upon his papers, the rekindled fire at his back, warming and restoring. Across the churchyard the children were racing about to keep warm, in their noonday break, George and John Bampfield running sticks along the railings round the Jeffries tomb, a group of boys – William Duggan, the Fletcher boys, little John Hollings and big Tom Meredith – playing tag, running like the wind and yelling when they were caught. Then Miss Hatfield appeared at the door and the bell came clanging out again; there was a scrambling down the bank behind the church and the appearance of another half-dozen children; the last tag was touched, the last stick rattled along the railings with her sharp reproof. The children lined up by the door and were counted. Then they filed in and the churchyard settled back to its quiet self.

Susannah's cat appeared from nowhere, walking up the path to their door and waiting. Miss Hatfield or Millie must go to let it in: he was calm now and the pain calm with him. He must get on with his work before luncheon, if luncheon could be faced.

Beyond the churchyard the top of Turner's wagon became visible as it made its slow way down the hill. Then it was gone, and the clopping faded. Clouds blew over the distant fields and parted: the sun of a winter morning, subtly changed in early February – sharper, brighter, more intense – lit the lichen on the top of the churchyard wall, the rim of a tombstone, the edge of his desk, beneath the windowsill. It lit the brass scales, a wedding present, which stood there for his letters. The graded line of weights was like a line of children, waiting in the cold by the schoolhouse door. He used them almost every day, opening the leather book of stamps, running his finger over the Queen's fine head embossed upon violet and scarlet and green, selecting and sealing and setting aside. He reached for the next weight: for the quarter-ounce letter, the two-ounce package of pamphlets. When he had finished, he lined them up again. He saw them sometimes as the children he still hoped for; sometimes as soldiers; mostly as weights.

Today, leaning forward as the bright sun touched the brass, he observed not these little brass figures but the dishes of the scales, balanced so perfectly upon their slender chains. He saw them as illness and health. Which would sink, vanquished, and which rise to take possession?

He picked up the smallest weight of all – the youngest child, the weakest soldier, bringing up the rear on the Crimean battlefield. He placed it on the shining dish on the right. He took his fingers away and the dish sank at once, as that sinful girl must have sunk into the lake at Burgage, the black water closing over her, her soul and the soul of the child within her descending into hell.

Leaping flames. Dark thoughts. Before him the little dish swung and sank; its brother rose up to God.

Illness and health, illness and health. Life and death, and which would claim him?

He took off the weight and set it back in its place. He picked up his pen, wiped the nib and began to write once more. Before him the dishes of the scales gleamed in the thin intensity of the February sun, as they resumed their balance, and after a while were still.

Between them stood the pillar of fire and the outstretched arms of God.

Luncheon. A mutton chop, a dish of boiled potatoes, a yellowing cauliflower. In the fields beyond the dining-room window – Parson's Plock, and Passey's Lower Ground – the first trembling lambs were bleating in the cold. The morning's gleams of sun had gone behind gathering rain clouds.

'For what we are about to receive, may the Lord make us truly grateful.'

'Amen.'

They raised their bowed heads, they slipped their linen napkins from their silver rings: another wedding present, each engraved with the elaborate B which also adorned his silver-backed brushes and the ivory-backed mirror which lay upon her dressing table. These things had belonged to his grandparents, long buried in the churchyard in Credenhill. Moving in here, a fortnight after their wedding – the thirtieth day of August, 1855 – he had thought, watching Millie and Susannah unpack the boxes, everything topsy-turvy and the door wide open to let in the late summer sun and air, to pass them on in time to his own children. He had watched Susannah, such a shy young bride, turn back the folds of black cloth which wrapped the silver – these napkin rings, those brushes, her own grandmother's gravy boat and salt and pepper pots and little mustard bowl – as if they were priceless, so careful was she with everything. He wanted to take her in his arms; when Millie carried the saucepans along to the kitchen, he did so.

'My wife, my dear wife. We shall be so happy here.'

He bent to kiss her; did he imagine her look of relief as the carrier knocked at the open door and set down the boxes of books? He released her at once; she smoothed back her hair with a blush. She was young and innocent; he had been a bachelor for too long; he must not frighten her with his urgent need.

He directed the books to his study; announced his intention of spending the rest of the afternoon in there, reassembling his library, a pleasant prospect, which quite quickly distracted him from that moment's unease. They had, after all, the rest of their lives in which to discover one another.

Millie was beside him now, spooning the boiled potatoes on to his plate. He raised his hand to stop her.

'Are you sure, sir? A little cauliflower?'

He nodded, reaching for his glass. The chop alone was an impossibility. Even to reach for water reawakened the pain. He pressed his lips together.

'Mint sauce?'

He waved at her in a spasm of irritation; he began to cough. What a filthy, horrible sound: he could feel the two women recoil. He felt for his handkerchief, he turned his head away, feeling, with every heave and gasp, a knife twisted deep in his spine. He spat profusely into the handkerchief; glossy green sputum filled it. He put out his hand; Millie was beside him at once with a glass. When at last he recovered himself, he saw Susannah's white face at the end of the table.

'Pray forgive me,' he said at last.

'You really are not at all well.'

'It will pass.'

All things must pass. Such relief, to think those words.

'Millie will be in town this afternoon,' said Susannah. 'Won't you, Millie? Should she not call on Dr Probyn? I'm sure he should come out to see you.'

He shook his head, blew his nose, felt calmer.

'It is Millie's afternoon off, is it not? I'll call on Probyn myself in a day or two. No need to bring him out now.'

And he smoothed the worn linen napkin over his knees, and picked up his knife and fork, nodding to Susannah to do the same.

'Thank you, Millie.'

She went out, leaving the door ajar. It had begun to rain, pattering against the leaded window. In Parson's Plock, the lambs were racing for their ewes. Rain and sheep and the sound of knife and fork on china. Blessed, ordinary things.

'And has your quiet morning restored you a little?' he asked Susannah. 'You have been reading?'

'Sewing. Mending school pinafores.'

'Ah.'

Here at the back of the house, the sounds of the children in the churchyard were less audible, though in spring and summer at luncheon time you often saw the bolder boys come scrambling over the stile from the Plock, where they were not supposed to go. No one was out there now, in this cold and wet.

'And you, Oliver? You have had a useful morning?'

'Writing letters.'

'Millie will go to the post. I'll tell her when she comes back.'

'Thank you.'

From the hall came the sound of the grandfather clock – his grandfather's clock – striking the half-hour. Then it resumed its ticking, measured and slow. He heard it as their conversation. Tick, tock. You. Me. A question, an answer, an absence at the heart. Where was the sweet to-and-fro he used to dream of when they first were married? He had imagined a continual flow, continual embracing, the babble of the children from the nursery. Was there still time?

'Susannah?'

'Yes?'

'Sometimes I fear that—'

Then Millie was in the room again, doing everything quickly today, that soon she might clear, and be off. He let her take his plate. He told her about the letters. The moment passed.

11

Spring came. The weather was like music. Silvery rain blew in drifts across the fields, chased by sudden sunlight, quickly gone again. The banks of the lanes were starred with primroses, the deep quiet woods now alive with birdsong, and the cries of the newborn lambs were everywhere.

Confined for so long to the snug, the one room small enough for him to heat, Richard opened up the house as Martha Price one morning suggested he might do. She fetched pails of water from the stream, eased open the long casement in the larger sitting room across the little hall. Spiders scuttled across the flags, and the beams were thick with cobwebs. She poked an old broom up the inglenook chimney and a flurry of soot fell down. There was almost no furniture in here, for the damp would certainly rot it, but with a good scrub, a bright fire, and a quantity of fresh air blowing through, it might become a place to use now and then. Bluetit and hawfinch were darting about in the mountain ash before the window; Richard left Martha with brushes and pail and went out into the garden.

The snowdrops, which had massed beneath the hawthorn hedge, were almost gone, but here and there a crocus bulb pushed through its cowl of earth, and the daffodils along the path would open at any moment: a single warm afternoon was all they needed. He opened the wicket gate set in the long wall beneath the mountain ash, and crossed the grassy drive through the next, which led to the orchard. And standing beneath the boughs of the Bramley apple tree, thick with wet blossom, he thought that he too might stand with upraised arms at the miracle of spring, were he at one with God and His creation.

He was not so: he felt estranged – from those around him and from God. He could not give thanks for something he must not wish to have. He could not ask for forgiveness for a sin he had not committed, though each night he took Susannah in his arms and fell asleep with her silken hair spread out on the pillow beside him.

He was a virgin, of course he was a virgin. These things had never been properly spoken of, ever: not even between himself and his father. He could not fully imagine them. But he tried to; he wanted to; and this, he knew, was sinful.

He would have said this to anyone who sought his counsel, though few parishioners did. He was young, he was new, he was the curate: he was someone to greet in the town and welcome on pastoral visits. He had visited now quite a number of the houses in the village: Miss Dorothy Wilkinson and her aunt, marooned upstairs in her old brass bed beneath the beams, to whom he had given the Blessed Sacrament; the Southwoods, after the funeral of the girl dragged out from the lake – to pray with them that a horror such as that discovery might never be visited upon the house again, that the household might live in peace.

They had stood in the library, their heads bowed, the servants all assembled. Richard knew that in effect he was praying that the ghost of Sarah Watkins might not return to haunt the grounds, though no one said this; he knew that he was on such an occasion second-best, when the older, wiser, better-known rector was not well enough to come out to comfort Elizabeth Southwood, the one who seemed most in need of it.

Miss Charlotte Southwood had flashed him a glance across the table at the luncheon that followed these prayers. He returned her smile, then concentrated on his soup plate. A curate as poor as he had few prospects; Miss Southwood must expect to marry well and would surely do so. If he as a single young man were briefly of some interest, this was only because there was, as it happened, no other single young man at the table that day.

Dearest Verity, There is a young woman here, rather well born, of some spirit, who puts me in mind of you. I think that for a moment she has entertained the fancy of courtship, but of course I am far out of her league, and besides ... besides, the truth is that my heart ...

114

He flamed at the thought. Her brother, in love with another man's wife. He could never tell them. He could tell no one.

He went on his round of visits. He sat in the parish council meetings and talked about woodworm and deathwatch beetle and read the quarterly accounts for the distribution of parish relief. He took out a guinea subscription to Mr Stanway's new library, in the High Street; he spoke at a Tuesday evening meeting of the Bible Society on the Epistle to the Ephesians, and promised to read the tracts put out by the Baptist Chapel in Furlong Street. He took Sunday afternoon service in the dining room of the Kington workhouse, where two hundred paupers were housed; he visited the churchyard school, met Miss Mary Hatfield, who kept it, and made an arrangement to prepare three older boys for confirmation. He wrote his letters home, walked into town and posted them at the post office in Bridge Street, then made his purchases: a loaf from Morris's, next door; a chop from George Bayrell in the High Street. On Wednesdays he went to the market and came home with new potatoes and spring cabbage.

He wrote his sermons, he led the prayers; each Sunday he opened the lich-gate and wondered if he were in time to see her cross the churchyard for the service. He climbed the pulpit steps and sought her face. He waited in the porch for her to come out, almost at the end, for their eyes to meet in a smile; to take her gloved hand in greeting.

Then he walked home through the woods, and after supper climbed the stairs to bed and tried to pray.

Father, lead me to her, if it is Thy Will—

Father, teach me what is right—

He climbed into bed and blew out the candle. He folded her into his arms.

Now the world in spring bubbled all around him, and he was unable to worship, unable fully to pray. The great moment of Easter and the Resurrection approached: he lay beneath the ice, with darkness between him and God: a dissembler whom no one truly knew. It was Lent. He struggled to relinquish the idea of love.

Martha Price was scrubbing the flagstones: he could hear the rhythmic movement of the brush, could smell blossom and water and soap and the glorious fresh earth. He left the orchard and walked down the lane where the millwheel turned and voices sounded. The apple tree behind the Birley cottage, which in winter he had barely noticed, was now a mass of pink and white, towering over the thatch, the new-filled river rushing by. The mid-morning train approached and then came through with its piercing whistle; the blossom was cloudy with steam, like the ghost of a woman in a sweet spring gown – glimpsed, then disappearing into the mist.

The train was gone through. Birley appeared through the steam, drawing back the gates.

'A beautiful morning,' said Richard, and Birley turned, and touched his cap.

'Aye. She's better than she was.'

The pronoun, attaching itself to many material objects and conditions, still gave Richard pause: had someone been ill? Had he not seen Alice walking up past the house early this morning, on her way to school? Now she was eight, she had told him, and the winter gone, she was old enough to take herself to school and back. Then he realised that Birley spoke only of the weather, better after yesterday's gusts of rain. The door of the crossing cottage opened: Tommy came out with his engine, from which he was inseparable. He set it down upon the step and ran it back and forth.

'Still going well?' Richard asked him, and he nodded. From within came the sound of a door unbolted at the back, and a new light poured through the cottage as Mrs Birley could be heard dragging out basket and washtub on to the grass.

'The world is spring-cleaning,' said Richard to Birley, and he nodded.

'Not before time. 'Twas a long hard winter: we do need the sun and air.'

The phrase stirred something, like a song, or a line of verse long-buried since the schoolroom, but Richard could not place it, though he said now: 'I shall be seeing Alice this afternoon when I go up to the school to hear the catechism. I shall call on Mr Bowen briefly, but shall I then bring Alice back with me?'

'She goes to school by herself now,' murmured Tommy from the step where light and shade were dancing.

'I know, I've seen her. What a big girl she is become.'

'Eight is old enough to walk up through in springtime,' said Birley. 'But if you are coming back that would be a kindness to bring her. I'm never quite easy till I see her home.' He was lighting his pipe and the smell of the briar tobacco was very good.

'The woods are quite safe, though, are they not?'

'Safe as anywhere, I expect. You get some strange ones now and then; there's one or two will sleep there when the weather warms up.'

'Do you know …' Richard hesitated. 'Do you know the young woman who lives up on Rushock Hill?' Even as he spoke it he thought he was committing a betrayal: a woman who chose to live alone like that must have her reasons, though he did not know what they might be. Perhaps she dreaded discovery – yet she had sought him out, had she not? She had come down all this way and watched him, as he began his new life.

Birley was tamping down his pipe. Perhaps everyone knew her – yet no one had told him about her, nor her lonely retreat amongst the birds.

'Can't say I do,' Birley said. 'There's Martha Price's cottage, and then there's the Higgins place and then as you climb there's the Mortimers' farm. I don't think there's much beyond that. A woman?' He shook his head, as a carrier came down the lane towards the mill, and he and Richard stepped back. The cart was drawn by a blinkered chestnut cob, whose thick winter coat would soon be in want of clipping.

'I had thought about a pony and trap,' said Richard, changing the subject, 'when I first arrived. If you ever hear of an old one in want of a home … Or a dog. A dog would be a good companion.'

'So would a wife, sir,' said Birley drily, as the carrier went past, and Richard felt himself flush deeply. 'I spoke out of turn,' said the keeper, seeing this. 'Not like me, sir. I hope you'll pardon the impertinence.'

'Not at all, not at all. Spring has come – it is entirely natural.' He took off his hat and fanned himself. 'But I think I am still too young to be in want of a wife. This is my first position, I am only just arrived—'

'That's right, sir. Plenty of time.'

'He'm building a nest,' said Tommy all at once from the step.

'Who's that, then?' Birley asked, and Tommy said: 'Him over there in the hedge.'

And they stood in the warm spring sunshine watching the darting in and out of a thrush, skimming the air with a beak full of hay and scraps of wool, while all around them came the sounds of the river, pouring down over the weir beyond the bridge, pouring through the great slats of the turning wheel of the mill, as the carrier came to a halt and the chestnut cob shook his head and the calling of lamb and songbird filled the air.

'This is as lovely a place as any upon earth,' said Richard at length, and Birley nodded.

'It is today.'

Then they parted, and Richard walked back to the house to thank Martha Price for her morning's work, and to eat his bread and cheese at the open window, while the warbling world sought out its mate and the daffodils began to open in the sun.

18th March 1861

The wind is blowing so fresh and alive across the fields; everything quickens: in the world; in me. Birley told me this morning that I was in want of a wife, but this, I fear, is something I shall never have.

What would she do, were I to speak? What could become of us? And Bowen himself looks so drawn and ill: how can I ever think of such things? It is a travesty of all I have believed in.

Yet I see her, here with me, walking across the wet orchard grass all strewn with blossom, lifting the latch, coming in to be close before the fire, climbing the stairs with me, to be closer still.

He slammed shut the journal, he slammed shut the drawer and turned the key. He dropped it into a little brown jug on the mantelpiece, which a woman would have filled with primroses. He took down his hat and coat and went out down the path to the stream, tumbling over itself through the gap in the hedge. He could see wet violets, there, beneath the thorn. The cries of the lambs tore the air. He walked up the track beneath trees just brushed with a painter's green, in a passion of self-reproach and shame.

From somewhere deep in the woods he heard the rumble of a cart, and the cackle of hens. In winter everything had been so breathless and still that you could hear the slightest footfall; now a myriad of sounds came from farm and homestead, and before he had reached the highway he had greeted a man and his boy chopping wood in a clearing, an old biddy out with her basket, collecting primroses, and the farmer from the top, come down with his dog to check the last lambing ewes.

Yes, he was the new curate. No, he had not drunk primrose wine, but thought his grandmother used to make it, and he should like to try some. Yes, the lambs woke him at dawn, but he did not mind for he was content to be here in his cottage by the stream, and had a good woman to help him and much company to look forward to, as the spring and summer came, and the evenings lightened.

He lifted his hat, he bid them all good day, he came out on to the highway feeling steadier, seeing the fields on the far side pricked with a sudden mass of young green corn, and a scarecrow of sacking and straw flap in the wind, with a hat at a comical angle.

Dearest Emily, Forgive me for not writing for a little while. I confess to have been feeling rather out of sorts, but today is a wonderful spring day, and I feel much refreshed.

A carriage and pair came trotting briskly past. The wind blew and as he came down the hill and rounded the corner he could hear the racket of rooks in the churchyard. His stomach tightened. Was she there? Would he see her today?

At once he reproached himself. Three boys were waiting for him, to be prepared for confirmation, were they not? This was his task; he must collect himself.

'Rehearse the Articles of thy Belief.'

'I believe in God the Father Almighty, Maker of heaven and earth …'

'Very good, Thomas.'

He was a curate, he was a man of God, his life had, as every life must, its own particular purpose. He touched his father's prayerbook in the pocket of his coat: man and book as steady as the rock whereon the Church was founded. Ahead, the weathercock on the tower of his own church swung to the east, towards his old home and family. Oh, how he missed them all!

He came to the entrance to the churchyard path and heard, from the laurel-screened house across the road behind the laurels, the sudden sharp slam of a door.

What was that … What need, on a bright spring day, to slam a door? Was wondering this a part of his pastoral duties? For a moment he hesitated, recalling the pinched, shrinking little face of Mrs Prosser. Perhaps he would call on them later. Perhaps he would not. He was almost late.

He had come to the top of the path; he pushed open the lich-gate. Across the churchyard he could see, at his desk, the figure of Oliver Bowen, gazing out. He lifted his hat: he must call, either before or after his catechism class. He was late: after. And he turned to walk along the empty path towards the schoolhouse, seeing only then a tall thin person at a graveside, his hat held before him, his head bowed, his black coat drooping a little at the hem.

Alfred Arndell.

Richard stopped. The depth of the young man's loneliness and misery was almost palpable: he was set apart; he did not know what to do with himself; he had not known that life could be like this.

Daffodils blew amongst the graves, sun and shade played over the bright new grass. Arndell, in mourning, was black as a rook. His shoulders were shaking.

Richard found his own eyes filled with tears.

'Mr Arndell?' He cleared his throat; he walked towards him. 'Mr Arndell?'

He came up beside him, saw the little bunch of primroses laid beneath the stone. His arm went round the thin shoulders. Arndell could not speak. Richard did not try. At length he said simply: 'I am so very sorry.'

Arndell nodded. 'It is hard.' He took out his handkerchief, and wiped his eyes. 'Almost a twelvemonth. I ask myself why God wanted this for her. For us. Not even a little one to comfort me – but then, I would not want him motherless.' The handkerchief went back into his pocket. Across from the schoolhouse they could hear the children, chanting. ''Tis a sweet sound,' said Arndell, 'though when I was in there I was as restless as any. I met her there, my poor little girl. We courted from

120

when we was fourteen. I never thought …' He moved away from the foot of the grave and Richard moved with him, on to the path. 'What do you think, Mr Allen? Why should the Good Lord let this be?'

Richard was silent. He said at last: 'In truth, Mr Arndell, you have more real experience in life than I have. I am sure that God moves with a purpose – yet, I can give you no real answer, save that your Lizzie is happy now.'

Clerical phrases. Platitudes. What use the catechism against such grief?

Arndell looked at him.

'Happy?' he said, and his loneliness fell like a cloak about them both. 'I hope she is,' he said, 'for I upon this earth could not feel more abandoned.'

And he nodded to Richard and walked away, along the path beneath the yews, and up to the vicarage, upon whose door he knocked, and was admitted by Millie. The door closed to.

Gone to seek counsel from an older, wiser man. Someone he knew and trusted.

Would he be given better answers? What answers were there?

Richard's hand closed round his father's prayerbook, with its slip of paper marking the pages of the catechism.

'What is thy duty towards God?'

'My duty towards God, is to believe in him, to fear him, and to love him with all my heart, with all my mind, with all my soul, and with all my strength; to worship him, to give him thanks, to put my whole trust in him …'

He walked to the schoolhouse door, scraped the mud from his boots, and lifted the knocker. Thirty chanting voices drew breath, and were instructed to resume.

'*These* are the *cap*-i-tals of *Eur*-ope …'

Miss Hatfield was taking the class, and although sometimes she came to answer the door herself, bidding the children be good as gold, today it was not she whose footsteps sounded in the hall, and who lifted the latch, but Susannah.

Richard's stomach rose and fell like a bird on the air.

'Mrs Bowen.' He took off his hat. He bowed. 'Good afternoon.'

'Good afternoon, Mr Allen.'

12

He thought of her all the time, yet when he saw her now she seemed like a stranger. She smiled at him. Smiling at one another was something they did often. Yet how great was the gulf between everything he shared with her in the seclusion of his mind, and the remarks they made to one another when they met.

She took his hat. He thanked her. He took off his gloves; he saw she looked drawn and tired. Though weeks had passed since the skating party, and her tears, brushed quickly away, she had not recovered herself: he sensed this now, as he had done at each subsequent meeting – in the church porch after a service; when he called at the vicarage to see her husband; when from time to time he stayed on for luncheon or tea. Always there were other people present; there was a smile, but it was quickly gone; now, as he took his prayerbook from his pocket and unbuttoned his coat, seeing the rows of children through the open schoolroom door, he thought that those sorrowful words by the frozen lake were the only unguarded words she had ever said to him, spoken straight from the heart – 'She was expecting a child.' He had not known how to answer her, and in this sudden moment alone, hearing the tap of the pointer on the board, and the scrape of slate and pencil, he did not know how to proceed.

'How are you keeping, Mrs Bowen?'

'Quite well, thank you.'

'You are a little tired, perhaps?' He laid the prayerbook upon the hatstand shelf, whereon her own gloves rested.

'I have had something of a spring cold, but it is almost gone.'

'I am glad to hear it.'

He hung up his coat on a hook by the row of the children's small coats and cloaks and jackets, with Miss Hatfield's cloak on one side and Susannah's on the other. This was not her Sunday cloak, but an everyday wool in which to go down to the village, or to slip on when coming across the churchyard for her lessons here. It was worn, and had been out in all weathers: he noticed a little darn on one of the folds: something as intimate and distinctive as a scar, which made the garment exclusively her own. From the schoolroom the children's voices rose again, as they learned the great world by heart.

'Par-is, the river Seine. Rome, the river Ti-ber.'

'And Mr Bowen?' he asked her, as she stood waiting. 'How is he keeping in this bright spring weather?'

He might have been addressing an old woman in the village, leaning upon her garden fence; not this pale unhappy girl – yes, that was surely what she was – standing in the schoolhouse hall in a gown as grey as a winter afternoon.

'He is still not quite better. Dr Probyn hopes for an improvement as the weather gets warmer.'

'I'm sure we all hope for that.'

The boys at the back of the class were turning surreptitiously to glance at him, then back to the board: his confirmation boys, William Fletcher, Tom Meredith, John Bampfield, all no doubt itching for the escape from schoolroom routine he offered. He could see the patched boots drying against the schoolroom stove: no doubt they had been across the fields at dinner time. In forty minutes the bell would ring for the end of the day – how could he prolong this minute now?

He said: 'I saw young Mr Arndell on my way across.'

'Did you?'

'He tells me it is almost a year since he lost his wife, that they were at school here together. Poor fellow, I fear I was able to offer him little comfort.'

How he despised himself now – discussing another man's sorrow in order to extend a conversation.

'Mr Arndell's grief is such that it is hard for any of us to comfort him. I am sure that you did your best.'

Susannah was looking at him directly. It was a good true answer. He looked back directly at her.

How long did they hold one another's gaze? Thinking about it afterwards, he knew it could not have been for more than a few moments, yet it seemed to go on for a long time, and in that gaze, clear and unsmiling, he knew that she too wished to prolong this encounter, and that, in some measure, his feelings for her were returned.

Well – he had always known this, had he not? It had needed only a moment alone, the smallest sign. Now she had given it to him.

Their lives, with this knowledge between them, now lay ahead, quite uncharted.

He said: 'Mr Arndell has gone to visit your husband.'

'Has he? Then I shall see him myself, perhaps, when I return.' She was moving towards the schoolroom door. 'Perhaps, when your catechism class is over, you might like to join us for tea?'

'I should like that very much. I had intended to visit Mr Bowen, only I promised my neighbour to conduct his little daughter home after school.'

'Alice Birley.'

'Yes.'

'You might bring her with you. Just for a little while.'

Then she pushed the door of the schoolroom wide, and he saw the blackboard, chalked up with the names of capital cities which he had never visited, just as for these country children they surely must always be as distant and mysterious as India. As London, even.

Paris. Rome. Madrid. Berlin. Warsaw. Prague.

They copied them down on their slates, they closed their eyes and chanted them, the girls in their blue cotton pinafores, the boys in their grey serge jackets, kicking one another beneath the benches. He smiled at his three fellows, gestured to them to rise, make their excuses, and come stumbling along the row towards him. He bid Miss Hatfield a very good afternoon, and thanked her; he felt happiness fill every cell in his blood as Susannah quietly followed him into the room. He thought: we belong together. He saw Alice Birley, up at the front, serious and careful as she rubbed at her slate. The spring sun was pouring through the window, and the room smelled of coal from the cast-iron stove. Dust floated in its shimmer of heat, as if in the shafts of light within a church.

Within a church, those shafts illuminating Norman stone or eighteenth-century oak looked holy, pouring from the heavens as a sign of eternal love. The dust danced within them like timeless human souls: before birth, in the dance of life, and after death. Here, in this warm schoolroom, with the texts and samplers and the old engraving of the young Queen upon her coronation hanging behind Miss Hatfield's high desk, the light was more diffuse, and its effect was of a painting, touching here and there the bent heads of the children. The smell of the coal was like that from the great furnace of the train as it came steaming through the valley, on and on.

Who knew but that these country schoolchildren might one day travel far from the place where they were born? As the new age of steam came rushing past even this quiet village, might it not bear them away, towards these cities upon the blackboard, towards an unimagined future?

He led his boys out from the class. They took their places in the little storeroom off the hall, filled with old primers, spare pinafores, boxes of chalk. They coughed and settled down; he could see them nervously running the week's catechism questions through their minds. Would their future still hold God, he wondered, he who had always thought that God held the world entire. Would the old answers be enough?

'What is thy duty towards thy Neighbour?'

'My duty towards my Neighbour, is to love him as myself, and to do to all men, as I would they should do unto me: To love, honour, and succour my father and mother: To honour and obey the Queen, and all that are put in authority under her ...'

John Bampfield came to a halt, twisting a button upon his flannel shirt.

'To subject myself to all my governors,' prompted Richard.

'To submit myself to all my governors, teachers, spiritual pastors and masters: To order myself lowly and reverently to all my betters ...'

For a moment, listening, Richard remembered Christmas morning, standing at his bedroom window, watching the sheep move slowly over the hillside in the frost beneath the stars. Would people still remember, a thousand years from now? Would they still care for

Bethlehem? That had been his first moment of doubt. Another had been today, in the churchyard, struggling to find an answer for a young widower bewildered by death.

But now – now, observing the farmers' sons before him, the sweet, open face of John Bampfield as he struggled to recall that he must keep his body in temperance, soberness and chastity, must labour to get his own living; as he listened to Tom Meredith, whose boots showed his socks, though he tried to hide it; rewarded William Fletcher's flawless response with a 'Good man, William,' and saw the blush of pleasure – now he let his mind flash to Susannah, to the long pure look which had passed between them, saying, in silence, everything.

He knew he would return to it, over and over again.

How could God not lie within such happiness? How could such happiness not belong with God?

By mid-afternoon it was growing cold again, the sun almost gone and the weathercock creaking in the wind as he left the schoolhouse and walked with Alice through the churchyard towards the vicarage. Behind them the children were streaming down to the lich-gate, though a few ran past them – 'Excuse us, sir!' – to push through the gate in the north wall, which opened into Parson's Plock and the footpath across the fields. Always, as she lined them up after ringing the bell, Miss Hatfield bid them leave quietly, and walk nicely; always, they broke away and set off at full tilt.

'What a noise they make,' said Richard. 'Almost as noisy as the rooks.'

Alice nodded, with a polite little smile.

'I expect you are anxious to get home yourself,' he said. 'Do you mind making this small excursion?'

She shook her head, but he could feel her shyness, away from everyone, with the prospect of grown-up talk.

'We shan't be long.' They turned up the path towards the house. 'I told your father I should call on Mr Bowen after school, so they will not worry. Come, take my hand.' She did so; and his own nerves quietened – for yes, he was nervous now, filled with a strange mixture of elation and apprehension. Within his leather glove he felt Alice's own small woollen one, and remembered the way she had twisted and twisted a finger of it in her longing for the doll at the market stall.

'How is Peg?' he asked her. 'Forgive me – I mean Victoria.'

'She is well.'

'Does she ever come to school?'

Alice shook her head. 'We are not permitted to bring our playthings.'

'Of course not. But I expect she misses you.'

'I think she does.'

'And how does she occupy the time?'

How sweet to talk like this, how quickly he could feel himself drawn into Victoria's long lonely day and the loving reunion at its close; how easy it was to imagine her taking her place at the supper table, and the crust she might like to eat – as if he were reading a children's book, or even writing one. As if he had a daughter of his own.

'What stories does Victoria like best?' he asked, as they came to the porch, and then he saw through the window on the left the sheen of pale hair within the shadowy parlour, and did not hear the answer.

She was waiting for him, perhaps had watched him and Alice walk hand in hand along the windy path. Had he dreamed that long look between them? When she reached home, had everything seemed blessedly familiar, as she hung up her cloak in the hall? Or did she turn in its gloom to look at the closed door of her husband's study and ask herself—

'Mr Allen?'

'Alice, I'm so sorry.' She was looking up at him as they stood on the threshold of the porch, with its rusty bootscraper and broken flags. There was the knocker: he knocked, smiling down at her.

'You were lost in thought,' she said.

'What a grown-up phrase.'

'Miss Hatfield says it to me.'

'Does she? And what do you—'

And then Millie opened the door and the dull light behind them showed the brass pot of ferns, the face of the grandfather clock, the engraving of a man half dead, brought back to life with the touch of Christ.

THE MYSTERIES OF GLASS

'Good afternoon, Mr Allen, sir. Hello, Alice. Here's someone come to see you, I think.'

Alice, as Richard ushered her in, saw the vicarage cat appear from nowhere, and her face lit up.

'Samuel!'

'Have you known one another a long time?' Richard asked her, taking his hat off, following her inside.

'Samuel's older than you are, isn't he, Alice?' said Millie, taking her things. 'He lived here even before Mr and Mrs Bowen.'

Alice nodded, kneeling upon the drugget, her arms round the cat as he rubbed her cheek with his.

'He has a *very* loud purr!'

'Indeed he does,' said Susannah, from the open parlour door.

'Mrs Bowen.' Richard bowed.

And this is a tableau, he thought, as he handed his hat and gloves to Millie. An engraving after a painting by Millais or Wallace. *The Child's Best Friend.* The little girl, the cat, the smiling servant; the solidity of that clock; the fond parents observing their daughter's innocent happiness. We might all be models for such a scene – the kind of picture my mother likes. And then, as the door of the study slowly opened, and Oliver Bowen leaned upon its frame, the picture changed: no longer a simple domestic interior but a morality tale, after Hunt, perhaps. *The Husband's Discovery.* It wanted only the young wife's dissolution into tears, her kneeling before him in a flood of shame, while her lover hung his head.

'Good afternoon, Allen.'

'Good afternoon, sir.' Richard flushed. How could he let his mind run away like this? He took off his coat, with his father's prayerbook deep within the pocket. 'How are you today?'

'Well enough. Mr Arndell has been keeping me company.'

'Yes, sir.' Beyond him, Richard could see Arndell's gaunt figure at the fireside, his pale, tear-stained face. Again, he felt a rush of self-reproach: that he should be already so self-preoccupied, while a man his own age was suffering such pain. He nodded towards him; Arndell smiled wanly.

'Will I bring tea to the parlour, ma'am?' asked Millie, turning from the coat-stand.

'Will that suit you, Oliver?' Susannah asked him.

Another tableau: she at the door to the parlour, with its piano and writing desk, and heaps of sewing, the cat now disentangling himself and making his way through there; he at the entrance to his study, lined with books and filled with papers. *Husband and Wife*, and between them a cold dark hall.

The grandfather clock struck the half-hour. Alice had scrambled to her feet and stood uncertainly, looking after Samuel but not daring to follow until she was told.

'Tea in the parlour,' said Oliver Bowen, and Richard could feel how he fought for breath and how magnificently he won the battle. 'Mr Allen …' He indicated the room behind him, and Richard stepped forward. 'We shall join you directly,' Bowen said to Susannah, and then, as if seeing her for the first time, 'Good afternoon, Alice.'

'Sir.' She dropped a little curtsy, then quickly followed Susannah into the parlour's warmth.

The study door closed behind them. Arndell half rose, then sank again into the high-winged chair. Books were heaped on the table beside it: glancing at the pile, Richard saw one or two new bindings, set upon the worn volumes of Tennyson and Wordsworth, which always lay there. Bowen indicated that he should take the chair opposite, with the castor in need of mending which made the whole unsteady. Richard sat down carefully, as the rector made his way to his desk. It was heaped with papers, as usual: with notes, with bills on a spike, with tracts from the Episcopalians and books from the Kington Reading Room. Beneath the window, beside his lettercase and book of stamps, the set of little brass weights and scales gleamed in the fading light. An upturned tumbler stood upon a carafe.

'Mr Arndell and I have been discussing the Will of God,' said Bowen.

'Sir.'

Bowen looked at him. Arndell gazed into the fire. 'The Will of God is something we may not question,' Bowen continued. He was sitting at an angle to his desk, and he leaned upon it, his hands clasped before him. 'We know that our passage through this world is often difficult, that we are beset by obstacles, by temptations.' He paused.

'Sometimes the very best of us will doubt and question. But such doubts and uncertainties—' He drew a breath, and then another; then broke visibly into a sweat as a spasm of coughing seized him.

'Sir—'

Richard rose, and went to him. The cough filled the room, bubbling horribly.

'I'll go for water,' said Arndell, and made for the door, but Bowen banged on the desk, shook his head and gestured, gasping, at the glass and carafe, which already stood there. Richard held him; Arndell poured water into the glass with a trembling hand. Bowen drank, his shoulders heaving. He fumbled for his handkerchief; at last he was calm.

'Thank you.' He waved them to return to their chairs; he wiped his brow. 'It passes,' he said. 'It always passes. God is helping me through, as He helps each one of us.' He took another sip of water. 'His Will is perfect and pure. We in our blindness may not be able to see his design, but we know it is there; that it is our duty to keep to the path, to accept what ills befall us. Our duty. "Lead us not into temptation" – doubt is one of those temptations, perhaps the worst of all. We must resist. We must be strong.'

'Amen,' said Alfred Arndell quietly.

'Fine words, sir,' said Richard. 'Thank you. They are worthy of a Lenten sermon. Will you preach them as that, this Sunday?'

Bowen rested his head in his hands, leaning upon his heaped-up desk. The carafe was empty. His clothes hung off him. He said slowly: 'I am not well enough to climb the pulpit steps. Not at present. We look to you to guide the flock, Mr Allen. For you to restore certainty when some lose their way in the wilderness. For you to bring them home.'

'Amen,' said Arndell again, and then: 'I have come home, sir, thanks to you. I do feel stronger now.'

'I am glad to hear it.'

There came a tap at the door; Millie entered.

'Please, sir, Mrs Bowen is sorry to interrupt you, but the tea has been standing and Alice Birley must be taken home.'

'Indeed. Gentlemen ...' Bowen waved them from the room. 'I shall join you directly.' He leaned upon his desk once more, looking out to the darkening churchyard, where shadowy daffodils blew amongst the graves.

And Richard took tea with Susannah and Alice and Alfred Arndell, who commanded the conversation, and took it upon himself to pass the muffins.

'Your husband is the finest man alive, Mrs Bowen. I have never heard such good strong words, have you, Mr Allen? I know that Mr Bowen can seem stern at times, but 'tis better to be stern than weak, and he has done me a power of good. My Lizzie would not want me to maunder and weep for ever – I must be strong too. Do you hear me, Alice Birley? Do you know in whose house you are taking tea? The house of a great good man. You will remember that when you are grown.'

'Yes, Mr Arndell.'

The cat lay curled upon the hearthrug, the fire blazed, the clock in the hall ticked steadily.

Contentment, thought Richard, a little detached part of him observing the scene as a canvas. *At the Fireside*. But though with a tiny part of his mind he was able to look upon the parlour thus, he knew he was taking refuge from turmoil. A sick man had reproved him: he was in no doubt of that. He had been told to give guidance, not tentative answers to grief and fear. He had been charged with the work of the parish. Not just a young curate but a deputy, a man.

'Mr Allen?'

Susannah was regarding him from the other side of the hearth. The firelight played across her face; her eyes held a troubled question, which must be acknowledged, answered.

He returned her gaze: once more, for a moment or two, the whole world fell away. This day had changed everything.

'Now you are both lost in thought,' said Alice.

He walked her home through the woods. Millie had lent him a lantern; its beam swung between them on the path. Alice held his other hand; rook and pigeon beat through the dusky trees. Richard thought of all the questions he had turned over in his mind that day, of his three boys stumbling over the catechism's certainties.

'How many parts are there in a Sacrament?'

'Two; the outward visible sign, and the inward and spiritual grace.'

'What is the inward and spiritual grace?'

'A death unto sin, and a new birth unto righteousness ...'

What step towards sin had he and Susannah truly taken in that long, unveiled exchange of glances?

It was growing dark. How comforting to hold a child's hand in his; how sweet to be a father, taking his daughter home.

'Not far now,' he told her, and heard her suppress a yawn. What a long day she had had.

And he thought of all the children in that crowded schoolroom, their heads bent over their slates, copying the names of unknown cities, beneath the framed texts that had been part of his own childhood. *The Lord is my Shepherd. Jesus said: Follow Me.* Beside them, the calm face of the young crowned Queen gazed dreamily out of a painted frame from forty years ago, her hand on a balustrade, while the great British lion slumbered at her feet.

'What should you like to be when you are grown?' he asked Alice, but this she could not answer.

13

He had gone. It was dark. Millie was moving about in the kitchen, washing up the tea things; soon, she would come through to light the lamps and move the household towards evening, and supper, and reading by the fire.

The fire in here was low; she should make it up. The lamp was unlit; she should light it. She should draw the curtains against the windy churchyard, she should cross the hall to her husband, who had not joined them for tea. His cough, even behind the closed door, had been terrible to hear: he must be resting; she must go and see.

Susannah sat in the button-backed chair by the fire and did none of these things. The sinking flames shadowed the parlour she knew so well: the convex mirror above the mantel, the wooden cross and china dogs upon it; her husband's wing chair across the hearth, the cat now stretched out towards it on the rug; her davenport, her sewing basket.

Everything looked different now. She was different now.

Beside her chair stood her table of books. *The Imitation of Christ*, given by her parents at her confirmation and always kept by her. John Clare's *The Shepherd's Calendar*, such pretty verses. The novels which came from Mudie's, to the new library in Kington: *Scenes of Clerical Life*. *Doctor Thorne*. Now there was another, the first volume of Mr Eliot's new novel. She had sunk herself into it, nursing her cold for a whole long day at the start of the week, doing nothing for once, for a childless woman, even the wife of a rector, could be ill if she must. The novel was called *The Mill on the Floss*, and featured a wilful girl. It was said that Mr George Eliot, its author, was in truth a woman, and lived in London with a man who was not her husband.

Susannah covered her face.

Before her, the cat rolled over on the rug, and brushed the hem of her gown.

'Oh, Samuel.'

She bent to pick him up. What a weight he was. She buried her cheek in his soot-black fur, laid him upon her lap.

'I must be very wicked,' she whispered.

The wind stirred the trees in the churchyard, the dense dark yew, the towering elms. It was spring, it was dark —

'— *And there is no health in us.*'

A line from the Confession, murmured each Sunday in that freezing church.

'*We have erred, and strayed from thy Ways like lost sheep.*'

Her husband's voice led them through the familiar words; she knew them by heart, she had always known them, murmuring them like poetry, wondering what to confess. Now she knew, as she listened for Richard Allen's quieter, younger voice, rising and falling, like tenor to bass. To think of him as she did ...

'*Look down upon us, we beseech Thee, as we stand in this place of sin ...*'

That ruined girl had stepped out into the dreadful blackness of the lake.

Susannah covered her face again, as the icy waters rose.

He woke at the tap on the door.

'Mr Bowen, sir?'

'Millie.' The room was quite dark, the fire almost out. 'What time is it?'

'Six o'clock, sir.' And even as she spoke the clock began its measured chime in the hall. She had lit the lamp there, and stood in the doorway now against its light. 'I thought I should come to see how you were.'

The last stroke sounded.

'Thank you. That was kind. I meant only to close my eyes for a few minutes.'

'You haven't been well, sir, you need the rest. Shall I light your lamp now? And see to that fire?'

'Leave it. I've been in this room long enough for one day.' He rubbed his face, he sat up, and the pain raised its head in its lair. He put his hand to his mouth.

'Sir?'

He shook his head, feeling old. 'Nothing.' He was forty-six. There were younger men lying out there beneath the grass.

'Shall I help you, sir?'

'Not yet. A glass of water.'

She moved in the shadows towards the desk; he heard the chink of tumbler and carafe. Then she went out, leaving the door open wide. The clock ticked, the lamp glowed. Across the hall the parlour door was closed. He could hear the gush of water into the stone sink in the kitchen, and was suddenly parched. Why had Susannah not been to see him? Who had been here today? Allen. Allen and that poor weak fellow. And the Birley child.

'Here we are, sir.'

The glass on the papier-mâché tray. 'Thank you.' He drank and drank.

'Ah, that's better. Is Mrs Bowen in the parlour? I must go and keep her company.' Once more he made to get up; this time, strengthened by the long cold drink, he was able to do so.

'Mrs Bowen is not feeling well, sir. She has gone upstairs to rest.'

'Oh. Oh dear.' He stood there for a moment, quite taken aback. 'What a household. I had thought she was feeling much better.'

'You know these spring colds, sir. You think you've shaken them off and then you get chilled outside, or sit in a draught, and they take hold all over again.'

'Yes. Yes, of course they do.'

'I'll make up the fire in the parlour, I'll bring you your supper on a tray. Would that suit you?'

'Yes. Yes, it would. Thank you. What a household,' he said again. 'You must find us dull.'

'I should never think that, sir.'

'You're very good, Millie.'

He walked slowly into the hall; he paused at the foot of the stairs. He should go up there, and see how she was. But then he would have to come down again, and climb the stairs again when he went to bed.

They were narrow and steep, like the path to heaven. He must conserve his strength.

Millie was behind him, closing the study door. He walked across the drugget, glancing up at the picture of Lazarus, which Susannah had thought rather sombre for a hall, but which he had felt offered hope to all who came here. Even the dead could be healed by Christ's miraculous power. Behold the great beauty of that outstretched hand, that look of holy love which promised everything.

'Heal me now, Lord,' he murmured, feeling the pain of this little exertion uncurl within him and begin to gnaw. 'Heal me now.'

14

P alm Sunday, 1861. The woods filled with paper-white anemones; catkins swaying over the stream; the birds a concert hall. The lambs and the ewes cried for one another long after dusk, and Richard was woken by them long before the dawn.

Susannah. Today I am to conduct the old service we all so loved as children. What a strange occasion it is, so full of singing and joy in the procession, as if something radiant must lie at its conclusion, when all the time the shadow of the Cross lies over it, and death awaits Our Lord. Yet it is made domestic and familiar, through the presence of the donkey, the carrying of the palm crosses fashioned in Sunday School.

This morning I shall see you again. The grass sparkles with dew before my window on to the field, the trees are in such glorious fresh leaf, the full-throated birds a miracle. I feel the presence of God in every note they sing, in each call of the lambs, each dissolving white cloud in the pearly sky. I feel Him in every breath I take and in my love for you, which, though it is something we must both know is forbidden, fills my heart with such happiness that I cannot believe but that God in His goodness, in His own time, might one day bless us both.

He blotted the page of his journal. He closed it, he locked it away. Then he bowed his head, closed his eyes at his desk.

Father, forgive me. Forgive me. Let me but pour my heart out here. Let me but dream of her. And help me to find a way through—

Through the open casement window at the front came the sweet rushing sound of the stream running past his garden, beneath the lane and out into the woods. From where, amidst water and birdsong, he now heard something else. A footfall, then another. He got up, he went to look. And through the woods' mist of green, in the gentle morning light upon dark earth, mossy trunk and the paper-white flowers, he saw her.

Her hood was back and her hair was down. She was carrying a basket. She could be any country woman, out gathering wild mushrooms, or primroses for wine, while the dew still lay upon them. Yet he knew that this was not her only purpose, and that she had meant him to see her.

He lifted the slender iron bar of the casement, and let it fall upon the sill. A finch flew out of the mountain ash. The woman amongst the trees stood still.

Richard, in his father's cassock and white tie – so she would see he was a churchman, or did she already know this? – unlocked his front door and walked down the grassy path to the gate. A pheasant croaked, deep within the woods. He opened the gate, and a sheep behind the thorn hedge trotted quickly away, her lamb bleating after her. He crossed to the bank where the stream entered the woods, and climbed quickly upon it.

He called out: 'Good morning.'

She did not answer, but he could see her quite clearly now, standing beneath the cathedral of trees, watching his approach.

His breathing quickened. He had an impulse to do something he had never done in his life: to cross himself, as if he were in mortal danger. It was a papist gesture quite out of keeping with anything in his past, and for an instant, as his hand went to his chest, he thought: how divided we all are from one another. We all must be children of God.

Then he lowered his hand, and said, as if it would protect him, 'This is a holy day.'

'What day is it?'

Her voice was low, with the same rounded vowel and softened consonant the Birleys had. Her face was thin, her eyes dark, like the loose hair falling to her shoulders. He had never seen a grown woman

140

with her hair like this – even Emily wore her hair up now. Except, he thought again, amongst the gypsies, camping in the long grass, lighting their fires. Perhaps that was all she was: a gypsy come down from her encampment on Hergest Ridge, to live by herself for a while.

Why should she do that?

He said: 'It is the day Our Lord rode into Jerusalem. Palm Sunday.'

She nodded. 'And then it is Easter.'

'Yes.' He hesitated. 'And then—'

'Then Whitsuntide.'

She knew it all.

'I remember,' she said, watching him. 'I remember from schooling.'

'I do not see you in church.'

'No.'

'And why is that?'

'The church put me in prison.'

'What did you say?'

'I said the church put me in prison.'

Across the great stretch of land between two parishes, St Mary's in Kington, St Michael and All Angels in Lyonshall, across the wooded hills, the open fields of the farms, where sheep and cattle grazed in the early morning sun, across stile and track and river, came the timeless sound of the bells, calling down the centuries, calling to prayer. Palm Sunday. The children would be gathering in the church-yard. His head was spinning.

She said: 'Every day of my freedom is holy to me now.'

He looked at her. He swallowed. He thought of her lonely shut-tered dwelling high up in the woods on the Rushock hill, beyond the farms, amongst the birds, the last house for miles and miles. He said: 'Are you in hiding?'

She nodded. 'I am, but it does not trouble me. The world means little to me now.'

'Yet you have sought me out. Have you not? I have sensed you watching me since the day of my arrival.'

'You are new here. You are not a man of the world.'

'I am a man of the Church. You have turned away from the Church.'

141

'But not from God.'

And he thought of her upraised arms, her look of rapture, as the trees all around her dripped from the winter rain, and the streams ran with melted snow.

The bells rang out, from one tower to another across the fields. In his own churchyard the children would be lining up behind John Blakely's donkey with homemade crosses, ready to process across to the church, as he had done as a child. As Susannah must have done, and perhaps this woman, standing before him beneath the soaring trees. Ritual and prayer united all of them, though she had broken away.

He said: 'I am taking the service. I must go.' He hesitated. 'May I ask your name?'

She looked at him steadily. 'Edith Clare. I trust you to tell no one.'

'I shall not. And perhaps I shall see you again?'

'Perhaps.' And she turned and walked away from him, going deeper into woods which she knew well and he was only beginning to know. He watched her: she took a turning towards the sound of the river. Then she was gone.

Palm cross and prayerbook. The children were all lined up at the gate, faces scrubbed, Sunday pinafores and jackets sponged and pressed. Their crosses were fashioned of sun-bleached reeds; at the front of the line John Blakely's old donkey stood like a rock. Miss Hatfield was holding his halter; she tried to disguise her relief as Richard came up the path, uncomfortably warm from the rapid walk in cassock, surplice and stole. Thirty-two faces turned towards him.

'I was delayed – I am so very sorry.'

The bells had fallen silent. Across the churchyard, through the open south door, the muted strains of the organ sounded; he could hear the rustle and cough of the waiting congregation.

'No matter at all, Mr Allen.'

'You are very kind. Good morning, children.' He looked along the line of them all, tiny Laura Middleship and Maggie Neve at the front, his great confirmation boys shifting from foot to foot at the back, their crosses held self-consciously before them.

'Good morning, Mr Allen.'

Their voices rose in chorus; he could feel their excitement and solemnity. Four or five children back, Alice Birley, grave and still, stood next to Jenny Neve; he smiled at her; he smiled upon them all.

'This is a special holy day. This morning we shall all process into church in memory of Our Lord's procession into Jerusalem. You all know about this day, do you not? And I am so pleased to see you all, to lead you into church with the help of this fine fellow.' He patted the donkey's nose; the bony head went up. A little ripple of smiles ran down the row. 'He is a good patient beast; I shall be talking to you about him in my sermon. Now – we are to sing a special hymn. Who will remind me which it is?'

'There is a green hill, sir.'

'There is a green hill.' Shy voices all along the line.

'Very good. God bless you all. Miss Hatfield, you are quite ready?'

She nodded. She was wearing a fresh spring gown; he smiled at her and she blushed deeply. Then she moved to let him take up his place before them all, and he opened his hymn book, though he knew the words by heart.

Miss Hatfield made a little clicking sound; the donkey stepped forward; everything began.

> 'There is a green hill far away,
> Without a city wall,
> Where the dear Lord was crucified,
> Who died to save us all.'

Their crosses held before them, they wound their way up the path, singing beneath the morning sky and the ungainly rooks, cawing and flapping in the elms; Richard up at the front, in billowing surplice and the green and gold stole of Passiontide.

They came to the fork in the path whose left arm ran towards the vicarage.

Richard, singing, glanced up towards the house. He saw a white face at an upper window.

He could not stop, he could not raise a hand in greeting, but how he felt the loneliness and exclusion of the sickroom, at that ivy-shrouded window. Had many of the children singing behind him also seen that face? Would their memory of a Palm Sunday led by the young curate be for ever marked by a man like a ghost looking out at them all as they passed?

> 'We may not know, we cannot tell
> What pains He had to bear,
> But we believe it was for us
> He hung and suffered there.'

The spring wind stirred the clumps of daffodils. They were approaching the porch. John Blakely's boy was waiting outside to take the donkey during the service. Within, Richard could see the bright gleam of the cross on its pole, as the verger stepped forward from the shadows and lifted it, ready for him to take, and raise high.

'*The church put me in prison.*'

For what? Had Bowen been amongst that company of men?

> 'Oh, dearly, dearly has He loved,
> And we must love Him too ...'

The words of the last verse came to an end; the children's footsteps came to a halt on the flags. Within the church, Richard could see faces from the pews at the back turn towards them all. Then Thomas Hatton began to play the fine tune of the hymn, Richard stepped forward, took the cross, and bowed his head. He carried it in through the door, he raised it high; behind him the children walked quietly through, and then the procession down the aisle began, with the hymn repeated and the congregation all raising their voices to join them. 'There is a green hill far away ...'

He felt the magnificence of the moment, one for which he had been preparing all his life, as he moved slowly down the aisle, the church filled with the ever-changing light and shade of spring through plain glass windows, dust spinning timelessly within it, while at the front stood the young woman for whom nothing in his innocent secluded life could ever have prepared him, nor her for him.

And if it were not a sin, to be so aware of her as he approached her pew, and felt her hesitant gaze rest upon him as he wished he might so gaze on her, then what was it, he asked himself, as he came to the transept, lowered and carried the cross through the screen and then turned to face his congregation. He was already lost. In truth, he had no place here.

'Palm Sunday. A man rides into a city on a warm spring day and is greeted by a crowd waving branches torn down from the trees on the dusty roadside. The air is full of the smell of fresh leaves; they strew his path and the ass he is riding steps over them, bearing him through the crowd as the sun rises higher and the leaves become fans in the heat ...'

Richard raised his eyes from the pages before him; he leaned a little upon the rim of the pulpit, and looked out over the congregation. All the children were returned to their own families now, and some, after the long service and the glory of the procession, were grown tired and restless. He could see Laura Middleship's eyes begin to close, and Will Fletcher running a hand round his neck to ease a tight starched collar. No matter; he had prepared this sermon for the children, he would deliver it, and in a moment they would be awake again. Dissembler though he was, he would do one small good thing this day. In her pew at the front, he saw her, looking up at him. He met her eyes in a glance, then looked away.

'This man will be condemned to death,' he said quietly. 'He will die parched with thirst on a hill outside the wall of the city, a common thief hanging on either side. He knows this, though all around Him people are shouting Hosanna! Hosanna! as the ass stumbles and sways beneath him. And for ever after, down through almost two thousand years, this animal, this ass from Palestine, this little English donkey, will bear upon his shaggy back the long, unmistakable sign of the Cross, for the man he carried was the Son of God, and he is marked for ever.'

They were with him now. As at Christmas, that donkey stepped in, in their minds, from the fields lying all around them, into this dilapidated church, with its woodwormy pews and rafters, maps of India staining the damp walls, rain dripping in through the gaps in the slates in winter.

'The sign of the Cross is something which marks this humble beast of burden, this patient animal. It marks his shaggy coat and it marks each one of us, each one of you, dear children, from the moment of our baptism, when it is made upon your forehead with water from the font. He died for us, He died upon the Cross that we might live, and at Easter, with the beauty of spring all around us, we celebrate His glorious Resurrection.'

Automatically, he turned the page beneath his hand, but he had no need to look down, for he knew how he was to conclude. And if he felt that in much of his daily life he uttered but clerical clichés, Richard felt in the pulpit now as though some real connection were working between him and his congregation. He saw the Southwoods intent upon him, from their locked pew with its worn baize lining; he saw, sitting close, Edward Turner and Effie Bounds, whose banns he had read this morning, and whose wedding, after Easter, he would conduct; he saw the Neves and Prossers, Bodenhams and Middleships and Bampfields; weary Miss Hatfield; intense young Alfred Arndell; the Birleys, with Alice and Tommy leaning against their mother and father, the Misses Jenkinson and the widowed Mrs Thomas and Mrs Meadham, side by side – he knew them all now, he saw that they were touched, as he had hoped they would be, by the quietness of his delivery and the simplicity of his message. He saw Susannah's sweet pale face, which he had thought so calm and pure when he first saw it, but which now looked so serious and troubled; he heard – oh, vanity! – his voice speaking into the hush.

'We are marked with the sign of the Cross upon our brow at baptism, and this morning, dear children of this church, you carried your own palm crosses in memory of the day on which Our Lord was greeted by the great crowd soon to turn against Him and send Him to His death. But the carrying of those crosses must be only the outward and visible sign of that which we carry, each one of us, within our hearts. Engraved upon them must be this holy symbol of Christ's love for us, and of our love for Him, our desire to serve and follow Him, to dedicate, indeed, our lives entire to Him.'

He picked up his pages, he tapped them together upon the pulpit's rim. He closed his eyes.

'The grace of our Lord Jesus Christ, and the love of God, and the fellowship of the Holy Spirit, be with us all, evermore. Amen.'

He heard the murmur of 'Amen' run through the congregation. Then he came down the steps and walked slowly back to his place behind the rood screen.

'Hymn number ninety-nine.'

The congregation rose to their feet; their voices resounded, echoing against the wood and glass and stone.

He stood in the porch; he waited to greet his parishioners. Thomas Hatton was running his fingers over a gentle tune from Tallis. Out they all came.

'That was a lovely sermon, Mr Allen.'

'Good morning, Allen. A fine service.'

'Oh, Mr Allen! I cannot tell you how much that meant to me!'

'You are very kind. Thank you. A very good morning to you. Miss Bounds – you are quite recovered now, I trust.'

'Oh, yes, Mr Allen, and it was such a joy to hear you read the banns for us, was it not, Edward?'

'Aye. Aye, it was. We're glad you'll be marrying us, Mr Allen.'

'I much look forward to it.'

At last she was there.

'Mr Allen.'

'Mrs Bowen.'

Her gloved hand lay in his. He could hardly look at her.

'Will you join us for luncheon?'

'Your husband – I fear he is not at all well today.'

'It will do him good to see you.'

'Are you sure?'

'Quite certain.' She drew away her hand, looked down upon the broken flagstones. The churchyard was full of conversation, and the sounds of the carriages beyond the gate. 'It will do us both good to have your company.'

'Then I shall be with you directly,' he said, and turned to greet the last few members of the congregation, as her gown rustled over the flags and the last notes of Tallis sounded in the empty church and then faded away.

Oliver Bowen had come downstairs. He was dressed. He sat by the parlour fire. Richard, admitted to this room by Millie, saw husband and wife on either side of the hearth, the fire bright, the brass fender polished, everything swept and fresh. The casement was open a little; daffodils stood in a jug.

What sweet domestic ordered life was this.

Susannah rose at his entrance. Bowen did not. Richard saw himself and Susannah briefly reflected together in the mirror above the mantel-shelf: small figures in black and grey enclosed within the whole of the room as if within a painting. He did not know what name to give it.

'Mr Allen.'

'Mrs Bowen.' He took her hand. Without its glove, his skin touched hers. It felt as intimate as if she lay naked beneath him.

'Good morning, Allen. I hear you preached well.'

'Thank you, sir.' He was blushing. He crossed to the other side of the hearth.

'Forgive me for not getting up to greet you.'

'Of course.' Richard took such a different, older hand. It felt hot and dry. 'How are you today, sir?'

'A little stronger, now I am downstairs. I was sorry to miss the service. The children all looked very fine in the procession. I was watching from the window.'

'Yes, sir, I saw you.'

'A spectre at the feast.' There was a silence. 'Well, now.'

Millie was at the door again, and the cat slipped in behind her.

'Luncheon is almost ready, sir. Will you take a little sherry?'

'If my wife and Mr Allen will join me.' Bowen looked up at them from the depths of the wing chair. 'I find it helps me a little. You don't mind?'

'Of course not.'

Sherry in the vicarage: this too was a part of him. And a little tray of engraved glasses was brought in, with the decanter.

'Your health, sir.'

'Indeed. Praise God the winter is over. Do sit down, Allen; it unnerves me to have you towering up there.' A flicker of a smile.

Richard sat on the ottoman, and the cat sprang up beside him.

'Samuel does not take to everyone,' said Susannah from her button-backed chair.

'Then I am honoured.' He ran his hand along the length of the animal's spine, saw her lower her gaze. The grandfather clock ticked in the hall, the cat purred, the rooks were a cacophany.

'They're hatching,' said Bowen, setting down his glass.

'Already, sir?'

They began a conversation about the incubation period, and how long after hatching the young might fly. He had had such discussions all his life about so many birds, but rook and elm and churchyard belonged together as entirely as bell and tower and weathercock. He could hear the weathercock now, amidst the chorus out there, turning and turning in the wind: towards here, towards his old home.

The bell rang in the hall; they all set down their glasses. As he rose, Richard's eye fell upon the heap of books beside Susannah's chair. She had hardly spoken. He saw the familiar Mudie's binding – it put him in mind of the novels Verity was always reading. How she and Emily had sobbed over *Jane Eyre*, and the death of Helen. He had read it because they made him do so, found St John Rivers a sanctimonious creature, whom he hoped never to resemble. And Rochester – did women really admire such men?

'You are reading a new novel, Mrs Bowen?'

Now it was she who blushed. '*The Mill on the Floss*. Have you come across it at all?'

'I fear I read very little fiction.'

So perhaps this would be a division between them. Or perhaps she would read to him from her novels and he read her some of the poetry he loved. Donne. Herbert. They could discuss it all.

'Who is the author?'

'Mr George Eliot.'

'Ah.' He remembered that name. '*Scenes of Clerical Life* – my mother quite devoured that a few years ago. It was serialised in *Blackwood's*, was it not?'

'Novels,' said Bowen, as the bell rang again. 'The novelist seeks to know the human heart.'

'Indeed, sir.'

'The novelist thinks he has access to the human mind. No one but God has that, Mr Allen.'

Richard saw Susannah bite her lip.

'And what are you reading, sir?'

'At present very little. I have ordered one or two things from London ...' He made to rise, waving away Richard's offer of assistance. He was on his feet. 'There we are.' He took a few steps; he cleared his throat. The clock in the hall began to chime the long three-quarter hour. He started to cough. Before the chimes had finished the cough had seized him.

Susannah's hands went to her mouth. For a moment Richard saw her look of real distress and fear. Then she was beside her husband, and he leaned upon her in a paroxysm.

'Water—' said Susannah, and Richard made for the door. Millie was already hurrying in from the hall with a glass and carafe.

'Here we are, sir, here we are ...'

The chiming clock, the purring cat, the freshly blazing fire – all this flew away. There was only this rasping, this bubbling, these dreadful sounds of illness. They helped him back to his chair; Susannah rubbed his curved spine as he leaned forward, heaving into a handkerchief. Millie kneeled, holding the glass to his lips. He struggled to drink; at last a few sips went down. He drank again, stopped coughing, leaned back in his chair, and closed his eyes. Spittle lay in the corners of his mouth. Susannah, kneeling, wiped it away. Millie took the handkerchief, and got to her feet. Bowen sighed. The sounds of clock and cat and croaking rook came into the room once more.

Richard watched all this and found he was shaking from head to foot.

'Forgive me,' said Bowen at last. 'I should not have come downstairs today – it was selfish of me. Foolish.'

'Hush,' said Susannah, still kneeling by his side. 'Hush – save your strength.'

His wavering hand went out to her; he laid it upon her head of pale hair. 'I save my strength so I might walk across the room.' He paused. 'Now I must save it so that I can talk. Soon—'

'Hush,' she said again, and rested her hand in his lap. His other hand went out to take it. In essence, she was now in his embrace.

They have been lovers, thought Richard, watching them. They are man and wife – she has lain in his arms, he has touched and caressed her. They have slept and woken together, while I have never so much as brushed a woman's lips with mine, nor ever wanted to, till I met her.

He turned away, to the open casement window. The wind blew over the bright spring grass; sticks fell from the nests in the trees. There was the path where he had led the children, there was the church where he had carried the cross. He thought: I should not be here, I am not worthy to be here – not in that church, not within this room. It is hopeless.

Little sounds came from behind him; he turned. Millie was gathering glasses and carafe, decanter of sherry, the tray. Oliver Bowen was gazing into the fire. Susannah had risen and was straightening her gown.

Millie said: 'Shall I serve luncheon, ma'am?'

Susannah looked at her husband. 'Oliver? Would you like a little luncheon on a tray? Would that be comfortable for you?'

He nodded. 'That would be kind.'

'I should go,' said Richard. 'Please – let me not intrude any longer.'

'You have had a long service, Mr Allen – you have been preaching – you must be hungry.'

'I can have luncheon at home. Mrs Price is very good – she always makes something.'

'Stay and eat here,' said Bowen from the fireside. 'My poor wife needs company.' He smiled thinly. 'Millie can be your chaperone.'

In the fields overlooked by the dining-room window, lambs raced about. With the bells gone silent, Richard Allen and Susannah Bowen might have been eating Sunday luncheon in any country home or farmhouse. The fire was lit. They took their places at the table laid for three. Millie removed the third place setting; Richard looked at Susannah.

'Shall I say grace?'

'Please do.'

They bowed their heads. He murmured the old words.

They unfolded their napkins. Millie brought in the soup. A little glass dish of primroses and violets stood in the centre of the table. Richard admired it.

Susannah said that the smell of spring flowers was indeed very sweet.

Millie said: 'I'll take Mr Bowen his tray, ma'am.'

'Very good. Thank you, Millie.'

She left the door ajar; they could hear her going back down the passage to the parlour, the murmur of voices. They drank their soup, and never in any meal he had ever taken had Richard so noticed the sounds of spoon upon plate, the pouring of water, the setting down of a jug. For the first time since he and Susannah had met, save for those moments in the schoolhouse, they were alone. He did not know what to say, where to begin. Where were his pastoral phrases now? He broke his bread, he praised the soup. Susannah said they were very fortunate in Millie. Millie returned, and took away the plates.

'How is Mr Bowen?'

'He has drunk a little soup, ma'am. He looks a little better.'

She brought in the roast; she carved it herself, sharpening knife upon steel.

'You are an expert,' said Richard, watching the slices fall smoothly away.

'Thank you, sir. 'Tis a lamb from the Burgage farm.'

In spite of everything, he was very hungry. Millie served spring carrots and new potatoes. The mint sauce was very fresh; a wreath of steam rose from the silver gravy boat that Susannah passed him. He remembered it.

He said: 'That was your grandmother's, I believe.'

'Yes.' She looked at him enquiringly.

He said: 'You told me that the first – no, the second time I had luncheon here – when everyone came. The Bodenhams and the Neves. Mr and Mrs Prosser.' And he had listened to them all, and listened for her voice. He said: 'Do you remember?'

'Yes,' said Susannah quietly.

Millie had left the room. He felt his heart begin to pound. He put down his knife and fork and looked at her. Susannah returned his gaze. Now there could be not a moment's more polite conversation.

They held one another's gaze, and if in those moments in the schoolhouse hall something had been acknowledged between them, now it was as if they were walking together through a great landscape, unfolding and unfolding before them.

Richard leaned his elbows upon the table, and let his chin rest in his hands – as if he were at home at his desk, with everything open and known between them, as if they had known and loved one another for a long, long time, and he were writing a sermon, thinking, looking out over his own field, with the oak just in leaf and the ewes and lambs calling for one another, as they were calling here. He continued to look at her, heard from a great distance Alice Birley saying in her clear grave way: 'Now you are lost in thought.' He saw that Susannah was trembling.

At last he said simply: 'My love.'

She gave an almost imperceptible little nod; she closed her eyes. Millie came into the room. She saw the plates they had barely touched.

'Ma'am?'

'Another few minutes,' Susannah said quietly, and Millie waited, standing before the dark carved sideboard, watching the fire.

Lamb and rook called into the silence. Down in the hall the clock ticked on and on. Somehow they finished the meal.

Bowen was sleeping before the parlour fire, the cat Samuel stretched out at his feet. Susannah said to Millie, come in to replenish the coal: 'I shall see Mr Allen to the gate.'

'Very good, ma'am.'

In the hall she took down her cloak from its peg on the stand – her good Sunday cloak, of dark wool. Beside it hung the one with the little tear, which she had mended, and her bonnet, whose ribbons hung down as if waiting to be run through her fingers, tied beneath her chin. He wanted to do all these things: drape her cloak around her shoulders, set her bonnet upon her lovely hair, tie the bow, kiss her mouth. He waited; he opened the door.

They stepped out into the churchyard. The wind blew over it, stirring the folds of her gown, her cloak, the hem of his father's cassock. Within just a few hours, the leaves were greener, the spring sun warmer. They walked beneath the trees. He wanted to have her slip her hand into the crook of his arm, to take it and press it to his side.

He said: 'May I call you Susannah?'

'Of course.'

'And will you call me Richard?'

153

'Richard,' she said. Title and surname were peeled away, their names uncovered. It felt as intimate as if they had undressed one another.

They walked on in silence.

At length he said: 'Susannah. Your husband is very ill. What we feel for one another – I do not know how to proceed. Just to think of you – I think of you all the time – it is against God's holy law.' She did not answer; he turned to look at her. They were away from the house; they had come to the fork in the path. One way led down to the lich-gate, the other led round to the empty church. He said: 'Is this not so?'

'It is. I am tormented.'

They took the path's fork to the church. Now no one could see them. Was that true? He looked round, saw only the blowing daffodils, the empty fields beyond the churchyard wall, the dark little villa behind the laurels, on the other side of the road.

He said: 'I have loved you since the first moment we met. It is like a homecoming.'

'Yes.' Her voice was a whisper in the wind.

'But I cannot bear to think of you so troubled. And your husband is a fine man, a good man. We are men of the Church, we are men of God. Sometimes I cannot but believe that God is with us. At others ... this morning I felt I was betraying everything – my faith, my life, my calling.'

'Then you are in torment too.'

'Yes.' It was true, though he had not thought to call it this. 'I do not know how to proceed,' he said again. 'This morning I told myself I must leave the Church.'

'No—'

'What else can I do? How can I remain here?'

She did not answer. Then she said: 'We have done nothing.'

'But we feel so much—'

'We have done nothing. Please don't leave.'

'What do you want me to do?'

'I don't know. But my life – my life ...' she made a sudden sweeping gesture, encompassing the church, the trees, everything within her. 'It is wicked, I know, but I want to think of you, to think of seeing you.' She stopped. 'Please don't go,' she said again.

A pony and trap came clopping up the hill. Sunday afternoon: an outing. They could see the tops of a hat and two bonnets, they could hear laughter. And what were the curate and the rector's wife doing, out in the churchyard together, so long and so deep in conversation?

'May I write to you?'

'How should I receive such a letter?'

He did not know.

'I must go. You must go. I shall see you very soon.'

'That is all I need to know,' she said, and as the pony and trap drew nearer she turned, and walked quickly away from him, her gown just brushing the grass as she stepped on to it, and walked between the graves towards the house.

He watched her. He waited until the trap had gone past, slowing as the hill grew steep. He was shaking again: he must pray, he must pray.

He turned towards the porch, wherein he had stood so many times, waiting for her to come in, to come out, to take his hand. Had he been dreaming now? After all these months of longing, had they really made their declaration?

He stepped inside. The porch was dark and cool after the warmth of the sun. He thought of the first day he had come here, of the icy cold, his nervous, grief-stricken state, his apprehension as he walked here to take up his appointment, and stole a few moments in the empty church.

Now, as then, he put hand upon the iron handle. Filled with every kind of emotion, he turned it and opened the door. And there came once again, like a reminder of who he once had been – innocent, believing, set upon a path, his whole life's work before him – that sublime and incandescent movement of air, that pure, unearthly choir.

15

The service of holy matrimony in which Edward Turner took Effie Bounds, his childhood sweetheart, to be at last his lawful wedded wife, took place on the second Saturday after Easter: on 13 April, in the twenty-fifth year of the reign of Queen Victoria, in the Year of Our Lord 1861.

By the end of this year, the country would muffle its bells, save for the one slow passing bell; would purchase or bring out from towering wardrobes the deepest mourning: for Albert, Prince Consort, patron of the arts and industry, guiding light behind the Great Exhibition, adored by the Queen and the little princes and princesses, had fallen into typhoid's dreadful fever, and been taken, at the age of forty-two, into the arms of God. On a dank December day, crowds lined the streets of Windsor as the funeral carriage rolled slowly across the castle courtyard to St George's Chapel. The long lonely decades of Victoria's widowhood began.

But today – today Queen and Consort were taking a morning stroll, arm in arm beneath the oaks of Windsor Great Park, and in Lyonshall the path from the lich-gate to the south door of St Michael and All Angels was strewn with fresh spring flowers. Primrose and violet, daffodil, prayermint and narcissi scented the air: here the young bride might take her footsteps as if on the very path to Heaven, brushing the petals with the folds of her pretty gown, whose cotton lawn had been purchased from Webbs in Kington; made up by Miss Jane Cooper, dressmaker, over three fittings in her little room in Bridge Street; and slipped on by Effie this morning in her bedroom beneath the thatch. House martins were nesting in the eaves; chinks of morning sunlight touched beam and bedstead and the heap of lacy veil. Down in the village street, someone went whistling by.

A wedding! A sweet spring wedding! After the snow, the cold, the winter rains; after the dreadful discovery beneath the frozen lake at Burgage; after the racking, draining months of illness endured by Oliver Bowen – the prospect of this day had cheered the whole congregation. Mr Bowen had been well enough to publish one set of banns; at Easter he had entered the church on his young wife's arm and been strong enough to lead the prayers, but it was Mr Allen who preached the Easter sermon, with its great subject of Resurrection.

' "If ye then be risen with Christ, seek those things which are above ... Set your affection on things above ... When Christ, who is our life, shall appear, then shall ye also appear with him in glory ..." '

The words of St Paul were spoken with such fervour. And yet – though the Easter morning was so fine that the church was filled with light; though it struck so gloriously the very rim of the pulpit as he stood there – did they imagine it, or did Richard Allen look pale enough to be himself on the brink of sickness?

Today, however, as he stood outside the church awaiting the arrival of the bride upon her father's arm, his robes stirring in the morning breeze, it was generally agreed that whatever had troubled him two weeks ago must now have quite departed.

'Good morning, Mr Allen!'

'A fine day!'

'Indeed, indeed.'

As the bells rang out, Richard greeted everyone: the Neves, the Middleships, the Bampfields, their children scrubbed like pennies; the stout lawyer Bodenham, and his stouter wife, puffing even with the walk from their waiting carriage; Skarratt the clockmaker, and all the little Skarratts, running up; Miss Dorothy Wilkinson, bringing news of her aunt's better spirits at last, with this fine spring weather – though she was, of course, still in her bed, and likely to remain so. How glad she would be of a visit! How glad they both would be! He promised to call within the week.

Carriages clattered along the highway, going to Kington or Pembridge. One or two stopped at the path of the church, and made the steep climb up, but most of the guests were on foot, walking up the long hill from the village, the air alive with conversation. As for Richard's neighbours: Birley must miss it all for the Saturday trains, but here were his wife and children, and Alice's serious little face lit up at the sight of the flower-strewn path. He raised his hand, and watched them walk towards him.

'Good morning, Mrs Birley. Good morning, children.'

'Sir. Mr Allen, sir.'

A blush and a bob from Lily Birley, the children on either side.

'How pretty you look today, Alice,' he told her. 'Is this the first wedding you have attended?'

'Yes, sir.'

'And the first I have ever conducted.' He took her hand. 'I believe I am almost as nervous as the bride.'

'I am sure that is not so, sir,' said Mrs Birley, as more guests arrived.

'Oh, but I assure you it is,' he said, and then she was distracted by Tommy, all at once darting away, and Richard turned to greet the Prossers, who had only to cross the road from the house behind the laurels, yet who looked, even today, somewhat out of sorts.

'Good morning, Allen.'

'Good morning, sir. Mrs Prosser ...' Richard took her thin little hand in his. Did it tremble a little? Was she quite well? 'How are you keeping?' he asked her gently, for her nervous, pinched appearance had always troubled him.

'Oh, very well, very well indeed, thank you. How kind of you to ask. We are all so looking forward to this.'

'You know that it is the first wedding service I have ever taken,' he said again, as another carriage and pair came clip-clopping up the path.

'I am sure you will conduct it beautifully,' said Mrs Prosser, and then her husband took her arm, and she flushed, and they both were gone into the porch, where the ushers were waiting, and Richard looked to see the Southwoods descending from their carriage, the horses tossing their heads though the martingale held them tightly. Too tightly? Had Prosser held his wife's arm too tightly? For a moment, within the tumult of his own feelings, Richard felt a stab of real anxiety. He must call on them – on her. Then the Southwoods were entering the churchyard from the west, and Alfred Arndell was walking along the path from the lich-gate, a daffodil in his buttonhole. Brave fellow. As he watched his approach, saw the pale determined face beneath the hat, Richard thought: before I came here, I could only imagine love. All my experience was of family affection. I so grieved to lose my father, but to lose a wife – to lose the very heart of your life ...

And at once he was filled with emotion, at an image of Susannah ill, Susannah slipping away from the world, and he unable to be at her side.

'Mr Allen?'

'Mr Arndell. A very good day to you.' Richard shook his hand; he knew he was flushing deeply.

'You are very warm, Mr Allen. Even with my walk here I still feel the April wind.'

'Indeed, indeed.' He floundered. 'How are you, Mr Arndell?'

'I am strong in the Lord,' said Arndell, replacing his hat. 'I expect Turner is waiting inside?'

'He is. Rather nervous, I believe.'

'He's a lucky fellow.' And Arndell tipped his hat at the Southwoods as they approached, and took himself into the church.

'Good morning, Allen. A splendid morning.'

'Sir.' Richard shook Southwood's hand: he bowed to Mrs South-wood, and to Will and Charlotte, who inclined her head, then adjusted her gloves at the wrist.

'A quite perfect day for a wedding,' said Elizabeth Southwood, and for the twentieth time that morning he agreed that indeed it was and said that the families were within and Miss Bounds arriving with her father within the quarter-hour. And was Will soon to return to Oxford, after the Easter vacation? Will said that he was, and his parents added that of course the wedding they were most looking forward to after this was Will's own marriage to Miss Georgina Debenham, though that could not take place until he had completed his studies in '62. Charlotte, of course, said James Southwood, checking his buttonhole, must be in want of a husband for very little longer, for with the May balls she would turn any number of heads.

'Father!' said Charlotte Southwood, and Will laughed.

'James!' said their mother.

'I am only speaking the truth,' said James Southwood mildly, but Charlotte's colour was very high, and his wife shook her head at him. The single status of a striking young woman on whose finger one would expect to see the loveliest engagement ring was not something to which a father should draw attention: all this hung in the fresh spring air as reproachfully as if the words were spoken.

'Well, well.' Southwood cleared his throat. 'And how is poor Bowen this morning?'

'This morning? I have not seen him, sir,' said Richard. 'I think perhaps with the change in the weather he is a little better.'

'Certainly at Easter he looked stronger,' said Elizabeth Southwood. 'I believe that Dr Probyn has prescribed a sleeping draught which also eases the cough. That is what Susannah tells me. Ah, here she is! My dear ...'

And she turned to greet her, as Susannah, in a gown the colour of a summer cloud, with a cluster of pink silk rosebuds pinned to her breast, came walking along the path from the vicarage.

'My dear, you look enchanting.' Elizabeth bent forward to press a kiss on the pale cheek beneath the bonnet. 'How good to see you. James – Mr Allen – does Susannah not look much refreshed?'

'Indeed she does,' said Southwood, raising his hat, and Richard bowed his head.

'Good morning, Mrs Bowen.'

'Good morning, Mr Allen.'

Their eyes met only for a moment. As his heart began to pound he was shocked at how easy it was to dissemble.

'I hear your good husband is much improved,' said Charlotte.

'And the great load of anxiety you have borne for so long is slipping away from your shoulders at last,' said Elizabeth. 'How brave you both have been.'

'You are all very kind, but—'

'But Mr Bowen is not with you,' said Southwood. 'On this happy day he is not able to join us?'

'I fear not. He was so hoping to do so, but he is still not quite as strong as we would wish. He had a restless night. I have left him sleeping.'

'Oh, my poor Susannah.' Elizabeth pressed her hand. 'We were so hoping—'

'You are very kind,' Susannah said again.

And listening, Richard felt for a moment as if he were observing a game of croquet: each right remark clicked in turn through the right hoop: We are so sorry. You are so kind.

Was this unjust? Were these not genuine expressions of warmth between friends? And yet – when had Susannah ever been able to say how she really felt?

And as they stood there on the sunlit path, amidst the jangle of harness and peal of bells, the rush of spring wind across the fields and the scent of cut grass and crushed flowers filling the air, he saw her, standing in just the same place on Palm Sunday afternoon, the churchyard empty, the daffodils blowing, her pale young face alight with passion.

'*But my life – my life … I want to think of you, to think of seeing you.*'

'Allen? You are gone very quiet.'

'And look, they are here!' Elizabeth was turned towards the gate where Effie Bounds, upon her father's arm, stood beneath the lich-gate roof, just arrived from their walk up from the village. How sweet to walk to your wedding! How good, on a fine spring morning, to click open the gate of your childhood home, walk on your father's arm along the village street where as a child you had bowled your hoop, and up the hill to the church where you had been baptised, where your childhood love was waiting, in a borrowed morning suit. Richard looked at Effie through the sun. Even at this distance, even through her veil, he could sense her mingled nerves and excitement. A lich-gate roof was built to shelter a bier, set down upon its slow progress to the grave, but today it sheltered a young bride, moving her posy from hand to hand, touching her veil for a moment, and then, on the arm of good John Bounds, stepping out on to the path of flowers. Tears pricked his eyes; he raised his hand in greeting.

'We must go in!' Elizabeth Southwood was ushering them all: she and her husband moved quickly into the porch, with Charlotte just behind them.

'Mrs Bowen.' Richard stepped aside; he gestured for Susannah to precede him.

'Thank you, Mr Allen.'

Her gown brushed his robe; his voice and hers were murmurs within the echoing porch; he held, for a fleeting moment, her elbow in the cup of his hand as she passed through, and felt as though an arrow had passed through him, piercing his very soul.

Then the bells were silent, and the church was hushed, as the Southwoods took their places, the last of the wedding guests, and he and Susannah walked down the aisle together, as if they were man and wife – as if, when all this were over, he might take her home, and up to their bedroom, and slip off that rustling cloud-grey gown and all that lay beneath it.

He ushered her to her pew. He walked slowly to the chancel steps. The air was so full of the scent of lilies, and he was so charged with emotion and desire, that for an instant he was swept by giddiness. Then he recovered himself, and turned to the congregation.

Here was the bride, and the strains of *Jesu, joy of man's desiring* came quietly to their close. Richard smiled down at Edward Turner, forbidden, like Orpheus, to turn and look at his beloved. Edward smiled nervously back, and for the last time ran a finger round his infernal collar. Beside him, his best man, Dick Bampfield, felt for the last time in his pocket. Then Thomas Hatton sounded the first great peal of the Wedding March, and Effie and her father came slowly down the aisle.

'Dearly beloved, we are gathered together here in the sight of God, and in the face of this congregation, to join together this Man and this Woman in holy Matrimony ...'

The church was hushed, save for the clearing of a throat, a small child's murmured question, quickly quietened: save for the concert of birds in the churchyard, distant but insistent, now the organ had fallen silent. Richard heard his voice tremble, and struggled to steady it again, as he took them all through the stern reasons for the ordination of matrimony: 'For the procreation of children ... for a remedy against sin, and to avoid fornication ... for the mutual society, help, and comfort, that the one ought to have of the other, both in prosperity and adversity ...'

Did they sense he was not fit to say these words? Could they know, as God knew, that with every breath he took he thought of her?

'Therefore if any man can shew any just cause, why they may not lawfully be joined together, let him now speak ...'

Before him, he felt bride and bridegroom stiff with tension, yet what had they to fear? Almost a hundred had come to see them wed, families who had watched them grow up and known them all their lives. And as he thought this he was swept with a sudden hunger for home, for his father to be alive again, and all of them gathered in church together for the first wedding in his own dear family. Who would it be? Who might be brave enough to take on Verity; which fortunate man might win tender Emily's heart? As for himself—

I shall never marry, he thought. Could that be true?

No voice of dissent disturbed the silence. His gaze swept the congregation, passed over Susannah's still pale face, returned to the couple before him.

'I require and charge you both, as ye will answer at the dreadful day of judgment when the secrets of all hearts shall be disclosed, that if either of you know any impediment, why ye may not be lawfully joined together in Matrimony, ye do now confess it.'

Edward Turner gazed at him, as rigid as if he were in court. Beside him, beneath her cloudy veil, with its primrose garland, Effie Bounds gave the tiniest shake of her head. He smiled at them, let the moment, with its dreadful threat, pass away. Now they could proceed. Now might be spoken the sweet solemn beauty of the vows.

'Wilt thou have this Woman to thy wedded wife ...'

'I will.'

'Wilt thou have this Man to thy wedded husband ...'

'I will.'

He knew the first tears were being wiped away: by Effie's mother, Edward's mother, by a sentimental aunt, and he felt a wave of affection for two shy young people, known to one another always. This was their day, saved for, dreamed of, here at last, and who was he to dwell for an instant upon his own longing and transgression? He was but three or four years older than either, but he had a role to fulfil, and would perform it from the heart.

And he stepped towards them, and took and joined their hands.

'Say after me ...'

'I Edward Henry take thee Euphemia Mary ...'

'I Euphemia Mary take thee Edward Henry ...'.

'In sickness and in health ...'

'To love and to cherish ...'

'... and thereto I plight thee my troth.'

Gently he loosened their hands, and turned to where Dick Bampfield was standing, upright as a tree, but with a dreamy gaze: not, in truth, quite with the occasion – just as his young brother John was wont to drift away in the catechism classes. Richard nodded at him; Dick came to with a start, and felt in his pocket. After all this – to lose his place in the service! A blush crept up from his collar; he withdrew his little box from his pocket, and thrust it forward; recalled he was to open it himself and quickly drew it back again. He fumbled with the clasp – a good young carpenter used to saw and chisel, not this fiddly thing. Richard saw Edward glance across, and knew how often, in years to come, they would recall this moment.

'There you were, fumbling with that box—'

'And he would not open, blimming thing.'

But it sprung open now, and as Dick started once more, and made to take out the ring, it slipped between his fingers and fell, with a tiny sound, upon the flags.

Gold upon stone – and where exactly was it?

Every best man's nightmare.

A little ripple of anxiety ran through the pews, shot through here and there with delectable mirth, immediately suppressed.

Where was the blessed thing?

Scarlet with embarrassment, Dick kneeled down. Richard and the bridal pair stepped back. Everyone gazed at worn and ancient lettering. 'Here lieth Benjamin Braithwaite, 1749–1783'.

'To the end of my days I'll not forget that name.'

'Bet he was having a laugh at us all.'

'I wasn't laughing then, Dick Bampfield, I wanted to crown you—'

'I wanted to crown myself.'

All this lay ahead, in the wedding breakfast. Now, Samuel Cooper, landlord at the George, was polishing a hundred glasses in the bright spring sun, and his wife and daughter laying a hundred places on ten trestles, while Dick, upon his knees, felt with caprenter's calloused fingers over every inch of stone.

Richard raised his head and looked at the congregation. Neither he nor they knew what was to be done, whether he should speak. Speak, and break the beauty of the liturgy with some humdrum phrase? Stay silent, and have everyone's nerves on edge? He watched the Bampfield family, stiff with the awfulness of it. Their Dick! Would that boy never do anything right? He saw little Mrs Prosser white with vicarious anxiety while her husband glared. He saw Susannah bite her lip, and he looked away, gave the reassuring smile he knew they all needed, cleared his throat and said: 'We shall find it, have no fear,' just as Dick muttered audibly, 'There!' and pounced, as if upon a rodent.

Sighs of relief in the pews.

'Well done,' Richard said quietly, and let them all draw breath. Then he took the ring from Dick's sweating fingers, and gave it into Edward's shaking hand.

'Say after me. With this Ring I thee wed ...'

'With this Ring I thee wed ...'

'With my body I thee worship ...'

Did he imagine it, or did he feel Susannah's gaze upon him more intent than it had ever been?

'With my body I thee worship ...' said Edward Turner, blushing to the roots of his hair, so fiercely brushed with water to lie flat for once, and Effie, beneath her veil, was pink as a rose.

'In the name of the Father, and of the Son, and of the Holy Ghost. Amen.'

Edward slipped the ring at last upon Effie's trembling finger; at last they kneeled before him, and Richard, filled with every kind of emotion, read the prayer.

'Send thy blessing upon these thy servants, this man and this woman, whom we bless in thy Name ... that they may ever remain in perfect love and peace together ...'

He placed his hand upon each head; he joined their hands once more. Then he spoke the great concluding words, which bound them to one another, no matter what, or who, might come into their lives.

'Those whom God hath joined together, let no man put asunder.'

☆

The organ sounded, the bells rang out; Edward and Effie, husband and wife, walked arm in arm up the aisle almost to applause. Following them and their families, as everyone began to talk and gathered up psalter and hymnal, Richard's gaze was fixed ahead, falling, as so often, upon the ringers at the far end, hauling down and letting the ropes slip through their hands – with a movement not unlike the steady rhythm of milking, so sure, so practised. They were ringing Grandsire Doubles, a splendid triumphant peal, perfect for a wedding. And what a relief to see their certainty, their concentration: Jeremiah Morgan, Ted Blomely and William Middleship there every Sunday, red-faced and puffing a little. Let him rest his gaze, his mind, upon the good men that they were. And he smiled to thank them and went out into the sun, and waited for her touch. Here they all were, crowding up to the newlyweds outside, as their families fussed around them.

'*What* a lovely wedding!'

'My heart was in my mouth when he dropped the ring – did you not feel almost *faint* with sympathy?'

'Surely it must be somewhere, that was what I told myself—'

'Well, indeed it must be somewhere, you foolish thing!'

'But that Dick Bampfield – 'twould have to be he.'

'Dick! Dick! Feeling better now?'

Richard listened, he smiled and shook hands, he stood and watched Edward kiss his bride, her veil now thrown back and her eyes quite sparkling.

'You are coming to the wedding breakfast, Mr Allen?'

He turned to see Miss Wilkinson upon Miss Hatfield's arm.

'Of course. I should not miss it for the world.'

'You took the service so beautifully, if I may say so – you must have had an anxious moment!' Miss Hatfield was blushing: what an awkward thing she was, away from the classroom.

'But you know, dear, once it was found,' Miss Wilkinson confided to her, 'I could not help but feel that losing the ring made it all rather *special*, somehow. Does that sound strange?'

'No, dear, I know just what you mean.'

Two middle-aged spinsters – rather as maiden aunts and bachelor uncles sometimes had a greater bond than parents with their children, were they not enjoying it all almost more than anyone? Richard half-listened, turned to greet the Bodenhams, the Southwoods, the Birleys, watching Tommy run about with little Jimmy Neve, shaking hand after hand. Where was she? The churchyard was as full as he had ever seen it, the scent of spring grass and daffodils was everywhere, the air full of laughter and conversation, and soon they would all be leaving for the walk down the hill to the George. Even now – yes, Edward and Effie were stepping away from the porch towards the path, and he saw a sudden fumbling in purse and pocket and then the shower of petals, falling on swept-up hair and swept-back veil, scattering over Edward's borrowed morning suit, as they made their laughing way to the gate. All began to follow.

Where was she?

He turned to rake his eyes over the crowd, felt his stomach somersault as she walked all at once towards him, detaching herself, he saw, with a graceful little 'Excuse me just for a moment' from Liza Neve's eager chit-chat.

'Mr Allen.'

'Mrs Bowen.'

He looked down upon her upturned face. He met her gaze, he took her hand, the world around dissolved.

'You are going to the breakfast?'

'I am.' He cleared his throat. 'And you? You are able to join us?'

She shook her head. 'Oliver needs me. It would not be right.'

'Indeed. Of course not.' He was still holding her hand in its glove; it felt as natural as if he held it every day of his life, as charged with sensation as if he were about to kiss her. Gently she withdrew it from his grasp. As she did so, he was all at once aware of eyes upon them – and should he not always be alert to this possibility? What was he thinking of, to stand gazing down at her, her hand in his? – and he turned to see Prosser's gleaming little eyes swivel swiftly away as he pressed his wife forward through the throng on the path.

'Perhaps you might visit us, on your way home?' Susannah asked quietly.

'Should you like that? Would it be convenient?'

'If Oliver is well enough, I'm sure he would be glad to see you. We both would be.'

'Then I shall call. Thank you.'

And she smiled, and moved away, and he watched her bid farewell to Liza, and the Southwoods, and walk across the grass and on to the path to the vicarage, where an upper window stood open to let the dancing air of spring into a sickroom.

He was not well enough to go downstairs – that is, he was not strong enough to make the long climb up again. But he would not lie in this bed for a moment longer. After the restlessness of the night the sheets were tangled, his pillows damp with sweat; already, after hours upon the lumps and cavities of the mattress, his muscles were so stiff that he could hardly rise; and he must rise, he must fight, he must not succumb.

'Sleep,' Susannah had said from the doorway, as the bells began to ring. Propped upon the pillows he gazed at her, dressed in a gown that made him think of heaven – cloudy, airy, full of light. Flowers were pinned to her breast: were they silk or miraculously early rosebuds? Silk, she told him, running the ribbons of her bonnet through her fingers. They were her mother's, she had kept them wrapped in paper, he had seen them before. He was sure she was right. Sleep, she said again, and crossed the room to open the window wide. The whole house smelled of soot; his nostrils were full of it, and of the smell of his own body, and unwashed linen, and something indefinable, horrible, always there. Was this how he smelled to her? After the night's interminable hours, after winter's long confinement, how fresh and alive was that air at the window now.

He turned his head, saw the tops of the elms and the rooks flying in, flying out, against the morning sky. At a pause in the ring of bells he could hear their cries, and the songs of finch and thrush and blackbird, the approach of carriages on the road below, and the bleating lambs from the plock behind the house. All the Lord's bright world around him. He must rise, must give thanks.

Susannah was leaning a little out of the window, watching the guests walk up the path. He could hear their voices; then the bells rang out once more. He drew in a breath of the blessed air, felt the cough begin to take him. He caught her look of revulsion, instantly become concern, like a field of long grass beneath the wind, swept one away and then another. He struggled, he fought, he heaved and hawked into the dreadful bowl beside him.

She was at the door. She waited. He fell back upon the pillows.

'Forgive me …'

She put out a hand, too far away to touch him. 'You must not speak of forgiveness – I know how it torments you. I should go – shall I go?'

'Of course. Millie will come up?'

'I will send her. And I will return the moment the service is over.'

'The breakfast – will you not wish to go to that?'

She shook her head. 'I could not leave you for so long.'

'It will do you good.'

He saw a little expression cross her face – hesitation and something more. Then she said quickly: 'It will last for hours – much too long. Go to sleep now. I shall be here when you wake.'

He closed his eyes. It made him think of childhood illness – the firelight playing on the wall, the figure of his nurse in the chair, always there, always waiting, rising the moment he murmured from his fever. The memory both comforted and repelled him – that he, in manhood, should long for his wife's kindness as for a kindly nurse.

When he opened his eyes, she had gone, though he had heard no departing footstep, no rustle of her gown. He lay there, the bell beside him. His body felt curiously light, as if his very bones were losing weight. Perhaps they were. And yet – when he tried to sit up, and swing his legs on to the floor, he could not manage it. He made to lift the bell, fumbled and felt it slip from his fingers. It landed with a dull little chink on the boards.

'Lord,' he whispered, and felt his eyes fill up. Why? That something which should ring out brightly had then such a dead dull sound? This could reduce him to tears?

The bells in the tower had fallen silent. The churchyard was empty of voices, save for the birds. Blessed, beloved, bright-eyed thrush, hopping about on the grass—

'Sir?'

Millie was at the door. She bore his sponge, soap and a towel, a steaming bowl.

'How are you feeling, sir?'

'Oh, Millie …'

Shameful that she should see him weep; his chest so full of phlegm that it was dangerous for him to do so. He closed his eyes again and let the tears seep through; he clasped his hands to pray and clenched them, bone on bone.

She took away the filthy bowl of spit, and the chamber pot. She sponged his face with warm water, helped him off with his nightshirt and left the room for a clean one, that he might wash in private. Cool air met wet skin and he shivered, sponging weakly. When she came back, the bed was wet with drips and he exhausted: she dried him, slipped on a clean nightshirt, helped him slowly, slowly across the room to the chair at the window. He sank; she tucked the blankets round him.

'You're very good.'

'I'll bring you some breakfast, sir, that's what you need.'

'Only a very little.'

He waited, hearing, just, the faint sound of singing from within the church: 'Love Divine, all loves excelling …'

In truth, he could hear only the tune, but he knew the words by heart, as he knew everything by heart, could not remember a time when hymn and psalm and liturgy had not run in his veins.

> 'Jesu, Thou art all compassion,
> Pure unbounded love Thou art …'

He and Susannah had sung the words at their own wedding; everyone chose it, like the Twenty-third Psalm: God spoke through those words to them all.

'Here we are, sir.' Millie was back with a dish of porridge and the creamer upon the worn red tray. Had that been a wedding gift? He let her settle it upon his knees; he contemplated eating.

'Mind, sir, it's still very hot. Shall I pour you the cream?'

Threads of steam rose softly into the air and drifted out of the open window. Even they were beautiful: so frail against the light, so lovely in their movement this way and that, melting so delicately into nothing. Now they were gone.

171

'Do try a little.'
He lifted the spoon to his lips. Yes, it was very good.

> 'Changed from glory into glory,
> Till in Heav'n we take our place,
> Till we cast our crowns before Thee,
> Lost in wonder, love and praise.'

I am dying, he thought, as the last verse faded. Lord, be with me always. Slowly he put down the spoon.

'Sir?' Millie was straightening the rumpled bed, smoothing the pillows. She turned, saw him leaning back in the chair, gone pale. 'Can you not eat a little more?'

'In a moment.'

Beyond the window, the breeze stirred the boughs of churchyard elm and yew. It brought in the smell of earth and narcissi and prayermint. He heard the croak of a jackdaw. Oh, how precious every little thing.

She had crossed the floor, was kneeling beside him, lifting the spoon to his lips.

'Try, sir,' she urged him. 'Try just a spoonful more.'

He tasted, and with each new mouthful felt a little life come back.

'Thank you, Millie, I can manage now. What time is it?'

The service was ended, and everyone come out. From his chair in the fresh-made room he watched them, the tray taken down and glass and carafe beside him. Joyful bells and good young couple: he knew them, solid and true, and now the churchyard was alive with voices as they stood arm in arm in the sun, big Dick Bampfield getting a ribbing for something, Prosser reproaching his wife for some misdemeanour, Allen greeting everyone and the children racing about.

And where was she?

There, with the Southwoods, and there with dull old Bodenham, there with a Skarratt child who had fallen, and with poor young Arndell, pacing about like a crow. Carriages waited at the gate, and on the road below: he could hear now and then the snort of horses, the shifting from foot to foot. He watched it all and then, as Edward and

Effie began to walk to the gate and were pelted with petals, he leaned back again in his chair listening to their laughter and the children's cries and running footsteps, all mingled with the bells. Soon she would be home.

Should he tell her what he felt in his bones? Would they pray together?

A little sound came at the open door and he turned to see the cat stepping across the threshold. It made him cough, and should not be up here.

'Go away – shoo.' He waved a hand. 'Shoo!'

Samuel looked up at the quilt and made to leap: must he ring for Millie again? He clapped his hands, and the cat slunk beneath the bed. Well, let it stay there until she returned. And he sank back on to the pillow at his head and looked out once more across the churchyard.

At first he did not quite absorb what he saw. His wife and the curate in conversation, as they often were. And then – how? By the tilt of her head as she looked up at him, by the length of time Richard Allen held her gaze, by the way her hand rested in his? It was all and none of these things – he noticed what he might have noticed over and over again, each time they were together, perhaps from the very first day Allen came to the house, and how could he not have allowed himself to understand?

The churchyard was emptying, the bells were approaching the end of the ring: he knew Grandsire Doubles by heart, as he had always known everything by heart. Except for this.

Allen had released Susannah's hand; she had turned, and was walking back to the house, stopping to say goodbye to someone – he could not see whom, and it did not matter.

He sank back upon the pillow and let the sounds of the world come up.

173

16

The sun was almost gone, slipping low behind house and barn and tree as Richard climbed the hill up from the village. Though the walking warmed him, the air was much cooler now, a wind beginning to cut across new-sown ploughland that lay to the left of the highway, stretching away to the hills. It rustled the hedgerow, just in leaf, and stirred the clumps of laurel shrouding the approach to the Prossers' villa. A few dry leaves, the last of winter, blew out across the ground towards him, and he stopped, and looked up the drive to the house.

The Prossers had come to the wedding breakfast but left the moment the speeches were over, rising from the trestle where all others were still laughing and talking. Sam Cooper's jugs were coming round again, but Prosser the verger, he told his table, must be away, must see that the church was in order for tomorrow's Sunday service, after the wedding. The path must be swept, the stove banked up and hymnals and prayerbooks tidied. People sometimes left things behind at weddings, so caught up were they with the occasion: he must gather up a fallen glove, a pair of lorgnettes, perhaps, or child's plaything, for some children were permitted by their parents to bring in a doll or soldier, though he himself never had allowed it when his own son was a boy.

'Mind you don't find a ring, Mr Prosser!' shouted out one of the Skarratt lads, and Dick Bampfield half rose to reach across and thump him, then sank down to the bench once more, scarlet in the face with laughter. 'Thee's awash with this cider, Bampfield!' called Jim Skarratt. 'Not like thee,' returned Dick, and the table roared.

Between the benches, Philip Prosser was urging his wife to the door.

'The Prossers' son,' said Richard to his neighbour, the lawyer Bodenham. 'Mr Bowen told me he lives in Hereford. I think I have never met him.'

Bodenham was reaching for a custard tart, for the wedding cake slices had been small, to feed so many, and he had a frame to fill. 'Young Prosser does not visit often,' he said, his fingers hovering.

Richard thought best to wait for a reason for this, but none was given. 'There are other children?' he asked, observing Tilda Prosser's anxious little smile of farewell to the bride and groom, as her husband ushered her out.

'I believe there was a stillbirth,' said Bodenham, taking a mouthful of crumbly tart. 'Perhaps more than one.' He brushed his lips. 'Women's matters, Allen, my wife knows more than I. A good many years ago now, in any event.' He turned as the Cooper jug reached his elbow. 'Ah, very good, Sam, very good. Allen, will you take another glass?'

Richard shook his head. He had drunk but one, with the toasts, and unused as he was to liquor it had gone quite to his head. And he let the jug pass with a smile of thanks, and watched the door swing to. What a bleak life for the Prossers, then, with only one son for their years of marriage, and he gone away and rarely visiting. And that house holding ghostly little shadows of stillborn babes. No wonder, perhaps, that Prosser was often so sharp, and his wife wore such a thin brave air. Oliver had told him nothing of their circumstances when he'd arrived, and was taken to visit them – indeed, had made it clear he did not wish to discuss them. And was that because Richard was so young and inexperienced, or because, as he had thought then, to speak of another childless house was perhaps too painful? And as the laughter rose around him, and someone began to sing, Richard allowed himself to enter in his mind the vicarage, wherein Susannah must be sitting with Oliver, and awaiting with every hour his own arrival. How soon might he slip away?

'I must say, Allen, for a man who barely touches a drop, you are quite as far away as if you had been drinking all afternoon.'

He came to with a laugh, and half rose as Southwood patted his shoulder.

'Forgive me, sir – perhaps it is because I drink so little that it does indeed make my head swim.'

'Well, what's the harm? Sit down, sit down. You did very well, if I may say so – a most lovely wedding, and that little difficulty with the ring quite smoothed away. Well done.'

'Thank you, sir. I was privileged to be able to conduct the service.'

What a prig, what a platitudinous prig, but Southwood did not seem to think so, and shook his hand, saying they were all off in a moment, and bidding him come over to Burgage for a game of croquet when the weather grew really warm. They would all be so glad to see him.

'Thank you, sir, I should much enjoy that.' Richard looked around. In truth, quite a number of the older gentry were beginning to leave now, and perhaps he himself would not be missed. On the contrary, perhaps the villagers were waiting for him to leave, so they might really begin to enjoy themselves.

But no – for Dick's father was drawing a bow across a fiddle, and John Blakely had begun to blow upon his pipe, and in a moment Sam Cooper was pushing wide the door to the snug, and as a little jig struck up Edward and Effie Turner made their way through and began, amidst much laughter and clapping, to trip across the boards.

And what a happy sight that was, and how it struck suddenly to the quick. Richard watched as they skipped and bowed and turned away; he watched as Skarratt and Bampfield, Fletcher and Meredith and Neve pushed back the trestles and rose in their ones and twos, swaying a little, stumbling a little, but taking to the floor, each with a girl with whom to link an arm or hold a hand – a sister, a cousin, a sweetheart, as the musicians got into their stride and the strains of fiddle and pipe sounded fast and faster still. Those at the tables were clapping and stamping their feet; Effie Turner's lips were parted as she skipped and twirled, and her eyes bright with excited happiness; Edward was flushed and panting and both had quite forgotten to be shy. And Richard, observing them, observing the younger children scramble to join the fun, in his mind's eye put himself amongst them all, Susannah's hand in his, his arm about her waist, the two of them in perfect time together, as the music rose and fell. He closed his eyes, allowed himself for a moment or two this delicious, carefree dream.

177

'Mr Allen? Mr Allen, I pray you come and join us.'

A hand was upon his arm; he opened his eyes to see Will Southwood grin down at him. 'You may not sit and slumber, Richard Allen, man of the cloth or no. My sister tires of dancing with her brother – will you not enjoy the pleasure of her company?'

Richard flushed, and rose. 'Pray forgive me,' he said again. And was he destined to go through his whole life asking forgiveness for each little lapse? Must he, at twenty-four, continually sound like some foolish boy, or bumbling cleric a generation older? 'I fear I was for a moment thinking of something else entirely,' he said, then flushed still deeper, both at his indiscretion and at Will's dry, 'Really? And what might that have been?'

'No matter,' said Richard, as the noise rose all around them. 'But I fear I am about to leave – I have promised to call in upon Mr Bowen.'

'Poor Bowen looks like a ghost these days, but I am sure he will last long enough for you to enjoy yourself a little. Come, you stiff fellow.' And Will drew him into the crowded snug, where Charlotte Southwood was deep in conversation with Maria Bodenham, a full young woman in a full blue gown, whose figure suggested an eventual silhouette not unlike her father's. Will said so; Richard had to smile. Charlotte was fanning herself with her glove; turned and saw their approach through the throng and smiled too – smiled back, as it seemed, to one delighted to have the opportunity of her company. And Richard, as he knew he must, made a bow before her.

'May I have the honour?'

'You may, Mr Allen,' said Charlotte Southwood, and gave him her hand.

And so it was not Susannah whom he drew on to the crowded little floor, not Susannah whose slender waist his arm encircled, as other couples flew up and down around them, not another man's wife, whom he longed to take in his arms, but a striking, vivacious, well-born young woman, with whom he felt clumsy and out of keeping, unable to mark time as he should, or to lead her and partner her as she wished. And as they dipped and bumped into one another and into other people, he had a sudden insight, as clear as the water of the stream before his cottage, of what harmony must be, must mean, what joy it must bring – and how terrible it must be in a marriage if it were not there. For it should be something as simple and natural as breathing, he could see this now, a fitting together in delight, as if this body were made for this other, beloved body, this hand to be placed just so, in just this place, on this curve of the cheek, in this crook in the arm, on the unimagined beauty of this little breast. And he knew that for him and Susannah it would be like this, and that they would never tire of one another, just as he knew, in this awkward, ill-matched coupling in a country dance, that he could never please Charlotte Southwood, spirited and exciting – yes, he could see that – as she was.

'Forgive me,' he called through the music, for the third time in an hour. 'I am so clumsy, most dreadfully out of practice.'

'Not at all,' said Charlotte, laughing, and in that laugh he could see Verity once again – flashing, impatient, funny and fierce – and he almost liked her. As why should he not, after all? She was clever and beautiful, was she not? Must it matter, here, at a country wedding, that she and he were not made for one another? Might they still not enjoy each other's company? And with this thought he all at once relaxed, and with more assurance spun her round in the crook of his arm, until they both were laughing, as the music stopped at last.

'Miss Southwood.' He bowed before her. 'Thank you so much.'

'It was a pleasure,' she said, quite out of breath. 'In the end,' she added drily, and he recognised her brother's humour, and liked it; and here Will was, portly Maria Bodenham at his side.

'Well, you are almost one of us, old man,' he said, clapping Richard on the shoulder. 'Is this not merry?'

'Merrier than an Oxford ball,' said Charlotte, 'or at least I find it so today.'

The jug was going round again, the fiddler and piper wiping their brows with enormous handkerchiefs, and the window of the snug flung wide to let in the fresh spring air. Four o'clock on an April afternoon, and the sun beginning to sink.

'I must go,' said Richard, seeing this, and thinking of Susannah. I shall tell her, he thought, straightening his clerical white tie. I shall tell her how I danced, thinking only of her, and the way we fit together.

'Go?' cried Will Southwood, catching the jug as it passed. 'How can you go, when Edward and Effie are still with us? Edward! Effie – Mrs

Turner! Come here and tell the man who conducted your wedding that he must not think of leaving.'

Edward and Effie came up, laughing, hand in hand.

'We must thank you, Mr Allen, for the service, must we not, Eff?'

'Indeed we must,' said Effie. 'We was so nervous, and you made it all so fine. Even with the blessed ring – did he not calm you, Edward?'

'I don't know that anyone could properly have calmed me then, to tell you the truth, Mr Allen,' said Edward, as open and happy as any new husband could be. 'But you did most certainly help us.'

'Well, well,' said Richard. 'It has been as lovely a wedding as I have ever attended. And if you had known how nervous *I* was, conducting my first—'

'We should never have guessed that, should us, Eff?'

'Indeed we should not.'

'I should,' said Will. 'He's nervous now, just look at him, trying to make his excuses.'

'Well, well,' said Richard again, and heard his father's voice in his. 'If Mr Southwood will permit me, I shall wish you both enormous happiness.' He rested a hand on each shoulder. 'My blessings on you both. May God guide you and keep you always.'

'Thank you, sir. Amen.'

'Thank you, Mr Allen.'

A little hush had fallen, with his gentle words, felt as deeply as any he had ever spoken, for was it not a great bond between them, the first couple he had ever married, and they so innocent and true, taking the greatest step of their lives through him? And if he himself were anything but innocent in his heart, if he longed, now, to have Susannah beside him and to slip away with her for a kiss as intense and deep as on any wedding night – well, no one knew that, and no one ever would.

'I must go,' he said again, and felt Charlotte's eyes upon him. 'Thank you all for a wonderful day.'

And as fiddle and pipe struck up once more, he shook Will's hand, bowed over Charlotte's, bade farewell to all around him, warmly thanked the parents of the bride and groom, and slipped away at last.

And now, on the steep slope of the hill, far up from the village, with the strains of the dance no longer audible, Richard stood in the cold of the late afternoon and watched the skittering dance of a few dry laurel leaves blowing about in the wind. Across on the other side of the road, the bank of the churchyard rose beyond the wall, and where this morning it had been filled with life and warmth and the joyous sound of the bells, now, in the ebbing light, the tower stood dark and stern. Soon it would be time to light the lamps: perhaps, in the sickroom, one was already lit, or a spill had been set to the fire on a cold spring evening. Or perhaps Oliver had come downstairs, was feeling a little stronger. If that were so, there would be no chance to talk to Susannah freely, no hope of lifting her hand to his lips and drawing her towards him.

His stomach fluttered anew at the thought of this, but then he was filled with shame. What manner of man – a man of the Church, who had just conducted the holy service of matrimony – would sit thus, and think and do thus, while an invalid coughed and groaned? And all the turmoil that he was growing used to as an inescapable part of each day flared up once more as he stood by the rustling laurels, when for a little while, in the wedding party, he had felt only calm true love – and a sudden, unexpected liking.

He must cross the road, he must go to where she was waiting, but he hesitated a moment longer, as the dry leaves blew about restlessly at his feet, and he all at once covered his face, thinking: I want to be free of this. And again he prayed: Lord, help me through. And then, as he stood on the darkening road, he heard from the villa, set back so deep behind the screen of laurels, a sudden, terrible sound – a scream, no, a series of screams, piteous cries of terror – and his hands fell from his face and then he was frozen, listening.

'No – no no please – I beg you – no no please – dear God you're hurting me – stop it stop it stop it – *help me!*'

Richard flew up the drive. The villa was unlit and the wind was rising: somewhere a shutter banged and banged. Was that a shutter, or did that dreadful banging come from within the house? He pounded upon the door.

The silence then was as sudden, and almost as terrifying, as the screams that had brought him here, and he stood on the unlit step shaking from head to foot.

'Open up! Open up!' He lifted the knocker and thundered, iron

181

upon iron. 'Open up in there!' Then came the sound of sobbing, unstoppable, on and on. Then the violent slam of a door.

Should he go for the police? How could he, when they were miles away down in Kington? Should he break in? He trembled and shook, and the thundering sound of the knocker, and of his own voice in the gathering dark, went through him like blows. 'God help me, Lord help me,' he prayed aloud.

All at once a lamp was lit in the hall, and the stained-glass panels in the door were illuminated in blue and green and gold, like the glass in a chancel window, and through them he could see, just, Prosser's little figure moving towards him. A bolt was slid back, and a chain unfastened. Then the handle turned, and Prosser stood before him.

'Mr Allen—'

'Mr Prosser,' said Richard, moving into the dim fall of light on the step. 'What in the name of God—'

'My wife is unwell,' said Prosser flatly. He brushed at his clothes, wiped a secretion of spittle from the corner of his lips. 'I am shocked that her cries are so loud as to alert a passer-by.'

'Perhaps it is as well I was alerted. I heard … I heard—'

Prosser shook his head. 'It is good of you to concern yourself, but there is no need for alarm. This has happened before. I shall send for the physician.'

'How?' asked Richard stupidly. 'Who will you send? What is wrong with Mrs Prosser?' His words tumbled over themselves; he could hear his voice shake. 'I heard sounds such as – such as—'

'My poor wife suffers from a nervous condition. She is prone to attacks of weeping and distress. I find it most upsetting. But our maid will return directly and then I shall take the trap to Kington. Probyn will come with a draught.'

'Shall I go for you?'

'No, no, you need trouble yourself no further. As I say, this has happened before.'

Richard hesitated. Prosser was speaking more calmly now, his whole demeanour less agitated, though his eyes, even in the dim glow from the hall, seemed unnaturally bright. Richard shivered on the step, recalling the words of his neighbour, down in the George: greedy old Bodenham, reaching for the custard tart. 'A son, who

182

rarely visits – one or two stillbirths, I believe – women's matters ...'
Was it grief that had loosened the mind of poor little Tilda Prosser?
Or was her husband concealing the truth? Never had Richard more
longed for the counsel of his parents than he did now. He must write
to his mother; he must look to the wisdom of her experience.
Women's matters – what, in truth, did he know of those?

'May I not see your poor wife?' he asked carefully. 'Might it help her
to have me offer words of comfort? To say a prayer with you both?'
Was this what Bowen had done in the past?

Prosser was emphatic. 'You are very kind, Mr Allen, and also very
young. My wife is far too unsettled to see anyone but those she knows
well. As I say, our maid will return directly. And now I must bid you
good night.'

He stepped back into the hall, and made to close the door. For a
moment Richard looked beyond him, into its shadowy depths. Where
was she? Was he really right to leave her? Then Prosser nodded, and
the door swung firmly to, and with its closing all the other sounds of
the evening, now bitterly cold, returned: the wind stirring the laurels,
sighing in the trees, the skittering of old dry leaves, the cries of the
lambs in the dusk and the new young rooks from the churchyard, all
at once most comforting, hopeful and familiar. And he turned and
hurried back down the path, crossing the highway at a tilt and running
up the path towards the lich-gate.

Lamps were lit in the vicarage. A fire flickered in the sitting room,
its reflection playing brightly upon the panes. When Millie answered
his knock he almost fell into her arms.

'Why, whatever is it, Mr Allen? You look as if—'

'It's nothing, nothing – at least ...' He stepped into the hall. He
had used to think of it as a dull, dark place, with its hatstand and
fern, stuffed hawk and sombre picture. Then, like everything else in
the house, it had become charged with radiance, with Susannah's real
and imagined presence – her footsteps crossing it, her hand knocking
on the study door, lifting down cape or bonnet, her voice calling
down to the kitchen, or up the stairs. Now, after that glimpse of
gloom within the villa, with the memory of those piteous cries of
terror, the whole vicarage felt like the sweetest home: that bright

fresh fire crackling beyond the parlour door, the daffodils on the parlour table, the cat upon the hearthrug and Millie taking his things.

'Thank you. Thank you so much.'

'Mr and Mrs Bowen are both upstairs, sir. I know they are expecting you.' She reached to hang up his hat. 'I hear it was a lovely wedding.'

'It was, it was. And the reception quite delightful.' He could feel himself growing calmer. 'How is Mr Bowen this evening?'

'He's a little tired now, but he had a good day. He watched you all in the churchyard from his window, and I know that pleased him.' She was smoothing the folds of his coat upon the stand; then she turned to look at him. 'But you, sir – you are quite out of sorts.'

'Better now, better now, thank you. I was – startled by something – no doubt it was only the wind.' For he could not think it right to discuss a private matter with a servant, not even with Millie, good as she was.

'He can rise something powerful up here, can't he, that wind? Sometimes I lie in my bed and imagine all sorts of things, listening. Must be worse for you, sir, down in the woods.'

'I've grown used to it. And I'm quite recovered now. You're very calming, Millie, very good and true.' And indeed, at that moment, had she been a servant in his own household, he would almost have embraced her – certainly as a boy he would have done so.

'Thank you, sir. I'll tell Mrs Bowen you're here.'

But the door of the bedroom upstairs was already opening, and Susannah calling down quietly: 'Is that you, Mr Allen?'

'It is,' said Richard.

She was above him, and he below – here they were, calling to one another, and for a moment he had the sense of them within their own house, their own home, with she about to run down and greet him with a kiss and he to fold her in his arms at the end of the day, to take her through to the fireside on a cold April evening, and draw her down on to his lap.

All this came and went as quickly as a leaf blown about in the wind. She descended the narrow stairs, her hand upon the rail.

'How good of you to call. Millie? Will you bring Mr Allen some tea? Yes, Mr Allen? Have you time to stay a little?'

'I have. Thank you.'

And as Millie went down the passage to the kitchen, Susannah pushed wide the parlour door, and gestured towards the fireside, where the black cat Samuel made his little sound of greeting.

'Our chaperone,' said Richard, without even thinking about it, and she at the same time murmured, 'Samuel can be our chaperone.'

They looked at one another.

'How alike we think,' Richard said with a smile, and then, as he asked her, 'How is your husband?' Susannah's voice joined his: 'How are you, Mr Allen?'

'We must disentangle ourselves,' he said quietly, as they entered the parlour. 'May I sit down?'

'Of course. Please ...'

He sat in Oliver Bowen's high wing chair and she took her place opposite, in the worn velvet button-back, the cat stretched out before the leaping flames.

'Mr Bowen is—'

'He has just fallen asleep. I have been reading to him a little.'

'It must have done him much good to have you with him.'

'I hope it has. We have had a very long quiet day, have we not, Samuel?' She bent towards the sleeping cat and began to stroke him, and he stretched out at her touch, and began to purr. Richard watched her pale head bent towards the flames, and he felt the room charged with everything they could not say, and could not do. 'And the breakfast?' she asked him, without looking up, and he saw the colour deepen on her face, though whether this was due to her consciousness of his gaze, or the warmth of the fire, he was not certain.

'The breakfast was very fine,' he said. 'Very touching. I will tell you all about it.'

Oh, what a sweet domestic phrase that was, betokening such affection, such easy familiarity – 'Come here, come here, let me tell you all about it,' with long unbroken hours ahead, by a fireside such as this.

'I shall like to hear it.' She looked up, and her smile pierced him. He felt then as if in this small exchange each had the same thoughts exactly, and as if they were opening another door, into a future of endless conversations, deepening their knowledge of one another, growing closer and closer. The turmoil of which he had longed to be

185

free quite ebbed away: there was only this calm true certainty, and he knew that whatever became of them, this moment, so simple and real, would always stay with him, like a bookmark on a particular page, which told him: this is love.

'But first I must ask you something,' he said, and he could feel her long to take his hand, to listen carefully.

Footsteps along the passage; the chink of china; a tap at the door.

'Come in, Millie.' Susannah leaned back in her velvet chair; she gestured at the table beside her, clearing her little heap of novels. 'This will do very well.'

Millie put down the tray; she set out cup and saucer, and a plate of seed cake. 'Thank you. I shall manage now.'

'Yes, ma'am.'

She went out, leaving the door ajar.

Did she know? Did she guess? Richard watched Susannah pour hot tea, and took the cup she gave him. At the window behind him he could hear the wind again.

'What did you want to ask me?' Susannah's voice was quiet, and he knew she must expect a question about her, or about themselves.

'The Prossers,' he said slowly, lifting the cup to his lips, and he saw her frown. 'What do you know of them?'

She shook her head. 'Very little. They have lived here a long time, many years longer than we have. Mr Prosser has long been verger here – I believe that Mr Bowen finds him reliable. I think him rather – rather sour, though I should not say so. His wife is a nervous person, is she not? She seems anxious to please him.' She paused. 'And of course – of course they have no children at home, now their son is grown. Perhaps the house feels rather empty.' She lowered her gaze.

Had they longer to spend together, were they quite alone, Richard would have gently asked Susannah now: 'As this house has felt, perhaps?' But they had not such time, and he did not ask it – and, after all, both knew that this was so.

'On my way here, as I was about to cross the road, I heard—' He stopped, all at once unable to bring himself to describe those dreadful cries, that wild and endless sobbing. 'Mrs Prosser,' he said carefully. 'Is she ill? Does she suffer from – how shall I call it? – some kind of nervous affliction?'

'I believe I have heard something of the sort. Yes, I believe she is sometimes given to such attacks.'

'She has told you this herself?'

'No. No, I believe Mr Prosser has mentioned it to my husband. He said something once, but Oliver did not think it serious. You said you heard something? What was that?'

Richard put down his cup.

'A woman in distress,' he said slowly. 'But perhaps – perhaps it is as everyone says: Mrs Prosser is sometimes unwell, and will soon recover.'

'Why, what else could it be?' asked Susannah.

The fire burned, the cat stretched, upstairs Millie was closing the shutters. Soon it would be dark, and soon he must leave for the long walk home with a lantern.

'Nothing,' he said, and let his gaze rest upon Susannah. How innocent she was, and how untutored he himself was in anything but questions of the spirit. In this vicarage home, whatever it might lack, goodness was at its heart: in Oliver's stern certainty, in Millie's steadiness, Susannah's sadness and longing. Looking at her now he allowed the memory of those cries to fade, let himself dwell anew upon her countenance. Susannah held his gaze, and there began then, in the firelit parlour, the great intimacy not of conversation, nor of an embrace, but of silence, which Richard began to discover as one of the most erotic gifts that life could offer. For with whom but a beloved could a silence hold so much? With whom but a lover could each breath, each long, long gaze, and thought unspoken, promise the world entire?

And so, as the firelight played upon them, they went on gazing into each other's eyes, searching, finding, searching again, while outside the cold April wind stirred the trees, and across the darkening highway the house behind the laurels now was silent.

17

April shook itself into May, a month marked in Richard's
memory by many things, each betokening some happiness
or contentment: schoolroom verses, inscribed by the girls at
an open window; his mother humming as she altered Verity's gowns
for Emily and made up muslin and cotton into new gowns for each
of them; the taking of just one speckled egg from the nest of thrush
or blackbird to add to his collection. He remembered the minute
observation in school grounds or kitchen garden of each striped or
pale green caterpillar that might become Emperor, Admiral or
Fritillary; the taking out and rewinding of fishing rods, and the
setting out across the fields with his father on an exeat weekend: just
the two of them, his bag for the catch swinging at his side; ahead,
the placid river and the lengthening afternoon. And now, as the apple
and damson and plum trees in his orchard were snowy with blossom,
as the tight buds of oak and ash and elm unfurled in the sun, and the
woods were misty with bluebells, he heard the voices of his family,
coming and going as he went about his life, his garden.

'A swarm of bees in May, is worth a load of hay ...'

He was out in the orchard one afternoon, composing, or trying to
compose, his thoughts for a sermon, when he heard this cheerful
chanting from the lane, and at once was transported to the schoolroom of his childhood, all of them bent over their slates and Verity
murmuring as she copied: 'A swarm of bees in June is worth a silver
spoon ...'

He walked across the new grass to the hedge. Petals clung to his
boots, and fell upon his shoulders.

'A swarm of bees in July is not worth a fly!'

'Hello, Alice.'

She was swinging hands with little Jenny Neve, walking home from the long day at school, sustained by chanting, and keeping step. Had Emily and Verity really been as small and young as this?

'Sir. Mr Allen, sir.'

'My sisters used to like that old rhyme – we all did. I am thinking of keeping a hive for my swarm of bees.'

'Yes, sir.'

'Have you been good today? What lessons have you learned?'

They could not remember, already the day become one of endless days, slipping away behind them like the dissolving sun.

Then: 'Mrs Bowen read us our Bible story.'

'Ah.' How everything in him contracted, hearing her name. 'And which story was that?'

They looked at one another. Alice's dark hair fell thickly to the shoulders of her pinafore, through which Susannah's needle perhaps had passed in a dutiful morning of mending. Jenny's fair wisps were in want of brushing, and her boots were most fearfully scuffed. He wanted to kiss them both.

'The story was of two disciples,' said Alice.

'And someone walks with them,' added Jenny.

'And who is that person?'

'They do not know. Then later He breaks bread with them, and vanishes. Then they know it was Jesus, come back to be with them after His death.'

'Very good, both of you. And can you recollect the place where they were going? The road they were on?'

But this they could not remember, and he saw how tired they were, how they longed to be free of questions, and play, as they had been about to do when he interrupted them.

'The road to Emmaus,' he told them gently. 'It is told in the Gospel according to St Luke.' And he bid them farewell, watching them from behind the hedge as they ran off hand in hand, no longer in step and no longer chanting, for he had interrupted and taken that away from them, with his questions about the scriptures. So that he could think of Susannah's voice, taking them through a story he had always loved?

Was that why he had persisted, to see how well she had told it? Or was he more cleric and schoolmaster than he was a man, fastening upon each opportunity to enquire, examine, have children do his bidding?

He walked back across the grass beneath the trees, brushing the boughs, with their weight of blossom, thinking of the mystery and poetry of that story, of the shadowy presence of a stranger, joining two companions on a dusty road in the hills beyond Jerusalem, engaging them in conversation as they approached the flat-roofed city, all at once after supper slipping away – no, vanishing – leaving them to look round, to look at one another, to realise.

Perhaps this should be the subject of a sermon: the way God came, the way God went, or seemed to go, but was always here, always waiting, watchful and loving.

The early summer sun was sinking: he saw the dark shapes of the sheep with their lambs passing the hedge in the rise of the field beyond the orchard; he saw his own shadow, here and there on the grass, on the trunk of a tree. He paced about, drinking in the smells of the animals and the grass crushed beneath his footsteps, thinking of his sermon, and of where Susannah might, if she were here, advise him to set a hive, in this merry, merry month of May, when all seemed possible.

' "*And thus it passed on from Candlemas until after Easter, that the month of May was come, when every lusty heart beginneth to blossom, and to bring forth fruit …*" '

In the quiet of the late afternoon, he heard from years and years ago his father, reciting marvellous lines from Malory's *Le Morte D'Arthur*, as they strode out over the fields on their fishing trip. What a good fine voice he had had – made to sing hymns, to deliver a sermon, made to declaim great lines of verse, great prose.

' "*Therefore all ye that be lovers call unto your remembrance the month of May, like as did Queen Guenevere, for whom I make here a little mention, that while she lived she was a true lover, and therefore she had a good end.*" '

'*Father! You know it all by heart!*'

Now he knew it too, it had never left him, and he thought sometimes that every line of legend, verse or scripture that ran in his veins was inflicted with his father's voice. Would that his life might run its course with the same kindness, generosity, certainty and

191

purpose. And pacing beneath the apple trees, as his shadow length-ened, he recalled not a cheerful recital of Arthurian legend but the leading of a congregation in the Creed, as all faced the light east window and declared: 'I believe in God, the Father Almighty, Maker of Heaven and Earth …'

Oh, the great certainties of the Creed, and the beauty of the benediction, as the service ended: 'The Peace of God, which passeth all understanding, keep your hearts and minds in the knowledge and love of God …' How, with his father's loving voice in their ears, could his congregation not leave the church uplifted? How could his children not feel strengthened all their lives by him?

Was it the shock of his death that had left his son so open to all emotion? So yearning for that great chasm to be filled that he fell in love within months, in a way that transgressed everything? In memory now, Richard passed the door to his father's study, often a little ajar, that his family might feel him amongst them while he worked. He heard the low murmur of a voice in prayer, though the words were indistinguishable. There were public prayers, there was private silent prayer, and there was this, like a conversation with God, perhaps, a question and answer at the desk, between fire and window.

'Father?' He saw himself tap at the door, saw – oh, so longed for – his father's smile of welcome. 'I have something to tell you, now I am a man—'

Impossible, unimaginable, even with him. For as the sun slipped low behind the hills, and the world was for a moment rimmed with gold, as quickly came the dusk, and the lichened trunks of the apple trees were clothed in violet shadow, the boughs thick with blossom now become like ghosts. And he saw, as he made to go in to the house, another study, wherein a sick man coughed and groaned, a man who in generation and beliefs could be his father's brother.

He had come to the gate. A little clump of prayermint grew at the foot of the post, and its faint scent came up to him in the twilight – something like mint, something like lily of the valley, something like itself. He bent to pick a stem or two, pressed it to his lips. The pale clustered flowers in their leafy hood put him in mind of Susannah. Everything did this, for she never left his thoughts, but this little plant especially now: delicate, pale, half-hidden, but with a core of such intensity, releasing a scent which went wafting all around him, as he stepped through the gate and on to the long grassy path which ran alongside the cottage from the barn down to the lane.

The orchard gate swung to behind him; he stood drinking in the flower's scent, the sounds of the sheep and the stream, the sight of the darkening hills.

'Susannah,' he said aloud, for to do this offered in some way relief from his longing, and he saw her face as it had been when they last were alone together: seated on either side of the parlour fire, gazing at and drinking in one another, on and on and on, until a bell rang faintly from upstairs, and Millie appeared at the door with his things and he took his leave, that Susannah might go to her husband.

And as that evening after the wedding had been marked both by love's silent gaze and by those cries of terror from an unlit house, so now, all at once, the evening hush was pierced by the shriek of a whistle at the train's approach, and when he turned he saw the billowing clouds of steam pour from the funnel, rise above the trees and go drifting into the dark.

He went indoors, set the stems of prayermint in a glass of water, lit the fire, for the evening now was quite cold enough to require it. While his supper warmed he made his notes for a sermon on the theme of God's constancy, taking as text the story of The Road to Emmaus, feeling as if Susannah, through the children, had sent him this as a gift.

And it came to pass, as he sat at meat with them, he took bread, and blessed it, and brake, and gave to them.

And their eyes were opened, and they knew him; and he vanished out of their sight.

And they said one to another, Did not our heart burn within us, while he talked with us by the way, and while he opened to us the scriptures?

'Unseen, invisible, ever-present,' wrote Richard. 'We see Him not, but He is always there. Do we recognise Him when He walks amongst us, in whatsoever guise? Do we feel His guiding spirit?'

193

Quick lines, as they came to him, his quill in fresh ink for the text he would take as his conclusion, the mighty last line of St Matthew's Gospel: 'Lo, I am with you always, even unto the end of the world.'

He bowed his head. He slipped back his Bible in its place upon the sill, and sat looking out across the darkening field. Truly, was he fit to preach upon this theme? To preach at all?

He pushed back his chair, fetched a dish of Martha Price's rabbit stew from the range, said grace alone, as always, and ate his supper, reading by the oil lamps as he did so, one of life's true solitary pleasures. By the time he had finished, and was quartering an apple, the windows on to field and lane were black, though when he rose to fasten the shutters he could see the first stars, and a sliver of moon. He banked up the fire, and sat down to write a letter.

6 May 1861

Dearest Mama,

I pray that you and my dear sisters are keeping well, and now that the weather is warmer at last I pray I might see you all here for a visit. The summer promises to be so lovely: already the days are grown longer, and the sun has brought out every leaf and bud, while the song of the stream by my garden and the sounds of the river and turning wheel of the mill are the constant accompaniment to my walks and writing.

This afternoon I have thought much of my dear father, his goodness and steadiness – I found myself remembering our fishing expeditions and am determined to take out my old rod and see what the sparkling Arrow may bring forth. So – while my memories of Father reawaken my grief, they are also so happy that I feel strengthened too – we fished together, so I shall fish now, and continue what he taught me: just one little thing amongst so many.

He read this through and marvelled that in all his inner turmoil and preoccupation he could send home such a picture of tranquillity. Now he must turn to the true subject of his letter. And he blotted the page, and continued.

194

All this is good, but as the evening stars appear, I must turn to
something less pleasant, seeking your counsel, dear wise Mama,
though I trust that what I have to say does not distress you.

You will remember the wedding I conducted, about which I
wrote to you? I described it all, but I did not tell you how that
sweet day ended.

Now he began to do so, his nib racing over the paper, and his heart
racing too as he relived it all: the skitter of leaves at his feet in the cold
spring wind, the ebbing of light, and then, as he stopped for a
moment, those screams, those pleas for mercy. The Prossers had been
in church each Sunday since: she looked pale and drawn but then this
was how she always looked, and when he enquired after her health,
out on the path with the sounds of the organ fading, she said she had
been unwell but was quite recovered. And she took her husband's
proffered arm and hurried away to the gate.

Dear Mama – someone said these were women's matters. What
do you know of nervous conditions? Do you think it possible
that buried grief may reawaken in a sensitive mind into visions of
cruelty? Brutality?

He stopped, for this was why he had not written of all this earlier:
did he want to rekindle his mother's own fresh grief, to fill her with
anxious thoughts about the future? And yet, who else could he ask?
There was already so much poured into his journal, withheld from
his letters home – 'I am in love – we long for one another – it is
hopeless – in my heart I have already broken the Commandment' –
he felt his colour rise even to think of putting such words on paper.
But if he could not tell his family of the true workings of his heart,
might he not confide his fears for a shrunken, cowed little woman
within his congregation?

So he wrote it all out, and felt relieved at having done so, and
concluded his letter with the hope that his mother would forgive him
if he caused her any pain, with the hope of her advice in her reply,
and with the tenderest expressions of affection for her and for his
sisters.

'Tell Verity and Emily I shall write to each one of them soon. And am intending to start a hive, and learn about making honey.'

He kissed the pages, blotted, inscribed and sealed them, and set them aside to take to the post in Kington. And then, seeing in the gentle glow of the lamp the paper-white flowers and viridian hood of the prayermint in its glass on the desk before him, he unlocked the drawer, withdrew his journal, and into its pages poured out to Susannah everything he could not say to her, nor send to her house in a letter: everything he longed for with every passing hour in this lonely place – for it was lonely, there was no denying it, as the night deepened and the fire sank low and all he could think of was her.

Next morning he must go into Kington: to the post, to a meeting, leaving Martha Price up to her elbows in glinting soapsuds, every shutter and casement open to the sun, the cottage flooded with light.

'I could take that letter for you, sir, if you need. I'm in town myself this afternoon.'

'No, no, that's very kind but I have a meeting, and shopping to do.' He paused on his way out, taking pleasure, after last night's solitude and longing, in this domestic scene: the heap of washing upon the kitchen flags, the swishing of water in the tub and the iridescent foam of bubbles, floating away now and then through the open window. Martha's sleeves were rolled up neatly, her sacking apron tied round her middle with a good firm knot.

'How well you set about things,' he told her. 'How accomplished you are. That rabbit stew last night was quite perfection.'

'He'm shot in the garden by my Joseph,' said Martha, lifting the weight of a streaming bedsheet. 'Him and his brother – all through the young spring cabbages they were.'

'Were they now? Well, you thank your Joseph for me, Martha. And thank you for keeping this place so comfortable for me,' he added, as a swallow went swooping past the window and up towards the barn. What a day, what a morning! The swallows were come!

'The swallows are come,' he said, with a sudden real lightness of heart. He strode towards the open kitchen door. 'It makes me feel as if this house is blessed.'

''Tis a blessing to have you here with us, sir,' said Martha, and he bade her a warm farewell and went out into the quickening world, bluetit and finch and swallows darting, the notes high and low of sheep and lambs calling to one another in the sun, the blackbird upon the apple bough. He did not venture into the shadowy barn, but it did delight him, as he walked down the lane, the sound of the stream behind him and the splashing of mill wheel and river ahead, to think of the swallows in there, building their nests on the beam.

Beside him the woods stretched away with their carpet of blue, pigeons murmuring high above the trees. In Richard's pocket lay his letter home, with its dark disturbing story, but on a morning such as this it was impossible to think of such things, the sunlit mossy lane and leafy hedgerows leaving nothing to be desired but the presence of his beloved, her hand in the crook of his arm and a little girl like Alice Birley skipping along at their side. For a moment the longing for such fulfilment – his wife, his life's partner, their own dear child – stopped him in his tracks, and he stood there wondering: is this how women feel? Do I forget myself, my calling, to long so much for this?

From somewhere over the fields behind him came the mew of a buzzard, high in the summer clouds, and with its thin cry he thought of another woman, one who had so startlingly disturbed him on Palm Sunday morning but who ever since had been almost eclipsed in his mind – by his and Susannah's declarations, by Easter, and his struggle to conceal from the congregation the drama of his inner life, by the wedding, the screams from that house at the close of the afternoon, by every little thing which made up his daily duties.

But he thought of her now – Edith Clare – as he rounded the bend in the lane and walked towards the crossing, and though he knew that her hiding place was two or three miles away, up in the wooded Rushock hills, he found himself looking for her here: up through the trees which soared from the miraculous blue of the ground; across the sheep-speckled fields which led to town and highway; over railway track and mill and rushing river, and even at the great weir whose water poured into the Arrow's pools: as if, on this perfect May morning, he might glimpse her again – watching him, seeking him out, as he had sensed, hearing that footfall in the woods that winter day, that someone was doing from the first moment of his arrival.

☆

On market days Kington was crowded with carts and shoppers, the air filled with the lowing of the confined black cattle and the shouts of the auctioneers. Today, an ordinary weekday, the town was its quiet little self, the children all in school, the market hall and cattle pens empty and swept, just a few matrons or serving girls passing in and out of the shops, and a knot of three or four people waiting for the coach to Hereford. Hammering rang out from Merediths Foundry as Richard walked by. The cottage doors of Nail Row, adjoining, stood open to the summer light; a moth-eaten rug had been hung over a garden wall; two old fellows sat smoking in the sun. They touched their hats to him but he knew, as he called out good morning, that this was just their everyday good manners to a passing gentleman or cleric, not because they were part of his congregation. If they went to church at all, it would be to St Mary's, the Kington church, to whose vicarage he was bound this morning for a meeting of the clergy and councillors of three parishes.

This was a regular part of his duties: to deputise at meetings for Oliver Bowen when illness or other claims detained him, and this was the second time he would be giving his apologies to this particular gathering, which met to discuss issues common to them all: the Reverend Oliver Bowen, rector of Lyonshall; the Reverend Stephen Ingram, rector of St Mary's, Kington; the Reverend John Maddock, curate to the parish of St Andrew's, Presteigne, whose incumbent, elevated and appointed to serve as Dean of Windsor, was scarcely seen these days. Fortunate indeed that young Mr Maddock was so earnest in his duties, keeping up the spirits of the congregation, raising funds for a Ragged School, gathering in the barefoot urchins and teaching there himself.

The County Gaol was in Presteigne, with the House of Correction next door. The magistrates' quarter sessions met there; it was but ten years since the stocks were taken away. But though there was poverty, as everywhere, and though thieves and vagabonds and fallen women were housed there, the town was also, Richard had been told, pretty and well kept in many parts, with some fine old houses.

Well, there was more time, now the days were longer, to travel further afield: to Presteigne; to Radnor; to Hereford, where he would surely soon be required to report to his appointing Bishop upon his progress – somewhere else where he must appear as just another sound young curate, finding his feet.

But now – now he had the morning duties of a good young curate to attend to, and must be on time for this meeting, to begin at ten. As he came to the corner of Bridge Street and the post office, a clock struck the three-quarter hour and he slipped his letter home into the box, bestowing a quick kiss upon the seal.

'A letter to your sweetheart, Mr Allen?'

He turned to see stout Mrs Bodenham, the lawyer's wife, observe him with a wry little smile as she came out of the bank, and felt himself flush bright scarlet.

'Mrs Bodenham, good morning.' He raised his hat as she came across. 'Indeed – you catch me in a sentimental gesture to my family.' He spoke only the truth, but he felt his heart pound as though he were lying to conceal the gravest deception. 'How foolish you must think me,' he stammered, as a horse and his rider clopped past.

Mrs Bodenham put a hand on his arm. 'My dear Mr Allen, how you blush. Your family are fortunate indeed to have such a loving son. You must miss one another greatly.'

'We do. With the loss of my dear father it is hard for them, I think, to have me take up my first appointment far from home. But still—' he heard himself sound steadier – 'I am hoping my mother and sisters will come to visit, now that the summer is here at last.'

'We shall much look forward to meeting them. We shall be able to tell them what a success you are making of your time with us!' Mrs Bodenham patted his arm again with her fat gloved hand. 'You must not mind my teasing you, Mr Allen – we all so admire you that we cannot help but consider on which fortunate young lady you might bestow your eye. You danced with Miss Southwood at the wedding party! I know my dear daughter was hoping for a turn with you herself! But perhaps you have someone in mind whom we can only guess at?'

'Mrs Bodenham ...' Once more he was overcome with blushing. 'You must forgive me – I am on my way to a meeting at St Mary's.'

'I know you are,' she said, lifting her skirts a little as they crossed the street. 'Is my husband not attending it?'

'Of course he is. How forgetful of me.' All he had thought of was a room full of men, some of whom he knew, most of whom he had met but once or twice. Bodenham, as a councillor, often came to these inter-parish meetings. So did Southwood. And Prosser. Had he really become so wrapped up in himself that he could fail to remember this?

'Mrs Bodenham,' he began cautiously, as they walked along the High Street, 'may I ask you – what do you know of Mrs Prosser?'

'Tilda Prosser?' said Mrs Bodenham, shifting her reticule to the other hand. 'Now there is someone who would be glad of a son to love and care for her, as you care for your dear mother. What a disappointment that boy has turned out to be. But why do you ask?'

'Oh – nothing of consequence.' He could feel his heart begin to race: he was on dangerous territory. And in any event, he could see ahead the hands of the town clock moving towards the hour. 'I fear I shall be late – will you excuse me?'

'I shall. And I must cross over to Webbs – I am meeting Liza Neve, to look at fabrics. Summer dresses! You have no idea, Mr Allen, of the longing for dresses and the agony of fittings.'

But Richard said that he had, recalling Verity's shrieks of irritation as a misplaced pin jabbed her narrow waist and their mother implored her to keep still. And he lifted his hat, and bid Mrs Bodenham good morning, as she pushed wide the door to Webbs' shadowy interior, with a clang of the bell cast at Merediths, and he glimpsed its great oak counters and bales of cloth. He walked on up the street, greeting here and there a familiar body – Mrs Middleship, going into the bakers; Miss Wilkinson, shopping for her aunt; Jeremiah Morgan, limping out of the druggist on his stick, though his rheumaticky old body held up each Sunday for the ringing.

Ordinary people, of whom he had grown fond. A useful meeting to go to; tasks to be done. What a relief to think of everyday things for a while. As a clock began to strike ten, and he quickened his step, turning up the hill towards St Mary's, he heard again Mrs Bodenham's arch enquiry: 'A letter to your sweetheart, Mr Allen?' And he blushed anew to think what it would mean if he had, indeed, been posting such a letter, and if someone other than Susannah were to find it. It is all madness, he thought, hurrying up the hill.

And then, as a fair-haired young woman came walking out from Passey Place towards him, his heart turned over. Even a fleeting resemblance made him catch his breath: it was as if Susannah lay within his very bloodstream, his whole being quickened by every little thing in the world about him: the scent of a plant by his orchard wall; a glimpse of fair hair beneath a sweet straw bonnet. She was here, she was there, she was always with him.

He came to St Mary's vicarage gate; he unlatched it, and walked up the path. Lady's mantle spilled on to the flags, the first summer bees were droning in and out of the lavender. He could see, through the dining-room window, men in white clerical ties like his, men in good grey suits, all assembling round a polished table, papers before them. He lifted his hand to the knocker and willed that Susannah, just for an hour, might set him free.

'Ah, Mr Allen. Good morning.'

'Good morning, sir. I fear I am late.'

'Not at all, not at all, we are only just assembled. Come and take a seat.' Stephen Ingram gestured to the last vacant chair, and Richard, pulling it back, surveyed the faces around the table and agreed that yes, he had, he believed, met everyone before. He nodded to a couple of Kington councillors, to Maddock, an open, friendly fellow, flanked by the verger and warden of Presteigne; to Bodenham and Prosser, whose eye he could not meet. Pleasantries were exchanged, the lovely May weather remarked upon, papers tapped together. From beyond the open window came the lazy clip-clop of a horse and rider ambling downhill in the sun, and a house martin came swooping towards the eave.

'The swallows are come to my barn,' said Richard, with an absurd little rush of pride, and there were murmurs of approval, as if he himself were responsible, and a brief discussion of when they had arrived last year, and when the first cuckoo had called.

'Now, then, gentlemen.' And Ingram asked the meeting to consider the agenda before them, fair-copied by his wife for each of them. There were five or six items, beginning with apologies for absence. Richard made apologies for Oliver.

'How is he?' asked Ingram, noting this down. 'I feel I must visit him

201

soon, poor fellow. What a long time it has been. You are conducting all the services these days, Allen?'

'Most of them, sir. When Mr Bowen is strong enough, of course, he takes them himself.'

'And when was he last strong enough?'

Richard could barely remember. Bodenham thought it was months, save for Easter morning. Heads were shaken.

'You are in much the same position as our friend from Presteigne, Mr Maddock, here.' Maddock, across the table, gave a self-deprecating little smile.

'How blessed we are to have such fine young men to help us. Mr Allen, you must let me know if there is anything I can do. And do send poor Bowen our very best. Ask if he would like a visit. Now, then.'

With apologies from James Southwood, attending a meeting in Pembridge, and from Ambrose Lilwell, a member of the Presteigne parish council, business began. Churchwardens' accounts were received and compared; a scholarship to Lady Margaret Hawkins School was recommended for a Kington boy, Albert Shaw, the brightest of his year all through elementary school. 'I shall be happy to propose this to the school trustees,' said Ingram, wiping his pen.

The seasonal summer arrival of gypsy caravans up on the race-course on Hergest Ridge was noted, and with it the need to lock every barn and outhouse, for a scythe, a saw, a hammer and box of nails could disappear as if lifted by the wind, with never a footprint on the grass to show for it. 'And the women will not leave you alone,' said Bodenham, leaning back in his chair, and then, amid laughter, 'if you receive my meaning. They are everywhere in the town, are they not,' he added, 'with those bunches of overpriced heather and bangles?'

'Too insistent,' said Ingram. 'Too pressing.'

'Wanting to tell one's fortune,' said Prosser, feeling in his pocket. 'Coming too close.' He made a little moue of distaste, and Richard looked at him. Their eyes met, then Prosser's swivelled away. And as the talk went on – of begging barefoot children, pickpocketing at the races, dogs roaming into the town and scavenging like foxes after dark – Richard's concentration was lost, as he thought of those cries, those rustling laurels, that long dark drive to the house. And while the gypsy talk went on, he thought too of Edith Clare, as he had thought of her early this morning, walking down the mossy lane with the misty stretch of bluebells beneath the trees. Not a gypsy, travelling with horse and dog and caravans, sights which had enchanted him as a boy; not exactly a hermit, though she lived as a recluse, for she had sought him out as a hermit would never do. What, then? If he went walking up in the hills again – a glorious thought, now that summer had come, with the promise of skylarks – would he see her again? Did she want him to see her?

'… snoring in the pew after matins,' said Stephen Ingram, and Richard came back to earth with a start. Another troublesome traveller had been found thus? But no – this was a man on his own, a disreputable old fellow come out of nowhere and sent on his way, only to disrupt Mr Onions' Temperance Meeting in the Assembly Rooms. Harmless enough – too drunk, indeed, to offer resistance to a night in the cells, but now he was out, and sober, and they all should keep an eye.

Next item: the preacher Ebenezer Spurgeon was expected to set up his tabernacle – the word was pronounced with some distaste – at the annual Summer Fair. The usual crowds from far and wide could be expected.

'This is something we do need to watch for, Mr Allen.' Stephen Ingram put his hands together, as if in prayer, and leaned on the polished table. 'The man is barely educated, yet he has a tremendous force of delivery and a most unwholesome preoccupation with the fires of hell, such as is guaranteed to terrify a child. And I fear that children and young people do hear him – the more simple-minded families are drawn to him. Last year I found Nancy Savaker weeping inconsolably, certain that the fires awaited her.'

'Was that not the young person who was found in the lake at Burgage?' asked John Maddock, frowning. 'The poor woman who drowned herself?'

'That was Sarah Watkins,' said Prosser. 'I had to order her coffin.' Richard looked at him. Prosser felt in his pocket again and took out a peppermint. 'Do you not remember?' he asked Maddock, twisting off the paper. 'That was the maid who took herself and her unborn child to hell.'

A little silence followed this remark.

Then Ingram said quietly: 'A dreadful thing.'

'But hell and damnation are what she deserved,' said Prosser. 'Spurgeon may rave, Mr Ingram, but there are things that must be said, and things that must be punished. Perhaps the Savaker girl had good reason to weep.'

The paper went into his pocket, the peppermint into his mouth.

And what a thin, cruel little mouth it was, thought Richard, watching him, and how venomous were those words. New as he was to this gathering, hesitant as he was to draw attention to himself, he felt now a rising tide of emotion. A churchyard conversation in winter came flooding back to him: the Sunday of his first service, the air freezing, frost on the grass between the graves. Prosser was holding forth, as they walked across to the vicarage for luncheon: on the Presteigne Gaol crowded with thieves and vagabonds, on the sinful young women held in the House of Correction. Richard heard Tilda Prosser's nervous interjection – 'At Christmas, in this season of goodwill my dear, then … there are poor girls whom I am sure do not deserve such long confinement…' He heard Prosser's snort of disgust. And he remembered how anger had risen within him, as it was rising now, and he heard himself quote all at once, as he had quoted then, the great words of Christ, on charity: 'For as much as ye do unto them, ye do it unto Me.'

His words fell into silence. He was shaking, as he had shaken on hearing Tilda Prosser's cries. Everyone looked at him.

'I mean to say,' he continued, flushing to the roots of his hair, 'that perhaps it does not behove us to judge so harshly, Mr Prosser. We have so little experience ourselves of the states of mind which drive such tragic things. As Christians, as men of the Church, it behoves us to look for the good, does it not, to reach out to those who suffer as Christ bade us to do—'

'Mr Allen.' The palm of Prosser's hand struck the table, and water from his glass leaped on to the polished wood. People shifted their papers quickly. 'I do not need *you*—' and how he stressed that pronoun – 'I do not need *you* to preach to me, nor tell me of my duties as a Christian.'

'Gentlemen, gentlemen.' Stephen Ingram moved his own papers

away from the spreading pool of water. Bodenham felt for his handkerchief, and could not find it. 'I am sure there is no need for discord,' Ingram went on. 'Mr Allen? Shall we collect ourselves?'

Richard nodded; he swallowed. 'Pray excuse me,' he said, as his heart pounded. 'I do not know why I was so …'

Across the table, John Maddock gave him a sympathetic glance.

'These are grave issues,' said Ingram. 'In theology and in life. Questions of sin and punishment arouse our passions; perhaps some of us around this table differ in our views, but I am sure no distress was intended. Mr Prosser?'

'Indeed not,' said Prosser. He shifted the peppermint from one side of his mouth to the other, and his lips tightened. Watching him, Richard wondered: what is it like for Tilda Prosser to hear her husband's footsteps in the drive? What does she feel as he returns from his duties in the church, opens the front door into that echoing hall, and calls her name?

'Let us proceed,' said Stephen Ingram. 'Item number six.'

And they proceeded, though in what item six consisted, Richard scarcely knew, and he could not look at anyone. So he looked instead at the table, and the little pool of water. It lay on the polished table like something made of glass, holding the darkness of the wood beneath, and the perfect summer light.

The meeting was concluded; refreshments were taken; John Maddock hung back, accompanying Richard from the room as the others went ahead. Ingram saw them all out.

'My apologies, sir,' said Richard, at the open front door.

Ingram shook his hand. 'It is good to see passion and conviction. Remember to give my very best to Mr Bowen. And his dear wife. She must be anxious for him.'

'Sir.' He went out into the porch. Beyond its cool shade the garden at noon was dazzling. A bumblebee went sailing by. Maddock came out.

'You spoke well,' he said, as they stepped out into the heat.

'You think so? I fear I was too hasty.'

'Not in the least. I find Mr Prosser very difficult myself. I am glad you spoke out.'

They walked down the flagstoned path, the scent of the lavender and the hum of the bees all round them. Bodenham and Prosser were going down the hill, a horse and cart slowly climbing it on the far side, the farmer letting the reins go slack, nodding in the sun. He tipped his hat to this group of clergy and gentlemen. Another house martin went darting towards the eaves, and Richard followed its flight. My swallows, he thought. I shall walk home and lunch in the orchard, and watch them come and go.

At the gate, Maddock said: 'We should meet. Would you like to meet?'

Richard looked at him properly for the first time. He was two or three years older, open-faced, fit from walking. He put him in mind of his old friend Arthur Symes, whom now he never saw. They smiled at one another.

'Come over for lunch one day,' said Maddock. 'Come now – why don't you come now?'

Richard almost said yes. He felt with the invitation a lightening of the spirit such as he had not felt for months, save when those sweet birds came swooping into his barn this very morning. How good it would be to spend time with someone like Maddock – someone like himself, indeed: young, gone into the Church's especial life, but bolder than he, he could sense that – bolder and more buoyant in spirit, throwing himself into service: that Ragged School, those children.

'Do say yes. I've nothing to do until teatime. I'd like to get to know you.'

'And I you,' said Richard, as they set off down the hill, but something prevented him seizing the moment. Yes – it would be very good to walk on easily into the town in conversation, up to the Presteigne road, and stride on between the fields, going somewhere new, with a new friend. He needed it – something carefree and lighthearted. And yet he would have to withhold so much, disguise so much. Did he want to begin a new friendship thus? For a moment he wanted nothing more than walk to Maddock's house, fling down his hat and throw off all his hidden life. He wanted to say to him, trusting his open, good-hearted face: I am in turmoil. I am in love. I don't know what to do.

But no sooner had he thought this than he was awash with fear.

Maddock was someone he had met but twice, who might have all kinds of local connections, who might be deeply shocked, might feel it his duty to—

No.

And as the slow clip-clop of the horse and cart faded, and a clock struck the hour, he said: 'Might we do it another time? I should really like to come, but my desk is piled high with papers.' And contained a locked drawer, and a leather-bound journal with a scarlet ribbon to mark the pages, wherein he poured out his heart.

He felt his wretched blush begin to rise, but Maddock said easily, 'Of course, of course, I know how it is. But we'll walk on together now for a little while, will we not?'

'We will.'

And they passed through the town, where shop blinds had been drawn out to shade the pavement, and a cat lay curled in the window of the wool shop and boxes of early cabbages and earthy new potatoes stood outside, at a penny a pound.

'No doubt from the wool shop garden,' said Maddock. 'I think I'll have some.'

And they each bought a couple of pounds of potatoes and a cabbage, and walked on, past Webbs and the bank and the butcher, talking as easily as if they had known each other always. By the time they had passed the foundry, and set out along the Presteigne highway, Richard had told Maddock of his father's death, described the house in Ironbridge where his mother and sisters lived now, and learned that Maddock was also, as he had guessed, the son of a clergyman. The family came from Rutland, where his married sister still lived near their parents, with her lawyer husband and three children, dear spirited little creatures whom Maddock greatly missed. He had three brothers: one in the mission in the East End of London, one up at Oxford, and one still at home and at school, and impatient to leave both and go to Africa.

'I once wanted the missionary life,' said Richard, 'but with the death of my father it did not feel right to go so far.'

'Indeed not. What a blow that must have been for you all. And your sisters? Tell me about them.'

The sun warmed their backs as they walked and the air was full of the smell of grass and cattle. It was almost too hot: they took off their hats, and fanned themselves.

'Verity is quick-tempered and clever,' said Richard. 'And Emily tender-hearted and passionate – she's the youngest. I love them both dearly.' He stopped all at once as Maddock put a hand on his arm.

'I can hear a lark.'

Richard listened. 'Yes. So can I.'

At first there was nothing to see, and then they made it out, rising into the haze of heat two fields away, a madly fluttering speck whose dizzying, open-throated song carried right across the land.

'Glorious,' murmured Maddock. 'Summer is truly come.'

They walked on between the hedgerows, alive with sparrows, bluetits, finches. Beyond, as they passed one field gate and then another, they could see the cattle ambling through the thick fresh grass towards the trees, the water trough. Sheep speckled the hills; buzzard were circling in the blue.

'Perhaps I shall meet your sisters one day,' said Maddock striding along.

'That would be very good.'

They came to the signpost to Bullocks Mill, and the long lane winding down.

'This is where I leave you,' said Richard. 'One day you must lunch here with me.'

'I should like that very much.'

They shook hands, stepping back on to the grassy verge, as the Presteigne coach came up behind them. 'I believe I shall take it,' said Maddock, and put out his hand.

'Whoa!' The driver slowed the horses and pulled up some paces ahead; heads turned from the top as Maddock ran, and swung easily up on the steps.

'Goodbye, Allen!' he called, and waved his hat as he took his seat.

'Goodbye!' called Richard, waving back as the coach set off again, and he stood by the signpost, watching the horses gather speed, hearing the hoofs upon the tarmac as one more sound amidst the beauty of the day, noon just tipping towards afternoon, the lark just audible still. He had made a new friend: how good that felt. He breathed in the scents of warm grass and meadow flowers, made to cross the highway, then stopped as the butcher's boy came clopping along in his cart.

'Morning, sir!'

'Good morning!' called Richard. He waited to let him pass, and as the boy rode on, whistling, thought that on a morning such as this Edith Clare would be out in her garden in the woods, or walking deep into the hills. Were he to turn round now, and follow the path up to Rushock, he might come upon her.

But the sun beat down upon him, and the thought of the coolness of walking home by the river was irresistible, and he crossed and entered his own lane, passing field and gate and high-banked hedge, which now were all familiar to him, so many times had he walked along. Just in the morning's warmth the lacy flowers of cow parsley had opened out, and the banks were cloudy and white.

And here, coming round the long steep bend, panting with the climb and the heat, was Martha, her basket upon her arm. She looked up and saw him.

'Sir.' She had not the breath to say more.

'Good day again, Martha. Is it not warm?'

''Tis very hot.' She stopped where he was waiting, and wiped her face on a cloth from her basket. ''Tis as hot as it's been all year. Good drying weather, mind – I've pegged them all out, sir, and done a good clean. And I baked a new loaf and drawed some fresh water – expect you'll be glad of that, when you gets home.'

'I shall be. Thank you so much. You'll be glad to be home yourself, I think, and rest a little.'

'They'll be waiting for their dinner,' said Martha, folding up her cloth. 'Ah, well, best be getting on. Good day, sir.'

'Good day, Martha. I shall see you tomorrow.'

And she went on up, as he went on down, and soon he could hear the river, and the turning wheel of the mill and the rush of the weir. He came to the bridge, where tendrils of toadflax grew, and leaned upon its sun-warmed, lichened stone, watching swallows skim over the rocky shallows, while the cattle stood motionless in the field beneath the trees.

Well. Now he had his solitude. Now he could begin once again to dream. And as a few hours ago, when he set out, he had thought that the loveliness of the morning wanted only Susannah at his side to make it perfect, now he thought it again, willing her presence here, and he let himself murmur her name, watching the weir's great fall of water pour on and on.

'Susannah …'

He spoke her name so softly, and indeed it was so full of vowels and sibilants that it was made for whispering, for hush, for an intimate drawing close. He buried his face in his hands. Was he to spend his whole young manhood thus, yearning for someone he must never have, foregoing camaraderie and friendship so he might have time to dream? Was this a wise life for any man? And for a man of God—

Speedwell and star of Bethlehem grew amongst the grass at the base of the old bridge wall, and a little clump of prayermint. He moved, and brushed against it, and its faint scent rose towards him and he groaned. Then, from a distance, came the whistle of the train, and he leaned out further at its approach through the woods, and watched the clouds of steam come billowing through the verdant trees, and drift and dissolve amongst them, now here, now gone into the summer air.

'Susannah.'

At last he left the bridge and walked on down the lane. Birley was pulling back the gates as he reached the crossing.

'A lovely day, sir.'

'Is it not?' said Richard, though now he was no longer sure how glad he was to be coming home to the long full afternoon. Well. He would take a jug of water and Martha's fresh loaf into the orchard, with a hunk of cheese; he would rest, he would pray beneath the trees, he would watch the swallows and try not to think of her. This evening he would write another sermon, one that could stand for the following week, and take as his text Christ's words on charity. Let Prosser fume amidst the congregation: let him hear.

And he bid good day to Birley, and went on, rounding the bend towards the cottage. The bluebells' miraculous stretch of colour lay beneath the trees; the pigeons made their throaty soft croo-croo; ahead, the sun was so intense all at once on the open fields that even beneath his hat it dazzled him, and he shaded his eyes. Amidst the brightness, with the sounds of sheep and birds and water all around him, he thought he saw a figure at his gate. Then he knew that this was simply what he so longed to see: Susannah there, Susannah waiting for his return, that he might take her into the house, tell her everything, hold her to his heart.

He walked on a few paces, stopped.

There was indeed a woman at his gate, and though at first he thought: It is Edith Clare; she has come to seek me out; he knew, with a glimpse of pale hair beneath a bonnet, who in truth it was, and felt himself held in some timeless, extraordinary, dreamlike place, as Susannah turned towards him.

18

A greenfinch flew out of the woods. It rose and fell on the air and vanished into the orchard. Richard, who had stepped back as it flew before him, now stepped forward again, slowly, as if he were mesmerised. He came to the gate. The dazzling sun beat down.

'Mrs Bowen ...'

'Mr Allen.'

'You have come here alone?' He thought she was trembling as she gave a little nod, biting her lip. 'Mr Bowen has sent for me?'

'No. No – he is sleeping. Millie is there.'

She pressed her hands to her face.

From somewhere within him, mingled with his joy, a thousand voices sounded a whispering chorus: *This is most improper* ... They came from the church of St Mary's, Ironbridge, from the church of St Michael and All Angels, from his parents, his sisters, his school and theological preparation for this life; from everything he had ever known.

He looked about him. The farmer from the top came down twice a day to check his lambs. Now that summer was come, there were people about in the woods and lane quite often – walkers, mill and farm workers, sweethearts, seeking seclusion.

There was no one here now. And Martha Price was gone.

'You are displeased?' Susannah looked at him from beneath her bonnet and he saw how afraid she was, guessed what it must have taken to leave the vicarage – on what pretext? – and go up the hill, not to walk or catch the coach down into Kington, but to turn off, quickly, glancing about her, and make the long walk down through the woods.

He said: 'I am overcome.'

But what should they do? If they sat in the garden, anyone might see them. If he took her into the house …

He held out his hand. 'Come.'

And he led her, not through the wicket gate by the stream, up the little front garden to the door, but through the open five-barred gate, up the long grassy path between the house and orchard. White sheets hung in the sun where Martha had pegged them between the apple trees; Susannah's gown rustled beside him. In the midday heat the prayermint by the orchard gate had closed its tender flowers: it wanted dusk, or shade, like the clump which grew in the shade of the bridge; it wanted the brush of a passer-by, or the touch of a hand.

He gestured towards it, saying quietly: 'That flower is my emblem of you.'

'How is that?'

'I shall tell you.'

They came to the back of the house: its shade fell in a deep cool square upon the grass. He drew her towards the porch door, and opened it; his hand beneath her elbow, he guided her in, as he had guided her in through the porch of the church, on the day of the Eastertide wedding. Then, he had felt pierced to the quick by her closeness; now, he could hardly believe she was here.

He took off his hat, and hung it on the hook. He unlocked the door to the kitchen. The windows were open, the flagstones swept and washed, the empty washtub drying in the sun. The new loaf stood beneath a cloth on the table, beside stone jug and plate. He looked at it all through her eyes and saw its simple beauty. The door to the snug stood open, and the sun from the front of the house fell on to worn red rug and the table and chair where he ate.

'Come.'

He pushed the door wide; she entered the little room, and looked about her: at the rug before the hearth, the hearthside chair; at the brown jug on the mantelshelf, and the family portrait, with its ferns and backdrop, and Emily about the collapse with laughter; at his desk;

his shelf of books overlooking the field; at the glass which held the stems of prayermint.

'At last I see it all.' She gestured to the photograph. 'This is your family?'

'Yes.'

'Will you tell me about them?'

'Later.' He drew a breath. 'It is extraordinary that you are here. I think of you all the time. This house – this room – they are full of you. You are never out of my thoughts.'

'Nor you from mine.'

He did not know what to do next. Was she waiting for him to act? How should he act? He swallowed.

'May I – may I put down my bag?'

'Of course.' He leaped to take it from her: such a small pretty thing, lace and cotton and warm from her clasp on that long anxious walk in the heat. He set it on his desk. Astonishing, to see it there. He said: 'You must be thirsty. Will you sit down? May I bring you some water?'

'That would be very kind.' But she did not sit down – she followed him into the kitchen, and stood in the doorway, watching him take glasses from the cupboard, pour water from the cool stone jug. He turned, saw her framed in the doorway, still in her bonnet, in a summer gown the colour of a hazy sky. He wanted to keep her there for ever. He wanted to take her in his arms. How should he proceed? He gave her a glass.

He said, as they drank: 'I almost did not come home this afternoon. I have made a new friend.'

'Oh?' A flicker of anxiety crossed her brow. 'And who is that?'

'John Maddock, the curate of St Andrew's in Presteigne.' He gestured towards the snug again. 'Let us go through. Do you know Mr Maddock?'

'We have met, yes. He is spoken highly of.'

'I like him. He invited me to lunch, after a rather stormy meeting.'

'Stormy?'

'Prosser was there.' He stopped. To bring Prosser's name, his presence, his mean vindictive spirit into this room now, with Susannah come to see him – it sullied everything. 'Never mind,' he said, taking

215

her empty glass. 'But I was glad to grow acquainted with Maddock on our walk out of town.'

'And why did you not have lunch with him?'

He put both their glasses on the table where he ate. The book he had been reading after supper last night still rested there. When he had eaten, he had written his long letter home. Then he had written in his journal, a love letter to the woman who now stood here, waiting for his touch. Was that so? Was that, in truth, what she wanted?

'Richard?'

To hear her speak his name ... From some forgotten place he heard his mother say to them once: 'I knew I loved your father when I heard him speak my name.'

'Richard? Why did you not go?'

He spoke to the copy of *Le Morte D'Arthur*, with its faded gold lettering and worn green leather. His father's copy, opened many, many times by his beloved hand. If his father could see him now ...

'I did not go,' he said slowly, 'because I was too afraid I should talk of you. And I wanted to be here alone, and think of you, and try to summon your presence.' He looked up at her. She was watching him intently. 'Now you are here.'

'Yes.'

'Because ...'

Now it was she who could not look at him. 'Because – the morning was so beautiful – I thought: I shall dare to go to him. Just once ...' She was whispering now; she covered her face. 'I fear I was doing great wrong.'

'You were very brave,' he said quietly.

'Foolish.'

'No.'

He moved towards her, and a bluetit flew out of the climbing rose at the window. The sudden movement startled both of them, as the bird had been startled by him. He went to the window, and quietly closed the shutters. Now there were shadows everywhere, barred with light from the gaps between the panels, the deep-set little window above his desk, looking on to the field. A ewe trotted past it.

Susannah said, with a little smile in which he sensed both happiness and anxiety: 'She will tell no one.'

'Nor I,' said Richard, and moved towards her again.

The summer warmth came into the shadowy room through the open kitchen windows. Susannah made to take off her bonnet; he watched her unfasten its ribbons with slender trembling fingers. He wanted to help her. Somehow he could not. After all these months of thinking of her, dreaming of her, of untying a ribbon, unfastening a row of buttons, letting cloak and gown and petticoat fall to the floor – he could not even take off her bonnet. He watched her lift it from her coiled pale hair, and look about her.

'Give it to me.'

He took it, and set it on his desk, by her little bag. Astonishing again, to see it there, dove grey upon his sermon papers, before the glass of flowers, in the place where for months he had dreamed of her, poured out his heart to her in his journal, kneeled and prayed about her, for her, for both of them.

How must he pray now?

She was smoothing her hair. She turned towards the mirror, and then all at once it was as if she did this all the time, as if he were entirely used to this, quite at ease – as if he often came in here and found her glancing in the glass – and he knew he would feel each time as he did now: this girl is completely beautiful. I shall always want her.

A thin line of light struck the glass, dancing with a myriad specks of dust. She moved, and it caught her coils of hair, and the clip which fastened them. He wanted to speak, he could not. He thought he could hear her breathing, fast and light. Then he moved to stand behind her, slipped his arms about her shoulders, drew her back into him. He rested his cheek against hers, felt the softness and warmth of her skin, her silken strands of hair against his beard.

How deep this silence now.

He looked into the glass and there met her own long gaze. Neither smiled, neither spoke. The mirror showed them two young people, the oaken beams on the wall behind, a picture, a little jug. As he looked and looked, unable now to resist drawing her closer and closer still, he thought that the shadowed glinting glass might, if they looked long enough, reveal their future: side by side, moving from youth to their middle years, their children about them; to old age, their children gone, and they still here together.

He touched her face, he heard her sigh, heard the pigeons in the woods across the lane murmur and murmur amidst the leafy boughs. He turned her to him, lifted her face to his.

'May I kiss you?' Her eyes searched his, and were filled with fear and longing. He drew her closer still. 'May I?'

'Yes. Yes.'

Their lips met, in a single gentle kiss. He closed his eyes. Their lips met again.

He thought: My whole life has led me to this moment, where once he thought: My whole life leads to God.

He drew her to the fireside chair; she sank upon his lap, laid her head upon his shoulder. Her weight upon him was a little heavier than he had imagined: no girl had ever sat on his lap save Emily, and she was light as a bird, and they so easy with one another, brother and sister talking about everything as they had done all their lives. Now he could hardly speak from emotion, hardly breathe. He had not been able to imagine Susannah's warmth, her realness, the way his arm would curve just so about her waist, the way she would move a little to settle herself, how he would harden beneath her. He had dreamed of stroking her hair, kissing her forehead, running his hand over and over her face, tracing the outline of soft pale eyebrows, the frown lines between them (made from reading by candlelight when she could not sleep? Made from anxiety?) and the grey-green eyes whose gaze he had met over and over again for months: in church and churchyard, with people all about them; across the crowded market in the town; on a frozen lake, in a schoolhouse hall, across her husband's dining table and her husband's parlour fire.

Now their moment had come.

Now they could look at one another freely – no need to glance up at a footfall in the passage, knowing that Millie might come in at any moment; no need for him to scan the guests at a wedding, lest someone – who? – had noticed the curate and the rector's wife in such close conversation. Now he could do all the things he had so longed to do, as she lay in his arms, and he began to do them, knowing from her glance, her gaze, her closing eyes, her sigh, that every touch he gave was what she wanted: for his fingers to caress the shadows beneath her eyes – where no one so young should have such shadows – and the bridge of her narrow nose, her flushing cheek, her mouth, her mouth, her mouth.

He put a finger on her throat and drew it slowly up to her chin, and over her lips, and down again to where the pulse in her throat beat so fast. He did it again. He stroked her like this over and over, as if stroking a cat – her cat, who so often had been their companion. She lifted her face to his, and he kissed her. He kissed her again. He kissed her again. He kissed her again and then as if it were the most natural thing in the world, though it made him gasp, so intimate did it feel, so shocking, their mouths opened into each other, their tongues met, and met again, entwined, and then he was drowning, dissolving in desire, plunging into and into her mouth as if to enter her entirely, as if to possess her soul.

He drew away. 'Susannah—' She drew him back. His hands were in her hair; he heard her clip fall to the hearth. With coil and tendril slipping like silk between his fingers it was as he had dreamed – her hair spread out on the pillow beside him, beneath him, her limbs all around him, her nightgown slipped off and the two of them naked, naked, and he going into her, into her—

He felt himself harden like a rod beneath her now.

'I love you, I love you—'

Then urgently, unstoppably, exquisitely, all these months and months of yearning came through him like a flood, in a gasping tearing rush as if a swollen river burst its banks, and he was pumping and bucking beneath her, snatching his mouth away to groan in sounds he had never heard, and could not imagine came from him, and then he was lost to everything.

He lay back in the chair, panting. He heard this as if from a great distance, and as if from a great distance knew what had happened and was filled with every kind of feeling – release, relief, exhaustion, happiness, guilt, shame, emptiness, completeness. He drew her to him again, felt her sink against him, opened his eyes. The room was swimming with shadows and points of light.

'Forgive me ...'

He had said these words so many times, to so many people, over

219

such little things. He could feel his heart thumping against his ribs. This was not a little thing.

'Forgive me.'

'Sssh!' Her fingers were on his lips. He kissed and held them. 'There is nothing to forgive.'

He heard an enormous sigh. It was his. He said: 'I have never – you are the first – I have never even kissed—'

'I know. I know.'

He looked down at her, there in his arms, everything he had ever wanted. He said slowly: 'I am completely in love with you.'

'And I with you.'

He held her, he rocked her like a child. Tears filled her eyes.

She whispered: 'I did not know—'

'Nor I.'

He could feel her heart beating and beating beneath his hand when he laid it – there, just there – on her breast. He gazed down into her eyes; she gazed up at him, his hand upon her breast, and her hand upon his cheek.

'You're my wife, you're my child, you're my lover …'

Her eyes closed.

'Look at me.'

She looked, and within that gaze he began once again to walk with her in love's great silence, as if beneath the soaring nave of an empty cathedral, or high on the hills, between one country and another, beneath the vault of heaven.

Someone was walking past the house. He froze. Who was it? Could they have heard his cries? Were they noticing, now, the shutters closed in broad daylight? How could they fail to do so?

'Richard?'

The footsteps faded. He heard their retreat up the lane, through the woods. He saw that the patches and chinks of light in the room had changed, had grown deeper: it must be mid-afternoon. Soon the children would be coming out of school.

'Richard?' He saw she was listening too.

'It's all right. They've gone.' He kissed her face. 'How are you, my beloved?'

'Very happy. And afraid.' She raised herself in his arms, slipped off his lap. 'I must leave.'

How was she to do that? How on earth was she to do that? If she left alone, and were seen to do so, what other interpretation could there possibly be for her presence here? If he left with her, would that not also look extraordinary? Less so, perhaps: it would raise questions, but he could answer them: Mr Bowen had sent for him, they were walking back to the vicarage together – yes, Mr Bowen was still unwell …

He thought all this through as she smoothed her gown, as he bent to retrieve her hairclip from the hearth, and pass it to her. And as she moved to pick up her bag, and from it take her brush, with its ivory backing, he remembered an afternoon in February, a cold wind blowing across the churchyard as he conducted Alice Birley to the vicarage for tea. He remembered how, as she ran to embrace the vicarage cat, and Susannah came to greet him, and Oliver coughed in his study, he had seen it all as a series of paintings, those domestic interiors – *Contentment* – such as his mother liked; or those with a theme or moral, like Millais, or Hunt, whom his father had so admired: *The Husband's Discovery*. He imagined another such painting now: *Deception*, and was filled with shame at the easy lies he was concocting, the ease with which they came to him, while Oliver Bowen lay on his sickbed, awaiting his wife's return.

'Richard?'

She was brushing her hair, putting it up again before the glass, the hairclip in her mouth. What a womanly thing. He lay back and watched her, as if he were lying in bed, as if they had just been lovers – true, full lovers – as if they were man and wife, and he observing her on one single day in a chain of days and nights, running on and on, marked by passion and domesticity.

'What are you thinking?' She fastened the clip; she turned to look at him.

'Many things. Many different things.' He rose from the chair, and came to stand behind her again. He was aware of his dampness and coldness: he must wash, he must change. He put his arms round her; she rested her cheek against his; once more they looked in the glass. How far they had come, in so short a time.

221

'Tell me some of the things,' she murmured, reaching up behind her to stroke his face.

'How you can leave in safety. How I don't want you to leave.' He drew a breath. 'In truth, how very wrong this is.'

She frowned; she turned to him; he could see how swiftly she was swept, as he was, from happiness to distress.

'Richard – what are you saying?'

'I don't know. I don't know. How are we to proceed? What must we do?' Even as he asked her, he knew the answer. 'I must pray,' he said, lifting her hand to his lips. He kissed it. 'We both must pray.'

She nodded. 'God will guide us. He will show us what is right.'

'You have all the certainties of your husband.'

There. Now Oliver stood in the room beside them. How strange and disturbing that felt.

'And you do not?'

'I did. Now—'

Footsteps went past the house again. She looked at him.

'I had thought this valley so remote, unvisited.'

'In winter. But now, with the sun, with the train, with the woods to explore and roam in – people do come and go.'

'You know them?'

'Some of them.' He kissed her hair. 'I know the workers at the mill, and the Birleys, of course; I know the farmer from the top, Mr Dickson. Most of the families who have houses up in the woods I know by sight now. And there is someone—'

He stopped. Something made him stop. Whoever, whatever Edith Clare might be, she had her reasons for her seclusion, her reasons for seeking him out.

'*The church put me in prison.*'

'Who?' asked Susannah, gazing up at him. 'Who else do you know?'

'I'll tell you another time,' he said, as the footsteps faded. 'We must go, must we not?'

'You are coming with me?'

'I am. I think it is best. But first – I must disappear for a moment.'

And he left her to pick up and fasten her bonnet, and went up to his bedroom, searching from behind a half-closed shutter to see who it was who had passed the house, but seeing no one now, only the sheep in the sun. He pulled the shutters properly to, and quickly washed himself at the stand, and used his chamber pot, slipping it back beneath the bed, wondering if she too might need to use it. What unimagined intimacy was this? Was this married life? While the shutters were still closed he stood looking round the room, so simple and plain, so male, monastic, even. He tried to imagine Susannah up here, as he had tried so many times to do, but now with more accuracy, and more hope. Then he heard the afternoon train puff along the track, with who knew what passengers, come at the end of the afternoon to fish or walk near here? He reopened the shutters; he closed the door.

When he came down, she was looking at his photograph, her bonnet replaced, her gown smoothed.

'You said you would tell me ...' She touched the glass.

He told her, pointing to each one of his family in turn, coming last to Emily, ready to laugh as only Emily could laugh.

What would she think of him now? This was something he could not contemplate.

'And you?' he asked Susannah. 'I know nothing of your family. We must spend a whole day talking.'

'Another day. Now we must go.' She touched the glass again. 'How I should like to know your sisters.' She turned, stepped far back into the room as he undid the shutters, caught sight of the stems of prayermint. 'You said that was an emblem? An emblem of me? You said you would tell me why.'

And he told her, drawing her into the kitchen, right at the back where no one could possibly see them, unless they came walking up through the woods from Kington, and down from the fields behind the barn, and this he did not think of. For the last time that day, perhaps the last time for many, many weeks, he drew her into his arms and kissed her, long and deep. 'Because prayermint is such a beautiful name,' he said at last. 'Because it is so shy, and half hidden, and delicate. Because it needs the touch of a hand to release its clouds of scent ...'

Susannah began to cry, so quietly against his chest that he thought she must be used to crying quietly, and this inexpressibly moved him.

'My love, my love ...' He held her and held her.

223

'I don't want to leave you. I don't want to go—'

'I know. I know.'

At length they drew apart. He found a cloth and dipped it in the jug; he wiped her tears away, wiped her whole face, as if she were a child.

Or a communicant, he thought all at once; as if this were a kind of sacrament. No. He put down the cloth: that was surely a blasphemy.

And he kissed her brow. Sheep went past the window on to the field, one by one, glancing in, moving on, in an endless line. 'They do this two or three times a day,' he told her, as the line went on and on. 'They move from one field to the next, they have long paths in the grass which they follow. I'll show you as we go.'

She nodded sadly. He closed the kitchen door, took his hat from the peg and led her through the porch, with its besom, and boxes of wood for the fire, and skates upon a hook.

Outside, it was grown cooler now, the shadows of cottage and barn stretched long and black over the grass, the light beyond them full and deep. The swallows were swooping low for insects, soaring back up to the barn, swooping in through the gap above the door like arrows. It felt like a lifetime since this morning when he had noticed their arrival, Martha Price up to her elbows in glinting soapsuds and he, in the long mossy lane with its carpet of bluebells beneath the startling green, thinking only of Susannah, of her arm in his and their little girl running before them. He stopped as they came to the gate. A little girl was walking down the lane towards them now.

'Good afternoon, Alice.' He felt his stomach plunge.

'Good afternoon, Mr Allen.'

Her pinafore was dusty, her shoes were worn right down, she was carrying a drooping handful of bluebells. She stopped, and looked at them.

'Hello, Alice,' said Susannah. He could feel her steady her voice, sound ordinary and calm. 'Have you come all this way by yourself?'

'Yes. I do so most days.'

'And sometimes I have the pleasure of your company, do I not?' said Richard, coming out on to the lane. 'Today Mrs Bowen has made this long walk down to fetch me to a meeting.'

To lie to a child. To lie to Alice. He touched his white tie as if to say: I tell the truth. No one questions me. In that moment he hated himself.

Alice nodded.

'Those flowers are for your mother?'

She nodded again.

'They look thirsty. How is your friend Jenny Neve?'

'At home with the toothache. I'm thirsty too,' said Alice.

'Run along home now.'

'Yes, sir.' And she made a half-bob and ran off, her worn shoes pattering on the hard-packed earth. At the bend, she stopped and looked back for a moment. Then she was gone, and there was only the tinkling of the stream and the sound of the sheep trotting and stumbling over the stones of the stream bed and on up the sloping field.

He and Susannah walked slowly up the lane, alongside the animals on the other side of the hedge. The verges were massed with cow parsley; clouds of midges hung in the air, and he waved them away with his hat. For a while they walked in silence. When they came to the highest point in the lane before it turned, he stopped, for from here you could see right over the hedge, and follow the old worn paths of the sheep, which he pointed out to her, so they had something neutral and ordinary to talk about, lest anyone heard their voices. She followed the line of his finger, nodding as he spoke. From here too, they could look down upon the cottage, its windows now deep in shadow.

There they had been.

Beside him, Susannah said quietly, 'Will she tell? Do you think she will tell?'

'I don't know,' said Richard. 'Perhaps she thought nothing of it.' He paused, looking out over the hills in the deepening light. 'I did not like lying to her.'

She bit her lip. 'I should not have come.'

'Don't say that.'

'It was selfish. It was foolish. It puts us both in danger.'

He could not answer that. And they turned and climbed on through the woods, filled with light and shade and song, with the

225

murmuring pigeons and here and there the rumbling sound of a cart, or barking dog, or footstep.

They said goodbye on the highway – a little way down towards the church – and quickly, he lifting his hat, she with a little nod: as if they had come upon one another by chance, as if it were nothing that she now walked on down the hill alone, without maid or friend or husband. He walked back up to the top of the lane, turning just once to watch her descent; then he plunged down into the woods.

And herein lay the beginning, the true beginning, of an adult life, the life of a man, of which he now knew he had understood nothing: which went this way and that, and where nothing was simple or without its shadow.

If he had thought before that he was falling from grace, and entering sin's darkness, what must he think now, when rapture and guilt coursed through him? He tried to imagine saying to Susannah: I love you, I shall always love you, but we must put an end to this – now, now, before we go one step further. Even if he could bear to do this for himself – and how could he bear it? – he could not think of her face, of her life, as he turned away from her. Would it not, in human terms, be almost sinful to cause so much pain?

He came to the lane's long turning, from where, at its end, he could stand and look down upon the cottage. The afternoon was sinking into its deepest hour; the sheep on the hills were bathed in gold. It felt as if everything in the natural world, so full and quiet, affirmed the day's great discovery of love: in this hallowed, immortal light, it felt like a benediction.

Yet how can this be, he asked himself, walking slowly on, when God must surely be turning away from me? And on whose terms do I live now? On mine? On God's? All my life they have been inseparable.

19

She was come home: he could hear her footsteps on the church-yard path. He struggled to lift himself on the pillows and could not. He waited, his head turned towards the open bedroom door; he heard her enter the house, and softly close the door. He could not raise his voice to call her; he pictured her taking off her bonnet, slipping it back on the stand, smoothing her hair, preparing herself to come up stairs to greet him. How? How did she thus prepare herself?

Millie was coming out of the kitchen; their murmuring voices sounded. Though he could not hear what was said he knew they would be discussing him, and the kind of day he had passed, something he himself could barely remember. He had slept, he had woken, and learned she was gone into Kington; he had longed for her return. He thought he had eaten something.

What time was it now?

'Susannah?' He tried to call her, felt the cough begin to rise. He swallowed, lay very still, tried again in a whisper. Ah, that was easier. It sounded as if they were about to share a secret. How sweet, how intimate, such a thing would be. 'Susannah ...' Whispering as the sun went down, as if the night were theirs.

'Oliver?' She was coming up the stairs, her gown rustling against the banister along the landing. She was here in the doorway, her face filled with anxiety.

'My dear ...' He wanted to hold out his arms, but could not; he turned his hand so it lay palm upwards towards her. She did not take it – perhaps she had not seen the gesture, perhaps his whisper fright-ened her.

'How are you?' She came in, stood looking at him for a moment; then she sat down in the chair by the open window, so he had to turn his head to look at her. The sinking sun touched the tendrils of hair at her temple, showed a young face filled with anxiety and the struggle to show him only calm enquiry.

He nodded, trying to reassure her. 'Much the same. What time is it?'

'Almost five. It pains you to lift your voice?'

'Today it does. Whispering is no effort – is it hard for you to hear me?'

'No, not at all.' She leaned back in the chair; they smiled at one another, husband and wife talking quietly as his long illness drew towards its close. He tried to think that this was how it was.

'And you?' he whispered. 'What have you been doing? You were gone quite a while, I think? How was the town today?'

'Oh – it was – it was much as usual.' He saw her colour rise. 'Summer is really come at last. I found it very warm.'

He nodded; he observed her. 'Indeed, I see you are flushed from the sun.' Was this what caused that ever-deepening colour?

Footsteps sounded along the path to the church, and the tap of a walking stick. Susannah turned to look out of the window.

'The ringers are come.' He watched her lean towards the casement, and call out quickly, 'Good evening, Mr Morgan!'

He heard old Jeremiah stop with the others on the path and call up, 'Evening, ma'am!' and the voices of Ben Neve and William Middleship join him. 'A lovely evening b'aint it? How's Mr Bowen today?'

She turned back towards him. 'Oliver? How shall I tell them you are?'

He saw her deepened colour fade; he heard the lightness in her voice now that others were there: bell-ringing practice; normal life. Was her relief because these things went on despite his dreadful illness? Did routine help her to stay calm? Or was it, he wondered all at once, because they had moved from the subject of how she spent her day?

'Oliver? What should I say to them?'

He met her gaze; he did not speak. Lo, how that blush began to rise

228

once more. He closed his eyes, he shook his head. 'Tell them I am resting.'

He heard her say this, the light tone gone from her voice. He pictured the men all lifting their hats as they called out their good wishes, and then they walked on up to the church, and he heard the lifting of the heavy latch, the swinging wide of the great south door. More footsteps from the lich-gate, as the others came to join them: walking up at the close of a perfect summer day, the rooks beginning to settle and the life of the church going on and on. Tuesday. Bell-ringing.

In here, Susannah was silent now. He thought she had folded her hands within her lap.

After a little while, she said: 'Millie is making some broth.'

'Very good.' And indeed he could smell it.

'Oliver?'

He could not look at her. Later he would, later he must. Not now. He heard her rise from the chair; he let her think he was falling asleep, and heard her soft retreat across the boards.

It was growing cooler: he felt the change of air at the window, and opened his eyes to look upon the sinking evening sun, fiery upon the glass, touching sill and treetop. Then the bells began to ring, tumbling and falling and rising through the air, pealing out across the church-yard, out across the fields, calling and calling, from earth unto the heavens.

'Lord,' whispered Oliver. 'Lord, be with me now.'

She entered the parlour; she closed the door; she let a long sigh escape her.

'Lord, Lord—' Her hands went to her lips.

With its one window on to the churchyard, and in the deepening summer evening, the room was a cool darkened place, touched here and there with mellow light – on the waxed oak of the table at the window, on the brass fender, on the convex mirror above the mantel, wherein she saw herself now so small and distant, as if she had passed quite through the glass and were now in some mysterious country, being drawn further and further away from all she knew.

Would she come back?

She crossed the floor, and the little figure in the glass came to meet her. She stood before it, searching her small reflected face for a sign. Could others see what she had done, what they had done together?

Her fingers traced the outline of her lips, as his had; stroked her cheek, stroked her hair, ran over the beating pulse in her neck. She closed her eyes, heard him murmur her name, drawing her closer and closer still. These things had truly taken place, though now, returned to this familiar room, with the great sound of bells ringing out through the summer air, she could scarcely believe it. Yet they had – they had – and because of her. Because she had dared to go to him.

Susannah searched her face in the glass again. She thought: I scarcely know you. You are someone I had not known was there.

The bells pealed on and on. Listening to them now, poised on the brink of this new knowledge, and afraid, it seemed that they rang from the past in an unbroken chain, calling her back: this is where you belong, and have always belonged – within the church, where what you have done is unthinkable.

'I have sinned,' she whispered, into the shadowy room, with its gleams here and there of light. 'I shall be punished – I should be punished.' Yet the prospect of re-entering her life, of relinquishing such undreamed of happiness – it was unendurable.

There stole then into her mind a thought so wicked she could hardly let it form: he is so ill. Perhaps, one day we shall be together …

'Lord, help me. Lord, save me.'

The bells rang down to the close of the peal, and fell silent. She heard her own voice in the hush, and her hands went to cover her mouth. In the great fight then, to suppress her sobs, she thought: my punishment is begun.

That night was the worst of his life.

At nine, he fell asleep by candlelight. He had taken some broth; Millie had sponged his face, put on a clean pillowcase and taken down the chamber pot. She had left him his spitting bowl, washed and covered, and a fresh carafe of water.

'I wish you a very good night, sir.'

'And you, Millie. Thank you.' Since taking the broth, his voice was a little stronger.

Susannah came up to say their evening prayers.

'At the going down of the sun, and the coming of darkness, Lord watch over us …' He murmured the words as the candle burned into the shadows and Susannah kneeled on her side of the bed, her head bowed. All their married life they had done thus, he on the one side and she on the other: in health, when afterwards he had taken her into his arms, and felt her struggle to conceal her fear (was it fear? Was it only that?) and now in sickness, when he must pray upon the pillows, and could barely lift his head.

'Our Father, which art in heaven, Hallowed be thy Name …'

He heard her voice whisper into her hands; he thought he heard her stumble over lines engraved upon her soul since childhood, as on his.

'And forgive us our trespasses, As we forgive them that trespass against us. And lead us not into temptation; But deliver us from evil.'

When he whispered the Amen he could not hear her; when at last she lifted her face and rose he saw in the candle's steady light that it was flushed and streaked with tears.

'Beloved …' He held out his hand.

She wiped the tears away, over and over, standing motionless, as if it would be dangerous to move, her back to the shuttered window, the light upon her face. Now he could look at her.

'Come here.'

She turned to feel in the top drawer of the chest for one of her mother's handkerchiefs; he watched her find one, and wipe her eyes and blow her nose. He thought: her tears are so close to the surface; perhaps she has already cried today. Beyond this he did not dare to think.

She came to stand beside him; he held out the other hand; this time she took it and her face crumpled once more. He could not tighten his grip as he so wished to, he could only let her hand rest in his and watch her fight back her sobs.

'My love—'

'Don't!' From what unstoppable feeling did that cry break forth? She took away her hand; she covered her mouth; she wept; he waited.

At length he said slowly: 'I am very ill, but you must not be afraid.'

'Oh, Oliver—'

'Sit down.' He touched the quilt; she sat; he took her hand again.

'Look at me.' Now, in the candlelight, he could meet her gaze; he could feel what an endurance it was for her to meet his own.

And now – now could he speak, and tell her what he knew, or guessed?

He could not.

What purpose could it serve, save to lose still more of her? Did he want her to be afraid of him, to dread his questions, to burn with shame? He thought: I have her now, her hand is in mine, we are husband and wife, and tonight she will sleep beside me. In the sight of God, what we have is sacred. No matter what another man might want, he does not have this. No matter what else she might want. I shall pray for her immortal soul, that she may return to the path of righteousness. And to me.

He said aloud: 'What we have is sacred.'

She had lowered her gaze; she did not answer him.

'What we have will last for ever: that is what marriage is. Nothing can take that from us, not even death.'

He felt the word enter the candlelit room as if on silent footsteps, and remain here, the first time it had been spoken between them. He had spoken it before, in many different rooms, as lives came to their close, for this was part of his calling: to help in the passing from this world into the next – the lives of the very old, the very young. There came before him the face of Lizzie Arndell, breathing her frightened last with Alfred, her poor young husband, beside her, his face almost as ashen.

'*Mr Bowen. Thank God you are come*—'

He had prayed with them until dawn broke, and took her into the arms of God. He had buried her on a windswept winter morning, with the mighty words with which all Christian souls were buried: 'I am the resurrection and the life, saith the Lord: he that believeth in Me, though he were dead, yet shall he live: and whosoever liveth and believeth in me shall never die.'

Now his own time approached.

'Oliver?'

Now she was looking at him; and even in the shadowy light he could see how dark her eyes were become, how still she sat.

He said again: 'I am very ill, but you must not be afraid. God is beside us both.' He could not bring himself to speak death's name again, and he knew he had no need. She understood. She knew.

And he let her think, as she bowed her head again and permitted him to lift his hand to her cheek, and for a moment stroke it, that his apprehension of her weeping and distress related only to this: illness, approaching death, her fear of losing him.

He must have fallen asleep, her hand in his. He woke to find her gone, but the candle burning still. She had set the little clock beside it: he saw it was almost ten. Where was she? He lay, feeling a fever begin to rise, and the sheets begin to cling. How could she bear to share such a sickbed, and how could he allow it? Yet how could he not want her here beside him?

'Lord, bring her to me.'

He waited, unable to call. Was she sleeping in the cold spare bedroom, opposite Millie's little room? In all their married life, in all his illness, they had never slept apart, though he had often, in the last few months, got up to go and sit there so as not to disturb her with coughing. Now he had not the strength to make that journey.

He waited. He listened. An owl called in the churchyard, then another, from a different place. Then the first one called again. Owl to owl, like husband to wife. Here I am. There you are. We shall always be together. He tossed on the pillow. Where was she?

'Susannah?'

She was here, she was in her nightgown, she was coming into the room with scarcely a sound, carrying her candlestick, pale as a ghost in the flickering light.

'Beloved—' He held out his hand.

'I have woken you?'

'No. I was waiting for you.'

She turned back the quilt. She slipped in beside him.

'How are you feeling?'

'Much better, now you are here.'

She blew out her candle; he reached for her hand; she gave it.

He thought: God is in this room. He will see me through this night.

He heard her breathing grow steady and slow; he heard her yawn; he knew she had fallen asleep. He let his own candle burn down beside him, felt his fever rise and rise.

Midnight. Midnight? It could be any hour. He woke soaking, gasping, raging with thirst and fever. All he could hear was his own dreadful breathing, all he could see was the glimmer of the moon. And he was on fire: the flames consumed him.

But somewhere in this house was water – he knew it – someone had put it somewhere – had let down a bucket, into a channel of darkness—

He flung out an arm towards his table – had someone not sunk a well just there, beside him?

There was a crash; there was the sound of water trickling.

'No, no, no—'

They must not take it from him now – he had only this moment discovered the source.

'No, no, I beg you!'

'Oliver! Oliver, whatever is it?'

Susannah was sitting up beside him. She fumbled for a match. 'I'm here, I am here.' There was light at the bedside, there was her frightened face.

'Water – water—'

She flung back the bedclothes; she ran; he heard her calling, 'Millie! Millie!' How that cry sounded through the house. 'Millie!'

A banging on a door, a stumbling down the stairs—

'Water—'

Into his mind there flew the small scrap of a text – a line, a verse. What was it? What did it say?

Then she was come back to him, was here, was lifting him in her arms, holding a glass to his lips. He drank, and drank again, and all the world's waters came pouring into this room – the Red Sea parting, the dove flying over the glassy Flood, Christ in Galilee, walking and walking upon that silver sea, and Christ in Samaria, resting upon an old stone well in the burning noonday.

'Whosoever – whosoever—' He heard his voice crack, saw Millie in the doorway, her hair all awry and her shawl clutched round her; saw the little scrap of text come whirling through the shadows.

'Whosoever—'

Millie was beside him. Now there were two women beside him, the one so young and pale and afraid, the other a comforter, a comforter – and here was that text, that marvellous line, hovering just above him. He reached for it – he drank again.

'Whosoever—'

'I must go for Dr Probyn, ma'am.'

'Don't leave me! How can you go in the dark?'

'But look at him, ma'am.'

The sound of water, more water pouring – the glass to his lips once more.

'Whosoever drinketh of this water shall thirst again—' There, he could see it quite plainly now. 'But whosoever drinketh ... of the water that I shall give him ...' How did it go on? He gazed at them both, beseeching. 'The verses – how do they end?'

'But the water that I shall give him,' said Susannah, her voice trembling, 'shall be in him a well of water springing up into everlasting life.'

He closed his eyes, he sank upon the pillow, and the waters lapped at him, gently, tenderly, as if to keep him safe. Then he began to cough.

'Millie!'

'It's all right, ma'am, I'm here.'

The hideous bowl before him again, the filthy heaving into it.

The room began to spin.

'Now then, Bowen, what have we here?'

He opened his eyes. The room was brighter; an oil lamp stood on the chest, turned high. Probyn stood beside him, his hair and the beard on his tired plump face unbrushed.

'You are—' He wanted to say the man was just risen from his bed, but the words would not come, and his voice was too faint.

'I am here,' said Probyn drily. 'Now then.' He took his hand into his own warm palm, he felt for Oliver's pulse – and Oliver himself could feel how fast it beat, could feel his heart racing and pounding, and hear his gasps. Susannah and Millie stood at the foot of the bed, their arms about each other. He wanted to reassure them, and could not. Something was crouching malevolently upon the quilt, black and gaping. He had not the strength to enquire what it could be. He heard his gasping go on and on and on.

Probyn looked up from his fobwatch and released his hand. He felt in his bag – ah, this was the crouching black creature, its jaws agape. How fever did transform the world. As once before, he had a floating memory of childhood illness, his nurse so patient by the fire, while the knots in the wood of the tallboy snarled. Somewhere, now, a ship was calling across the water – could that be so? It came again.

Probyn was untwisting a paper, tapping it into a glass.

'Have we a spoon?'

Millie was gone like a shadow.

Susannah came to the other side of the bed. Now he could not see her, for he could not turn his head. Was it flame or water that licked him now? That ship that called – was it calling him? Where were they to go? When he closed his eyes, he saw darkness, and brightness. With every gasping breath came the pain in his chest, his spine. He felt the cough begin to rise.

'No, no—'

'Sir—' Millie came panting back into the room.

There came the pouring of water, the tinkle of silver upon glass.

'Now, then, Bowen, my good fellow …'

Probyn's arm went round him; he was lifted from the pillows.

'Drink this.'

Drink ye all of this; for this is my Blood … Do this, as oft as ye shall drink it in remembrance of me.

The glass was at his lips; he gasped and struggled to swallow something vile.

Drink this in remembrance that Christ's Blood was shed for thee, and be thankful.

'Come on, dear fellow.'

He swallowed, he heaved, the bowl before him.

'Keep it down, keep it down …'

He brought up the cough, the phlegm, the powder, heard someone run from the room, brought up a shining clot into the vile bowl, and than a spray of scarlet. It fell upon the quilt like summer rain.

Then it was over. Then he fell back.

☆

Morning was come. Morning was come, and he was here to greet it. He gazed upon the bloodstained quilt, the lamp on the chest, the text above: 'Lo, I am with you always, even unto the end of the world.'

'Oliver?'

She was here, she was seated at the open window. He could not turn his head but he looked towards that corner. She was still in her shawl and nightgown.

'How are you?'

She rose and came towards him, her hair tousled and her face so drawn. He could not speak, but he lifted a finger.

'Water?'

She lifted the glass to his lips. It tasted stale, but he managed to swallow a sip. Then another.

'More?'

This he could not manage. She set down the glass and kneeled at the bedside.

'You passed a dreadful night – Dr Probyn came – do you remember?' He thought he did. 'Millie went with her lantern to the Prossers. Mr Prosser drove into Kington in the trap.' She took his hand. 'Dr Probyn will come every day to you now.'

He listened, he nodded. A little sound came at the door.

'Here is Samuel,' said Susannah, turning. 'He is come to see how you are.'

She stretched out her other hand, and the cat came towards her. Oliver could hear the beginning of a purr at her caress. She turned back towards him with a gentle smile, and the moment felt all at once as close as any in their married life – no, closer: she in her nightgown beside him, his hand in hers, the sun come into the room and the cat contented.

'Your fever is lessened, I think,' she said, watching him. 'Dr Probyn said he thought it might, he said he thought ...' she hesitated, then glanced down at the quilt. 'He said he thought that the release of blood might help you.' She took her hand from him, she rose. 'Millie is sleeping – later she will help me to change the sheets, and bathe you. Dr Probyn said when you woke I was to help you to eat, to give you some strength. Do you think you could take a little gruel?'

He did not know. He felt filthy, exhausted, the smell of the room

237

and of his own body deep within his nostrils, and she about to leave him. For her to go from the room now – just as they were so close and quiet …

'I shall be back very soon. Samuel? Shall we have breakfast now?'

And then they both were gone, and he lay there unable to move or murmur, close to weeping. He was abandoned, a tiny craft upon the waters, drifting alone towards an unknown shore.

When she came back she bore a little red tray, a blue-patterned bowl upon it. As once before, he thought those threads of steam quite beautiful. Life, they said, rising so gently. Life, life.

Susannah set down the tray, she propped him up, she lifted the spoon to his lips.

'This will do you good.'

He swallowed. The cough lay waiting. He swallowed again: she had sweetened the gruel with sugar and something else, something he knew, which made him think of Christmas. He looked up at her.

'Nutmeg,' she said, dipping the spoon again. 'Nutmeg and cinnamon.'

He nodded, and took another spoonful. He did not cough. Was everything foul and filthy come up from him now? Had he turned a corner? Life, said the sweet warm gruel, slipping down like honey. Life, life, life.

'You are eating well!' She smiled down at him, and he gazed up at her, feeling nourishment and warmth seep into him.

'Another spoonful?'

He took it. That was enough. He lay back upon the pillows.

'Thank you.' He heard his whisper, thin as a thread of steam, and then: 'I so love you.' He heard that too, could not remember when those words were last spoken between them. He said them again.

Susannah's eyes filled with tears. He held out his hand, but she did not take it.

'I must – I must—'

She was gone from the room. He heard her swift footsteps down the stairs, the closing of the parlour door, and he knew she would be weeping by the unlit fire, still in her shawl and nightgown, the day becoming lovely at the window, as it did at the window here, open on to the churchyard, the rooks, the morning air.

Was this the Lord's last test of all? Not only to try him – nay, torment him – with illness, with glimpses of death, but to take away human love just as he glimpsed a return?

Clouds blew past the window. What was He trying to teach him?

I am the Way, the Truth and the Life. He that believeth in Me shall not perish, but have Everlasting Life …

Hear what comfortable words our Saviour Christ saith—

How many times had he murmured those words at the Communion table, pressing the wafer Host into upturned hands, then offering the chalice?

Take, eat, this is my Body, which is given for you …

But now?

Must he face his own end alone?

He had no child. Was even his wife to be taken from him?

Oliver closed his eyes. Once more there came to him that vision of a tiny craft, sailing out upon the waters. As a child he had pictured such a stream of light from Heaven: all his life he had been nourished by this eternal prospect. Now – now, all at once he saw only darkness, and a ship upon black waters without star or compass.

'Lord,' he whispered, and heard his voice sigh into the empty room, with the smoky globe of the lamp upon the chest, the drift of dust on the floor, the empty grate and the blood – his own blood – upon sheet and quilt. It began to rain; it began to come in at the open window.

'Lord,' he whispered again, and heard only the voice of a man in a room, which went unanswered.

It was Millie who came to bathe him and make him comfortable. She, like Susannah, had the face of one who had been up all night.

'You are very good,' he whispered. 'I fear I am become a dreadful burden.'

'Never, sir, you could never be that.'

She turned back the dirty sheets, and where once she had left him to sponge himself in private now she must lift him, and lift his gown, and offer the chamber pot just in time, for he was about to flood the mattress. Oh, what shame. And he let her wash him, as intimate as any wife could be, and draw a clean nightshirt over his head, and then half carry him over to the chair that she might strip the bed.

'Mrs Bowen—'

'She is sleeping, sir.' Millie tucked the blankets round him. 'Do you want me to call her?'

'No, no, let her rest. She is in the spare room?'

'She is. I have made up a fire. I shall make one in here in a moment.'

He had not the strength to thank her again. He lay back against a cushion, so grateful to be clean. While she tugged off the bedclothes he contemplated the length of the passage between this room and the next, opposite Millie's own small bedroom. Susannah slept but yards from where he sat: it felt as distant as Africa, somewhere he could never journey now.

A heap of sheets and blankets fell softly to the floor and dust was everywhere. He covered his mouth, closed his eyes, saw that pitiable vessel sail away to darkness.

'Sir?'

He began to cough. She was at his side in a moment.

'How foolish of me—'

The bowl was before him. It all began again.

Probyn returned at noon. May's glorious summer warmth was given way to clouds and rain: Oliver could hear the doctor shaking out his cape in the hall, telling Millie how his horse was left beneath the trees.

'Shall I wake Mrs Bowen, sir?'

'No, no, she will need all her strength – let her sleep while she can. Give her this book when she wakes.'

What book was that?

He came up the stairs with his heavy tread.

'Now, then, Bowen, how are we?'

Oliver was returned to bed, the sheets and pillowcases fresh and clean, and the fire leaping. Such comforting things, but he was not comforted.

'You are well cared for,' said Probyn, setting down his bag. 'I am glad to see it. And how are you feeling, after your interesting night?' He took out his stethoscope, rubbed the cold metal plate in his hands.

Oliver watched him. How many times had Probyn pressed that

thing to his chest in the last twelve months?

'Put it away,' he whispered.

'I should like just to listen—'

'Put it away.'

Probyn looked at him, holding the rubber tube between plump fingers. Oliver met his gaze, as the rain came driving against the glass. Had there been sun? Had there been summer? Had he himself once been fit and strong, and asked his father's oldest friend if he might take his daughter's hand in marriage?

'How long will it be?' he whispered.

Probyn put down the stethoscope. It lay on the quilt with its arms outstretched. He rested his hand on the rail at the foot of the bed. Then he came and took Oliver's hand in his, paper white against firm flesh.

'With the loving care you have from your dear wife – if you can keep down food and medicine – you might last the summer. Other- wise – perhaps not very long.' His thumb stroked the back of Oliver's hand, thin as a bird. 'You are strong in faith,' he said slowly. 'God is with you.'

Oliver closed his eyes. The rain fell hard against the glass. Once again came the vision of that lonely, lonely vessel, borne away. It assailed him, it would not leave him; it seemed to say: This is the truth: there is no light from Heaven. At the end, this is all we have.

'No, no—'

'Hush.' Probyn's hands enclosed his own. With their warmth he thought of the story which, like the streaming light from Heaven, had sustained him all his life.

'Lazarus ...' he whispered.

Down in the hall, where he had not been for weeks, where perhaps he would never go again, hung that old engraving. How many times he had passed it, entering his study, leaving his study, glancing up or standing before the miracle of Christ's outstretched hand, His healing touch, His light in the darkness as a dead man came to life.

And now—

'Christ is gone from me,' he whispered.

'Never,' said Probyn, clasping his hand. 'This is illness, Bowen; that makes you think such a thing. Be strong, my dear fellow, be strong in your faith as you have always been. Come, look at me.'

Oliver opened his eyes. Probyn was bent over him, stroking his hand. Fatigue from a broken night was there in his brown eyes, but sleep would restore him, he was strong and fit, as Oliver once had been. How could he know the truths that illness told?

'Now, then,' he said, and released his kindly grip. 'I shall help you all I can, and your dear good wife and your maid will nurse you.' He folded his stethoscope, and slipped it back into its case. 'I am leaving powders for much stronger draughts, which you are to sip very slowly: they will help you to sleep. You will take some now. Here, let me help you.'

He was tapping a paper: a foul-coloured powder fell into the glass. There was the wretched tinkling of the spoon, a sound which should be comforting but which made him heave. 'Here we are, here we are, come now ...' He was eased into Probyn's good strong arms, the spoon was at his lips. 'Just a sip, that's a good fellow, let that go down. Marvellous. And just one little sip more ...'

'I can't, I can't—'

Probyn pressed his hand. 'You can. You can. Do it for your wife, Bowen, do it for her.'

He did it. He swallowed the hideous spoonful. He did it again.

'Now gently, gently ...'

And gently he was eased back upon the pillows, spittle on his lips and his stomach churning.

'Well done. Well done, old fellow. Keep that down and you will wake a little stronger. Now, then ...'

He was screwing up the paper, fastening his bag. Oliver lay with his mouth clamped shut, willing and willing the potion to stay within him. For her. For Susannah. Let him fix on that.

Probyn was watching him. 'Excellent. What a fine patient you are. And I shall be back tomorrow. You will soon grow tired of me.'

He gave him a smile, he fastened his bag, once more he patted his hand. Then he walked to the window, and stood looking out at the rain. 'I believe it is easing,' he said. 'My horse will be glad of that.'

When he woke, he saw Millie tending the fire. He lay watching her do this, poking in kindling, dropping on little pieces of coal with the tongs, so as not to disturb him. The room was full now of afternoon sun: when he turned to the window he saw the bright drops shining on the glass, and the green of the tops of the elms was green with a new intensity. Such things had always seemed an affirmation: lo, the storm passes, and the world is made anew. Could he rediscover these beloved certainties?

'Millie ...'

She set down the tongs, was beside him in a moment. 'Sir? How are you feeling now?'

'Calmer.' He saw her relief. For a little while he said nothing, just let himself float upon gentler waters. Ah, how good that felt. Then: 'In the night,' he whispered, 'in the night it seemed a ship was passing.'

'Ship, sir?'

'Something was – something was calling – a horn, a ship's horn.'

Millie frowned, then her face cleared. 'The owls, sir? I think it was them you heard, they was very loud.'

'Ah. Thank you.' Was that all it had been? The hoot of an owl become a foghorn? This was fever's horrid alchemy – a doctor's bag become a monstrous creature, an owl become a ship, become a metaphor ...

He closed his eyes again. The vision of that lonely craft was gone. He felt weak but a little better. Had God returned? Surely God would return to him now.

A sound at the doorway. He turned, he looked. Susannah stood there.

'My love ...' He held out his hand.

She flickered a smile; she came into the room. She was washed and dressed now, her hair put up into its coils. Yet how pale and drawn she looked still.

'How are you, Oliver?'

'Calmer,' he said again, and remembered something. 'Probyn lent you a book? What book was that?'

'Miss Nightingale's *Notes on Nursing*.' She slipped past Millie, and went to the window, where the rain still shone. 'Dr Probyn much admires her, he says she will help me. I have been reading a little while you slept.' She pushed at the casement, and the drops flew out from the pane. 'She believes in fresh air above all things.' She fastened the catch on the sill, and turned to him. 'Does the air not smell sweet after rain?'

It did. It bore in the scents of the fresh wet earth, the summer grass, old stone. He turned to look at her. He said slowly, for everything felt slow: 'You and Millie – you knew of fresh air, did you not? What else does Miss Nightingale say?'

'Many things.' She sank down into the chair where this morning he had heaved and spat. 'That all hurry and bustle is painful to the sick. That it wearies the very sick to be read to.' She paused, recollecting. 'That the nurse must sit always within the patient's view, so he has not painfully to turn his head to look at her …'

'She thinks of everything.'

'She does. And you – you sound better. Your voice is stronger. Shall Millie bring you some broth?'

'If you can keep down food and medicine – you might last the summer …'

He nodded. 'Thank you, Millie.' Miss Nightingale was right – it was a great effort to turn from one to another, and he did not do so. He wanted to go on looking at his wife, this thin pale creature doing her duty, reading *Notes on Nursing*, dreading the night ahead. But perhaps, with this new powder …

Millie had gone from the room. In the quiet he could hear the fire's crackle, and the dripping of the trees. The sun was sinking, and Susannah's milky hair was turned to gold.

'My love,' he said again, and willed her to hold his gaze.

Part Three

20

May 1861

Dearest Richard,

How glad I was to receive your letter, and I am replying at once, on two counts. First, we are determined to come on a visit! The weather is so glorious now, and we have been far too long without your dear company. I have one or two meetings to attend, and Verity wishes to complete a little course of study begun with a charming tutor, of whom I shall write to tell you more. Or perhaps she will tell you herself. But in early June we shall be with you, if you can accommodate us – might the good woman Martha Price prepare our rooms? Or should we stay in Kington? Is there a good and affordable hotel? I shall wait eagerly to hear.

But lest you think that the prospect of seeing you makes me so happy that I have not fully read your last letter, let me assure you that I read it with very serious attention, and was disturbed to hear of the distress of the poor woman you describe. I am disturbed for you, too, that something overheard should make you so anxious. In truth, I cannot tell if those cries were indeed hysteria, or if some dreadful violence was being done against her. Either seems possible, and in either event it seems she needs a friend.

I am sure you know that sometimes deep unhappiness is accompanied by shame – one dare not let friend or neighbour have the truth; one keeps up a front – and this, alas, is how despair or cruelty go undetected, until it is too late …

☆

A summer Saturday morning, the postman come whistling up the lane. Richard was out in the orchard, breakfasting beneath the apple trees. He saw the man's hat skim the hedgetop, rose to walk down the path to meet him at the gate.

'Morning, sir. Another fine day.'

'Indeed. Thank you.' He took the sealed envelope, felt himself melt for a moment at the prospect of Susannah's hand upon it, saw at once that it had come from home. And as a thrush tugged at a worm in the grass, he began a little conversation about the birds, the weather, the lambs gone off to market, such as any country curate might have with a country postman on a lovely summer day. Then the man tipped his hat, said he'd better get along now, and went walking back down the path, and on up the brimming lane beneath the trees. His whistle came clear through the soft summer morning, and then it faded, and Richard took his letter back to his seat beneath the boughs, and broke the seal, and read it.

How might he reply?

Dearest Mama, Since I last wrote to you, I have lost my heart entirely …

Dearest Mama, Since last I wrote to you, I have held another man's wife in my arms and kissed her so deeply that my body and soul dissolved …

Dearest Mama, I am lost, I am lost. I think only of her, of her mouth, and the way that it opened beneath my mouth. I dream of her beneath me, above me, of myself within her, within her …

Dearest Mama, I cannot pray, except to pray she will come to me, stay with me. You do not know me. I no longer know myself …

The letter lay before him on the table, amongst breadcrumbs and preserve, and he put his head in his hands and groaned aloud. What should he do? What must he do?

Birds came and went in the boughs above him. From far down the lane he heard a little voice singing. That was Alice, out of school on a Saturday morning, out of the crossing cottage, and playing on the grass.

'She is young, and she is pretty,
She has the keys to the golden city.'

248

Was that what she sang? Was she singing to Victoria, perhaps her only toy?

And had she told her mother what she had seen four days ago? Pretty Mrs Bowen come out of the curate's cottage, the two of them alone? There came now another little voice, less distinct but no less happy on this sweet May morning, when all God's creation might open itself to the sun: Tommy, conducting his engine along the track to Kington, the furthermost edge of his world.

Richard got up, and cleared his breakfast things. He took them indoors, and left them in the stone sink for Martha, who soon would be here for her hour on Saturday. He carried his letter from home into the snug, and sat at his desk, before the little glass of fading prayermint, and uncapped his bottle of ink.

Dearest Mama,

This is wonderful news! Of course you must stay here: to fill this empty place with you and my dear sisters would be my greatest joy. As for poor Tilda Prosser, I wonder if I can arrange for you to meet her. I can think of no one who might more sensibly be able to give her affection and guidance ...

'Morning, Mr Allen.'

Martha, arrived already, entering the porch.

'Good morning, Martha.'

He ended his letter, he signed and blotted it. A sheep looked in at his window as he reached for the sealing wax. Martha came in.

'Am I disturbing you, sir?'

'Not in the least.' He struck a match, and watched the dripping wax. 'I am just into Kington,' he told her, turning to see the square comfortable shape in the doorway. 'I am to the post – and to do a little shopping. There.' The letter was sealed, and the ewe had gone stumbling past. Last night, one had cried and cried for her lamb, long after darkness fell. 'Now, then,' he said to Martha, 'I have had splendid news, though I fear it will mean more work for you.'

'What's that, sir?'

And he told her, pushing his chair back, slipping the letter into the pocket of his gown. His mother and sisters were to come on a visit;

he had told them all about Martha, and how well she looked after him; and now might she make ready the other two bedrooms? The one was large enough for his mother and elder sister, the little one beneath the sloping ceiling just where Emily might like to lie, pretending she was a child again …

He heard himself run on, listened to Martha's account of linen, and how, for just a few days, all this was possible, how she would be happy to do this for him, how she would like to meet his family, having so often dusted their photograph and wondered, if it was not impertinent, if she might meet them one day.

'You shall, you shall,' said Richard. 'How good you are, Martha; how fortunate I have been in you.'

And he bid her good morning, knowing that neither she, nor the postman, nor anyone he might meet in the town today would ever guess what river of emotion lay beneath this calm and clerical exterior. He took down his hat in the porch, he stepped outside. Swallows went skimming before him. He saw one dart out of the barn. Would it do any harm if he slipped inside?

It made him think of boyhood, and his father, as he walked across the grass. It made him feel better, ordinary, innocent again – a curate, a naturalist, an ornithologist, someone like Maddock, who so had loved that lark – to open the latch on the worn barn door, and step quietly inside. He stood there, adjusting to the dimness. Chinks here and there in the weathered boards let in shafts of sunlight: dust motes spun within them, as they spun within the church. He watched them. Were they less beautiful, here? In this secular space, this wholly ordinary, country space, which once had housed a pony, was dancing dust the symbol of life and death he used to make it, or simply itself? Without the great presence of God behind them, might things not hold their own beauty, and mystery, simply through being themselves?

He moved in further, drinking in the smell of old wood, old apples. Cobwebs hung everywhere, caked in dust and become as thick as string. He looked up, as if into a soaring nave. There. There they were, a row of mud-caked nests along the beam, and there – yes, as his eyes adjusted he could just see the beak, the perfect dark curve of a motionless head, bright eyes, in every one of them. They watched him. He watched them, keeping absolutely still. What a timeless precious sight they were, keeping life – life! – so close and warm and hidden, until the right time had come. Then a male bird, with a beak stuffed full of insects, came swooping in, and saw him, and turned and was gone in a flash.

Richard stood very still. Would the bird return? He waited, then he stepped out to the grass, shadowed by the barn's great height, and quietly latched the door. At a little distance, down on the long path, he stood and watched, and waited, and just as he was about to give up, the swallow came swooping back. Like an arrow it made for the gap above the barn door and was gone into it.

And Richard turned in relief, and walked down the path to the gate, which the postman had left open, and on down the lane towards the railway crossing. He thought of the sermon he must give tomorrow, of the face in the pews he would hardly dare to glance at as he delivered it; a face that now he knew quite differently: no longer pale and restrained and anxious but ardent – so ardent! – so loving and open and filled with desire. He would not dare to look at her lest his own face betray them to the world; he would fix on a point above them all, and preach on constancy.

'Just as the swallow is hidden in the barn, and waits night and day upon her nest; just as Christ walked as a stranger beside his disciples on the long dusty road through the hills to Emmaus, and then disclosed himself – so God is with us, unseen, but constant: always beside us, never forsaking us, there until the very end, and into Eternal Life …'

These were the words his congregation wanted. These were the thoughts that had guided him all through his life. Who was he now to think he might preach differently? Was he to lean upon the pulpit and confess: I am taken by love and passion far from such conviction? I am no longer certain I can live within the Church. I am no longer certain it is God who moves the world …

He rounded the corner.

'Good morning, Alice.'

'Good morning, Mr Allen.'

They were there in the grassy garden behind the low stone wall. Tiny doll clothes were strewn about them; the scarlet paint on the engine was chipped away. The Worcester apple tree, which in early spring had been clothed in pink blossom like a girl in a gown, now towered over them, leafy and full, and beyond them the river went slowly by, filled with spring rain, and glinting.

On a hard chair at the open back door, their mother sat sewing and watching. He touched his hat to her; he blushed quite uncontrollably. But if Lily Birley had been told of something scandalous she gave no hint of it, only her shy quick smile of greeting, before she bent over her mending once again. And he stood watching them all, his blush and his fear diminishing, drinking in this gentle domestic scene. *Contentment. The Crossing-Keeper's Garden.* Was it sentimental to see it thus? Was he sentimental to long for such children as these?

And here was the train, puffing in from Leominster, and the sound of the river was gone, and the turning mill wheel faded, and the steam was clouding everything – river and tree and gabled roof and garden, mother and children and worn wooden toys – as if what was here, now, seen with such intensity, was all at once disappeared, swept away, and gone for ever.

The town was full of shoppers. Everywhere he looked, he hoped to see her. There was a lovely face beneath a bonnet. There was a glimpse of silky hair. He thought: if I see her I shall beg her to come home. But no one was her. No one could ever be her.

'Allen! Good morning!'

James Southwood was making his way through the throng, with Gauntlet at his heels. 'Good to see you.' He shook Richard's hand. 'How are you keeping?'

'Very well indeed, sir, thank you. Enjoying this marvellous weather. And I've had some good news,' he added, running his hand over Gauntlet's greying head. 'My mother and sisters are to come on a visit – I had a letter this morning.'

'Splendid. That's splendid. You must certainly bring them to see us. We must send the carriage. I don't know how you manage to walk everywhere as you do, Allen, but we should love to see them. Croquet, that's the thing. Croquet and tea on the lawn. Charlotte would be so glad of new company, and she is a fearsome creature with the mallet.'

Richard laughed. 'I can imagine, sir.'

They stood amongst the shoppers, talking easily in the sun. How good it felt: he was part of things now, there was no doubt about it, and the prospect of seeing his mother and sisters made welcome at Burgage Manor on a summer afternoon – something to divert them, something he could give them, through his position here – it was pleasant, it was satisfying, it was how things should be.

'And Bowen?' asked Southwood, stepping back as the mail coach came rolling down the street. 'I hear he is none too well again. I saw Probyn earlier, hear there've been one or two calls in the night.'

'Oh?' Richard bent to the dog once again. 'I fear I did not know that.' He felt the wretched flush creep up. 'I shall see Mr Bowen tomorrow,' he said to Gauntlet's head. 'I shall call on him after the service.'

'Of course, and I'm sure you will bring him comfort. We're very fortunate in you, Allen, glad to have you with us. And poor Bowen – we must hope this warm weather will do him good. A chair in the sunshine, that's what my wife would say. Speaking of whom ...' He glanced up the street to the clock tower. 'Must be getting on. We'll see you tomorrow.' He raised a quizzical eyebrow. 'I must tell you that Charlotte enjoys your sermons, Allen, and she does not enjoy them all.' And he was gone off up the street, Gauntlet slowly following.

Richard stood watching him go. The morning's warmth and the town's lively Saturday atmosphere felt suddenly distant, as if he stood in a little pool of darkness, here on the crowded street. A summons to Dr Probyn in the night – how grave that must have been, how frightening.

'Good morning, Mr Allen!'

That was Liza Neve, coming along with her basket full of packages.

'Morning, Mr Allen, sir.'

That was Dick Bampfield, lugging a sackful of seed.

Richard greeted them both, and then he collected himself, as he must, for he could not stand here gazing about him like some vacant boy. He posted his letter. He purchased a ham, just a small one, to last him through the week. He made himself think about feeding the family, when they arrived, decided to consult with Martha, pay her for extra produce from her garden, encourage her Joseph to take out his gun to the rabbits. He bought a quarter-pound of cheese, and a half-pat of butter, and he did all these things, and thought all these things, while a worm of anxiety burrowed away all the time. He bumped into people he knew at every shop front; he made small talk as every good curate should. The clock outside Skarratts showed quarter to twelve; outside the carpenter's shop he saw a hive.

It was beautifully made, and it calmed him. He thought of it standing in the corner of his orchard, up at the far end, where the grass was long and thick. He crossed the street, ran his hands over its sloping top, warm from the sun. Through the open door he could smell sawdust and resin; behind the dusty window stood a row of crocks, labelled in copperplate hand: Herefordshire Honey.

The carpenter came to the door in his apron. Richard made his enquiries: how much for the hive; who could teach him about bees; must he purchase a hat and a net for his face and such things as beekeeper's gloves? He described his orchard, with its secluded far corner. Might this not be just the place for a hive?

The carpenter listened and answered, and the town clock struck the hour. He directed Richard to the secretary of the Kington Beekeepers Association, out on the Hergest Road, and said that the hive could be delivered after four o'clock today, if that suited.

'That would suit very well,' said Richard. 'I shall go out to Hergest next week.'

By now it had grown very warm. He took off his hat, and fanned himself.

'Step inside if you wish, sir.'

He breathed in the cool woody smell. Saws hung on hooks, a plane stood on a trestle. Untreated timbers were propped against a wall, there were spindles and settles and benches. There was a shelf of wooden toys.

'May I?'

He picked up cows and carts and caravans. He found a little cradle with a hood, and had fixed on this, and a haycart for Tommy, and was about to pick up and pay for them both. Then he saw the hoop. It hung on a hook on the plastered wall and was covered with dust. He took it down, and blew the dust away. He ran his hand over its smoothness, and plainness.

'Have you a stick?'

The carpenter looked amongst lengths of dowel and beading.

'I think this should do, sir.'

Richard took it. He set the hoop upright and gave it a tap. On the uneven boards, with their heaps of sawdust, it ran but a few feet before it fell. But out in the lane, with the hard-packed earth of summer – how it would bowl along.

He thought of the lie he had told Alice, how unquestioningly she had received it.

Mrs Bowen has made this long walk down to fetch me to a meeting.

Hateful. Shameful. Well – if he never had a daughter, let him give this child a hoop. If he did nothing else for Alice Birley ever again, let it roll through her innocent childhood and let her remember him – please – only for this.

The lane was deep in shade as he walked home, the hoop hung over his arm, for the trees were growing full, and the hedges dense. He could smell cut grass and pipe smoke as he came past the mill from the bridge, and as he approached the crossing cottage he saw that Birley had been at work on the verges with his scythe, now propped up in the porch. The swathes of long grass lay drying in the sun like new-mown hay, and behold – Richard had a haycart. He took it out of his knapsack, stuffed it full, felt like both boy and father.

He crossed the lane to the cottage garden and looked over the wall. There they all were, the children flopped down in bare feet beneath the apple tree, Bob and Lily Birley on the kitchen settle, pulled out into the sun. The sweet-smelling smoke from Birley's briar was rising in dreamy puffs in the warm still air; bread and cheese and a pitcher of water stood on a table in the shade, and a couple of sparrows were quarrelling over the crumbs. He coughed, and they flew up into the tree.

'Good afternoon. Forgive me for disturbing you.' The Birleys looked up at him; he saw now that the children were fallen asleep. 'Might I have a word?'

'Come in, Mr Allen, do.' Lily Birley nodded at the gate. Foxgloves were springing up beside it.

'No, no, I won't disturb you. But – I hope it is not too much of a liberty – I found one or two little things in the town which I thought that the children might like.' He rested the brimming haycart on the wall; he slipped off the hoop from his arm, and felt for the stick in his bag. 'May I leave them with you?'

The Birleys got up from the settle and came across the grass.

'That's very kind of you, Mr Allen.' Lily picked up the haycart. 'They'll love that, won't they, Bob?'

'Aye.' Birley tamped down his briar. What a rich heady smell it gave. 'The hoop's a fine thing,' he said slowly. 'Alice'll enjoy that.'

'Let me waken them,' said Lily. 'Won't you come in for a moment?'

But he did not want them woken, so deeply and softly asleep in the shade while the light fell all around them.

'Let them have them when they waken by themselves,' he said. 'I shall like to think of it.' And he stayed for a few moments longer, talking of the town, the carpenter, of how his sisters still had their hoop in the loft at home, and how they were coming for a visit. Then he bade them farewell and walked home, and in his orchard stood in the sun-warmed corner where his hive would stand, and his bees come forth to feed on the flowers in the lane: rosebay willowherb, foxglove and cuckoo flower, cow parsley, jack-by-the-hedge and gentle prayermint, whose scent had come up to him just now, as he opened the orchard gate, and made his heart turn over.

> A swarm of bees in May
> Is worth a load of hay.
> A swarm of bees in June
> Is worth a silver spoon …

Oh, the beloved voices of his childhood, calling now like the song of the river, running past Alice's garden, out to a distant sea.

Just after five, a cart came down the lane. Richard was out in the front garden, the door to the cottage opened wide to the sinking sun.

'Evening, sir,' said the carter, pulling up.

'Good evening.' He walked out to the lane. A cloud of midges hung about the horse's head. The hive lay in the cart. 'May I help you with it?'

'If you don't mind.'

Together they lifted it down, carried it up the long path and through the orchard.

'I thought here,' said Richard, nodding towards the far corner. He could hear the old horse tearing at the grass on the verge, and the voices of the children, carrying up the lane. They set down the hive in the long grass. The light was honey gold.

'He'll do nicely there,' said the carter.

When he had paid him, and watched him turn the horse by the stream, and clop away, Richard went back and observed his hive with a sense of achievement. He lifted the lid. He ran his hands along the ridges where his trays of bees would lie: cell after cell of God's most purposeful creatures. Yet even as he considered it all – the sailing out on currents of summer air; the murmuring amongst foxgloves, lilac and lavender, in the ceaseless production in the darkness of the hive – he thought, as he had thought of the swallows in the barn: might these creatures not live their busy, complex lives whether or not God's hand was there to guide them? Was not the purpose and pattern of bees so clearly inscribed upon their brief span here that they had only to follow it, almost as a machine followed all its tasks?

The great machines of the age – those marvels shown ten years ago at the Great Exhibition in London: the cotton spinners, the printing machines, the talking telegraphs, the mysterious glass daguerreotype – all these still required a man to watch and guide and work them. But might the day not come when they had no need of human hand? And might the day come when all creation could be seen as guided, not by God, but by itself, by nature's own great forces?

Was this not what Mr Darwin was writing about?

'I trust I am not to find I have taken on a curate who finds this heresy in any way attractive.'

Oliver Bowen's stern caution, on his first afternoon at the vicarage, as Richard ran his eye over the scathing dismissal of Darwin's work in the *Quarterly Review*. A winter sun, a glass of port, an endless list of duties after lunch. He had known, even then, with the very first sight of her, that their lives must intertwine. Was human love – forbidden human love – really taking him so far now from the love of God, from the very idea of God?

In the deepening of the evening, the light so intense and still upon the orchard, these thoughts gave him real disquiet. He walked slowly back to the house, and in the shade and cool of the snug stood looking at it all: the place on his desk where her bonnet had rested amongst his papers; the mirror whereon they had gazed as if for ever upon two faces set so close together; the hearthside chair wherein they had made their discovery of passion. The room was full of her presence, her absence.

Richard sat down at the desk, and looked out over the great expanse of the field.

'Lord,' he murmured, closing his eyes, struggling to find again that great connection between solitude and prayer, between man and something so much greater. 'Lord, show me how I must be.'

But within him now he could feel no answers, and as he sat there, hearing through the open door on to the lane the familiar sounds of bird and sheep and stream, he knew that in his struggle to reconnect with God, and with what had once been so clearly the duties of his vocation, he wanted only Susannah's footstep on the path. He wanted the sound of his whispered name on her lips, her miraculous reappearance, that he might enfold her in love's deepest and most intimate embrace, as dusk gathered all around them and the world sank into sleep and secrecy. If his voice could but summon her now ...

He pulled out his journal, he picked up his pen.

Beloved Susannah,

It is early evening. All day I have thought only of you, and everything here returns to me your presence – the desk, the glass above the fire, the fireside chair wherein we lay and kissed, and gazed, and kissed again, our love declared at last.

Could human love bestow such fluency? His pen flowed over the pages; with every line he was lost more deeply in memory and desire.

My only wish is to hold you close once more, to listen to all that is in your heart, to comfort you in what I know must be such lonely, difficult days and nights.

'Susannah.' He groaned her name aloud. 'Susannah, my love, my own—'

A little sound came from behind him. He turned. He froze.

'Alice.'

She was there in the doorway, the hoop in her hand, the summer evening air all round her from the open door.

'Has no one ever taught you to knock?'

The words were out before he could stop them. He saw her small face crumple.

'Forgive me.' He rose from the chair. 'I did not mean to speak so harshly.'

She was scarlet. 'Mother said I might come to thank you. I did knock, sir, but you did not hear me.' She turned and went out, catching the hoop on the door and snatching it free.

'Alice – don't run away—'

He followed her into the garden, but she ran down the path without a backward glance, the hoop bumping against her pinafore.

'Alice—'

She had lifted the latch on the gate, she was running home, and how could he follow her there? He would have to lie – lie again: not just to her, but her parents. And what most possessed him, as he watched her go? Remorse, at having hurt her, or fear of what, in the silence of the evening, she must have overheard?

'Dearly beloved ...' He rested his hands upon the pulpit; he surveyed his congregation. On this warm May Sunday, the last before Ascension Day, there were summery bonnets, flowered gowns and children's dresses: they blurred before him as he fixed his gaze on the worn polished door of the Southwood pew. So many eyes to avoid: he had been so aware of this as he greeted them all at the entrance: not just Susannah's – and she had arrived so late that he was gone inside and opening his prayer book before he saw her – but the eyes of the Prossers, and now the Birleys.

His fingers shook as he held his papers before him.

'Dearly beloved. The theme of my sermon today is constancy. And also charity, that great gift of one man to another which St Paul raised so high in his letters, and which Our Lord wanted each one of us to hold in our hearts and lives. I link these two great ideals for no better reason than that each, in different ways, has seemed important to me in these last few days.'

He spoke on: of Christ's miraculous appearance after death to his

259

disciples on the hot and dusty road to Emmaus, showing Himself as always here, always with us, as constant as the swallow upon her nest. 'His love, like the love of God, flows on and on, like the sparkling Arrow, our own fine river where the mayflies are dancing now.'

He turned the page. What did it mean, to write thus, and speak thus, reaching out, he knew – from their upturned faces, the sense of concentration – to the hearts of a country congregation, if, in his own heart, lay fear and even faithlessness? Oh, how much sweeter, and fuller, and richer it was to believe. How did a man who truly lost his faith endure such absence at the heart of life? All these things ran through him, as he read on.

'I turn now to the theme of charity, reminding us all of Christ's great words recorded in St Matthew's Gospel, where he speaks of setting upon his right hand those who are righteous, summoning them into his Kingdom:

'For I was hungered, and ye gave me meat: I was thirsty, and ye gave me drink: I was a stranger and ye took me in: Naked, and ye clothed me: I was sick, and ye visited me: I was in prison, and ye came unto me ... Verily I say unto you, Inasmuch as ye have done it unto the least of these my brethren, ye have done it unto me.'

He leaned upon the pulpit. He had promised himself he would speak out, and he would do so, and let his words find their mark where they should.

'Dearly beloved, let us never forget those amongst us who are frail, those who are frightened, those who need our kindness, and tender care, no matter how lowly, how outcast, how unable to ask for these things themselves. On this lovely summer morning, I conjure from winter's darkness the memory of one so afraid that she took her own life.' He sensed a little ripple of unease amongst the pews. 'I want to suggest that dreadful though this act may be, so dreadful that burial must be beyond the churchyard walls, it must not drive compassion from our hearts.'

He turned the page; he made himself speak the words upon the next.

'It is easy to condemn the weak, the foolish, the sinful. It is easy to think of them as outside our own lives, but each one of us is capable of sin, has done things of which we are ashamed, and for which we seek forgiveness, And as Christians, as God's children and disciples, we are required to reach out, to understand, to forgive. We are required to live our own lives well, and to remember, above all, that our duty is to those who are closest to us. Within our own homes there should be no fear, no unkindness. There should be'– he felt his heart thumping in his chest – 'there should be no cruelty.'

Somehow his voice stayed firm. He could not look at any one of them, but he felt the silence before him as deep as the water in a well, and he knew they were hearing every word.

'Christ is among us, Christ is constant. Let it be on His love that we turn our gaze; let us watch over and cherish, and love one another as he bade us to do.' He paused, let his words sink in. 'And now, may the peace of God, which passeth all understanding, be amongst us and remain with us always. Amen.' There was a murmured 'Amen' from the pews. He raised his eyes. It was over. 'Let us sing together Hymn number five hundred and twenty-four.'

Thomas Hatton sounded the first strains of the tune; Richard tapped his sermon papers together and descended the steps, as the congregation rose to their feet, turning the pages of their hymnals.

'Come to our poor nature's night,
With Thy blessed inward light ...'
He walked up the steps to the chancel.
'We are sinful – cleanse us, Lord,
Sick and faint – Thy strength afford ...'

He resumed his place, he began to sing. As he dared to look out across the pews, he saw Tilda Prosser's tense little face had gone quite white, though she sang out alongside her husband.

For a moment Prosser's eyes met his. For a moment, in the sunlit church, they seemed to glitter: like those of a creature long hidden in darkness, suddenly caught in the beam of a lantern – discovered, dangerous, ready to strike.

'You spoke of us.' Susannah addressed the flagstoned path in a passion. 'You spoke of me, my duties.' They were walking back to the vicarage, the service ended, the last little knots of people still talking

261

in the sun. He had shaken every hand that was offered him. Not each one was.

'No,' he said quietly, urgently, now. 'I was not thinking of that.'

'Then of whom? You seemed to speak to me directly. "Each of us is capable of sin, has done things of which we are ashamed."'

Her voice was so quiet he could hardly hear her, but he did hear her, while the Prossers, on the other long path, reached and passed through the lich-gate; while Edward and Effie Turner stood talking to Alfred Arndell beneath the trees, and the Southwoods and the Bodenhams climbed into their waiting carriages.

'Beloved.' Like her, he addressed the sun-warmed stone, wanting only to take her into his arms, to enfold and comfort her. 'I was speaking of people quite other than us.'

'But of whom? And how could you? It felt as if you were uncovering all we had done and laying it before the congregation.'

He stopped on the path. This might be their last opportunity to speak intimately all day: he felt no danger, as long as they were quiet, for people were used to seeing Mr Allen go to the vicarage for Sunday luncheon, used to seeing Susannah Bowen accompany him there, to visit Mr Bowen in his illness.

'I did not for one moment intend to address you in that sermon.' Yet how could he have been so thoughtless? How could his words not have pierced her to her heart? 'Look at me. Look at me. Please.'

She glanced up and he saw how pale she was again, how close to tears.

'Darling. Beloved. Forgive me. I was not thinking of us.'

'But how could you not?' Her voice broke. 'You spoke of shame. I have been in torment – and Oliver has been so ill.'

Tears fell on the path. And now they were in danger, for surely someone must see her shaking shoulders, see how close they stood to one another.

Someone had. Elizabeth Southwood came hurrying up.

'My dear, I was in the carriage. We were about to leave when I saw you—' She pressed Susannah's hand. And though she gave him a sympathetic smile, Richard felt as clearly as if it were spoken: Stand back, you are not wanted. These are women's matters.

And so he stood back, and listened to the murmurs of enquiry –

how really ill was poor Mr Bowen, how might Susannah be helped? He saw her tears fall freely, her struggle to prevent them turn to real sobbing and it moved him deeply. It made him think of his sisters, and the tears that he, as a boy, must never shed, but which he had witnessed all his life – over a rabbit hanging in the pantry, over a sum, Helen's death in *Jane Eyre*, the struggle to control a temper. And then, with what shock, the tears of grief and mourning at his father's death. Even then, he must swallow back his own, be a man, look after them all. How they had wept when he left to come here.

He paced up and down on the flags. Across the highway, he saw the Prossers walking up to the laurel hedge, bright with new shoots. He saw Prosser's arm go round his wife, as if to guide her. Then they had disappeared up the path, and with the calling of the rooks he could not hear their footsteps.

'Goodbye, Mr Allen!' Edward Turner was calling, raising his hat.

Richard raised his hand in return, watched Edward and Effie walk hand in hand through the lich-gate, watched Alfred Arndell walk slowly down to his Lizzie's grave and stand there in the sun, his bony hands clasped before him. What had Arndell made of the sermon, he wondered, as he watched his head bow down, and he answered himself at once: *Too soft-hearted. There is right and there is wrong, and we must stand by what is right, Mr Allen. Some things are not for us to forgive: only God can do that.*

He turned back to the two women. The Southwood carriage horses were tossing their heads. Flies were everywhere.

Susannah was growing calmer; Elizabeth Southwood had proffered a handkerchief, a little vial of salts. He could hear her offering to visit, to be on hand at any time, perhaps to seek a new physician …

'No, no, Dr Probyn is very good. And Oliver likes him.' Susannah was wiping her eyes, she gave a watery smile. 'I am so sorry – you are so kind …'

'You look quite exhausted. How I should like you to rest.'

'Millie has been very good.'

'I am sure of it. But perhaps – would you like to come and stay for a night or two? We could find a nurse for Mr Bowen; you could be cared for—'

Susannah shook her head. 'You are so kind,' she said again, 'but I

263

should not like to be away from Oliver now.'

Listening, Richard thought: Is this because she would also be far from me? Or is she regretting every moment of our time together? Has Bowen, in his illness, driven me away? He glanced up at the bedroom window. It was open to the sun and air – something he seemed to recall his mother saying that Miss Nightingale advised – but no pale face was watching.

In truth, how was he to conduct himself on this visit to the sickroom now?

'Mr Allen.' Elizabeth Southwood was beckoning him across. 'Mrs Bowen is feeling a little stronger.'

'I am pleased to hear it.' And he smiled at Susannah – a public, clerical, sympathetic smile – and she gave a wan little glance in return.

'I shall leave you to conduct her home, and I shall trust you not to tire her or Mr Bowen with your visit.'

He bowed. 'Indeed, I shall try most earnestly not to do that.'

'I know you will.' And she kissed Susannah's pale cheek beneath the summer bonnet – oh, what a pretty thing it was – and bade her send for help at any time it was needed. Then she walked back to the carriage where her husband stood waiting for her, as if he too knew that tears were for women, and must not be disturbed.

And Richard approached Susannah once again, and under the gaze of the Southwood family – climbing into the carriage, waving, calling to the coachman – accompanied her to the vicarage. Lilac bloomed at the door. He wanted to tell her: Remember that I love you. He wanted to ask her: And you? Have your feelings changed? But these things felt too enormous, too weighty, in the face of her distress, and besides, the door was open now, and Millie standing there.

'You are certain he wishes to see me?'

'How strange it would be if you did not visit him.'

That was no answer, but then his question had not been direct. Behind it were the others: Have you told him? Does he know? Could he guess?

'Susannah—'

In the crowded dark hall, with its clock and its ferns and stuffed bird, and its picture of a dead man brought to life, Richard touched her arm and as she looked at him he tried in his gaze to ask her all these things. She made a little gesture, which he could not read.

'Come.' She turned to climb the stairs. He followed, his hand upon the rail, hearing Millie clatter about in the kitchen. Susannah stopped at the open bedroom door.

'Oliver? Are you awake? Mr Allen is come to see you.'

There came a murmur. Richard followed her to the threshold. He had not known what to expect. He hardly dared to imagine this room, this heart of married life, this invalid. Now he was shocked. That hollow face, white as cambric upon the pillows in the high iron bed. And did he imagine it, or did he see, as Susannah went quickly to the bedside, a look from Oliver Bowen to the doorway where he stood, and another questioning glance at her, as if to ascertain what might be between them?

'How are you feeling?' Susannah took his hand, and even from here Richard could see how thin it had become, how light. He saw, too, how gentle and tender she was with him, and as he took in the rest of the room – the chest, the lamp, the texts, the chair at the open window – he was minded of another Sunday, Palm Sunday – not so long ago, though it felt a lifetime. They were all in the parlour before luncheon, and Oliver seized with a horrible spasm of coughing. Susannah had been at his side in a moment, kneeling, holding him, held in his sick embrace. Richard had thought then: They are man and wife – she has lain in his arms, they have slept and woken together. He had thought: It is hopeless.

And even though on that very day they had declared their love, he thought all this again now as he saw the shrunken shape of the limbs between the quilt, the way Susannah held that hand and smiled in reassurance. He looked away, towards the open window. Someone – Millie? Susannah? – had set a jug of lilac on the sill; it caught and held the sun, and its scent came drifting into the room. He could hear slow footsteps leaving the churchyard: Alfred Arndell, leaving his Lizzie's grave at last. Would he ever wed again?

'Do come in, Mr Allen,' said Susannah.

He entered, creaking on the boards. She moved away from the bedside, and he saw on the little table, with its Bible and bell and candlestick, its glass carafe, the corked brown bottle, dark with

265

medicine. He stood at the end of the high iron bed, and saw the text above it: 'I am the Way, the Truth and the Life. He that believeth in Me shall not perish, but have Everlasting Life.' He touched his white tie, moved his father's prayerbook in his hands, looked at the sunken face before him.

'Good morning, sir.'

Oliver's fingers moved on the quilt. He murmured something.

'Sir?'

He murmured again. Leaning forward, Richard caught: 'The Visitation of the Sick.'

'Sir.' He clasped the prayerbook. Did Oliver really wish him to go through this? 'Do you wish me to—'

Oliver shook his head. Not just his limbs, but his hair, his whitened beard, were thinner now. 'I meant only – the formalities are observed.'

'Sir.' Richard shook his head. What could he say? 'I am not here only for formality.' Hypocrite. Hypocrite! 'I hear you have been very ill,' he said carefully. 'I am so sorry. You must tell me everything I should do within the parish—'

He broke off. Susannah was moving towards the door, her gown brushing the faded rug.

'I shall leave you both to talk. Do come down, Mr Allen, when Millie rings the bell.'

'Of course. Thank you.'

He turned to her, but she did not meet his eye, and as she left he heard her soft reproach to the cat on the landing: 'Samuel! You must not come up here. Shoo, downstairs.'

'How was the service?' A weak voice from the pillows.

Richard returned his gaze to Oliver. This was the tall strong man who had shaken his hand so firmly, less than half a year ago? He was shrunken, sunken, a broken reed.

'The service went well, sir, thank you.'

'You preached on …?' Such a faint quiet voice, but the terrible coughing was gone, it seemed, with that vile-looking medicine.

'I preached on constancy,' said Richard, and because he could not move, as he had done in the sermon, to speak of charity, and Tilda Prosser's pinched white face, and the glitter in her husband's beady eyes, he added: 'And of faith.' And he told him, for he knew he must

266

not tire an invalid by making him ask questions, of how Alice Birley had heard in school the story of the Road to Emmaus, how Mrs Bowen had told it to the children – he felt a dull blush rising – and how, he added quickly, he had likened the invisible presence of Christ to the swallows secluded in the darkness of his barn, knowing that such pictures touched his congregation.

'And are you strong in your own faith, Mr Allen?' The question was a whisper.

'Sir.' Richard swallowed. 'Do you doubt that?' he asked, but everything in the last few days came flooding into this sunlit sickroom – Susannah in his arms; the immortal gold on the hills when he walked home without her, wondering if he still was close to God; his shameful lie and reproach to Alice; his sense that the world, like a great machine, could spin on and on into the future whether or not God stood behind it.

'Do you doubt my faith?' he asked again, for he did not know what to say.

And Oliver said quietly from the pillows: 'Answer me.'

Richard felt his heart begin to thud. Was Oliver asking this question because he could not ask another? What was he really trying to do?

He said slowly: 'Sir. There is not a man alive who has not sometimes felt ...' He swallowed. 'Perhaps even you yourself—' He stopped. Was it cruel to speak of doubt to a man so gravely ill? He read again the text above the bed, the words which for so long had been engraved upon his own heart: 'He that believeth in Me shall not perish, but have Everlasting Life.' In truth, he could not imagine that Oliver Bowen had ever doubted.

'Even I myself ...' The voice from the pillows was not without a gleam of irony, but as Richard met his eyes again, he saw a shadow pass like a dark wing over Oliver's drawn face. 'Sometimes – I am so ill – sometimes I feel that Christ is gone from me—'

The words hung like dust in the air. From downstairs came the sound of footsteps, a door unlatched. From out in the churchyard came the smell of sun-warmed grass and yew and lilac, the ceaseless cawing of the rooks. In here there was silence, as Richard, young and in crisis, gazed across the expanse of patched quilt and mended linen at a man approaching death, reaching out for comfort.

He thought: I should take his hand. I should take his hand and kneel beside him and pray. I should give him the certainty and strength he craves. And he thought: I cannot do it. I have deceived and betrayed him. Perhaps I shall do so again. To deceive him now, on this, at the gravest time of his life – it would be unpardonable. Let someone else – Stephen Ingram, John Maddock, the Bishop of Hereford, even – someone true, someone real, someone whose faith is like a rock, let them kneel beside Oliver Bowen, and do right by him.

Not me.

And he said, very slowly and carefully: 'Sir, I know you would wish me to tell you the truth. I cannot feel that Christ would ever leave your side. If there be truly an eternal life, then I am certain He awaits you there.'

'If. But—'

'But – sometimes I think that …' He could not stand here, gazing into those sinking, dark-ringed eyes. And he moved away from the foot of the bed, and went to stand by the open window, looking out over the churchyard, over the fields. Summer clouds sailed slowly through the sky; from somewhere he could hear John Maddock's dizzying lark song, rising and rising and rising through the blue. On such a day as this, did faith not give unity and meaning to it all? And yet—

' That the world is beautiful – is this not enough?' he said quietly, but loud enough for Oliver to hear him. 'Is the world not here for us to see and rejoice in, no matter if God or nature fashioned it?' The scent of the lilac – from the bush by the door below, from the jug upon the sill – came wafting in. 'See this,' he said slowly, touching its creamy spires. 'See the light shine upon it, making the flower so full. Smell the sun on the grass. Does it matter if we cannot believe? Are these things in themselves not something to fill the heart with gladness, whether or not God made and cares for them?'

A sound came from the bed. Downstairs, the bell began to ring. Luncheon. He turned back into the room.

Oliver was weeping.

'Sir—' Richard stopped still. With every step he took, every word he uttered, he hurt everyone around him. 'I have distressed you – I am so sorry.'

Put yourself there, said a voice within him. Put yourself there, upon the pillows; there, with your strength quite gone; there, as the hour of your death approaches. See, then, how you want to think of the world.

'My life,' whispered Oliver, as the tears ran down his face. 'My life, my life—'

Richard stood quite helpless, stricken with self-reproach and sorrow.

'Forgive me,' he said, as he had said so many times, and never more fervently than now.

Downstairs the bell rang again.

'Send my wife up to me.'

'Yes, sir. Of course.'

'And, Allen—'

'Sir?'

'You need not come again.'

Down the narrow staircase, out through the open door. No, he would not have luncheon, though Millie was very kind, and he was sorry. No, he would not return this afternoon. Susannah was white as a ghost as he took down his hat, and her eyes now beseeched him: When would they— How would they—

'Good afternoon, Mrs Bowen.'

Out across the churchyard, striding along to the church. He pushed wide the door, and if there were music or air to greet him he did not hear it as he flung himself into a pew and buried his face in his hands.

'Lord, Lord—'

No answer came to him, and he did not know what, in this new turmoil, he might ask or dwell upon, nor how long he knelt there.

He grew cold. He stood up. The sun had gone in, behind those summer clouds, and the church was darkening. How could he distract himself? What should he do?

He did something he had not done for a long time. He walked up the aisle and through the dim-lit chancel. He made his way to the organ. Had Thomas Hatton locked it? He had not. Had he locked all the music away in the stool? He had not.

269

Richard pulled out the first sheets that came to hand: Charpentier's *Messe de minuit*. Haunting and tender, unspeakably sad. He had sung it at school.

He put it before him, settled himself on the stool. He pulled out a stop or two. He began to play.

What sweet, unbearable melancholy was this. The music filled the church, filled him. He played on, played on, through every crowding thought: that he had come as close to adultery as any man might come; that he had lied and spoken harshly to a child he loved; that he had pushed a man close to death towards despair. That he was still in love; that the sight of Susannah's white shocked face as he brushed past her had cut him to the quick; that he was on the brink of losing his faith and everything that had nourished and sustained him all his life.

When the *Midnight Mass* came to an end, he began it again.

At last he stopped. He drew in a deep breath, and rested his head against the organ pipes. Then he sat up. How dark the church had become. He turned to the tall east window above the altar, to which all services inclined, towards which all congregations looked as they recited the words of the Creed: 'I believe in one God ...' At the window the sun rose, at that window the light of God appeared.

As he looked now, he saw that the afternoon had changed entirely from the morning's radiance. The light was quite gone, quite drained away. He turned to the windows over the choir stall, where the glass was plain. So heavy, so purple-dark were the massing clouds beyond that it felt as if the world had been abandoned.

So. This was the world without faith. This was darkness, without hope of light. Was this what Oliver dreaded? He felt it enter his bones.

And from within all the questions he had asked himself in the last few days, now, as Richard fixed upon that clouded, leaden-lit window, one question seemed to strike him to the heart. How did solid earth become translucent glass?

The answer, with its meaning, came as he bowed his head once more. No man who betrayed his calling as he had begun to do could escape some punishment. Earth became glass through purification by fire.

21

He was gone: he was leaving her. She watched him stride from the church down the path towards the lich-gate, without even a glance at the house: not up at the bedroom, where Oliver slept restlessly; not at the parlour window where she stood, twisting and twisting a fold in her gown. She wanted to call him, she wanted to run to him, and how could she do either? Millie might hear her, a passer-by might see them – though who, beneath this sudden thundery sky, would go out walking now?

He had come to the gate; he stood beneath this gabled roof, looking out across the highway and the fields. His gown blew a little in the rising wind; he put up a hand to his hat. Did he not know she must be watching him? Would he not turn back? Her fingers went to the window latch, fell to her gown; she knew her hesitation was not only through fear of being seen or heard, but fear of him. Fear of him! How could this be true?

She looked at his silhouette beneath the tiled roof, at the shape and height of him, which for so many months had occupied and filled a space within her like a figure within a mould: fitting exactly, sinking into place, as if it had always been meant to do so. For months she had learned him by heart, observing everything: his walk, the weight of his tread on the flags as he came down the aisle to begin the service, or on the steps of the pulpit as he climbed to deliver his sermon. She had looked at slender hands, as they rested on lectern and pulpit; as they turned the pages of the Bible, of hymnal and psalter; as they raised the chalice, or held it to her lips, as they folded in prayer, or were laid on the head of a child. She had watched them run over Samuel's spine as he lay stretched out on the ottoman, or before the fire; week after week, she had rested her own gloved hand in his, after the service; had dared to look into those hazel eyes whose gaze at the congregation seemed always to avoid her own. When he had held her hand, when their eyes met at last – oh, how the world fell away. And that he had returned these feelings, that he had loved her ...

Wrong though it was; wicked though it was; unimaginably beyond everything that had nourished and contained her, it gave her life its meaning.

And now—

Now he was white with anger and distress. Now he would not look at her, but must snatch up his hat and leave the house in a passion, as if he might never return. Now he must stride into the church as if shouting: Do not follow me! Leave me alone! And if she were to call to him, if she were to run to him, out from this dark sick house with its groans and smells and dreadful need of her, would he turn upon her, seek to blame her, raise his voice and tell her that all was over between them?

'Richard ...' She let his name escape her in a whisper. She felt her heart pound as she lifted her hand once more to the latch, but he was already leaving the shelter of the lich-gate porch, though the sky was so leaden and dark that surely a great storm must break at any moment. And yes, the first drops came splashing on to the path, and the first distant rumble of thunder sounded over the fields. Surely he could not walk home in this, surely he would come back now for shelter, would take her hand and draw her to him again, and say how he wished he had not hurt her.

But he did not come back. In a moment the brim of his hat was gone as he made the descent to the highway, and then the sky broke open and the rain came pouring down. She heard it batter the slates, saw the rooks beat their way to the tossing trees, saw the lilac bush bow down beneath the weight of water. Millie was running from the kitchen and up the stairs, to close the sickroom window; Samuel came wailing for her as the first great clap of thunder tore the air.

She pressed her face to the streaming casement, and closed her eyes. Let storm and wind and water shake the world.

☆

Though he ran for the trees he was soaked through in moments. He stood beneath a sycamore overhanging the highway from a field of barley, and, through the water streaming past his hat brim, watched the rain swirl down the hill and hammer in slanting rods the cornfields across the way until they, like the barley, lay flattened and broken. This morning their fresh bright sunlit green had seemed to betoken hope and promise, had calmed his nerves a little as he walked to deliver his sermon. Now, as the thunder pealed, it felt as if the very crops must, like all else, be brought low.

And indeed there was something purging in this storm, this opening of the heavens: if the world had been abandoned, as it had felt in that sinking, leaden, dreadful approach of darkness in the church, then let it be hammered, and battered, and tossed. If lightning were to strike him, let it strike.

Lightning did not strike him, though it flashed above the hills, though the thunder tore the sky asunder, rent the veil of the temple asunder, shook the earth. For perhaps half an hour he stood there, within its raging, and when at last it grew fainter, and rumbled away, and the curtain of rain blew aside and into the distance, he was chilled to the bone, and his teeth were chattering. As he stepped out from beneath the tree his boots squelched, and he wrung out half a tankard of water from his hat. There was nothing for it but to walk the mile and more home, and he set off up the hill, and then down the long lane through the woods.

The trees dripped all around him; his boots stuck in the soaking earth; he must over and over again step aside to avoid the pools of water in the deep ruts from carts in the track. He heard no carts now, no dog or voice from the farms, only the dripping from the boughs, the stirring wind, and everywhere the reawakened birds. The sun came out, a jay flashed past, a pheasant croaked, blackbird and finch and thrush were flutes among the leaves. Everything soon was dappled in the light.

When he came out on the turning above the fields, the sheep were grazing as if the storm had never been. The grass was thick and lush, and its wetness shone. And the sky now held a rainbow, misty and miraculous, an arch across the valley through which a dove might pass.

Richard did not expect to see a dove, nor any kind of sign he might interpret as a blessing, but though he was shivering as he made the descent to the cottage, it did feel as if something huge had happened: an insight into what it would mean to yield to unbelief, to absorb and endure that, and suffer it, and how it felt now to have life and hope rekindle.

The stream before the garden was so full that it brimmed above the banks. He held his misshapen hat beneath the tumbling fall through the hedge until its creases were full, and shook it out. Inside the cottage he lit the fire, stoked the range, set the kettle upon it. He stripped off every sodden garment and when the fire was burning well rubbed himself dry and in fresh underclothes and cassock stood waiting for the kettle to boil, looking out of the kitchen window on to the field.

The sheep were filing past it, one by one, on their evening move up to the hills. On and on they went, steady and slow, and when the last had gone he saw a pheasant come stepping over the soaking tussocks from near the stream bed, looking this way and that, cocking his head at every fresh scent or sound. The rain had not quite gone: it blew in its last gentle drifts across the field, and in the evening sun the rainbow shimmered. And Richard stood watching it all, the glossy grass, the glittering rain, the pheasant stalking through. As colour and light and water came and went, it felt like the rise and fall of faith, of love – now here, now gone, now returning, now at rest.

Behind him the kettle had come to the boil and the room was cloudy with steam. He made tea, took it through to the snug, and drank it at his desk. He wanted to write to Oliver – *Sir, May I ask your forgiveness for failing to think of how my words might sound...*

He knew he could not, for the next letter running through his reawakened blood was to Susannah.

And the greatest illumination of the day, that punishment – purification by fire – awaited him, was something he now struggled to understand, as he kneeled and tried to pray.

22

The cottage, all at once, was full of preparations. Martha beat rugs, shook out the old feather beds from the other two bedrooms, long unused, and hung them to air in the orchard. Feathers blew over the grass. With the passing of the sudden storm the summer unfolded yet more full, the days blue and cloudless and the cuckoo calling, the nightingale calling, May melting into June, and woodbine and dog roses scenting the lanes. Martha unpacked the linen chest, washed the worn sheets and had every window open. She washed the glass, and every time a casement was pushed open or drawn shut a dazzling piece of grass or sky swung in the pane.

Richard thanked her, and helped her, and watched each part of the place become homelike and welcoming. He dragged the mildewed ottoman from the larger sitting room and stood it to air in the garden, where it looked outlandish. He thought it was the kind of thing the children would enjoy, sitting on indoor furniture in the open air, as he and Verity had once slept out on a chaise on summer afternoons, recovering from childhood fever. He pictured Alice swinging her legs above the grass, unwrapping Victoria's winter cloak so she could take the air; he pictured Tommy, scrambling about on bulging horsehair. But he did not invite them up to play, and when he passed the crossing cottage he did not glance towards the door or garden. And when, in the mornings, Alice ran past his gate and climbed the lane through the woods on the way to school she did not look back. He did not know what she had heard, he did not know what she had told, but he knew he had frightened her, and he could not put it right.

Now there were two houses which he could not visit.

He walked into town, and took the coach out to Hergest Ridge. As he sat up on top in the sun, and heard the larks and watched the hills unfold, and the train puff through them, whistling, he thought that in other days he would have been gloriously happy with all this, his sisters beside him, and a carefree day ahead. All he could hope for now was to give his family a carefree time when they came, a time to remember always, which he would not darken with his inner life.

The coach pulled up opposite a cluster of cottages climbing the hillside, and just by the entrance to the lane up to Hergest. He would walk up there when he had concluded his talk of bees, and he jumped down from the coach step, his knapsack bumping against him, and crossed the highway as the coach set off again, rattling towards New Radnor. The sun beat down, and he fanned himself as he walked up through the hamlet. The bee-keeper was an old fellow out in his garden, full of hollyhocks and foxgloves, and the hum of the bees was everywhere.

'Morning, sir.'

'Good morning.' And Richard clicked open the gate and became the curate-naturalist once more, as they talked about gloves and netted hats and swarming, of how to smoke, and how to extract the comb, and then the honey. He left with a jar weighting down the knapsack, and the promise of trays of bees delivered by the end of the week.

By the end of the week, the family would be here, and he must take the service, explaining how ill Mr Bowen had become, and how it was not possible for them to meet him. He must introduce them to the congregation, and to Susannah, without by a single glance or gesture indicating what they had become to one another. He had not seen her since the day of the storm, could not imagine how they must greet one another only in public, and as he came out of the bee-keeper's cottage and crossed to the shady lane up to Hergest, he thought: my mother knows me so well – how will she not detect what lies between us?

He climbed the long lane to the Ridge. Wild bees droned in the unkempt hedgerows where yellow woodbine clambered: he beat away clouds of flies with his hat. He came to the foot of the open Ridge, smelled the sun-warmed turf and saw the sheep grazing between the clumps of bracken. It was very hot now, and his black gown clung to his back, but he walked on, leaning upon his father's stick, getting into his stride as he had used to do when they walked together of old. How his father would have enjoyed it up here, on this open grassy path, the sheep trotting over it, the song of the lark so clear upon the air, and the view, the great view as he came to the summit and looked out upon the forested dark hills of Wales, the glinting Arrow far below and here and there an inn or farm or chapel, on a path winding into the distance.

He was up on the great broad back of the Ridge, and ahead all at once he could see the gypsy encampment everyone had spoken of: the thin blue smoke rising from the caravans, the tethered skewbald ponies cropping the turf, the women tending a cooking pot. Washing was draped over the gorse, a few ragged children were playing with a terrier, a couple of dark-skinned men sat smoking in the sun. Again, he felt the sudden thrill of childhood – at the smell of cooking outdoors, the sight of those brightly painted homes, the freedom of it, the here-today-and-gone-tomorrow of it, with nothing but a rag upon a bush and a ring of burned grass to show they had been here at all. And again, for the first time in weeks, he thought of Edith Clare, and wondered if this indeed was where she came from.

But why should she leave them all, and hide away?

He turned and looked back to the town. From this height he could see the tower of St Mary's and make out the market hall. He could see the great expanse of common land beyond the bridge, and upon it what he had not seen from the coach as it climbed Castle Hill: the canopies and booths and bunting of the Summer Fair, with amongst it all what he guessed must be the Tabernacle, a marquee large enough to hold a crowd, come to hear Spurgeon the preacher preach: of fire and of damnation.

On this clear summer day, far above everything that so troubled and beset him, his mind, with the exertion of his body, beginning to ease from its perpetual disquiet, he saw again the face of Philip Prosser. He saw him shift a peppermint within his small cruel mouth, saw him thump upon the table in the Kington vicarage as Richard protested at his talk of Hell. '*Mr Allen! I do not need* you *to preach at me* ...' And he saw again the venomous glitter in Prosser's eyes as he concluded his sermon on charity, and the way, after the service, that his arm went so firmly round his wife as he guided her up the long shrouded path to their house.

Richard took off his hat. He wiped his face with one of Verity's handkerchiefs, and sought out the shade of the trees. Beneath an oak, he unfastened his knapsack and took out his flask of water and apple and bread and cheese. And he tried once again to calm himself, to eat a walker's lunch in the open air, while the sheep nibbled away at the turf, or put up their bony heads amongst the bracken, as if all were as well as it seemed to be, up here, in the cloudless peace of summer.

But he knew that everything awaited him when he came down: a dying man whose house he could not enter; a stricken pale girl whom he loved and could not comfort; a family with whom he must dissemble as he had never done in his life; the prayers he tried to say, which had no answers. And, through it all, a sense of real danger, though how it would manifest itself he still could not imagine.

The house was made ready: in two days they would be here. Everything smelled of soap and beeswax; desk and table and flagstone shone, china and glasses sparkled. He had scythed the long grass in the orchard and garden; his bees had been delivered in a box. Within a day they were sailing out of the hive and into the garden, into the hedgerows and fields. He watched them, and wondered that within so short a time they had a flight path, knew how to return to the hive. Because this was something innate, or because God guided them? Was setting forth and coming home a subject for a sermon? Perhaps a good sermon for the Sunday of his family's visit, journeying as they had across the country: he could make this his starting point, weave it into the journey through faith and doubt, while God always waited for the lost sheep to be found and brought safely home. And let no one ever know or guess how troubled his own soul had been, how in the summer darkness of the church it had seemed God was gone from the world.

It was early evening. Tonight he would settle at his newly polished desk to write. The stems of prayermint had faded, and he had pressed them in the pages of his journal, locked away. Looking now round the clean little snug it felt extraordinary that it had held such passion, and that no one would ever know of this, that soon his mother and the girls would fill the house, as it was meant to be filled. And as he paced about the airy, fresh-smelling rooms, the beds all made up and the pantry filled for the visit, he remembered the first freezing night of his arrival: how alone he had felt in this empty place, which felt now like a family home, wanting only his wife and children to call from room to room, to sit at the table and bow their heads for grace, to play in the orchard and read by the fire, to sleep upon pillows whose linen was stored with lavender: the children in their bedroom where a rushlight glowed, his wife in his arms, her hair like a flood of pale silk in his hands, and everything open and known between them.

Thinking thus reawakened all his longing. How had Susannah spent the days since he had left? What must she think of him?

He stood in the open doorway on to the garden, breathing in the scents of cut grass, of lavender and woodbine. If she were to come to him now ...

But the lane ahead was empty, though as he stood there dreaming the sound of voices came from beyond the turning to the crossing, and here were the Birleys, come to walk in the woods at the close of the day, Bob Birley's pipe smoke drifting through the air and Alice bowling her hoop before her as if nothing had ever troubled her, and the hoop were her favourite thing in the world.

Now he must break the ice, must he not, and resume all their easy old ways? And he called out good evening from the doorway and they stopped and turned.

'Good evening, Mr Allen.'

Tommy crouched down on the bank of the stream, and at once began to find things to drop into it, little bits of leaf and twig and grass. Alice made to bowl on up the lane in the deepening sunlight, but her mother put out her hand and she stopped, and said good evening as she was bid, and Richard's heart turned over at the sight of her, meeting his smile with her own grave gaze.

He walked down the path to the gate. A dragonfly hung in the lane. He said that in two days his family would be arriving, and he at the crossing gates to meet them.

'You'll be wanting help with the bags, I expect, sir.'

'I will. Thank you.'

He thought of that frosty walk up here as darkness fell, Birley's lantern swinging before them, and everything ahead unknown, unguessed at. Alice had been the very first person he saw, gazing down at him from the rushlit gabled window.

'I expect you're looking forward to this visit, sir,' said Lily Birley, her hand through her husband's arm. 'All this long time on your own.'

He said that he was, that he had missed his family greatly, that his sisters would love to meet the children, and have them up to play. And as they talked on, he felt no hint of reserve or speculation, only the familiar politeness and shyness which perhaps must always mark an exchange between a humble family and a man of the Church, though he had tried to break through this. If Alice had wondered about him, and been hurt by him, she had kept it to herself. And he felt his anxiety disappear like the smoke from Birley's briar, rising and dissolving into the evening air, though guilt still ticked away, that he and a child should share a secret, albeit one she could not understand.

He bade them farewell; he watched them walk on up the lane, their shadows lengthening as the sun sank low, their footsteps quiet on the earth and the hoop rolling steadily on and on, as if all were well with this corner of the world, and always would be.

Mid-morning, the sun climbing, he at his desk. Martha would not be here until afternoon, for everything was made ready, and she had only to set a loaf to rise for the morrow, and bake a pie. As he drafted the last lines of his sermon, and heard the distant whistle of the morning train, someone came walking down the lane. He did not look up, for he had grown used to people coming and going in these long fine days, and he wrote on: of returning to God after no matter how long an absence, how long a journey away from His love, like the bird to the nest, like the bee to the hive. He could hear the bees now, humming amidst the climbing rose at the window, and then he heard the latch of his gate being quietly lifted, and then he did look up.

Susannah was softly closing the gate behind her. She was walking up the path. It seemed to him, as his heart began to hammer and he rose from his chair, that a figure was moving through the trees behind her, but the woods were so dense now, so full of shadows, that he could not be certain, and indeed he could hardly think at all, except that he must let her in now, at once, before someone else came past.

She tapped on the door. He went to open it.

'Mrs Bowen—'

She stepped quickly in to the hall.

'Susannah—' A dozen questions were on his lips. So astonished was he to have her here once more that for a chilling moment she seemed quite out of place, a stranger, and he saw in her anxious glance that she sensed this, as they stood in the little hall, out of sight of the world and so close to one another, but without a single touch. How drawn she looked, how sleepless.

'I had to come – you must not be angry with me—'

'How could I ever be angry with you? I am only surprised – astonished. I was working. Come …'

He drew her into the snug. There was their chair. But he could not close the shutters in broad daylight once again, and she had only just arrived, and looked so fragile. 'Come,' he said again, and opened the door to the kitchen, where no one but the passing sheep could see them. He closed it: now they were safe.

He took her hand; he lifted it to his lips. Some of the strangeness melted.

'How long are you here?'

'Not long. I have lied to poor Millie again.' She shook her head. Then she took off her bonnet, and laid it upon the table. It stood between breadboard and jug, an extraordinary still life. Without it he could see more clearly the hollows in her cheeks, the still deeper circles beneath her eyes.

'You have been ill,' he said slowly. 'I am so sorry. Tell me.'

'Not ill,' said Susannah, but her voice shook. 'Just – so weary – so distressed.'

'How is Oliver?'

'Very weak – very pitiful and weak …' Tears filled her eyes, and his arms went round her. How she had lost weight – he could feel her ribs beneath her summer gown. He was filled with tenderness, stroking her hair.

'Tell me,' he murmured. 'Tell me everything.'

'Oh, Richard, he needs me so much – I cannot help but feel for him.' She began to cry. 'But I thought – I thought …'

'What did you think?'

'Oliver told me – he told me he no longer wished you to come to the house. Until then I thought you no longer wished to see me.'

'Hush, hush.' He drew her down on to his lap, on the hard wooden kitchen chair. 'I am so sorry that I left you as I did. You know I shall always wish to see you. Always.' He kissed her hair, he held her. 'But – I was so – how shall I put it? Filled with remorse, and shame. And then, in the church …' He stopped, for how could he describe to this weeping girl that darkness? 'One day I'll tell you. Go on. I am listening.'

'I thought you were dreadfully angry with me. I thought all was over between us.' She covered her face, weeping, and he held and rocked her, murmuring he knew not what, suffused with sadness. What must become of them? What should he do?

At last she gave a sigh like the passing of a storm, wiped her eyes, slipped off his lap. 'May I have a glass of water?'

'Of course.' He got up, took a glass from the shelf, filled it from the jug. She drank, and he watched her struggle to recompose herself. She gave him a thin little smile, and he gestured to the chair again. 'Come sit on my lap. Come back to me.'

But she shook her head. 'This week,' she said slowly, 'sometimes I have thought I can hardly bear to be a woman.'

'What?' He looked at her. 'How can you say that? You are the loveliest woman I ever saw.'

'But how must I live my life?' asked Susannah, and she moved to stand against the cupboard, and looked out over the field. A pair of pheasants were picking their way across the rough grass, the one so copper-bright and gleaming, the other the colour of milk and earth. She watched them, and Richard watched her. She said, 'All this week I have thought: he has turned from me, and I can do nothing. I am a woman – I must do nothing. Women must suffer, women must wait, women must follow, must be quiet and good, must never say what we feel.'

He listened. He thought all at once of Verity, of the temper she must struggle to control, and the drive he sensed within her – wanting what? Wanting what from her life?

And he said to Susannah, feeling something hugely important shift in what lay between them: 'Look at me. Look at me.'

She turned from the window and their eyes met. So many times had they held one another's gaze, searching and yearning, filled with desire. This was different. This now was steady and true.

'You can say what you feel to me,' he said quietly. 'Indeed, you must say it, or we are lost. How can we love one another if we are not open? I want only openness between us – I want to be able to tell you everything—' He realised he was speaking as if they were married, or about to be married. He realised that this was their first true conversation – not about sin, or passion, or what they must and must not do, but about who they truly were.

Her hands were held before her; a finger pushed her wedding ring this way and that. So loose was it now it seemed it could fall to the floor at any moment.

She said: 'You must understand that I have never been open in my life. I have never dared to be, never been taught or allowed to be. I have been taught to be good. And I have never spoken like this to anyone. Never.'

'And why do you speak like this now?'

'Because I have to. Because I must, or I shall sink beneath the waves. That is why I came.'

He watched her; he said carefully: 'For you – the pale gentle girl I fell in love with – for you to do so – to come here twice, alone – to dare to leave your home and come to another man – in truth, I am astonished.'

'No more than I.' She leaned against the cupboard and closed her eyes, and for a moment it was as if she were alone, and he had come upon her and were privy, now, to her great struggle. 'I have been on the edge of despair,' she said. 'Afraid I had lost you. Ashamed to long for you so, when Oliver is suffering as he is. In the end, I thought I must act or break. Something in me refused to break.' She opened her eyes and looked at him again. 'I am a little stronger than I thought.'

'So it seems.'

'And are you glad of that?'

'Yes,' he said slowly. 'I cannot help but be glad, for it has brought you to me again.'

She was still looking at him, and now it felt as if all their long exploring of one another until now had been between two much younger people – in love, yes; longing for one another, yes; but not with this new strength and knowledge. He felt everything between them growing, and deepening, layer upon layer; as if he had never known the meaning of their passion until this moment, as if they stood naked before one another, about to make love, in the certainty that they would go on doing so all their lives.

He could hardly breathe.

At length he said slowly: 'I love you completely. Utterly.'

'And I you.'

He rose from the wooden chair, and moved towards her. He said: 'Whatever happens, we can never go back from this.'

'I know.'

He kissed her, and he was lost. The room was full of light, and when he closed his eyes he felt filled with it, brimming up in him, dissolving him, body and soul. Somewhere, as he moved his tongue with an exquisite slowness, feeling Susannah answer and answer his every move with hers, he thought: God is with us, God lies within us, in this, in this, in this—

And then he heard running footsteps through the house, and a voice he knew better than any voice in the world calling out: 'Richard! Richard! We're here!'

The door flew open, and he leaped.

Impossible to know who was more horrified: he, at this sudden collision of worlds, Susannah, all colour draining away, or Emily, upon the threshold, her hands now flown up to her darling young face and her gasp the most heartbreaking sound.

'Emily. Emily—' It felt as if the world had ceased to turn. 'You were to come tomorrow.'

'We wanted – we wanted—' She was scarlet and stammering. 'We wanted to surprise you – we thought it would be fun …'

'Oh, darling—' What could he say? Beside him, Susannah was shaking like a reed. 'Where are the others?'

'Coming up the lane with Mr Birley. I ran ahead – I should have knocked, but I so longed to see you.'

He knew just what she had wanted: to run in and see him leap up with joy from his desk, to have him take her in his arms and whirl her round as he did when they were children. And now ...

He drew a deep breath and his arm went round Susannah. 'My sister, Emily Allen,' he said as steadily as he could. 'Emily, this is Susannah Bowen.'

He saw Emily's eyes widen, her sudden shocked flashing glance at Susannah's hand; he saw her light upon the ring, so loose upon the finger, and her scarlet face grow pale. Nothing in her gentle life could ever have prepared her for this.

'How do you do?' said she to Susannah, all the courtesies of her upbringing in her trembling voice. She held out her hand; Susannah took it.

'How do you do, Emily? I know you from your picture – I have longed to meet you.'

'Now you know,' Richard said to his sister, for there was nothing else he could say. He must move, he must act, he must go to the others, quickly. If his family must know, Bob Birley must never know, never.

He said, the words spilling over one another: 'You are very shocked, Emily – I am so sorry. This is how things are. One day I would have told you.' Would he? Or had he hoped – he no longer knew what he had hoped for.

Emily made a helpless little gesture. She said to Richard: 'Mama and Verity will be here any moment.'

'I know. I must go to them. Will you—' He looked at the two of them, standing in the sunlit kitchen as the sheep went slowly past. There was nothing to be done but live through this. 'Will you wait here? Or be comfortable in the snug, or the sitting room? I shall be back directly.' He lifted Susannah's hand to his lips. 'Then I shall take you home.'

And he left them, hurrying out to the open front door, hearing his mother's and Verity's voices, and Birley's slow footsteps, as he brought the bags. He ran to the gate, which Emily in her haste to see him had left standing wide. His bees were humming in the lavender and foxgloves, the dappled lane was all moss and lace and buttercups. He stood there, waiting to greet his family as they arrived in this corner of heaven in a country parish, and his heart was thudding and thudding at what he must do to them now.

'Richard!' They came round the bend and his mother saw him. Her

285

face beneath her hat lit up with happiness; beside her, Verity looked marvellous, no longer in mourning, wearing a gown he did not remember, and her straw bonnet. He held out his arms and she ran into them. Neither could speak.

'Here we are, then, sir.' Bob Birley was making for the open gate. The travelling bags were bursting at their straps. 'Will I take these into the hall?'

'No – no – just set them down.' He disentangled himself from Verity's fierce embrace and kissed her. 'Thank you, Birley, that was very kind.' He felt in his pocket. 'I should have been at the crossing myself – my family have quite surprised me …'

'A nice surprise, I should think, though, sir.'

'Oh, indeed, indeed.' He pressed a coin into his hand. 'Thank you again.' And as Birley tipped his cap to them all, and wished them a pleasant stay, Richard turned to his mother and was folded into the loving embrace of his childhood.

'Mama.' For a long sweet moment it felt that he had never left it, or her, or any of them, that his life in the past ran on and on, unbroken by his father's death or by anything that had happened since. 'Dear Mama.'

'Richard.' His mother drew away; she looked at him, long and full. 'My own dear boy. What a beautiful place you have brought us to at last.' She gestured at lane and field and garden, at the house, with its front door open. 'We have not disturbed you by coming early? It was Emily's plan – she was so excited—'

'Where is she?' asked Verity, making for the path. 'Emily! Come and help us!'

'Wait—' He put a hand on her arm. He said: 'I have something to tell you.' And he led them to the garden seat, and brushed away dust and leaves. 'Will you sit down?' They sat, looking at him enquiringly.

He said again, his heart like a mad thing leaping against his ribs: 'I have something to tell you – something important – kept hidden from you – from everyone.'

He took the greatest breath of his life, and began.

It was noon, the sun high and the woods gone quiet and still in the heat. Too hot for walking, but he must take her home. They had met, she and his family, all gathered together in the big cool sitting room, which until now he had hardly used, or needed to use, in his solitude.

'Susannah Bowen – my mother – my sister Verity …'

Everyone muted; everyone doing their best. No one quite meeting anyone's eye. Spots of colour flared on Verity's cheekbones as she took Susannah's hand, so briefly. Perhaps one day, far into the future, they might all be able to recall this day together, as friends and sisters, with, 'Do you remember …?' and, 'Oh, if you knew how we felt …' For a moment he dared to hope for this, then returned himself to the present, where no one knew what to say next. His mother was doing as well as she could, though he had not seen her so strained and white since the day of his father's funeral.

'I shall do my very best to understand—'

The buzzard was mewing over the hills: there was his mate. They all went to look from the window, and his mother began to talk of birds, and how Richard's father had known every call and song, how Richard had inherited his passion.

'My husband too,' said Susannah, as if she were at any tea party, making conversation, and stopped herself abruptly. 'I am almost too tired to think – please excuse me.'

Richard went to her side. 'Let us go.' He looked at his family, filling the room, all their joy and excitement quite drained away.

'Let me show you your rooms,' he said gently. 'I shall take Susannah home while you rest. Then we can have lunch. Martha is coming this afternoon to finish her baking. She wanted to have everything fresh to greet you, I know.'

'It's all my fault,' said Emily suddenly. 'All my foolish ideas.' And she burst into tears, ran from the room and went racing up the stairs. He made to follow her, but his mother put her hand on his arm.

'Leave her, Richard. Let me talk to her. Don't worry about our rooms.' She went to Susannah, and took her hand once more. 'I shall pray for you, my dear. We all must pray for guidance.'

All the brave reaching out for God's guidance, all through his life. He listened, he watched them, he went down the path to the gate. Swallows were skimming the lane, and the buzzard circled, but he could see no one about. The workers at the mill would be eating their bread and cheese at the back, looking over the river. Birley would not be out at the crossing until the afternoon train; Martha would not be here until two.

Inside the house, Susannah was waiting in the hall. He went to say goodbye to the others. Verity would not look at him.

At the gate, he said to Susannah: 'If we meet anyone, you have come to meet my family.' He glanced at her, gave her a wry little smile. 'As indeed you have done.'

She said sadly: 'If I had not come here you would have been spared – your mother and sisters would have been spared.'

'I shall make it right with them,' he said, as they began to walk. 'I shall try to. Of course they are shocked, but we can be honest now. Had you not come I should have been living a lie throughout their visit.' The lane was growing steeper. Swallows darted before them. They slowed down, walking very close. 'And had you not come,' he told her, longing to take her hand, 'you would not have spoken as you did. We know one another better, do we not? We are closer now, are we not?'

'I have never felt as close to anyone.'

They spoke to the lane ahead, not looking at one another, but as they walked he could feel her narrow hip beneath her gown, brushing against his own with every footstep. He wanted to take her hand and draw her into the woods, deep within their soaring shade, and find a mossy place above the river, and lie her down upon it, and himself upon her.

'What will you do when you reach home?'

'Tell Millie I needed fresh air. Go to Oliver.'

He said: 'Remember this. No matter that we do not see one another, no matter that we cannot be together, remember I am thinking of you at every moment, loving you at every moment.'

He looked round. Everything was hushed in the heat. He dared to put his arm around her.

'I want to kiss you. I want to kiss you—'

She turned to him, whispering something he could not hear.

But a little sound came from the trees – just a bird amongst the branches, but enough to make them start. And he dropped his arm at once and they walked on, leaving the sheep and the fields behind, climbing and climbing in lovers' silence.

23

So accustomed had he grown to coming home alone, so accustomed to his solitude within the house, that it felt quite extraordinary to return to it knowing that his family was waiting for him there, and that for the days of their visit he would have not one moment to himself. He had imagined conducting them round it, planning their activities, talking late into the night about everything, except that which was most important, and which he kept concealed. Now they knew it all, and were struggling to absorb it, and as he came down the lane after bidding Susannah farewell, he could not tell if in truth he were glad they could be honest, as he had told her, or if he would not much rather have kept his secret, and thus his privacy.

Every window stood open. As he drew near, he knew that if the morning's discovery had not taken place the girls would be waiting for him at one of them, as he returned from some meeting in the parish: would be waving and calling and running out to greet him. As it was, he could not make out either, and pictured Emily weeping into her pillow beneath the slanting ceiling of her little bedroom, Verity pacing and furious, his mother trying to comfort both of them, longing for his father. Somehow he must cheer and lighten their hearts, though his own was so full of Susannah he did not know he had room for even the smallest creature.

This feeling changed as soon as he opened the front door. Emily was sitting on the stairs like a child, her hair let down and her eyes red.

'What are you doing there, you goose?'

'Oh, Richard—' She got up and ran down to him, and he hugged her.

'Poor Emily. I am so sorry.' He led her into the sitting room, with its window open to the mountain ash, where the first berries were forming. Bluetits and chaffinches hopped about amongst them. 'Here,' he said, seating her upon the mildewed ottoman. 'Now you can tell me what you think of me.' And trying to lighten it all, and make her smile, he said, 'It seems I must spend the whole day soothing weeping girls.'

'Don't mock,' said Verity from the doorway, and her voice was cutting. She came in, and he saw her tremble with anger. 'Please do not mock us, Richard.'

'Verity—' He held out his hand but she did not take it, and he saw beneath her anger how hurt she was, and thought of Susannah's struggle to find the courage to speak as she had done.

'*Sometimes I have thought I can hardly bear to be a woman.*' Listening to her, it had been Verity he thought of, and as he looked at her now, her colour so high and her eyes bright with unshed tears, he thought: she wants much more than ordinary things. She always has done. She's burning with it.

He rose from the ottoman, squeezing Emily's hand. 'Where is Mama?'

'Resting,' said Verity coldly. 'With a headache.'

'Do you think she would like to see me?'

'No.'

'Verity,' protested Emily, getting up. 'You know that isn't true.'

'Come now,' said Richard. 'Let us not quarrel, please let us not quarrel. Let us have luncheon. I have a little table in the orchard, I can show you my bees.' He kissed them both.

'You are like Father,' said Emily. 'You are a peacemaker.'

'He is a fool,' said Verity. 'More than that.' She looked at him steadily. 'How do you imagine you can possibly proceed?'

'Let us have luncheon,' said Richard again. 'Then let us talk.'

They carried out trays and a cloth, and three kitchen chairs, and Martha's fresh loaf and the ham he had bought, and the cheese and the jug and a dish of plums. Plates. Knives and forks. Everything.

Then, beneath the apple trees, the visit began.

A letter came from Burgage Manor, inviting them to croquet. It came by a pony and trap, and to Richard's astonishment the driver announced that these were to stay with him for the duration of his family's visit.

'Good gracious. Are you sure?'

'I believe Mrs Southwood says something in this letter, sir,' said the driver, climbing down. 'They cannot spare me, but he's good and quiet.'

'Well, well. Please tell them I am delighted. I'll write, of course.'

Richard tipped him and, as the driver set off up the lane, stood reading the letter in the morning sun.

'I am sure your dear family will be glad of the trap,' wrote Elizabeth Southwood. 'Will it not make everything much easier? We shall be quite a little party when you drive over for the croquet: Will is here, with one or two Oxford friends, and Miss Debenham, of course, and James has invited John Maddock, the curate of Presteigne, whom I believe you know. We are so looking forward to seeing you all.'

The pony was flicking at flies. He was chestnut, with a blaze.

'Emily!' called Richard. 'Verity, Mama – come and see!'

The pony looked towards the house as they all came down the path. Cabbage white butterflies were dancing over the lilac.

'Oh, he's sweet!' said Emily, patting his head. The trap had been polished, and furnished with rugs.

'Well,' said Richard. 'Now we may go anywhere we please.'

He took them into Kington, and into all the shops. They tethered the trap at the end of the town, crowded with visitors to the fair.

'Would you like to visit it?' he asked them, but his mother shook her head.

'I think I am too old for fairgrounds, Richard. They weary me. I shall love to see the town.' And he waited in Webbs while she chose a length of lawn and cambric, and in Stanway's the druggist, while Verity chose lavender water for their mother and eau-de-Cologne for Emily. Everywhere, as they walked along the street, were members of his congregation: the Skarratts, the Bodenhams, who invited them to tea; Jeremiah Morgan, the Neves, the Middleships. And with every encounter came the delight at meeting Mr Allen's family at last, and appreciation of all he had been doing in the parish: the visits, the meetings, his inspiring sermons, the lovely way he had conducted the Turner wedding, and kept his composure when Dick Bampfield dropped the ring. Edward and Effie Turner would be in church tomorrow, of course; the Allens would meet them then. They would meet everyone.

And with every introduction on the crowded pavement, the smell of the cattle still in the air from market day, came the same observation: how good it was that Mr Allen had been able to assume so many duties with poor Mr Bowen so ill – desperately ill, it seemed – and his poor young wife so anxious.

And Richard, each time this remark was made, watched his mother and sisters grow tense and uneasy, and look to him to smooth the moment over, and listen as he dissembled. So that what for them should have been unclouded pleasure – pride in him, interest in all these welcoming new people, and this pretty market town – was shot through and tainted, he knew, with anxiety and shame.

How much more of this lay ahead, he wondered, as he drove them home. The verges of the lanes were thick with cow parsley and buttercups, the hedges pink and white and yellow with dog rose and woodbine and star of Bethlehem. Deep in the woods the cuckoo called, and swallows skimmed over the weir. As the trap springs creaked, and the pony clopped steadily on, everything should have felt innocent and contented. But his family were silent in the seats behind him, and though he tried to hide it when they reached the cottage, he was filled with sadness for them.

While Verity and their mother took their purchases inside, he and Emily unbridled the pony, and led him up past the barn and through the little back gate to the field. They watched him toss his head and bend to the grass starred with thistles and daisies. A few sheep had come through the gap in the hedge from the adjoining field, and were sleeping beneath the trees. Beyond, in the valley, cornfields went on for ever, beneath the Radnor hills.

'It's all so beautiful,' said Emily. 'I just wish—'

'I know.' His arm went round her.

'Mama is so upset, and Verity so angry with you.'

'I know. And you?' he asked her, watching the pony graze.

'I just wish,' she said again.

☆

That evening he tried to talk to Verity. They were all in the sitting room after supper, she and Emily with their embroidery frames, his mother with a book she was not reading.

'What is it?' he asked her, seeing it lie unopened.

'*Cranford*,' she said, with a little sigh. 'Dear Mrs Gaskell's *Cranford*.'

'Have you not read that before?' Surely he remembered it from boyhood, the way she had quite lost herself in each episode in *Household Words*. Then it was bound; now it lay in her lap.

'It's Mama's favourite,' said Emily, snipping a thread of new silk.

'Such a comforting book.' Their mother gave another little sigh, quickly suppressed, and looked out over the garden, where the light was deepening once more.

'Dear Mama.' He rose and kissed her. And another conversation about books came back to him all at once, from a Sunday in the vicarage. He could hear the voice of Oliver Bowen, stern and unyielding.

'*The novelist seeks to know the human heart. The novelist thinks he has access to the human mind. No one but God has that, Mr Allen.*'

Who could have imagined that so strong a voice should so soon become a whisper? How was Oliver now? How was Susannah? Though her presence was everywhere amongst them, no one was speaking her name, and he was beginning to bury it again, to cherish and keep it deep within him, away from everyone.

'A novel about everyday life,' Verity was saying of *Cranford*, with a little edge to her voice. She bent over her embroidery frame. 'Set in a village. Set in the past. Nothing dreadful ever happens in the past.'

'Verity—' Richard turned to her, but she did not look up. 'Come,' he said, and went to her, and put his hand on her shoulder. 'Will you come and walk with me?'

'Walk where?'

'Down to the river? It's so pleasant there in the evenings.'

'May I come?' asked Emily quickly, then bit her lip. 'No – I'll stay with Mama.'

'Why don't we all go?' asked Verity, tugging at a thread. 'If it's so pleasant.'

So they all went, for, after all, as their mother said, sending Emily up for her shawl, they could read and sew at any time, while here, in this lovely place, with Richard to conduct them—

And they set off down the lane towards the crossing. Richard and Verity walked ahead. The light was rich and full. A dragonfly hung before them; the birds were a symphony. They could hear the children's voices.

'Will you speak to me?' he asked Verity, as the gates came into view.

'I do speak to you.'

'You know what I mean. Talk to me. As we used to do.'

'Everything has changed. You have changed.'

'Not really. At least—'

'Don't be absurd.'

They rounded the bend. There was Alice, bowling her hoop up and down. There were her parents and Tommy in the garden, watching the river run by. Everyone stopped, everyone was introduced, and made remarks about the beauty of the evening, how they were finding it here, how the pony was settling down in his new surroundings.

'Perhaps the children would like to come for a ride,' said Richard. 'Would you like that, Alice?'

'Yes, sir.'

Did he imagine it, or was it only her shyness which made him feel that she did not want to come? It was her shyness, he decided, as they said good evening, and walked on towards the bridge. So many new people – not even Emily could make Alice talk in a group of strangers.

He drew Verity to him, as they walked on past the mill. From far across the fields a corncrake called, and as he bade Verity notice this he thought of John Maddock, and how he had stopped in mid-sentence to listen to the lark. Maddock would be at the Burgage Manor party. Perhaps he and Verity might take to one another ...

Her hand was through his arm now; she did not feel quite so fierce.

'Verity?' he asked her carefully. 'Mama wrote that you had a tutor now. Is he someone you like?'

'I like his subject, certainly.'

'And what is that?' he asked, and gazed at her when she told him. 'Greek? You are learning Greek?'

'And why should I not?'

'No reason at all, of course. Only ...' He floundered. Behind them he could hear his mother and Emily talking of the scenery, of the ways in which it was, and was not, like the scenery at home; of the cattle walking down to the river to drink; how darling were the little calves, and how loud the corncrake sounded in the evening quiet. He thought that this conversation was a refuge for them from the shock of Emily's discovery, and his revelation. But he also thought that this was the kind of talk which must make up so much of their lives, and that where Emily was sweet enough, and generous enough, to take part in it, and indeed enjoy it, it was not enough for Verity. And where he had thought to talk to her of himself, and his feelings for Susannah, trying to make her understand him, he saw that if he were to grow close to her again then in truth he must try to understand her.

They had come to the bridge. They stood looking out on the rushing weir, the swift flow of the river over the stones. Wagtails walked up and down by the shallows, where the cattle were drinking. Here, on countless occasions, he had stood and dreamed of Susannah. Even now, his gown brushed the fading clump of prayermint, and its last faint scent came up. But now, though Susannah never left him, he thought of his elder sister: bent over her books in the schoolroom, always ahead of them, always quick to answer, working things out, remembering everything. Greek and Latin ran in his blood: he could scarcely remember a time when they had not done so. But for the girls – studying was over almost as soon as they put their hair up. They had enough to equip them to teach little children, like Miss Hatfield, to be governesses, if by some chance they did not marry – but surely they would marry. Did Verity really want to—

'Should you like to teach?' he asked her, leaning beside her on the lichened stone.

'I should like to learn,' she said, and again there sounded that sharp little edge to her voice.

'You mean – you should like to be a scholar?'

'I should like to do all sorts of things, but none is possible.'

'Tell me.'

'Oh, Richard—' and now she was full of impatience – 'please don't trouble yourself. You are in the midst of something so appalling – so scandalous and disgraceful—' Her voice was shaking as she tried to keep it low. 'Please do not think you can distract me with talk of my own pitiful ambitions. None of them will come to pass. I shall not go to Oxford, or London, or study, or become anything at all—'

She was on the brink of scalding tears, and his arm went round her, as the others came up.

'Verity – darling—'

But she shook him off, and stood up from the bridge, and in a moment was stalking away up the lane, waving furiously at midges, her shoulders shaking.

'Oh dear,' said their mother, as she had said so many times in the past, when Verity flared up. 'What has brought this about? You have been discussing ...' She faltered.

'She is very upset,' said Richard, and so was he.

'I'll go to her,' said Emily, as she always did, and she ran up the slope, panting as Verity turned the steep corner by Downfield Farm, calling out 'Verity! Verity!' into the quiet.

'Lord, Lord—' Richard put his hands to his face. Was he really to lose the people who until he came here had been the dearest to him in the world? Could Verity, in her bitterness and disappointment, truly turn from him? Was this the beginning of his punishment?

'Dearest boy.' His mother's hand was on his arm, her voice as soothing as it had been when he was little.

'I have let you all down,' he said bleakly, and for once she did not answer straight away.

He thought, pacing over the bridge, looking up the lane towards the turning: if my father could see us – could see me – would he – might he – could he possibly understand? What would he think I should do?

His mother was talking quietly now, about forgiveness, and God's will, God's guidance. He tried to listen.

At last she said: 'I know you would not have let this happen if it had not been something momentous. Beyond that – in truth, I do not know how to help you. But I shall always love you, Richard. Always.'

The lump in his throat was so great he could not speak.

Then the girls were coming down the lane once more, and though Verity would not look at him she was no longer weeping. He did not know by what effort of will this was so – had perhaps always been so, all her life.

'*Sometimes I have thought I can hardly bear to be a woman.*'

What lay ahead, for Verity? Was she destined, like Miss Nightingale, for some great work? Without it, what could she do?

He brushed her tear-stained face with his lips, and she let him. They all stood for a little while, letting the sinking sun and swift-flowing river calm them, talking of innocent things – how long the swallows stayed, how far they flew to Africa. Then they walked slowly back down the lane, hearing, as they came to the mill, two quiet voices, a man and a child's.

Richard frowned. That was Alice's voice, but that was not her father's. 'Excuse me one moment, Mama.' He quickened his pace, and turned the corner.

Alice, in the evening sun, had rolled her hoop quite a long way down from the crossing. Now she stood with her hand upon it, holding the stick, and a mean-looking youth with slicked-back hair stood talking to her. What about? Who was he?

'Alice?' called Richard, and they both looked up.

'Lovely evening,' said the youth, and something about him put Richard in mind of someone he knew, though he could not think who it was, only that it was someone he did not care for. 'Just out for a walk,' the young man said lightly. 'Passing the time of day.' And in a moment he had smiled at Alice and turned aside, taking the path by the mill which led to the river bank, soon disappearing amongst the trees.

Richard stood watching him, and knew for the first time in his life what it was to feel the hairs on the back of your neck begin to rise.

'Alice, who was that?'

But she shook her head, and took up her hoop and ran with it, bumping against her side, back to the crossing cottage. And here was Bob Birley, come out to close the gates, for the whistle of the evening train was sounding in the distance.

Alice ran into the cottage. Richard walked quickly up.

'Mr Birley? Did you see the young man who was talking to Alice? I've never seen him before.'

'No, sir. I've been in the garden.' He shook his head as he drew the first gate across. 'I don't like her talking to strangers, I've told her, but we do know most people round here. What did he look like?'

Richard described him, his height, his lean sallow face and dark eyes, his oily hair. The family were approaching the gates and he waved to them to wait until they closed. Bob Birley listened, dropping down the catches.

Again he shook his head, and then, as the train came into view far along the track, he said: 'Unless that was young Mr Prosser. He does come back now and then, from Hereford. What would Wilf Prosser be wanting with Alice?' He turned to the porch. 'I'll call her—'

But Richard put out his hand, saying quickly, 'No, leave her, no matter at all. I was only curious.'

And then the train was upon them, the whistle shrieking, and the swirling clouds of steam hid everything.

Sunday, and he was to preach upon journeys, and coming home. Sunday, and he was to stand before his congregation, and Susannah. He had thought before his family arrived that his mother would surely guess what lay between them. Now she and his sisters knew it all, and must, like him, dissemble before everyone, be drawn into deception.

He and Emily pulled the trap from the barn after breakfast, and backed the pony in. Martha came down from Rushock again, to do the roast. The morning was cloudy, threatening rain after all this fine weather, and a few spots fell as they all set off.

'Whom will we meet?' asked Emily lightly.

'Everyone. Everyone wants to meet you. The Southwoods, of course – we can thank them for their kindness.'

The pony was snorting a little as the lane grew steeper. The rain began to patter through the trees.

'And, Mama,' Richard added, keeping his voice light, 'Mr and Mrs Prosser will be there. You remember that I wrote to you—'

'Ah.' His mother nodded, quickly understanding. 'Indeed I do.'

'Remember what?' asked Emily, and Richard floundered. No more lies, no more concealment – he could not endure it. Yet he could not bring himself to discuss his suspicions with the girls. What could they know of such things? And why, when they were already so disturbed by him, should they have to be troubled still further?

His mother was patting Emily's hand. 'I shall tell you another time.' And Emily, dear sensitive girl that she was, accepted this, while Verity looked on, and thought her own thoughts.

And Wilfred Prosser? Richard asked himself, as he lifted the reins and urged the pony on. Would he be there, watching and noticing, reporting back?

All night he had dreamed, and woken, and dreamed restlessly again, of that sallow, secretive face, the ingratiating smile. 'Lovely evening.' How swiftly he had vanished amongst the trees.

'Susannah will be there, will she not?'

'Yes. Yes, I am sure she will be.'

And they fell silent as the pony strained up the hill.

Outside the churchyard, they left pony and trap beneath a yew. None of the carriages was yet arrived. They put up their umbrellas and made their way along the path as the bells rang out.

'That must be the vicarage,' said Richard's mother quietly, as the house came into view.

'Yes. Yes, it is.' He glanced quickly across. Ivy and lilac were dark with the rain, everything closed against it. He looked up at the bedroom window, saw no invalid face looking out from the chair, no Millie or Susannah. Would he ever pass through that door again? The rain fell faster. 'Come.' He hurried them into the church.

All its patches of damp and crumbling plaster, its wormy rafters and chinks in the roof he saw now with their new eyes, as he had seen them on the winter day of his arrival, when Oliver Bowen had prayed he would serve it well. Rain was slanting against the glass, darkening everything. Someone had set a bucket to catch drips from the leak in the corner. There was Prosser, setting out the hymnals. Richard glanced quickly down the aisle. There was Tilda Prosser, sitting in their pew, and beside her – yes, a thin young man with slick dark hair was bending over his prayerbook. Across the aisle, Alfred Arndell, always early, was upon his knees.

From their place by the west door, beneath the tower, the ringers were tugging on the ropes. They nodded towards Richard as he showed his family round, and he murmured their names to his mother. 'You remember Jeremiah – we met him yesterday, in town.'

'Indeed, of course.' She smiled towards him. And then Prosser was beside them, hymnals in hand.

'Good morning, Mr Allen.'

'Good morning.' Richard could hardly look him in the face, but he must. 'May I present my family?'

'Indeed. Delighted.' Prosser set down the books, put out his hand, as Richard made his introductions. 'A pleasure to make your acquaintance, Mrs Allen. Miss Allen. Miss Emily. Welcome to St Michael's. No doubt Mrs Bowen will soon be here to welcome you herself, if her husband's health permits. Or perhaps—' he paused – 'perhaps you have met her already?'

Richard flushed. He saw his mother hesitate, saw his sisters turn to examine in great detail the plaque to the Hooper family.

Then his mother said carefully, 'Someone I am so looking forward to meeting is your own good wife, Mr Prosser. Will you not introduce us?'

'Of course. Of course. My son is here too, on a visit.' He led them all down the aisle, as Alfred Arndell rose stiffly to his feet, from prayer. And watching the exchanges between them all, the nods and bows, Richard saw that Tilda Prosser's usually pinched little face and anxious air were quite transformed today. 'My son, Wilfred,' she was saying with a happy smile. 'My son – he is home to see us.'

'I believe we met yesterday, did we not, Mr Allen?' Wilfred Prosser's voice was smooth and unctuous as the oil on his flattened dark hair, and he met Richard's eyes without a flicker.

'We did,' said Richard briefly, and then, as others began to enter the church, he showed his family into a pew, and made his excuses: he must greet the congregation as they arrived.

Thomas Hatton came into the porch soaking wet, shook out his hat and made his way to the organ. The Bampfields arrived, and Miss Hatfield, then the Bodenhams, Miss Bodenham's eyes very bright as Richard greeted her. Here were the Southwoods.

'The pony and trap are a blessing,' said Richard, conducting them down the aisle to meet his family. 'We cannot thank you enough.'

'Only pray for fine weather for our little gathering,' said Elizabeth, taking his mother's hand. She turned to Richard. 'And how is Mr Bowen today? I have invited Susannah to join us for the croquet, if he is well enough for her to leave him. How she must be in need of some diversion.'

'Indeed,' murmured Richard. 'How very kind of you.'

'You could bring her in the trap, could you not?'

'Indeed,' he said again, and then, as James Southwood demanded to know which of these two lovely girls was Verity, which Emily, that he might present them to his own dear Will and Charlotte, Richard completed the introductions and left them all to settle into their pews, and bow their heads.

As he returned to the porch, he felt as if he were treading on glass. That he must rely again upon his mother and sisters to behave as if they knew nothing, when at every turn and remark they must be filled with confusion and anxiety – it filled him once more with shame and sadness. As for the Prossers – what did they know, or suspect? That Prosser should send out his slimy-looking son to question Alice, to keep watch, perhaps, on his movements, his visitors—

Richard greeted Edward and Effie Turner. He greeted Miss Wilkinson, and enquired about her aunt. He shook a dozen hands, greeted the choir members, hurrying to change from wet clothes in the vestry, told a dozen people that yes, his family were here, and would so like to meet them after the service, and through it all he burned. The Birleys were not here. Perhaps it was the rain which kept them away, or perhaps they had listened to Alice's account of her meeting with a strange young man, and what he had asked her. What she had told him.

The choir was assembled, the churchyard empty, but for the sweeping rain.

And Susannah? Where was she?

He stepped to the entrance to the porch and turned to look out towards the vicarage. Its door was still shut, and the ivy dripped over the windows. Was Oliver so ill she could not leave him? Or perhaps it was too much for her to do: to dissemble and pretend, with each member of the congregation, while his family looked on.

Behind him the bells were finishing their peal. In a moment the single call to church would come. He must go in, he must go to the vestry, lead the choir and let his family, at last, see, at least upon the surface, everything he had been brought up to, everything he had been trained for, play out at last: taking his father's mantle, a true man of the Church. Somehow he must do this.

The single bell began to ring. The door of the vicarage opened. She was there, putting up her umbrella, she was hurrying through the rain towards him.

And at the sight of her pale face his heart contracted: they stood on the brink of he knew not what, but as she reached him, and put her hand in his, the recognition of love flooded through him again.

'Mrs Bowen.'

'Mr Allen.'

He drew her into the porch. She shook out and furled her umbrella; she left it standing against the stone seat with three dozen more. For an instant, to his eye, they looked like dark rooks, or an assembly – a funeral, a courtroom, a congregation – with everyone in black. Then he pressed her hand again, for no one now was coming across the churchyard, and the single note of the bell was ringing into silence.

'All is well?' he asked softly.

She nodded. 'How glad I am to see you.'

'And I you. Come.'

He turned, as the last notes of the bell died away, and conducted her towards the open door to the church, where all had fallen quiet, and where Philip Prosser was standing, just inside, by the shelves of psalters, ready to hand one to a latecomer with a smile, his sharp dark eyes observing everything.

Richard led the prayers, he led the hymns, he preached on coming home. He managed to do it all, announcing how glad he was to have his family here at last, praying for them, in a list of prayers which, every week, included those for the sick, and especially Oliver Bowen, their priest, in his long illness. Each week as he uttered his name he had felt ashamed, and full of pity. Now, though these feelings still possessed him, he heard it as his mother and sisters must surely hear it – words on the lips of a hypocrite and sinner.

'*You are in the midst of something so appalling – so scandalous and disgraceful—*'

He saw Verity's burning face, Emily's hands flying up to her mouth, his mother wrestling between love and shock. And as he murmured Amen, and the congregation murmured in response, he knew that no matter who else was watching him, though these feelings still possessed him, something of his punishment had begun.

302

☆

Croquet on the lawn at Burgage Manor. Sunday's rain had blown away, the sun was out once more, and as he drove the pony clip-clopping up the manor drive, with Emily beside him on the seat, some of his deep disquiet began to leave him. Cream and red cattle were grazing in the park, beneath the chestnut trees, roses rambled over the stone façade, doves walked up and down on the tiles.

'Oh, it's lovely!' said Emily, squeezing his arm.

Behind her, Verity and his mother sat with Susannah, whom they had collected from the vicarage, as Elizabeth Southwood requested. Verity had not spoken to her once, beyond a swift greeting. Verity was hardly speaking at all. Each time Richard tried to engage her she found some excuse – her book was upstairs, her sewing was in the other room, she was tired after walking, and must lie down. Verity never lay down. He gave up, but how grateful he was on this short journey to hear his mother making conversation with Susannah – about the weather, about her pretty gown, about the village, through which they made a little detour on the way, greeting Effie Turner in her garden, and Miss Wilkinson, coming out of the shop. Outside the George, two of the ringers sat smoking on the bench; they lifted their felted old hats as the trap went past, and wished them a pleasant afternoon. There was no one who might think it strange that Susannah was with the curate and his family, and though Richard glanced towards the laurels shrouding the Prosser villa as she came down the churchyard path, they were now so thick with summer growth that surely no one would see through them on to the church. And in any case, this was Elizabeth Southwood's request, that Susannah should have a few hours' diversion from the sickroom, and who might argue with that? As he drew up the pony before the house, and watched him look about him at his old home, and blow through his nostrils in the heat, he thought: Let us all have one happy summer afternoon. Let my sisters enjoy meeting new people, let my mother be looked after by the Southwoods, as she deserves, and let Susannah and I be with one another, play a little, laugh a little, try to lighten our hearts.

He helped them all down from the trap, one by one, and as his hand held hers, and their eyes met, he thought of the first time he had come here, to a New Year skating party. The snow had glittered beneath the winter sun, the skaters sped over the ice, and as she came flying towards him, her pale hair almost silver in the sun, he had known what for weeks he had been trying not to know: that he was in love.

And then came Effie Bounds' terrible scream, and the party had come to a standstill. Then, as he followed James Southwood out across the ice, came the old dog's dreadful howl.

But today ...

Today, even though he himself had not long reminded his congregation of that pitiful dead girl beneath the ice, Richard would not think of horror, or of fear. He would not. Here was old Gauntlet, walking slowly round from the stable block to see them, and here was James Southwood raising his hand, greeting everyone, summoning them to the lawn, to tea in the shade, to croquet. Come! Everyone was here!

And there, on the lawn behind the house, were tables and chairs and a snowy cloth beneath the juniper tree. There was the croquet all set up, and Will and Charlotte already at play, with three or four others, amongst whom even Verity must find someone to please her. Far in the distance, the sun glinted on the reed-fringed lake, where swans were sailing. A summerhouse stood open. And here was John Maddock, laughing, striding across the grass, his hand outstretched.

'Allen! How good to see you again!'

He bowed to Richard's mother, and to Susannah; he turned to the sister nearest to him, and took her hand.

'I believe you must be Emily.'

And she smiled up at him, as only Emily could smile.

All his life, Richard was to look back on that afternoon as fulfilling, almost entirely, its every promise. Every summer sound was there: the click of mallet and ball, and laughter and clapping from beneath the trees, the tinkle of porcelain cups and silver spoons, an old dog yawning in the sun. Doves fluttered between tiled roof and dovecote, somewhere the cuckoo called. There was his mother in a thickly cushioned seat, deep in conversation with Elizabeth; there was Verity, striking ball after ball through the hoops with deadly accuracy, applauded by her team, accepting tea from tall Leonard Barnard with a smile. Barnard was up at Oxford with Will, but he came from London. Richard heard him talking to her of John Stuart Mill, and his essays in the *Westminster Review* – had she by any chance come across them? Her father used to read the *Review*, she told him, as they walked across the grass.

There was Emily, laughing as he had not seen her laugh for a year, her hair ribbons half undone and her cheeks flushed as her ball bounced off a hoop and went rolling into the rough.

'You should be a cricketer,' said Maddock, striding over towards it, striking it on.

'Do you play a great deal?'

'I do,' he said, returning to her side. 'I captain the team at Presteigne – perhaps you would like to come and watch us there one day. You must arrange it, Allen, next time your family come.'

'I will.' Then Richard had a thought. 'Why don't you join us on a drive out to Hergest? On Thursday – our last afternoon?'

'That would be marvellous.' Maddock wiped his brow and smiled down at Emily once more. 'That is – if you would like that.'

Her eyes were sparkling. 'Oh, I should love it. We all should love it if you came.'

The distant hills were hazy in the heat. Looking across to them, Susannah at his side, and happiness all around them, Richard thought: perhaps I am mistaken in all my anxieties. Perhaps we are safe, and God has forgiven me. Perhaps – somehow – all will be well.

The game was concluded; everyone was taking tea, or strolling across the grass in conversation.

He turned to Susannah. 'Will you walk with me a little?'

She hesitated. 'We must be discreet.'

'But of course. We need not go far.'

And they did not go far, only a little way towards the summerhouse, where the grass was thick with buttercups.

'How is your husband?' he asked her gently.

'Dr Probyn feels he is more comfortable.'

'Does he say so himself?'

'He says very little.'

'And he spends his days …?'

'He rests, and when he is well enough sits in his chair. When he is well enough I read to him. He asks me to read from *The Pilgrim's Progress*; he says it makes his boyhood live again.' She was speaking to the grass. 'He wants only to have me with him, to have me hold his hand.'

'And does that—' he spoke carefully, imagining it all: her hand in Oliver's, the sickroom, the high iron bed, and she still – still? – sleeping within it, beside him – 'does that trouble you?'

She said, looking down at the long lush grass: 'I think of you at every moment. But he is still my husband, Richard. Ill as he is, how can my heart not go out to him?'

She turned, and began to walk back towards the house, where his mother and the Southwoods sat talking in the shade. Filled with emotion, Richard looked towards them all, and James Southwood looked steadily back at him, as if for some time his gaze had been resting upon them.

On their last afternoon, he drove everyone out to Hergest. The sun was high, the trap piled up with rugs and a picnic basket – lent by Elizabeth, and filled by Martha Price, who saw them off at the gate. This was the last time she would see them all, for tomorrow they would catch the morning train to Leominster, though she would be down at midday to clean and do the washing, after they had gone.

'Poor Mr Allen, he won't know what to do with himself without you.'

'It's true,' said Richard, climbing up to the seat.

'I hope you'll have me to talk to,' said John Maddock, who had come on the coach from Presteigne, and walked down the lane from the highway. The trap was almost groaning with the weight of them all. His hand touched Emily's, just for a moment. 'I shall miss having you to talk to,' he said lightly. 'I shall miss you all.'

Then Richard lifted the reins and they set off, down towards the crossing. His heart was in his mouth as they approached it. Alice would be in school, but would Birley, scything the grass again, turn his back on him?

He did not: he touched his cap and bid them all good day. Lily Birley was out in the garden with Tommy, pegging clothes upon the

306

line. She did not turn as the trap approached, but her work was half with the washing and half watching her little boy as he played close to the river. 'Good afternoon, Mrs Birley,' Richard called, and she gave him a little nod, still turned away.

The trees were thick and full above them as they drove on. They passed the mill, greeting one of the workers as he fastened back a door. Then they were over the bridge, and began the long slow climb.

'Too much weight, Maddock,' said Richard, as the pony strained. 'We should have met you at the top.' But in truth how glad he was to have him here, talking easily to everyone, making them laugh, doing everything for his family he should like to do himself: making them happy, in short. Even Verity could not maintain her silence.

'Shall you see Mr Barnard again?' he had dared to ask her after the croquet party, when they were all come home. She said that she thought he might write.

'So perhaps—' he was cautious – 'perhaps this visit has given you something, even though I have distressed you?'

'Nothing can make up for that,' she said, and bent to her sewing once more.

'I'll get down,' Maddock was saying now.

And Emily said: 'So will I.'

'We shall end up like Aesop's fable,' said her mother, laughing, as Richard pulled up and they both climbed out. 'Must we carry the pony now?'

But he did go much faster without them, and soon the trap was rolling ahead, and had reached the crossroads. Waiting for them there, Richard looked out towards the Rushock hills. For the first time since he saw the gypsies on the Ridge, his mind turned to Edith Clare. He thought: When this visit is over, I shall go to see her. Perhaps she knows things I do not.

The pony was bending to crop the long grass on the verge. The Kington coach rolled by.

'Here they are,' said his mother at last, and he turned to see John Maddock and Emily walking up the lane behind them, hand in hand between the towering hedgerows.

Up on the Ridge they spread out their rugs, while the pony stood waiting beneath the trees below. They unpacked the hamper, ate their picnic to the sound of skylarks, talking contentedly of nothing very much, watching the sheep moving in and out of the bracken, and one or two riders trot by, and break into a canter. The gypsies were all gone into the town, the caravans shut up and the shaggy wild ponies grazing. Verity went to give one an apple.

Emily said: 'Today is the first time I've been happy since Father died.' Then she put down her cold chicken, and touched her mother's hand. 'Mama – I'm sorry – may I be happy now?'

'Darling Emily. What else would a mother want for her children? What else would your father have wanted?'

'If only—' Emily said, looking at Richard, as he ate on the edge of the rug – 'if only you and—' She stopped, as he gazed back at her and willed her not to say another word.

'If only what?' John Maddock asked easily, leaning up beside her. Then he saw her scarlet face. 'I intrude,' he said quietly, after a moment or two, and said no more, getting up to brush off the crumbs from his gown, walking a little way away to watch the riders.

'I am so sorry,' whispered Emily to Richard. She was on the brink of tears, and her mother drew her close. 'I am so thoughtless and silly.'

'You are not,' he told her, but he was filled once again with sadness. Even up here, even on this lovely afternoon, with everyone at ease, the visit was ending as it had begun: with Emily's distress.

She recovered. Verity returned from the ponies. They all repacked the hamper and went walking along the Ridge. Maddock bade them listen to the curlew, pointed to a deserted chapel, spoke about breeds of sheep as a black-faced ewe came up. The sun was sinking behind the hills, and the sky was blue and gold.

'Does it not make you think of Heaven?' he asked them, and then, as they turned and made their way back: 'Poor Bowen,' he said all at once. 'To be so ill, in a summer such as this.'

As evening approached, they said goodbye at the crossroads. 'I shall wait here for the six o'clock coach,' said Maddock. 'Or perhaps I shall walk along until it comes – I am filled with energy after this lovely afternoon.' He took all their hands in turn, and Emily's last of all.

'May I write?' he asked her, and turned to Mrs Allen. 'I have your permission?'

'You do, Mr Maddock. It has been a delight to meet you.'

Then he jumped down, told Richard that he hoped to see him soon, and stood waving as he turned the trap and crossed to the other side. They plunged down into the lane once more, Emily looking back and back, and waving.

As they drove slowly on, between the scented hedgerows, the corncrake calling again across the fields, Richard said: 'If anything should come between you and he – if anything I have done should come between you—' he could hardly bear to think of it – 'I should never forgive myself.'

'Don't,' said Emily. Tears filled her eyes. 'Don't.'

Next morning, after breakfast, everything was a search for clothes, a strapping up of bags, an opening up again.

'How can three women need so much?' Richard asked them, sitting on Verity's bag while she tugged.

'How can we manage with so little?'

At last it was all done.

'Should we put them all up in the trap? Then I can drive it straight to Burgage.'

But they all, on this their last morning, wanted to walk down the lane, if he would only carry the bags for them. He would. How quickly the days had gone.

Emily went to say goodbye to the pony. The field was still wet with dew. Richard found her with her arms about his neck. The pony whinnied as he approached.

'Everyone is going home,' he told him. 'Even you.'

'Oh, Richard.' Now Emily's arms were about his own neck. 'I love you so much – we all love you so much. It's been so lonely without you—'

'Hush, hush. I shall not be here for ever.'

'But what will become of you? What can possibly happen?'

He could not answer that.

At the crossing he set down the bags on the little platform. Lupins and willowherb grew all along the track. Here was Birley, come to close the gates. They all said goodbye to him.

'And I wish you a pleasant journey,' he said, touching his cap.

There, in the distance, came the train.

'We shall pray for you,' said his mother, pressing Richard close. 'We shall all pray for you.'

Birley was waving his flag as the train drew near; it hissed to a halt and the steam and the morning sun were swirling clouds of light.

'Like a painting by Mr Turner,' said his mother. 'Your father so loved Mr Turner's work.'

She pressed her gloved hand to her lips, and Richard kissed her. He kissed his sisters. Then he and Birley helped them all in with their bags, and the doors slammed. Verity leaned out of the window. He took her hand.

'You do know I love you,' she said.

'I do. I love you too. And respect you. Hugely.'

She shook her head. 'Be careful, Richard. Please.'

Then Birley was calling: 'Close the window, please, Miss Allen,' and she drew back her head and pushed up the glass. The whistle blew, the train began to puff, and Richard, as the wheels began to turn, walked with it, then broke into a run. For perhaps half a furlong he kept up with them, stumbling along below the bank. Then he gave up, and stood there waving his hat, on and on until the last carriage could be seen no longer, and the last threads of steam were gone.

Never had the house felt emptier. In all his love and longing here for Susannah, he had conjured her to him, poured out his heart in his journal, felt her, so often, close within his heart. This was different. He walked from room to room. Emily had dropped a ribbon by her window; threads of embroidery silk clung to the ancient ottoman. He picked them up and put them on his desk. He washed the breakfast dishes, looking out at the barn where swallows no longer came and went, for all were now out in the lane, or skimming the waters of the weir and the river. He drank a glass of water, left Martha's money beneath a plate, and then he went to the barn and hauled out the trap. In the field he took the pony's halter.

'Come on, old fellow. Time to go home.'

He backed him into the shafts, and slipped on his bridle. Then he left the house for Martha to see to, and clopped slowly away up the lane. The morning was fair and fresh. He would return the pony to Burgage, stay for lunch if he were invited, then walk down into the village, where he did not go often enough. He would visit Miss Wilkinson's aunt, and pray with her. He would call on Effie Turner, see how she was enjoying married life. Perhaps he would call on Arndell. In short, he would resume his duties. Then …

Then he could not call in at the vicarage. He would walk back to the house and there think through everything. He would write to his family, write in his journal again. He would try to pray.

'Clip-clop, old fellow.' He chucked the reins.

It was after five when he returned home again. Though James Southwood was out at a meeting, Richard had stayed for lunch at Burgage with Will and Charlotte and their friends, and listened to Leonard Barnard talk about London, and a visit he had once made to the Carlyles in Chelsea. He thought: if Verity could love this man, he could offer her much. Could she? He had not John Maddock's radiant charm and good looks, but his seriousness was not earnestness, was something real and persuasive. As for Charlotte Southwood: she was much taken up with another Oxford man, Charles Carruthers, who hoped to go to the bar, and whose croquet had been vigorous.

All this distracted him. On his way up the hill from the village, later, after his visits, Richard found himself writing letters to his sisters in his mind as he used to do when he first came here, seeking thus to bring them close to him again, in his new life.

Dearest Emily, I miss you already. What joy it was for me to have you here. I have returned the pony to Burgage and I think he was very glad to be out in his own old stable block once more, with the carriage horses—

He stopped. In his mind he was writing now as he used to – when everything that had happened here was unknown to her, to any of his family. Now they knew it all, and he would never again be able to write of such innocent things without knowing that they looked between each line.

He had come to the foot of the churchyard path. Could he go up there? Could he knock on the vicarage door? As he stood there he felt as he used to do – his heart so full, his soul so consumed with guilt and longing, each time he saw her, each time he went to the house. Now they had declared themselves and he could not even approach her door.

He climbed the path, just a little way, and stood looking up at the house. Might she see him from the parlour? From the bedroom? Might she come out? He waited. No one came. As he turned and came back down the path once more, he thought he saw a movement in the laurels over the way, and his heart began to thump. What was he thinking of? He must walk purposefully up to the church or walk straight past it: to stand about here like a spy was fearful.

He came to the foot of the path. Across the way, a blackbird hopped out of the laurels. So – he had been frightened by a blackbird. As he walked on up the hill, and turned down into the woods again, he thought: this is diminishing me. If I continue thus, hesitant and fearful, I shall be less of a man, and everything good that lies between Susannah and me – for there is goodness there, is there not? – will become lessened too.

All around him the woods were full of song. When he came out and saw the house again, and the sheep moving slowly along the old paths through the fields, his spirits rose.

Inside, the house was clean and fresh. The floors had been swept, the beds all stripped down and the linen hung out in the orchard. As he gave thanks in his mind for this to Martha, and sat in the orchard eating the last of the pie, he let solitude settle round him again, and take possession of him. When he felt calm, he went into the house, and at his desk sat looking out at the sun sinking over the field. He brought back into his mind Susannah's presence here, and felt all his love for her begin to fill him again in quietude. He unlocked the drawer of his desk, and reached for his journal. Within its pages he would write to her once more, and search, as in prayer, for answers.

His hand felt again in the drawer, amongst letters and envelopes and sermon papers. He felt again. He pulled the drawer right open.

The journal was not there.

He looked again, he turned everything over.

It was not there.

Now his heart was thudding so wildly he could scarcely breathe. He knew who must have taken it, who must have watched the house until all had left it; who must have come creeping in, hoping to find evidence, before Martha came down the lane; who had searched for the key to his drawer and found it in that little jug beneath the glass, and now—

His groan filled the room. Then he bowed his head, and waited for everything to happen.

24

The letter, when it came, bore the Burgage seal. It occupied a single page.

Mr Allen,

You are required to appear before an extraordinary general meeting of the District Parish Council. This is to be held in the Kington Assembly Rooms, on 19th June AD 1861, commencing at 10 a.m. Clergy and councillors from the parishes of Lyonshall, Kington and Presteigne will be in attendance. The Bishop of Hereford has been informed.

I need hardly tell you that I write this with the very heaviest of hearts.

James Southwood

He set it down on his desk. The postman was still whistling up the lane; he could hear Martha, on her pattens, coming up the long path. It had rained in the night. He had hardly slept. Now the air at the open window bore in from his orchard and garden, and from every farm and field, the smell of earth, roses and lavender and woodbine, cattle, new-scythed grass. On such a morning might the world be made anew, might a lover write a sonnet, might a little girl run waving past his gate on her way to school. She ran past it now, and did not wave, nor turn her head. He watched her catch up with the postman, and the two of them walk easily on together. He thought: when I am gone, everything here will close around itself, back into itself. The trains will come and go, Alice and the postman will walk up through the woods, the sheep will follow the trails from one field to the next. It will not matter that I was ever here, except that people walking past this house might say: There was a scandal, once …

'Good morning, sir.'

'Good morning, Martha.'

She was setting down her basket in the porch, draping her shawl on a chair. Every time she came here, she did these things. Now, as every time, she put her head round the door.

'Terrible rain in the night.'

'It was.'

'She's lovely now, though. Lovely and fresh.'

He saw her glance at the envelope on his desk, with its seal. She was too respectful to question him, ever, but slipping the letter into his pocket, he said: 'I am still expecting to hear from home – this is but parish business.'

'Always plenty of that, sir. You must be missing them all, your family.' She looked across at the photograph on his mantelshelf. 'Even prettier in the life they are, Miss Allen, Miss Emily.'

He smiled. 'I shall tell them you think so.' Then he rose from the desk, saying that he would be out for a while, and she should lock up when she left. In the hours after the theft, he had thought to ask her: Did you see anyone? Did you hear anyone? Did you notice any kind of disturbance?

But she would have told him if she had, and he had no need to ask these things. He knew. And soon enough she would know too, and he would no longer be able to look her in the face.

He took his hat. He took his father's stick, where it rested against his fishing rod. He had not fished in the Arrow, and now he never would.

'Martha.' She was clearing his breakfast things. Water was heating up on the range. The gentle steam was like the breath of life.

'Sir?'

He wanted to say to her: 'If you should hear – when you hear – I hope you will not think too badly of me.' But even in his mind he could hardly complete the sentence, for it was one he might try to deliver to every single person he had met here, and there was not one who would not be horrified.

316

'Only – thank you,' he said. 'Thank you for everything.' And then, to keep his voice steady: 'Is it very wet underfoot?'

'Aye, sir.'

And he put on his boots in the porch, and went out over the shining grass, and down the long path.

He must pass the crossing cottage. He passed it, his heart beating hard. Birley was digging in the garden: a robin hopped about on the turned earth.

'Good morning,' said Richard, and Birley nodded. His spade sliced into the ground. 'Lovely and fresh now,' said Richard.

'Aye.' He did not look up.

That was all. That was all there was going to be, and the storm had not even broken.

As he walked on along the lane, Richard thought: perhaps it isn't true that the waters will simply close over it all. Perhaps for a long they will not close.

He came to the bridge and he turned and looked back. There at the gabled window Alice had looked gravely down upon this new arrival on a winter afternoon. Perhaps all her life she would connect him with a summer evening, the sudden appearance of a stranger as she bowled her hoop, the sun going down as he questioned and questioned her: What had she heard? What had she seen? When? How often? Only once? Was she sure? Perhaps all men, as she grew up, would be in some way tainted.

Richard leaned on the bridge and his face burned.

Here had Verity's clouded, clever face burned too.

'Please do not think you can distract me with talk of my own pitiful ambitions ... You are in the midst of something so appalling—'

That too was before the storm had broken.

His boots were crushing wet grass and kingcups. The faintest scent of prayermint came up. He bent down, picked the last white faded flower. It had seemed to betoken everything about his love: hidden, delicate, offering such passion at his touch. As he kissed it, and opened the letter in his pocket, and slipped the little plant within the page, he saw her: looking out over the field from his kitchen window, asking how she must live her life.

'... I have never been open in my life. I have never dared to be, never been

taught or allowed to be ... And I have never spoken like this to anyone.'

'And why do you speak like this now?'

'Because I must, or I shall sink beneath the waves.' She turned to look at him. *'That is why I came.'*

How strong she had shown herself to be. How strong she would need to be now.

He dropped the letter in his pocket, and walked on, up the steep turning past the farm and up the long lane beneath the hedgerows, white with star of Bethlehem, where John Maddock had taken his little sister's hand.

Emily, Emily.

'If anything should come between you—'

'Don't. Don't.'

He came to the highway, the crossroads. The morning coach to Presteigne was just gone past, and Dick Bampfield on the top of it, lifting his hat.

'Morning, Mr Allen! Lovely morning!'

Soon Bampfield would know, and his little brother John, whom he had prepared for Confirmation. Soon everyone would know.

He raised his hand in greeting.

Then he crossed the highway, and walked up the long winding lane ahead, where a farm dog barked and the cattle grazed in the fields on the lower slopes, walking on and on until barn and farmstead and the track to Martha's cottage all were left below, and he was up in the wooded hills, searching for Edith Clare.

The first time he had found her, her house was all shut up and the hillsides ran with water after rain. They ran so now, in every ditch and stream, but where before, in winter, the small stone house had been just visible through the leafless trees, now their full greenness and the dense undergrowth cloaked it so completely that he almost missed it. On this fine morning there was no thin blue line of smoke to rise from a chimney and betray her and it was not until he climbed, and climbed further, and was all at once come out to open country, that he realised he had missed it, and came down again. He looked along the banks by the woods once more, saw the ground beyond was thick with brambles. How deeply she had concealed herself. Then, as he caught the blue flash of a jay, he saw the house, and with his stick made his way through the undergrowth towards it.

And as he did so he asked himself again why it was that having hidden herself so entirely from the world she should have come down from here, and sought him.

The back of the house was windowless. He did not want to come upon her too suddenly. He skirted, as well as he could, until he was a good twenty paces away from the front. The shutters were open. The weatherbeaten door was open too. He stood in the midst of the trees, watching and waiting. Dishes of crumbs and scraps stood on the wall of her little garden, set with stones, where wild foxgloves grew. And all around the songbirds sang like flutes, like pipes, like the water running everywhere around him.

He moved, and a twig broke beneath his boot, but the ground was so softened by the rain it was almost soundless. The jay came flashing through the trees again, and its harsh cry made his heart start racing. Should he call? Approach and knock? Perhaps she had simply left the house to air, and was gone through the woods for mushrooms, or to beg from a farm below. Was this how she subsisted? Should he continue to wait, until she appeared and saw him, or would that frighten her?

'*The church put me in prison.*'

Why? What had she done?

Then he remembered her look of rapture and her outstretched arms as she lifted her face to the light on that winter day, in a gesture he had found both pagan and holy, and knew he had nothing to fear. After another few moments he walked quietly over the sodden ground, until he was close to the garden wall, where a rough piece of wood made a gate, and he called her name.

'Miss Clare? Miss Clare?'

Silence. He walked closer, set the makeshift gate aside, and entered the garden. Little pools of water were everywhere in broken crocks between the stones. There was a bench made from a plank set on tree stumps.

'Miss Clare?'

He walked to the door. He knocked, and looked inside.

At the turning of the stair he saw her.

She was coming slowly down towards him, and so unfamiliar was he with this shadowy interior, dappled with the light through the trees, that at first he could not see her face at all. He had an impression – loose hair, then a glint in dark eyes – nothing more.

'You have found me.'

'Yes.' He swallowed. He would not tell her he had been up here before, and watched her. He said simply: 'I have come to seek your help.'

She came further down, and now he could see her rough worn dress and sunburned skin. She reached the entrance. The floor beneath the rotting stair was but earth, though she had set stones here and there upon it. Even on a summer day he could feel the chill, the damp.

'Why do you need help from me? Why should a man of the Church need help from me?'

He said something he had never thought in all his life to say. He said: 'I may leave the Church.' In this quiet, unvisited place, the words almost roared in his ears. He knew it was true.

'And why is that?'

'I may have to.'

There was a silence. He thought: and are we now in some strange alliance? Both in some way outlaws? He wondered if this pleased her; for a whirling moment, exhausted as he was, on the edge of everything, with the world about to break about him, he thought: this is what she wanted. This is why she came to me.

Then she said slowly: 'But you are a man of God.' And then again: 'You are a man of God.'

He closed his eyes; he leaned against the door frame. Everything welled up in him. He could not speak.

She led him out into the garden, and covered the wet bench with sacking. A light wind stirred the dripping trees, birds came and went from the garden wall. He held his hat in his hands and turned it and turned it, as God once turned the world.

Where should they begin?

'You live up here because—'

'You have walked up here because—'

320

They began again.

He said: 'I am very troubled and anxious. As you see. I came here because I need to confide in someone who is outside everything, as you are. Whom I think I can trust.' She listened. A robin flew on to the wall. Richard gestured at the trees, the slope of the hill down into the valley, with its farms and villages and busy little towns. Kington, Presteigne. She had always known them, had she not? Before she began to live in hiding, she must have lived down there. Or was she—

'Sometimes I have wondered if you once travelled with the gypsies,' he said slowly. 'When I was a boy I found them somehow magical. I still do. They come. They go. They live as they please.'

She gave a little laugh, and the robin flew up. 'That is romance. A gypsy life can be as hard as any. And I told you – I was in school. Gypsy children do not go to school.'

He turned his hat. Each time he moved his feet the rich wet smell of the earth came up.

'Will you tell me, then, where you grew up? How much you know of the people here?' And as he asked her, a picture came to him of the churchyard school, of the children – of Alice – running amongst the gravestones to play fox and hounds, or grandmother's footsteps. Had this been the childhood of Edith Clare?

She said: 'I lived as a child below Norton Hill. You know where that is?'

He shook his head. There were still so many places he did not know.

'My father worked on the Norton estate – he was a gardener there. It lies outside Presteigne – if you walk there you can still see the cottage where we grew up, but none of us lives there now.' She sat looking out at the trees. Squirrels were racing through the boughs. 'There were six of us – more, but three died. Every day we went the three miles to school in Evenchurch. A clergyman used to come and teach us, to tell us the Bible stories and prepare us for Confirmation.' She looked at him. 'No doubt you do these things.' He nodded, thinking of John Bampfield's struggle to recite the Catechism, of how the sole of Tom Meredith's boot flapped as he swung his foot, how Will Fletcher had everything by heart.

'First, I learn to believe in God the Father, who hath made me, and all the world.'

Edith said: 'My mother had another child, another girl, and lost her. Then she fell very ill, and then she died. The clergyman at school used to comfort us. Our teacher had used to beat the boys, but he stopped them. He was a good young man, a kind man. We used to watch for his visits. I used to think that life was a terrible thing, but he made me feel I was loved by God, and my mother was in Heaven.' She was looking down at her hands now, and he saw they were cracked and chapped and bitten to the quick.

'Then my poor father too fell ill, and lost his position and was taken into the Hereford workhouse. We little ones went with him. My elder sisters were put into service. One of my brothers ran away, another found work on a farm in Monmouth. We were all scattered. My little brother and I went in with my father and we had a mean rough time in there. It turned us.' She stopped, then said: 'A wicked time. It turned and hardened me.'

He listened and waited for her to continue, trying to imagine it all: all this happening not so long ago, and not so far from here, but so far from the life he had lived. He tried to imagine her as a child, knew there were hundreds of children like her, perhaps thousands. John Maddock, no doubt, had children such as these in his Ragged School, barefoot little motherless creatures – the kind of children of whom he himself knew nothing. What kinds of things went on in the workhouse, the poorhouse, the orphanage? What was done to these children?

'Do you wish to tell me—'

'No.' Her hands were held tight in her lap. 'I never speak of it.' She looked out again through the dripping trees. 'Up here, I do not have to speak to anyone.' He waited, watching the squirrels leap so lightly from branch to branch.

She said: 'I ran away, like my brother Seth. I was hardened to everything. I took up with a fellow – he was homeless like me, he was sick, we were brother and sister to one another. When we got hungry we darted in and out of the shops. One evening when he slipped out of the bakers with a loaf I was so hungry and glad that I kissed him, long and full, and he kissed me back. It was the first time I was kissed by a man I did not loathe.' Her voice had dropped low, she was twisting her hands. 'Somebody saw us, someone passing by, and we

322

were taken in, we were sent before the magistrates. One of the men on the bench was a man of the Church, but not such a man as I remembered from my days at school. He was not a clergyman, but one who had made the Church his life, who served on every council, and every bench. He put me in mind of one who was in the workhouse ...'

Now he could hardly hear her, but must strain for every word.

'He had Jed transported for stealing. He kept looking and looking and looking at me, and he called me every name. He charged me with lewd behaviour in a public place. He sent me to the House of Correction, in Presteigne. When I was locked up tight in there, he came and forced me – he said if I told, he would have me hanged ...'

Her voice was a dark bitter whisper now, in the murmur of the trees. As he listened so intently, Richard felt gooseflesh rise all over him. He had no need to ask this man's name, for he knew, he knew, but he asked it.

'Why does it matter?' She was gazing at the ground.

'It does. It does.'

'His name was Philip Prosser,' said Edith Clare.

The wind had blown the rain away and the trees no longer dripped on to the earth. They walked between them, and the sun came slanting through.

'Why did you seek me out?' he asked her.

'Because I heard you were coming – I heard a new curate was coming.'

'How? How do you hear such things?'

'There are one or two people I still see, people I trust – we made friends inside. After, some went into service, some still had homes to go to. They bring me food and clothing.' She tugged at a leaf, and stripped it as they walked. 'One of them hid me after I escaped. Once I saw Prosser, and he saw me. Then I heard of an empty little dwelling, where an old man had died. I came up here. After a while I began to grow calmer. One night I dreamed about my mother in Heaven, and when I woke up I felt happy. I thought of the kindness of the clergyman who used to come to school. I thought perhaps he was one of the few good men in the world, and how he had helped me. I thought perhaps it was a sign – that I should come here, and have that dream, and think of him. I thought I might find God again, in a different way, and so I have.'

She was turning on to a path where the ground was drier, running between pine trees, overlaid with a carpet of needles. Foxgloves and ferns grew all along it. He saw that she knew every path, every glade and turning.

She said: 'When I heard you were come here, I thought I might see again if there was still goodness in the world.' She went to pick a foxglove, and drew it between her fingers, over and over again as they walked. 'I thought you might be as he was, Mr Westwood, the clergyman at school. When I saw you—'

He saw she was tugging the flowers of the foxglove from the stem, with her bitten fingers, as if she must have something to soothe and distract her. In this he saw how her childhood had never left her, how human and afraid she was, where before he had seen her as something almost unearthly.

'When I saw you, I saw your face was good. I knew you were a true man of God.' Then she stopped on the path, where the flowers of the foxgloves had fallen, and asked him: 'Why have you come to me? Why must you leave the Church?'

How could he tell her? How, after everything he now knew about her life, could he tell her: I am in love with a married woman – with the wife of the man I came here to serve. I have held her in my arms and we have been discovered. Soon, this will be in the papers, on everyone's lips. I shall be summoned before my bishop.

How could he tell her who was bringing all this about?

They walked on. He thought of the way in which she had said with such certainty, as he stood in the doorway of her hiding place: 'You are a man of God,' and how after all his turmoil this had filled him with such overpowering feelings of grief and longing that he could hardly stand.

Again he was silent. Then he thought that if he did not speak she would learn of all of it after he had gone, and surely that would break the last thread of her trust in men for ever.

So he told her himself, and watched her face, which he had seen open in rapture to the light of Heaven, now grow closed and dark.

'You have preyed on her – you have seduced and preyed on her—'

'Never. Never.'

'You have brought her low – you have brought your own self low.' She began to walk fast, snatching at ferns and flowers.

'You are mistaken,' he insisted, walking to match her pace. 'We are in love. This is love—'

Then the jay came flashing through the trees once more, and its mocking cry silenced every songbird. It landed: he could see its brilliant blue.

'Never tell anyone you have been here. Never tell anyone where I am.' She did not turn, she did not look at him.

'I will not – I will not.'

And he stood and watched her turn off the path, and walk quickly away into the ferny depths of the wood, as the jay shrieked again from the bough.

25

_____

'Now I saw in my dream, that by this time the pilgrims were got over the Enchanted Ground, and entering the country of Beulah, whose air was very sweet and pleasant, the way lying directly through it, they solaced themselves there for a season. Yea, here they heard continually the singing of birds, and saw every day the flowers appear on the earth, and heard the voice of the turtle in the land.'

She stopped, and looked up, her finger on the page. Had he fallen asleep? Awake or asleep, his breathing now was so fevered and fast.

'Go on,' he whispered, and his milky eyes slowly opened. 'The voice of the turtle—'

'I do not tire you?' She suppressed a yawn. 'Miss Nightingale believes it is very tiring—'

'Not for me.' A long pause, each word something to weigh – like a stone, like Pilgrim's burden. 'You may tell Miss Nightingale—' A flicker of a smile: the reading comforted him. His eyes rested upon her, sitting in the chair by the open window. 'What time is it?'

'Just after seven.'

'In the morning?'

'In the evening.' She opened the window a little wider. 'Can you not see the evening sun?'

He did not answer. Then, slowly: 'The reading is tiring you?'

'No, not at all.' And she bent to the page once more.

'In this country the sun shineth night and day; wherefore this was beyond the Valley of the Shadow of Death, and also out of the reach of Giant Despair; neither could they from this place so much as see Doubting Castle. Here they were within sight of the city they were going to …'

A sigh came from the pillows; she looked up again.

'Oliver?' She rose from the chair, crossed the room, bent over him. 'Oliver?' And now, yes, now he was asleep. Such a shallow quick racing thing had his breathing become – when he slept it was as if he were swimming underwater, just beneath the surface, through which he might break at any moment. Sleeping and waking, sleeping and waking – both were so restless now, save when he took, and kept down, the opium powder which Dr Probyn gave. Probyn would be here in an hour, to settle him for the night.

Susannah went back to the chair, and sank into it. She seemed to have been reading for ever; it seemed that the end of Christian and Hopeful's long journey was approaching. From her own childhood, she thought she could remember this, and turned the pages: how far was there to go? Would her voice bear up, if he woke, and wanted her to continue?

'… and drawing near to the city, they had yet a more perfect view thereof. It was builded of pearls and precious stones, also the street thereof was paved with gold; so that by reason of the natural glory of the city … Christian with desire fell sick; Hopeful also had a fit or two of the same disease. Whereof, here they lay by it a while, crying out, because of their pangs, "If you see my beloved, tell him that I am sick of love …"'

She covered her face.

In this room, now, was a kind of love played out: his love for her, which had never faltered, and, in his frailty and helplessness, hers for him. She dropped her hands to her lap once more; she watched him, an old white bony bird upon the pillows, his little breaths coming and going, coming and going. For so long that high iron marriage bed had held their lives: the prayers murmured on either side of it; the awkward, dutiful, horrible embraces beneath its worn darned sheets – horrible for her, shrinking from his touch; horrible for him, knowing this as he must. The bed had held their sleeplessness, their loneliness, the great absence at the heart of things, their longing for a child. She would never nurse a baby there. It had become a sickbed; now a deathbed. From it he would enter the shining city.

'*Sometimes I feel that Christ is gone from me—*'

Dr Probyn had told her that this was what he felt. Oliver himself had never told her this, and now John Bunyan was comforting him. Perhaps her, too.

Her eyes went back to the page.

'But, being a little strengthened, and better able to bear their sickness, they walked on their way, and came yet nearer and nearer, where were orchards, and vineyards, and gardens, and their gates opened into the highway. Now, as they came up to these places, behold the gardener stood in the way, to whom the Pilgrims said, "Whose goodly vineyards and gardens are these?" He answered, "They are the King's, and are planted here for his own delight, and also for the solace of pilgrims." '

Susannah got up, went to the open window, and leaned out. Last night it had rained, and today, though she had seen the landscape only from in here, it had been as full and fresh as any summer day she could remember. Now the sun was slipping slowly down over the distant hills, and Herefordshire's orchards and fields and gardens were touched with gold. From behind this dark house, which had held so much despair, she could hear the evening anthem of the sheep; within the churchyard the rooks were beating home.

She knew that everything was about to change, and that she, through all that happened, was already changed – beginning to inhabit someone she had not known was there. She closed her eyes again, and let herself for a moment leave this room, and enter again the long lane down through the woods, the house at its end, by the stream; the room where he was waiting for her.

The evening wind stirred in the elms, the rookery. It rustled the screen of laurels, across the highway. A horse clopped by, beneath the churchyard wall; beyond the laurels, she thought she heard a door slam to, breaking the quietness.

Then Oliver was whispering her name, and she turned back to him.

There was nothing he could do to warn her. He could not go to the house. Were he to write to tell her: I have been summoned – we are surely discovered – my position here is now impossible – then he must leave her to read such words alone. Could he cast her into such anxiety and fear, for him and for herself?

He could not. All night, he tossed in his bed. It seemed that all night the owl was hunting, all through the woods and out across the fields; that every time he thought he might sink into oblivion at last, he was summoned awake by those low cruel warning notes. He lay there as a mouse or a shrew or vole must lie: listening, waiting for the end.

Was she awake too? Was she offering a drink, a powder, words of comfort? Did Oliver's hand, that frail and bony thing, lie within her hand?

'He is very pitiful and weak ... I cannot help but feel for him.'

What a huge weight lay upon her. Was he now to burden her still more?

The owl called again. He had grown accustomed to it, yet now it chilled him as it had on the first night of his arrival, living alone for the first time, entering a new community of souls, leaving that little company of women.

Dearest Mama, my dearest sisters – Today I am to take part in my first service.

How they had all grieved to part from one another, yet how proud they had been for him. Now he, who had sought to live a good life, his father's life, was about to bring them low. Already, he had drawn them into secrecy and distress. Now it must all come out into the open?

'I know you would only have let this happen if it were something momentous ... in truth, I do not know how to help you. But I shall always love you, Richard. Always.'

As he lay there, so restless in the deep quiet dark, broken by the searching cry of the owl, it seemed that all the women he loved and cared for passed before him: his mother, enduring her new widow-hood so bravely; Verity, struggling to live a life so much smaller than the one she craved; Emily, who now, when scandal broke, might lose all prospect of her new-found happiness; Susannah, on whom all this now revolved, and who was waiting for him.

On so many nights he had lain here, and summoned her presence – into this room, this bed. He had played out a dream of her beside him, beneath him, of a life together in which such passion lay at the heart, became devotion, ran on and on.

But life with a man cast out, disgraced – he saw Philip Prosser's twisted little mouth, his glittering eyes in the pew, like a discovered animal, as Richard preached on constancy, on cruelty, thinking of Tilda's pitiful cries of terror. Prosser was after him, wanted him brought down. Was this something Susannah could bear? What would become of them?

Into the darkness now came Edith Clare: seeking her childhood glimpse of goodness in solitude, in hiding, amongst all the birds of the air. She had found a kind of peace; through him, she had rediscovered bitterness.

'*You have preyed on her – you have seduced her ... and brought her low.*'

This was how everyone would see it all, and surely Susannah must be tainted by it.

Yet she had come to him. She, the dutiful rector's wife – that pale, unhappy girl – had dared to do this.

'*For you ... to come here twice, alone – in truth, I am astonished.*'

'*I thought I must act or break. Something in me refused to break. I am a little stronger than I thought.*'

Then they must both be strong, and perhaps for the last time in this house, this bed, he drew her in his mind into his arms once more.

'*I love you completely. Utterly.*'

'*And I you.*'

'*Whatever happens, we can never go back from this.*'

Then they must not.

The sky was lightening: he could see through the chinks in the shutters, as the earth so slowly turned. As God once turned it – as Richard had always believed He turned it.

Did He do so still? Had everything he had done wrong taken him so far from God that truly he could no longer believe?

'*You are a man of God.*'

Could he still be such a man?

From deep within the woods came the first faint songbird's call. After a little while, another. It was almost dawn.

He pushed back the covers.

For perhaps the last time in this room, beside this bed, he kneeled, and tried to pray.

They were all waiting for him, seated on the far side of a great oak table, facing him as he was shown in by a clerk from the hall of the Assembly Rooms. At first they were but a blur of dark suits and gowns against the panelling, then he could make them out: the Reverend Stephen Ingram, rector of St Mary's, Kington; the lawyer Arthur Bodenham; James Southwood, his eyes very dark and grave; the Reverend John Maddock, curate of St Andrew's at Presteigne, whose gaze dropped to his papers; Mr Philip Prosser, councillor and verger from St Michael and All Angels, Lyonshall.

'Good morning, Mr Allen,' said Stephen Ingram, from the carved oak chair in the centre. 'Pray take a seat.'

There was only one to take: he took it, and sat before them. Ingram surveyed him. Richard met his searching look. He was here; he would face it all.

'It is my difficult duty to chair this meeting,' said Ingram. 'It saddens me greatly to see you called before it.' He shook his head; he turned to his colleagues. 'Gentlemen. Shall we open with a prayer?'

There was a murmuring of assent. Richard felt the first sweat begin to break.

'We shall not,' he said clearly.

'I beg your pardon?'

'I shall not join in any such prayer. There are those in this room with whom I do not wish to join. With whom I hope never to pray again.'

There was a ripple of disquiet.

'Mr Allen, the meeting has not even begun. Already you seek to provoke—'

'I seek to provoke no one, but I shall stand my ground.'

There was a pause. Then: 'Very well. Let us proceed.' Ingram tapped his papers; there came a clearing of throats, a sipping from glasses of water. Across the table Richard caught John Maddock's eye, and received a deep swift glance he could not read.

'This is not a court,' said Ingram. 'I think Mr Bodenham will tell us that it has no legal status, not as such. That is so, Mr Bodenham?'

Bodenham nodded, and his two chins trembled. 'That is so.'

'This is a hearing.' Ingram rested his hands upon the table. 'A closed, confidential hearing, Mr Allen, an extraordinary general meeting in which we, as senior parish councillors, require you to answer certain allegations. These are allegations which have shocked each one of us to the core. If they are found to have any substance, they threaten to bring you into the very gravest disrepute. I need hardly tell you that they threaten your position.' He cleared his throat again. 'Shall we proceed?'

Richard nodded. Already, the gown beneath his arms was soaking.

'Very well.' Ingram turned to James Southwood. 'You will be good enough to take the minutes of this meeting?'

Southwood picked up his pen. 'I shall.' He looked across at Richard, and in few people's eyes had Richard ever seen a greater sadness. He gazed back at him steadily: Southwood's eyes dropped; he looked away.

Ingram continued, 'Mr Allen, it is alleged that you have taken advantage of your position to seduce the young wife of the Reverend Oliver Bowen, vicar of St Michael and All Angels, Lyonshall. It is alleged that in so doing you have deceived a man so gravely ill that he has been unable to act as he would wish, to uphold his rights as husband, and that you have thus compounded the breaking of a Commandment by acting in the most dishonourable fashion it is possible to imagine. It is alleged that you have done all this while presenting yourself as a man fit to hold the office of curate in the Church of England, fit to conduct services, to offer the Blessed Sacrament, to conduct the great service of Holy Matrimony—' He stopped, and Richard saw that his papers shook in his hand. 'In short,' he said quietly, 'it is alleged that you have behaved in a manner so low and disgraceful that no member of this council could countenance your remaining here, if even some of this is true. What do you have to say?'

Richard had felt himself flush so deeply as this speech was made that now he was burning. His own hands shook as he placed them on the table.

'May I ask ...' He cleared his throat, he heard his voice already beginning to rise. He took a breath; he began again. 'May I ask who has made these allegations? And on what evidence?'

'We have had our suspicions,' said Ingram slowly, and then: 'Let me correct that. All but myself – I have never seen you, Mr Allen, except in parish meetings in my own house. I am not able to form a judgment. It is in this neutral position that I act as Chairman. Otherwise—' he glanced up and down the table – 'otherwise, I believe I am correct?'

'Not quite,' said John Maddock clearly. 'I myself have been – how shall I say? – I have been disturbed to be told of these things. As representative of St Andrew's, in the absence of Mr Palgrave, it is my duty to attend this meeting. But I cannot say that I have ever entertained the slightest suspicion of anything dishonourable, or even untoward in relation to Mr Allen's conduct.'

Richard flashed him a glance, but Maddock would not look at him. He was waiting, it seemed, to learn the truth. And when it came – then how would he respond?

'Very well.' Ingram was drinking from his glass. 'These suspicions have been entertained by everyone else?' No one denied it, and Richard felt his heart begin to pound. Had he really been watched all this time? Not just by Prosser, but by everyone? For how long? Had he really been so indiscreet that his every glance had been noticed?

He said carefully: 'Suspicions are one thing. May I ask again: what evidence do you have?'

'This,' said Prosser, and laid upon the table the leatherbound notebook, with its silken ribbon, which Emily had sent for Christmas, and which Richard had made his journal. Markers had been slipped within the pages. Even though he had known this must happen, to see it here – to see it here brought forth, exposed ...

He shook with anger.

He said, struggling not to raise his voice: 'That is a stolen item, Mr Prosser. That has been stolen from my house. How dare you – how dare you present it here?'

'Dare?' asked Prosser. 'You, Mr Allen, ask me what I dare? You, who have dared to deceive us all, ask how I dare present our evidence?' Spittle was gathering in the corners of his mouth; he dabbed at it. Then he opened the journal at a marker, and gave a salacious little smile.

'Gentlemen? Should Mr Allen be read the grounds on which we bring him here?'

Richard saw Maddock quickly turn away, but the others – the others leaned forward: only a little, but it chilled Richard and repelled him utterly. He said: 'Prosser, if you dare to read those words—'

But Prosser was already reading:

'My communion with God leaves me wanting ... I feel myself estranged from Him, and full of shame ... I see her here with me, walking across the wet orchard grass, coming in to be close before the fire, climbing the stairs with me, to be closer still ... I am in love ... we long for one another ... in my heart I have already broken the Commandment ...'

Richard was on fire. The silence in the room as Prosser read on was like the very ending of the world.

'All day I have thought only of you, and everything here returns me to your presence – the desk, the glass above the fire, the fireside chair wherein we lay and kissed, and gazed, and kissed again, our love declared at last. My only wish is to hold you close once more ...'

'That is enough!' Richard was on his feet. He lunged for the journal, but Prosser snatched it to his chest.

'Is this not evidence enough?' he asked the table. 'Could any man hear this and not condemn it? Are these pages not entirely steeped in sin? Could their author for one moment be judged fit to hold office within the Church?'

'Let him who hath no sin cast the first stone, Mr Prosser!' Richard was shouting now, beating upon the table. 'Let him who hath no sin—' His words came tumbling out of him, from one who had never shouted in his life. He, who once had cherished prayer and solitude, who once had thought silence a precious thing, who had been so in love and so in anguish for so long, was now in the grip of something uncontrollable.

'Mr Allen!' Ingram had pushed back his chair. 'I must ask you to sit down.'

'I will not!'

'Sit down!' And now Ingram's own voice was raised, and all around the table ran the words, 'Sit down!', 'Control yourself, man!', 'Do as you are bid!'

His eyes raked them all, this company of men, and he felt like a stag at bay.

'Richard.' John Maddock's clear quiet voice came through. 'Will you not sit for a moment?' He turned to Ingram. 'Is Mr Allen not to respond to these charges? To give us his account?'

'I am sure Mr Ingram does not need to be told how to conduct this hearing,' said Prosser, as Richard sank into his chair, and he wiped more spittle from the corners of his lips.

'Thank you, Mr Prosser. Thank you, Mr Maddock. Gentlemen – let us restore some order.' Stephen Ingram looked across at Richard. 'Will you try to calm yourself? You must know very well that we wish to hear what you have to say.' He waited, as Richard struggled to regain composure. He took out one of Verity's handkerchiefs, and wiped his brow. Beloved sisters – let them be spared all this. 'Now, then. How do you answer these charges?'

'With the truth,' said Richard, and the room went quiet. He looked at Prosser. Prosser looked at his papers. 'That journal, that private, intimate journal belongs to me. I wrote those words within it, and I wrote them of Susannah Bowen, and I am not ashamed of a single line, though I never thought that a common thief would enter my house, and that his father would read them before a gathering such as this.' He stopped, and the hush was almost palpable. And though he was so filled with emotion that his whole body shook with it, somewhere within himself he now was in control, just as his nerves before preaching a sermon vanished, always, once he had begun. He had something to say: he said it.

He said: 'When I came here, I thought of nothing but my own

inadequacy to the tasks that lay before me. This was my first position: I did not dream that it would be my last. I wanted to honour the memory of my father, who was as good and true a man of the Church as I have ever known. I wanted to serve the Church, and serve our Lord, as he had done. I wanted to serve Mr Bowen—' He felt a little ripple run through the room, as he drew close to home. 'I wanted to learn from him, and I saw that he, like my father, was an honourable man, a man fulfilling his vocation, though I think that perhaps he thought less highly of me. I was made very welcome, none the less – by him, by almost everyone. Especially, perhaps, by you, Mr Southwood. You have always been very kind.'

He stopped again, cleared his throat, and drank from the glass before him. He saw Southwood dip his pen in the silver-topped inkwell with enormous concentration.

He drew a breath. 'Something happened here which I could never have imagined or predicted, nor even wanted to happen. I fell in love. I fell deeply in love with someone who was not free, but who returned my feelings. We declared ourselves, we tried to do what was right.' He looked Ingram full in the eye. 'Susannah Bowen was not seduced. She is caring for her husband as she should. As she wishes to do. That I have done wrong to him is not in question, and it is something of which I am deeply ashamed. But I will not tolerate all this being salivated over by a man who is not fit to enter the portals of this or any church.' He turned his gaze to Prosser, whose own eyes began to flicker round the room as his sallow face went white. Had he not known he must be confronted? Did something in him want, at last, to be exposed?

'Mr Allen—' Ingram began, but Richard put out his hand.

'Pray do not stop me, for I shall not be stopped. You might think me a hypocrite, a sinner, and perhaps I have been. But I shall not leave this meeting without calling to account the man who has brought me here.' He looked around the table. No one but Maddock would meet his eye, and Maddock's own eyes were widening. Richard turned back to Prosser.

'It is you I speak of, you wretched man. You, Philip Prosser, who are the cruellest, the most wicked man I have ever known. You speak to me of sin? Look at your own life, Prosser, look to your own vile heart.'

'Mr Allen!' Ingram was rapping on the table, but nothing would stop Richard now.

'Look to your own poor beaten wife, Philip Prosser. Look to her!'

There was a horrid silence. Within it, after a moment, throats were cleared and glasses reached for. No one looked anyone in the face. Southwood had stopped writing.

'Why do you not minute this?' Richard demanded of him. 'Why, sir? Must a woman beaten half to death in her own home be erased? Must she be silenced? She shall not be, for I shall speak for her! I shall say her name! Tilda Prosser – do you hear me, gentlemen? When I am gone, will you look to her, and save her?'

No one could speak.

'Women,' said Richard to Bodenham, whose fat face shook as he looked away. 'Women's matters. Things behind closed doors. Things we would rather not think of, done by men to women too frightened to speak out.' His blood was up again, his blood was up. Never had he known such fury. 'I could say so much more,' he told them. 'So much more. I do not, because I wish to protect – I wish to protect—' And now he had to fight to control himself, for with another word Edith Clare's name would be in this room, and somehow Prosser would find her, somehow have his revenge.

And another name burned within him now, as he heard on a glittering winter day a scream far out on the ice, and silence – a terrible silence – fall. He heard the prayers, he heard Oliver Bowen, a good true man whom he had not wished to hurt or harm, even though he had – it was true – most shamefully done so, ask God to look down upon this place of sin.

And Richard asked now, directly of James Southwood: 'Which man here is the father of Sarah Watkins' child? Sir? Can you answer that? Might that be minuted?'

And then, as the colour drained from Southwood's face, and uproar rose all round him, Richard pushed back his chair and stood up and said to them all: 'You have no need to hound me from the Church. I love – I loved it. It was everything to me. My faith – the Church – they were my whole life. Now I am leaving.'

And he turned, and flung open the door, and strode from the panelled room, out into the panelled hall, with its portraits, and clerk at a desk, who looked up in astonishment.

'Sir—'

Richard wrenched open the door to the street. A horse and cart went by in the sun, a dog ran across, people were passing in and out of the shops. He was panting and shaking so hard he thought he must fall there. Then he strode on.

'Allen! Richard!'

Maddock was calling him, Maddock caught up with him.

'Richard.'

He shook his head. 'I am not fit for human society – I am not capable of conversation—' He walked swiftly on, looking at no one.

Maddock was walking fast beside him. 'I have only to say – I respect you. I am your friend, if you will still be mine. Write to me, or I shall write to you.' He grasped his hand, and held it. Then he let him go.

26

---

arly evening, and everything packed in his bags. They stood in
the hall, and the front door on to the lane stood open, letting
the hum of the bees, and the song of every beloved bird
come in. For the last time he looked around the house: at the desk
where he had kneeled and prayed, and poured out his heart into his
journal; at the chair where he had held her; the place in the kitchen
where she had stood, and spoken with such courage, when he had
known he would go on loving her all his life.

*Darling Susannah, my own true love, By the time you receive this letter I shall
be gone – but have no fear: I shall never, if you still want me, be gone from you.*

The storm may be about to break.

*I shall, when I see you, tell you everything. And you will tell me everything too,
will you not? We made our promise – we shall always be open with one another.*

*Beloved Susannah, I think of you with every breath I take. Know that I am
waiting for you, that I shall send for you, and I pray that you will still wish to come
to me.*

Until then – I am always yours.

He went out of the porch, and the swallows swooped low before
him as he walked across to the orchard, wherein he had struggled with
faith and doubt as he watched his bees come and go: because God bid
them, or because, for whatever reason, this was the life of bees.

He walked down to the gate, and stood there looking across to the
woods, where Edith Clare had so quietly walked, and watched him.
He looked down the lane, as the last train of the day came whistling
up from Kington, bringing the clouds of steam, and their marvellous
mystery. He thought of Alice, whom he would never see again,

towards whose gabled cottage he would never walk again – not now, to take the train, and not to say goodbye to her, for he could not bear it.

He walked back to the house, and took up his bags. He had left Martha her money, but no note, for she would not be able to read it. He hoped she would remember the last words of thanks he had spoken to her.

Then, for the last time, he made the long climb through the woods.

The sun was sinking, touching every summer cloud with holy light. The sheep were moving along the trails, on through the gate between the fields, on up the hill.

Richard walked up to the turning. He stopped, set down his bags, and looked back at the house. This, too, he would never see again and he heard himself murmur farewell.

Then again he picked up the bags once again, and walked on.

Dearest Mama, my dearest sisters, I do not know what the future holds: we none of us truly know that. I pray you will find it in your hearts to forgive me, and I pray that in time I shall find some new occupation. Perhaps – what do you think of this? – perhaps it is not too late for me to study the law? There are things I have learned here which in the midst of my own troubles have opened my eyes. There is a need – I might serve usefully.

In the meantime, now, I think of you all with every step I take. Soon I shall be home.

A wind was beginning to rise, a choir of air, sighing through the trees. He listened as he walked, remembering that incandescent song in the church, when, at great and important moments in his life, he had swung open its doors. Now, from tower to tower, the evening bells began to ring across the valley. He climbed on, listening. And though doubt and anxiety had so long assailed him, and a new life must begin, he asked himself now, hearing the rise and tumbling fall of the bells: Is that me calling God? Or is God calling me?